Noëmi's Reckoning

K McCity

Noëmi's Reckoning

Copyright © 2021 K McCity

ISBN:9798713342944

Dedicated to the Truffle Pack with all my love.

Time to assemble!

ACKNOWLEDGMENTS

A special heartfelt thank you to my incredible, massively talented editor, Emma City, for her help. My gratitude also to Emma City for the awesome book cover artwork.

Finally I must acknowledge Babe, who read this book first and whose support, encouragement and belief have held me up during all this time.

Cover design by Emma City ©emmacityart

Noëmi's Reckoning

PART ONE - REASONS

Toutes les violences ont un lendemain - Victor Hugo

Noëmi's Reckoning

PROLOGUE

GROSS MORON

4 January 2007.

'Had she been murdered?'

Noëmi McAllister joined Newcastle Green Academy part way through the school year, in January 2007, at the age of thirteen. Arriving at the grey school gates, her father checked the back seat of the car and handed her school bag over.

"Make sure you're on time, N. You've got your key?"
She nodded as he leant across and hugged her tightly.
"It's going to be tough for both of us." He sighed, holding her at arm's length. "You know why we couldn't stay in Kenmore. I'm sorry."
Noëmi closed her eyes.
"Be strong." He said.

She got out of their small red Renault and immediately a rowdy group of younger students pushed past her. Watching her father leave for his work, her throat felt tight and lumpy.
Noëmi walked towards her new school and thought to herself.
'There's nothing remotely green about this place.'

There had been too many changes. She was devastated to leave

3

behind her friends in Kenmore where she could wander freely amongst the Scots pine trees in the woods, paddle in the cold freshwater streams and climb the hills around Loch Tay. Even more so, she was distraught to leave the place where she had clear memories of her mother, where they had been so content and blissfully ignorant of life's cruel chances.

Arriving at her form room, students were sprawled over the tables and a strong smell of Lynx Africa filled her nostrils. The teacher looked up from her desk and gestured for her to come over. The bell went and the class settled.

"Right everyone this is Noëmi," called out her new form tutor to the class, pronouncing Noëmi, *"Nooo - me."*
"I'm sorry, Miss, there's actually a diaeresis on the 'ë'. So it's pronounced No-em-ee."
She thought to herself. *'What would be the point otherwise?'*
"Right, thank you. She's now joined the class and you need to be nice to her because her mum has just died."
A mouse before eagles; keen eyes of the convocation upon her.
She could hardly hear the rest of what her teacher said; only that a girl called 'Deanna' had been assigned as her buddy, and that the teacher mispronounced her name twice more.

Noëmi knew this brief factual summing up of her circumstances was going to make things even harder; *'the new girl with no mum'*, her eyes were blurred and her throat was even lumpier.
"Was she murdered?" were Deanna's first words.
"No, she had Leukaemia, cancer of the blood," Noëmi said simply.
"That sounds bad. First we have maths, I like maths," Deanna announced in a matter of fact way.
"Me too," replied Noëmi.

* * *

"Are you getting on okay in the lessons?" Her father asked as she got in the car after her second day.
"Yes," Noëmi said, slamming the red car door shut behind her.

She pulled the seat belt around her and sank back into the chequered fabric.

"You look very smart."

"My skirt's much longer than anyone else's Dad."

"Well it's good quality, from the proper uniform retailer and it'll last. Have you met some new friends?"

"Oh yes!" It was a half-truth. Noëmi hoped it would be enough to stop his questions.

When they pulled into their driveway, they sat staring into space. Eventually, Noëmi filled the silence.

"All anyone asks is how mum died, it's like they just want to hear some kind of gory story; a tragic but grizzly crime."

"Let me talk to the school," her father Donnie's voice caught in his throat, looking close to tears, he put his arm around her.

"Plus everyone's already got their groups, their friends. It's hard."

"We need to give it some time N, be patient, my office is not easy either. It's so quiet…"

"Try not to cry tonight Dad, please."

He tightened his hug and kissed her gently on her head.

6 February 2007. Each break time students would congregate in the quad area where there were flat wooden benches and areas of muddy grass. Paralysed by fear and the thought of looking stupid by being on her own, Noëmi would position herself next to a group of girls from her form. The girls were popular and self-assured; talking about weekend plans and older boys. She would sit by them reading, just on the limit. It was a busy place, where everyone would merge together. Noëmi was confident that she did not appear as an obvious hanger on.

This lunchtime they were joined by an eighteen year old student, wearing ripped jeans and a fringed black leather biker jacket, with a red and gold eagle embroidered on it. Deanna had told Noëmi all about him; he was 'John Ricketts-Dyer'. Actually, he should have been in Upper sixth but had to retake a year, following disappointing results in his exams. Tall, good looking with dark hair he was going out with a girl called Ellen, who was two years older than Noëmi. Ellen was small and delicate with a perfect complexion and soft, golden, curly hair.

Everyone knew that during the school charity week, the previous summer term, on pyjama day, Ellen and her boyfriend had arrived together in a double sleeping bag. They had zipped themselves up together and the rumour was that they had actually had sex in the sixth form common room whilst inside it. Technically Ellen would not have been allowed in the sixth form area, being under sixteen, but smuggled inside the sleeping bag, no one had noticed the lower school student was there. Noëmi was unnerved by how out of her league, daring and popular they were.

Sitting silently she noticed a gap had formed between her and the group. She considered what to do. Move closer uninvited? Or stay where she would be on her own in the quad? Suddenly her thoughts were interrupted by John Ricketts-Dyer in his leather jacket, moving right in front of her. He was peering straight into her face.

The whole scene fell silent as the entire group and other onlookers turned, stared at her and saw her for the first time. The tall sixth form student leant across and put his face right up against hers and said so all could hear;

"Who is this gross moron?"

John's audience all laughed, whilst a couple of girls who had spoken once or twice to Noëmi, also smirked and eventually laughed along too. Encouraged by the merriment he was creating he stared at Noëmi and shouted it out again and again.

"Who is this gross moron?"
"Who is this gross moron?"

Ellen looked at John and widened her eyes, although Noëmi felt this was more for how pretty she looked when imploring him, rather than for her feelings.

"It's a new girl, she's an orphan or something." Ellen finally said.

John laughed, put his arm around his girlfriend and swaggered off taking Ellen with him. Noëmi, body shut down, lowered her head and began to comprehend what had happened to her in front of everybody. She felt hot tears sting but luckily they did not leave her eyes. A space had now formed and the other girls had moved away from her and she was on her own.

She quietly turned and left to find the toilets.

'Had she been murdered?' She was not sure but she knew she may as well have been.

From then on, the incessant, humiliating, almost ritualistic baiting began and she was just known by everyone in school as 'gross moron' or sometimes just 'gross' for short.

CHAPTER 1 - SEPTEMBER 2016

Noëmi

More than 9 years later…St Wolbodo's School, Durham.

In spite of being a maths teacher, Noëmi had managed to horribly underestimate the time required to walk to the school. Flustered and running late, Noëmi had fifteen minutes to make it to her desk and get to the Monday morning all staff meeting.

Noëmi ran up the road, trying to manage her laptop bag and an umbrella against the pouring rain. She dodged sleepy commuters winding their way unwillingly to the station in one direction, and those trudging equally reluctantly to work in Durham city centre in the other.

Before she knew it she was through the door. Notebook in hand, Noëmi ran to the morning briefing, slipstreaming the senior management as they turned in from another corridor.

She walked, breathless, into the meeting.

'Thank God I'm in!'

She heard senior management file in behind her. Noëmi kept her head down, willing them not to see the hurried redness of her cheeks.

"In a rush this morning Noëmi?" quipped a familiar voice from behind her. She noticed the immaculate shine of his shoes before the friendly face. Frank, Head of Science, came and sat next to her.

"Oh Frank, I moved into my new flat this weekend. I thought the walk to work was two kilometres, not two miles."

"I'm just not going to ask how you got that maths degree, how was your birthday Noëmi?"

"Solitary, the usual, but things are changing. You know, I'm really feeling good about this year, Frank," she said as the meeting began.

The staffroom was trapped in time. No different from the previous year or any of those before. A large room filled with too few Seventies style chairs, in a number of pastel colours, now heavily coffee stained. These rough woollen seats were set out in small groups for staff members. There were rows of pigeon holes along one wall. A small set of work stations along another and a large picture window looking out onto the school playing field on the third. The fourth, Noëmi's favourite, was taken by a small kitchen area for staff coffee. Lucky enough to have been employed from June, Noëmi had already spent six weeks at the school. So she was familiar with the people and the set up. Even more so with the coffee.

"Good morning everyone and welcome back!" the Head Teacher, Maurice Mundy, a small, bespectacled man began, "the first point on the agenda is introductions…"

Noëmi flicked absent mindedly through her notebook not even glancing at the management team. After a moment, however, she realised that in this group must be the new Assistant Head, who was boldly coming in to improve the school. They had beaten Frank to the job.

"So unfair Frank," she had commented at the time.

"Well at least you have the preferred reaction, Val celebrated with champagne!"

"Typical of him, he doesn't want to share you with anyone or anything!"

Mundy's words fell faintly into the background of Noëmi's thoughts as she finally looked up at the group.

She saw a face she knew instantly.

Noëmi scanned the features and her blood froze. She heard nothing more apart from the confirmation that John Ricketts-Dyer, now known simply as John Dyer, life ruining tormentor, was joining the school as part of the senior management.

Maurice Mundy spoke as if he were announcing a celebrity.

"Let me introduce John, our bright young star who is coming in to lead us through the transition to academy status! We're so pleased that you're here John. I'm sure you know every trick in the book to make us a successful school!"

Faint laughter followed from the teachers.

"John has had a meteoric rise and is the youngest Assistant Head in the county if not the country. He has a mesmerising way with students as well as extensive subject knowledge in resistant materials."

"Undoubtedly an intellectual giant," muttered Frank. As Head of Science, he had no time for anything as nonsensical as *resistant materials*.

Noëmi tried to smile but could not. She found herself staring at 'John', feeling dizzy, incredibly sick but intently hanging onto every word.

"So, it's great to be here!" He clapped his hands together, "First thing I'll be doing is auditing all departments, observations, seeing what's what and tidying up the whole operation!" stated John with confidence. His voice grated on Noëmi.

"Getting rid of people then," muttered Frank.

"We need to have a tight ship to steer towards Ofsted and anyone who is not 100 per cent focused on riding this horse towards outstanding needs to throw in the towel immediately!" John stated boldly.

"Metaphorically messing with my head now," sighed Frank.

"Competent, consistent and committed teachers are what we need here," stated John with apparent passion.

"Of course." Frank rolled his eyes.

"So don't say I didn't warn you," John quipped with a wink, a point of the finger and almost a pantomime slap on the thigh. He then added "...and God bless," for his final flourish.

Again everyone chuckled.

The group dispersed for the training day, where students stayed home and staff had 'useful' preparation sessions.

Noëmi stood with feet of lead.

She could hardly believe after nearly ten long years that she was staring at John Ricketts-Dyer.

Then he was swaggering towards her to leave the staffroom. Panic rose to her chest. There was nowhere to go. No time to think. The image of him as the cruel sixth former was all she could see. Their eyes met.

John Dyer looked through her without the faintest glimmer of recognition.

Noëmi felt faint as he brushed past her. She found a seat and sat down, unable to talk. So many thoughts were in her head. She was thirteen years old all over again. Why did he have to be working in the same place as her? What was she to do?

He showed not even a flinch of unconscious recollection. His life had moved on. And so had hers. Noëmi was in a good place and that should be that.

'Just forget about it and let it go. Don't be a stupid child,' she reasoned. Her mind drifted back to those years, *'no I want my revenge.'*

Having gathered herself together, Noëmi moped quietly to the next meeting which would review the examination results. She walked to the school hall, a large traditional space with walnut cladding on the walls, a vaulted ceiling and a raised stage. A large wooden cross was suspended above the performance area, with a sizeable modern screen below it for presentations. Mr Mundy, Head Teacher, stood at an old style lectern.

John Dyer was sitting in the front row with the rest of senior management. Smiling, nodding, acquiescing, shaking hands, listening attentively, looking fascinated, standing up, giving warm pats on shoulders and making a fine impression at all the right moments. She examined him, the hair was dark and smartly cut, he was wearing an expensive midnight blue suit. He looked fresh faced and his jawline was firm. He spoke to people he did not know with ease and he oozed confidence. Wary of bumping into him again, she sat down with her maths colleagues and stared viciously at him.

Presentations followed, analysing the recent examination results and detailing areas for improvement. Hand-outs were shared, observations made and a range of pointless questions asked. In the queue for coffee during the break, Noëmi overheard a number of people remarking on the 'impressive' new Assistant

Head; one young teacher desperate to know if he was married. The other senior managers were smiling smugly to themselves, clearly happy with their smart new recruit. Already it seemed that John was forming friendships and allegiances.

The hot water urn ran out just as it was Noëmi's turn. With no hot drink, feeling quite suffocated, she went to get some air by standing at the hall's outside door that opened onto the school field. The September sun glistened on the damp grass and reflected off a small memorial plaque.

Frank found Noëmi and immediately expressed his frustration.

"Well useless would be a compliment given that I could be more gainfully employed simply staring at the wall."

Distracted Noëmi tried to think what to reply but came with nothing.

"You're very taciturn my dear, what's the problem? I think it may be more than realising you're wasting eight hours of your life stuck here!"

"Well you have a point Frank; I've just seen a ghost that's all."

"Don't talk to me about ghosts, Noëmi, they're everywhere, well for anyone with an interesting past that is. If you've lived a boring life then no need to worry!"

Frank was an intellectual, quick witted and kind man.

Noëmi thought that maybe she should be more relaxed, like Frank.

"Are we still all going out for a drink later?"

"Of course, my dear, but just our crowd, only people we can trust, need to let off a little steam after today!" smiled Frank.

"Will Val be joining us?"

"Ah no, he has a late night at the surgery, a couple of difficult root canal cases."

"Ouch, sounds bad."

"He still says it's an absolute breeze compared with teaching!"

"What being the dentist or the patient!"

"Both I think! You must have heard his rant about when he started training to be a teacher back in the day. God, one lesson with a bunch of thirteen year olds and that was it. Immediately he swapped courses to Dentistry! He couldn't stand the fact they talked throughout his class."

"No problems with that when drilling teeth!"

Frank laughed and looked at the schedule.

"Oh '*New Curriculum Information*' is next, this day just keeps giving!"

"Doesn't it just," smiled Noëmi, "I'll see you at The Swan and Three Cygnets later, about sixish?"

"Sounds perfect."

Back in the school hall, sitting in the next round of meetings, Noëmi did not listen to any of the talks of which the intent was either to inspire with unrealistic ideas or reprimand in a similar fashion.

She started to daydream about how she could get revenge on John Dyer. Her mind raced with ideas; get him sacked, reveal to everyone that he was a bully, accuse him of harassment and complain to Human Resources. Be smarter than him.

It was no good, none of this would work, it was easy to be an

14

Assistant Head, with hardly any teaching and all the power; he would inevitably do a 'good job'. Telling people about his treatment of her would make her look stupid and reopen all the wounds of humiliation. HR would need evidence of him being a pest and he was clearly going to keep his sheet clean here. *'Be smarter than him...'* she mused with this one.

A young art teacher went to the front to speak about gifted and talented students.

She noticed John Dyer eye up the teacher as she spoke. *'Such a pervert can't keep his eyes to himself.'* She thought about whether he would look at her like that. Maybe that was it? Make him fall for her and then reveal herself. She imagined playing on his weakness and humiliating him. Her plan was developing.

The day of meetings drew to a much needed end with a final mandatory all staff meeting in the hall. One of the administration staff was doing a register of the adults present.

"Ridiculous, how old do they think we are?" moaned Frank.

"This is just to check we've not all fucked off home," stated Noëmi, annoyed. She noticed Frank was looking at her curiously; she rarely swore.

"Or died of boredom more like," sighed Frank.

Maurice Mundy, Head Teacher, addressed the congregated staff and wished them well for the coming year. This gave everyone the impression that they were on their own, which indeed they were as he would be spending the year either hidden away in his office or 'out' for 'important lunch meetings'. John stood up and thanked everyone for the warm welcome he had received. Teachers then filed out to prepare their classrooms and their mark books, ready for the students returning the following day.

Noëmi went to her classroom where she spent the next couple of hours trying to organise her class lists, but she was unable to concentrate. She was exhausted before the term had even begun. With relief she turned off the lights and shut the door of her classroom just before six.

She headed to the Swan and Three Cygnets, which was a favourite of hers, being right on the river in Durham. She found Frank and a few others sitting together in the snug.

"Hello dear friends," she said as she sat down with them.

"Ah Noëmi, good to see you're on time for the pub!" joked Frank.

"Clearly I have priorities," smiled Noëmi.

"What did we all think then?" asked Charvi.

"The new Assistant Head is very young," said Brianna.

"What's his reputation?" asked Frank.

"No one seems to know," said Charvi, "I asked around, that new maths teacher Will knew him from when they were trainee teachers, says they were friendly."

"I'm sure Mr Dyer has fond memories of being a trainee, it can only have been yesterday!" said Frank sarcastically and the others laughed. "Mmm I think he's trying to be tough, snooping around the department meetings and looking sinister," he continued more seriously.

"He's not bad looking," said Brianna, whose mind was elsewhere.

"How does what he looks like matter?" asked Charvi.

"Well just saying," said Brianna defensively.

"He's vile," stated Noëmi and Frank looked at her intrigued.

"I don't like him, not at all," said Noëmi decisively.

"Well I would say you're a good judge of people, Noëmi, so I'm with you, and also he called me 'Dad' when I met him at the interviews for the Assistant Head position."

"Ageist!" Noëmi shouted,

"Well I was more offended that he thought he was good enough to share my genes, even in jest!" Frank finished his drink.

Everyone laughed.

"And I'll be leaving with you when he's Head Teacher," said Frank.

"Oh God don't say that," replied Noëmi.

"Nothing would surprise me in this place," said Charvi.

"Mundy's on the way out they say," added Brianna breezily.

"Who knows? But I'm already knackered and I've not even seen a student yet," laughed Frank.

The group continued chatting about their summer and where they had visited. Frank had been to Italy to visit his husband Valentino's family and they had travelled around Pompeii, Sicily and the Amalfi coast. Val consoled him when he did not get the promotion, by saying that it would only have 'interfered with' or indeed 'ruined' their social life. They ate well, drank red wine and immersed themselves in Italian culture and family squabbles.

"Well they're in a mandamento really aren't they?" Frank would comment.

Noëmi's mind wandered. She was missing her old school friend Marcus McKenzie more than anything and wanted to talk to him about the shock she had received today.

CHAPTER 2 - MAYA

Noëmi

Walking home, Noëmi was now determined to get revenge in its most brutal form. She imagined herself witnessing John Dyer's spectacular downfall. She would make him desperate for her, humiliate him and make him feel small. Yet this idea jarred with her as it would mean some kind of physical contact which she knew she could never do. There was no way she could ever allow him to touch her. There was a problem with her plan.

As she got to her flat, she carried on desperately trying to think, turned on the television and flicked through the channels. Her attention was suddenly caught by a documentary about 'catfishing' and she sat transfixed as she watched the scenario unfold. A catfish was when someone pretended to be someone else in order to deceive another. This was it! She would make him want her via a fake persona, torment him like a cat with a mouse between its paws, and then destroy him. She would play every relationship trick; ghost him, gaslight him, control him. What better downfall than to make him fall in love with 'her' and then deny him? She was suddenly a little bit shocked at her vitriol. Where was her forgiveness? *'That man deserves to be punished,'* she said to herself.

Now she needed to create a profile that would definitely entice him into her power. Noëmi grabbed her school laptop and scoured the internet for images. She found some but there were not enough for her to create a whole persona. What she needed was to lift someone's entire life so that she could use it to captivate John. She searched for 'sexy woman' images, but they were too extreme to be convincing. Suddenly she remembered. On her social media she was friends with a Polish woman called Magda, whom she had met once at a fitness event. Magda was a strikingly good looking woman, with an enviable figure that she liked to show off on her profile. In addition Magda did swimsuit and lingerie modelling and had no problem sharing her images with her social media friends. Magda had long chestnut hair and stunning green eyes, well set in perfect cheekbones. Looking at her photos Magda clearly had a zest for life. Luckily she had a variety of photos available, as well as a set of super sexy ones that would be handy too. To make things even better Magda lived far away in the south of England, and was in no mutual social circle, having only become a contact with Noëmi, after a brief meeting a couple of years earlier. She decided that Magda should now be called Maya.

She felt uncomfortable about what she was doing, as Magda had accepted her friend request and clearly trusted her. She brushed off a twinge of shame, *'Just ignore it, he deserves to be brought down, he has robbed me of my teenage years',* she thought to herself. *'The ends justify the means do they not? Magda will never know'.*

In recompense for feeling so guilty, she clicked 'like' on Magda's public profile picture and started work on Maya's dating profile.

'Hey Maya here! Part time model and fitness instructor. You'll find me on the tennis court or in the gym. Holidays for me, it's Ibiza clubbing, St Moritz skiing and scuba diving in the Red Sea. Work takes me everywhere!!! Last month it was New York, Stockholm and Barcelona. I also love to party and to meet new people, especially men who can keep my needs satisfied. Get in touch!'

Noëmi should have been sleeping in preparation for the long first day of term. Yet she was on a roll and totally absorbed in preparing her new persona; indeed she was quite impressed with her work. By the end, even she wanted to get to know Maya. Noëmi yawned and looked at the clock, it was 11pm, and she had to be up in seven hours. Yet she did not feel tired, her mind still distracted by the work of making Maya into the perfect decoy with which to bait John Dyer.

M and N:

Deeply engrossed in her preparation of Maya's dating profile, she heard a notification, could it finally be Jesse? She looked at her phone.

'Hiya N, how's school going? Would love to hear from you Mxxx'

It was Marcus, she was absolutely delighted. Noëmi looked up at the clock, realising that she had spent a further two hours on the profile. She wondered whether she was of sound mind to be so fixated with this man, however each time reason entered her head, anger chilled her blood, she sat up tall.

"That man will suffer," she said out loud with determined resolve.

Coming out of her stupor she pushed her laptop to one side, relaxed her body and called Marcus on her phone.

"Hey!" she said as he picked up.

"N, how are you? What are you up to? I've not heard anything from you for a bit, what's going on?" Marcus asked.

"Sorry, it's been busy. What time is it there Dr McKenzie?"

"It's about 7am, and doctor? I wish, still another year to go until I'm fully qualified, but hey Vietnam is awesome. We're up early to get out of the city to see the Củ Chi tunnels. It's where many North Vietnamese lived during the war, underground can you believe? Thousands of people...but I wouldn't have expected you to still be up as it's... what, about one o'clock in the morning there?"

"Yes, but I saw your message and I wanted to talk to you."

"Okay, I was making the most of the hostel Wi-Fi," he explained, "We go to the healthcare project in Phnom Penh tomorrow."

"You've been away nearly two weeks already, it's going fast!"

"Yes, another couple to go then back to Oxford to get ready for finals, what joy!"

"Mmm that'll be good."

"You sound distracted."

"Oh you know school...getting me down already."

"That's not like you Miss McAllister!"

She was silent, so he carried on, "Okay what's really the problem?"

"No nothing...Oh Marcus I've seen that Dyer person," she sighed, ready to tell him everything.

"What do you mean?"

"Do you remember that guy from school, John Ricketts-Dyer, that sixth former, that one who... you know..."

"Yes, yes, unfortunately, I do, good looking guy, tall, popular."

"Sounds like you fancy him."

Marcus laughed.

"You know he made a racist remark to me once, my mum complained, and he got suspended for a week." Marcus reminded her.

21

"I tell you he's awful, a bully and a racist, were you not mad at him?"

"To be honest I was twelve and not really sure why anyone would be bothered about the colour of my skin, now I know otherwise."

"Evil man," said Noëmi.

"Well he's out of our lives now."

"No! Not true, he's got some big job at my school, can you believe? He's dropped the double-barrel name thing, just Dyer now."

"Are you sure it's him?"

The silence made Marcus quite sure she knew it was him.

"Has he recognised you?"

"It would appear not, and he came right up close, looking straight at me."

"Well you have changed, remember your hair in school, I thought you looked lovely but it was very unique."

After her mother had died, Noëmi had cut her hair herself, in the same style that her mum had in the Eighties; a fluffy layered look which made her feel close to her mother. She refused to have it any other way and only changed it once she had left school. However, whatever her style choices, Marcus was ever supportive of her.

"Maybe I'll go back to that hair style one day."

"You can't, he'll recognise you!"

"Damn you're right, the hair stays," laughed Noëmi "But how are you M? What's Vietnam like?" changing the subject.

"Manic, hot, lovely people, the war history is unbelievable, the Vietnamese have suffered so much," said Marcus, clearly very taken with the city.

Noëmi felt envious and wished she could be with him.

"I'm looking forward to hearing about it all, we must go out when you get back, have some fun!" She bounced back optimistically, desperate to see him.

"Great idea, to get together that is. But I warn you when I get back, I may sleep the whole time, the final university clinical year is going to be the most anti-social and physically exhausting gig ever."

"Well, you tell me the weekend you get back and I'll look forward to it," replied Noëmi, wanting to encourage him.

"Great, I'll do that, but I have to dash now, getting the coach to the tunnels, what are you doing?"

"Oh, nothing much, just catching up on school work," she lied.

"Don't exhaust yourself, it's already late and term is only just starting," he replied.

The call ended and Noëmi felt glad to have spoken to him. Since his departure they had kept in regular email and messaging contact and she enjoyed hearing about his adventures. He replied with equal attention and awaited her news eagerly. Noëmi found that nothing was held back. Yet this morning, for it was now tomorrow already, she sat bolt upright in the silent darkness, her heart racing, feeling sick. She realised she had crossed a line and lied to Marcus for the first time in her life and in the nine years of knowing him.

"Well it kind of is to do with teaching... teaching someone a lesson," she justified to herself. Ignoring her conscience, she worked furiously on Maya's profile until 2am, only pausing once to search on the internet what the Củ Chi tunnels were.

CHAPTER 3 - NOËMI

Manon

Noëmi's mother, Manon Santoro, had grown up in the south of Italy, to Italian parents and she was named after *Manon Lescaut.* Having met Donnie McAllister at Edinburgh University they quickly settled down together. Parenthood surprised them early in their married life.

"Donnie, can we name her Noëmi?"

"That's beautiful like her, she's got your face, Noëmi, you know if we take the letters from our names we can make Noëmi!"

"It's a sign!"

"The extra letters could give us *Donna* as her second name, Italian for a woman," said Donnie.

"And the female version of your name! We have just one *N* left over!" joked Manon.

"Then that's her nickname as no one will pronounce her name correctly anyway!" he replied as he gazed at their beautiful daughter.

This confirmed to Manon that it was meant to be.

"Noëmi," she looked into her baby's eyes, "I wish you all the love, joy and happiness that exist in the world. I will always be with you on this brilliant adventure we're starting together."

However, their contentment was to be short lived, as fate had other ideas. Manon died from leukaemia on 7 December 2006, at the age of 38. Noëmi, who was then thirteen years old, had to move with her father to Newcastle, where his firm also had an office. And then it happened. John Dyer ruined her already ruined life.

Noëmi

6 November 2007... Your smile.

Now fourteen, Noëmi was feeling tired as she left school that day. Whilst she had not come into direct contact with John Dyer again, accounts of the incident spread wickedly around the school. Indeed a group of boys in her year, in awe of the sixth former, enjoyed the fact they now had someone to bully. They relentlessly tormented her with *gross moron* name calling. They followed her when they were bored, wrote on her school books and sent photos of her with vile comments around their group. Every day the comments got worse; *'Gross moron swot.'*

The drizzle seeped down constantly and the sky was gun metal grey; it was, after all, a typical day in November in north eastern Britain. Walking home she saw a fellow student Marcus McKenzie behind her. He was tall, good looking and had an athletic build. His smile was warm, his eyes were kind and his hair was soft and curly, worn stylishly in a short afro.

"No - em - eee, No - em - eee." She heard behind her, she looked round, Marcus was alone.

"Can you and your foul friends never just leave me be?" she scowled, rain was trickling down her collar and her hair was going frizzy.

"I only called your name. Had to get your attention somehow,

Noëmi."

She looked suspiciously at him.

"Why don't you join in with what all the others call me?"

"God no! I'd never do that, I hate how they treat you."

She was taken aback; he seemed to be so well brought up.

"What are you some kind of saint?"

"You did well in English today," he said, shifting his rucksack onto his other shoulder.

Noëmi was silent. She had not expected a conversation let alone a compliment and had no response. She looked round and he smiled at her.

"You always do well, you're the one to beat," said Marcus.

"Aren't I, in so many ways," replied Noëmi sarcastically.

"People don't always mean what they say."

She decided to let him know what she thought.

"Then why say it?"

He looked at her and then at the ground as he thought up his reply.

"Dunno it's just stuff, just stuff to say for that lot," said Marcus,

Noëmi grimaced. It rang true. From what she had seen at Newcastle Green, fourteen year old boys tended to just follow the crowd and join in with taunts without thinking.

Marcus continued; "I think they're not considering your feelings."

27

"No, really is that so?" she replied with a scoff, "Is this a joke? Is someone videoing this or something?"

"They really have damaged you haven't they?" he said genuinely.

Noëmi was incredulous at how thoughtful he was. She realised that he was very much his own person.

"I don't need you to feel sorry for me."

"No, I just want to talk to you that's all, I like that you're smart, you know stuff, in maths I heard you counting in Italian, no one else can do that."

"Maybe in Italy they can."

"Yeah but in Newky Green it's a thing,"

"God, anything beyond a two word sentence is a *thing* in that place," Noëmi replied.

Marcus laughed, "It's a mess, did you see that prize draw, for everyone with 100 per cent attendance, in assembly today?"

"And the winner was absent!" They said this at the same time.

Marcus laughed. Noëmi too, but then she checked herself, worried in case he was making a fool of her.

"I still don't trust you. I reckon this is a big prank."

"You can trust me," he said, putting his hands out physically manifesting his lack of artifice.

"You're doing well in everything too."

He was now walking beside her. "I need to up my game, I want to go to Oxbridge or whatever it was they were going on about in that talk we had, none of my family ever went to university."

28

"Same, I want to go there too, my parents went to Edinburgh uni and said it was awesome. It'll get me away from this nasty little place."

"You could get into the Oxbridge thing I would say."

"You're funny, you hang around with that useless bunch of haters but you seem alright."

They turned into the busy road.

"Anyway you'd better go now in case you get seen talking to me, terrible things could happen to you, your reputation would be destroyed forever. For me things can only get better."

"They will. We could help each other with work and that, go to Oxbridge."

"You know they're two places, one is Oxford and the other is Cambridge, they put half of each name together to come up with Oxbridge."

"You know all this. Now, you can help me get in."

"Okay, and what do I get out of it?"

"You get to spend time with me!"

"You're really annoying."

Noëmi swung herself round and saw he was smiling at her.

"If you're lucky you'll see me tomorrow!"

As it happened, Marcus lived around the corner, on the street next to hers in the High Heaton area of Newcastle. That evening, listening to some of her mother's favourite music, she looked out from her bedroom window and made out the lights of his home.

I have no friends, no-one to see
And I am never invited
But I am here, talking to you
No wonder I get excited

She began to relive the conversation and smiled to herself.

She thought of Marcus in a different way and from then on he would often wait for her on the way home from school. By the end of the year they met every day to walk home together. After school they would study hard at Noëmi's house, helping each other. They were delighted with how well they were getting on in their work and with each other.

The McKenzie house was a 1930s red brick semi-detached, with a bright scarlet front door, extended to accommodate the family: Marianna, her husband Anthony, their children Marcus, Jayden, Isaiah, Tianna, and Marianna's mother Raeni. Having arrived in the UK from Jamaica in 1948, Raeni's family had built a new life. Aware of the opportunities that schooling and qualifications gave people, Raeni valued education beyond anything else. Marcus, as the eldest grandchild, delighted in repaying her enthusiasm. Both parents worked long hours; so Raeni took charge of the children and would sit with them going over their school work to ensure they made the best progress. Her dedication left a marked impression on Marcus and he was inspired to see how far he could advance in every subject.

It made Noëmi smile that Marcus was the only student she knew who would smarten himself up, doing up his top button and straightening his tie, for when he arrived home from school. She soon got to know the high standards his mother had and how her children feared her disappointment more than anything.

The McKenzie family were vociferous, warm and welcoming, taking Noëmi and her father under their wing. They became close through her friendship with Marcus and would socialise regularly, with days out, picnics and meals together. For Donnie this companionship saved him from being consumed by grief and helped him manage the emptiness that had followed their bereavement. Marianna was kind and direct, asking Noëmi questions such as; *'You're so young. How do you have time to study and do everything around the house?'*

Often she would tell Noëmi, *'I admire your strength, child, your father is not well and I see you are also fragile.'*

Spring 2009. During their time at school, Noëmi and Marcus were in many of the same classes. By Year 11 the students were nearly sixteen and getting ready to sit their final GCSE exams. Their history teacher, Mrs Gomez, had found that these large children were getting harder to manage.

Standing, hands on hip, at the front of the class, almost hidden by a pile of text books, she raised her voice,

"To avoid my premature death caused by the inability of this so-called top set to listen, you will henceforth be seated in alphabetical order."

Moaning loudly, the students lumbered themselves into their seating plan, using the opportunity for silliness such as forgetting the alphabet and pretending to topple into one another; generally larking about. The register order meant Noëmi McAllister and Marcus McKenzie were going to be sitting next to each other.

"Finally, I love being a *Mc!*" joked Marcus as he swung his legs over the desk to take his new place.

"With no A!" she grabbed her things and quickly joined him.

"We Scots need to stick together."

"You're English and I'm Italian, well maybe half Scottish I suppose," she said in reply, smiling.

Their banter was soon interrupted by Rob Barr, from behind

shouting, "Marcus is about to be infected by gross," and many others laughing.

Marcus turned, annoyed, and shouted to Rob, "Why don't you just fuck off."

Noëmi went bright red and put her head down as the rest of the class either guffawed or gasped.

Mrs Gomez let out a small yelp, "McKenzie and Barr remain at the end of the lesson please."

"I'm so sorry it's all my fault," Noëmi said quietly to Marcus.

"Don't you apologise, that dumbass is the one who should apologise."

"But you're in trouble now, what if you get excluded?"

"I don't care about things like that, I hate this constant bullying, abuse and all that stuff."

Marcus

Mrs Gomez spoke to Marcus and Rob at the end of class.

"Marcus, I'm truly shocked by your language," she said.

"I'm shocked by Rob's constant bullying of a fellow pupil," he replied.

"This is not the time to be smart, you need to apologise."

Rob stood looking at his feet saying nothing.

Marcus looked between the two of them.

"I apologise sincerely to you Mrs Gomez for using that language, it was wrong. I'm sorry Rob for swearing at you but I'm just preparing you for the real world because if you bully people you may find that people will swear at you or worse."

"Is that some kind of threat?" asked Mrs Gomez.

"No merely an observation about human behaviour,"

"What's he been doing?" asked Mrs Gomez fairly.

"It's a thing they do to Noëmi McAllister, ever since she arrived at this school, name calling. It never stops, every day, it goes on and on. She has to walk all different routes round the school to avoid them. They write on her books, that's why her history book is covered now. It's been nearly two years already and they never tire of it." Marcus explained.

Rob found his feet even more interesting.

"I see, thank you for letting me know I had no idea. I'd have thought by Year 11 this kind of mean, immature behaviour would've stopped," she said exasperated.

"Me too, but please talk to her first, please don't call her dad, he's really not well," implored Marcus.

"Right, I understand. I'll look into this, have a talk with some support services and see what we can do to help her. But you mustn't swear Marcus, now off you go," she finished.

"Is he not going to get excluded?" asked Rob, speaking for the first time.

"Absolutely not, I'm grateful that he brought the abuse to my attention, now you need to help me clean my classroom after school for the whole of next week and we can discuss how to be kind to others as you do it." Rob rolled his eyes and handed over his diary for Mrs Gomez to write in the sanction.

Marcus soon found out that Mrs Gomez had thought it best to let his mother know about the incident. She had written a short email, without the full details, which caused a problem at home.

"Swearing? In class?" Marianna challenged her son.

Marcus remained silent.

"When did I bring a child up to behave in such a way?" She felt shame running through her veins and Marcus knew it.

Marcus said nothing.

"I have told you time and again how much harder it is for us. Everyone wants to think we're the bad ones, the people who are the problem, who cause all the trouble. We all need to avoid actions that can put us in the wrong light. Plus what does the Bible say? Turn the other cheek. What do you have to say for yourself?"

"I'm sorry," was all he came back with. He did not want to tell his mother about how Noëmi was treated at school lest she told Donnie and it upset him. Noëmi had carefully hidden from her father all details of the grim torment she was experiencing every day and Marcus knew it.

"You know I just don't think you're sorry, I think you're arrogant and selfish. What gives you the right to talk down to people? Swearing at another pupil."

"Nothing, I *am* sorry."

Marianna

He was made, by his mother, to write apologies to his teacher Mrs Gomez and to the student Rob. Marianna chose not to let Raeni know as she knew how upset she would be. He was grounded, although that made no difference as he was not going out anyway with the exams approaching. His mother viewed him with suspicion. She arranged to call Mrs Gomez, to discuss the incident.

"Thank you for your time and I want to express my sincere regret for Marcus' behaviour. My son has written a letter of apology, I hope you have it."

"Oh yes, Marcus gave it to me immediately. He gave one to the student as well, although I don't think he needed to. Really there's no need to worry. It was an isolated incident, but I had to let you know in case there's anything you've noticed in his behaviour which could indicate problems. Young adolescents are very vulnerable. He's the most conscientious and polite child I've ever taught so it was quite dramatic."

"But I don't understand why he did this?" explained Marianna.

"Did he not tell you?" Mrs Gomez was shocked.

"No, he just said he was *sorry*."

"He was standing up for a student who was being bullied."

"Oh!" Marianna was surprised.

"Yes, to be honest he really has been amazing. I've since found out that this student has suffered an awful lot, terrible, but I think his defending them has been a brave thing to do. So much easier to follow the crowd. You should be proud of him."

Marianna had no words; she chose a moment to talk to her son.

"I spoke to Mrs Gomez."

"Okay."

"She says you have been standing up for someone who is being bullied."

"Did she say who?"

"No. Do you want to tell me about it?"

"Yes and no."

"I understand, you have your own life, but is this other student in danger?"

"I don't think so, it's tough for them, their family doesn't know, they don't want to worry them, they do have friends."

"Yes, but this person needs help."

"It's okay Mum, they're okay, don't worry about them but it's just humiliating isn't it? Bullies defining someone like that, it sucks out the soul. Some sixth former started it all, he's left now but it just carries on and on. Imagine how it must be to go to school each day knowing you will be made a fool of by others for no reason. It's just annoying for me but humiliating for her."

Marianna left it, if she needed to know her son would tell her.

On the one hand she was proud of her son for his thoughtfulness, and on the other aware that he was growing up. She was not sure who the victim was, but she had a good idea. Noëmi did not have the confidence that most young people did and seemed to be jumpy and wary of others, plus she knew what a true and close friend her son was to her.

CHAPTER 4 - MOVE ON

Noëmi

18 August 2011, two years later. Throughout their time at school Marcus and Noëmi grew ever closer and increasingly dependent on one another. Sharing the same ambitions they were elated when A Level results' day brought well deserved success. For both their Oxbridge dream was realised. Ready to move on, sixth form students were all meeting up to celebrate, and toast future dreams, in a city centre bar that had organised half price drinks.

Marcus and Noëmi met at the corner of their roads and fell into a tender embrace.

"You're looking good in that dress, N,"

"You too, well not in a dress! Great shirt, you look very dapper Mr McKenzie!"

"Dapper! Well you look gorgeous Miss McAllister!"

"Ha! You're wearing that jacket!"

"Yes I know, remember your Dad dropped it round to the house!"

"How could I forget! Jacketgate!"

Together they headed for the city.

At the bar everyone was relaxed; the music was loud, the mood was buoyant.

Marcus' friends greeted him immediately, hugging and back slapping each other. The pair went their separate ways as they did not share the same close friendship groups. Noëmi was friendly with a couple of girls there, Ruby and Deanna.

"I failed maths," sighed Ruby, "I went out the night before with Kai; he was bored so we spent the evening at Best Golf."

"You play golf?" Deanna was all eyelashes.

"No stupid, it's a place for drinking and hanging out whilst the guys play snooker or hit baskets."

"Sounds fun, why don't you play?" asked Noëmi.

"Kai doesn't like me doing his stuff, he just likes me there."

Noëmi was a bit taken aback.

"Anyway, what about you? You're actually really friendly with Marcus, he's so hot. You know Charlotte from our maths group really likes him, can you put a word in for her?" said Ruby.

"He's so buff you can tell he works out," continued Ruby, checking her reflection in the window.

'Yeah he seems obsessed with the gym," agreed Deanna, smoothing her hair.

"So fucking fit." Ruby said, leaning back to finish her drink.

Noëmi felt uncomfortable, her palms got sweaty.

The bar got busier and hotter as more people pushed their way in. Noëmi found herself separated from the others so she stepped out the back door into the pub garden to get some air. The night was dappled but clear and bright. She popped her jacket on a wrought iron chair and looked up at the skies. She felt optimistic about the future for the first time since the death of her mother, *'Cambridge, can you believe it! Mum I'm going to make you so proud.'*

"Dreaming as usual? Look over there you can see Mars, it's redder than the other stars and planets," she recognised Marcus' voice and smiled at him.

"Astronomy expert now are you?"

"No, I got this new thing on my phone, Star Walk, look it shows you what everything is," he moved next to her and got his phone out to demonstrate the app to her.

"Getting ready to impress everyone at Oxford are we?" she smiled.

"Seems hard to believe it's happening eh?"

Noëmi leant on the wooden picnic bench and gestured at him to move next to her.

They were the only two from Newcastle Green Academy to have got into Oxford or Cambridge. The Head Teacher was beside himself with joy; their last Oxbridge success had been fifteen years earlier and now he had two students who had made the grade. Their picture together had appeared in the local paper that day. Noëmi loved to look at it as she remembered how Marcus had put his arm around her for the photo. It was such an affectionate and public gesture. Marianna had requested copies of the photo for everyone from the publishers. Both she and Donnie intended to put theirs into photo frames to be displayed proudly on their mantelpieces.

"I'm so excited," Noëmi confessed.

Marcus gave her a smile and sat on the bench next to her and put his feet on one of the iron garden chairs. "How far away are Oxford and Cambridge from each other? We must visit, see which one's best!"

"Two hours by car, but there's no direct train, I've already looked."

"Oh I see," Marcus laughed.

"I'm excited for a new beginning, you must be too? For me the time has come when I can slam the door on the past."

"No, I get that N."

"...but I'm no victim, I don't want you to feel sorry for me." She clenched her glass with both hands.

"I don't, I'm angry about the name calling thing though, it all says more about those haters than you."

"Just don't mention it. Doing well academically saved me...and... you..."

He moved in front of her and looked at her sincerely, "Am I in the past too?"

Noëmi laughed and replied "No, you've held me up all this time and never let me go, there's not a big enough word to say what you mean to me."

Taking her hands off the glass and he held them in his.

"Finally, I feel it's time we were properly together...all year we've been..." said Marcus looking down. The muffled sounds of music were thumping from the bar.

Noëmi laughed with embarrassment, "Oh my...yes...I would love..."

"Marcus get here!"

"Mate! shots now!"

She heard Marcus' friends shrieking from the other garden door, for him to come back inside. She saw the faces of his many friends.

'Not good enough for him'.

She threw her head back.

"Look we're going off to uni, don't get nostalgic, you should be planning your future like I am, not getting stuck in the past," she said casually.

"Noëmi, no, don't say that!"

"Time to move on." She looked straight ahead.

"No! Think of all the stuff we've done...helping each other, having a laugh, those jokes no one else gets... but Noëmi you remember that day, those times together... what we promised? It meant absolutely everything to us both, my feelings have never changed... "

"There's not even a train," She looked away.

"Noëmi, why won't you give it a go?"

"Marcus, I don't want to hold you back. You've already given up too much for me. You need to look forward, anyway it's unrealistic to expect a long distance relationship to work."

"That's just not true. God, now you're completely breaking my heart."

"Mate come on!" Two of his friends were coming over.

Noëmi turned away, as Marcus got pulled by his friends to join them, causing him to spill his beer over his shirt. With Marcus gone, the last of the bunch shouted *'Gross moron'* from a distance laughing.

Noëmi felt a sudden chill and went to fetch her jacket from the garden chair.

She bit her lip to stop it trembling, Marcus was gone. She wrapped her jacket around herself to stop herself shivering. Abruptly her phone pinged; her dad was outside to pick her up. Getting up she caught sight of Marcus who had freed himself from his friends.

He ran to her.

"Noëmi!"

"Dad's here, I have to go,"

"Already?"

"I can't get into the club, Digital, anyway. Plus you know he insists on fetching me now after that Christmas party. Bit embarrassing really, hope he's round the corner."

"Okay, wait! I'll walk you round to him." Marcus said quietly and put his jacket on.

They left the bar together into the cool evening which was lit by a clear sky.

Donnie thanked Marcus.

Outside, hugging him tightly, Noëmi said goodbye to Marcus who went to join his friends again. They saw Marcus walking away. He looked back over his shoulder at them.

"He's *such* a gentleman that boy! Always keeping you so safe!"

Noëmi was silent.

"How was the celebrating?" Donnie asked his daughter as she got into the red Renault 4 he had just got back on the road.

"Yeah good, it's just I can't go to the club because I'm not eighteen, eight days to go."

"Ah yes that's a shame," Donnie replied, "but they can be dangerous places, drugs, knives, and the other day I saw this terrible documentary. An arson attack on a club and the poor people could not get out. Many died. Just awful."

Noëmi was lost in her thoughts, looking out of the window at the blurry city lights. She caught her reflection in the car's mirror.

Arriving back at their semi-detached 1930s home, they said goodnight.

"You've done so well N, getting into Cambridge, things are really looking up for you!"

"Yeah, sure Dad, but sometimes it feels one thing gets on track only for another to derail. But Cambridge will be a new start. Night."

Ruby

Deanna and Ruby had noticed Marcus and Noëmi leave the bar.

"I hope he's coming back or do you think they're hooking up?" commented Ruby, cupping her glass in her hands.

"Reading books with each other, more like!" joked Deanna.

"I think there's more to that so-called friendship than they let on," said Ruby. "She's really cagey about him and he's always single, Charlotte got nowhere."

"They would be actually really cute together, they're well suited, the clever ones in the school," admitted Deanna.

"Yes but I think Marcus needs a bit of pre-university fun don't you? I mean Oxford sounds pretty boring and hard work."

Ruby was scheming.

Upon his re-entering the bar, Deanna, Ruby and Charlotte accosted Marcus en masse.

"Hey, well done, amazing result."

"You did so great."

"You're so clever Marcus."

"So fit and smart," Lots of compliments flowed.

"Thanks but well done and good luck for all your courses too!" he replied.

"Yeah whatever, you know what, we've all changed our plans and we're going to a house party at Ruby's now, cheaper and we can go on longer, your group's coming, why don't you?" said Deanna.

"Oh hold on I'll let Noëmi know she left as she can't get into Digital."

"Sure but don't worry, I'll message her the details, save you the bother, we'll see her there!"

"Thanks Deanna."

Noëmi

The next morning Noëmi was woken at 6am by her father.

"N, where did Marcus go last night?"

Face buried in her pillow, she replied, sleepily, "They all went to a club, Digital, in the town centre."

"He's not gone home, Marianna's beside herself with worry."

"But often people sleep over so she shouldn't be concerned."

"Yes but he never does, you know they don't allow that because of all their beliefs. He's never not come home before, she wants to call the police. I can just imagine how she must be beside herself, poor Marianna."

"Let me call him."

"He's not answering."

"I'll call Deanna."

She got her phone and called her friend.

Finally she picked up "Deanna where are you?"

"Ruby's… we had a gathering, why?"

"Where's Marcus?"

"In bed with Charlotte, why?"

Noëmi felt her stomach lurch; she sat up, paused and took in this news.

"His mum wants to phone the police," she managed.

"Don't let her do that, I'll go and wake him and Charlotte. I'll see he gets home straight away. Seriously, just make sure she doesn't call the police. There's all sorts of shit here, plus Ruby's parents have no idea, don't let her do anything stupid, bye Noëmi."

Noëmi turned to her pillow. She knew Ruby's luxurious, modern, detached home. She wondered what the beige leather sofas, soft cream carpets and ornate curtains in a gold chintz cotton, looked like now.

"Tell Marianna he's okay and he'll be home very soon," she reassured her father and she sank back under her duvet thinking about Marcus and Charlotte in bed.

An hour later, Donnie got a call from Marianna to say that Marcus had made it home with a raging hangover and could he thank Noëmi for helping out. Donnie left for work and Noëmi sat wondering what had possessed Marcus to spend the night with Charlotte.

* * *

Noëmi's phone rang. It was Marcus.

"What?" she replied curtly.

"I need your help."

"Why?" even more abruptly.

"I don't know what happened last night, you need to find out for me, I'm terrified I've done something wrong," He explained the situation and what he remembered from the night before, which was very little.

"Why are you asking me? Maybe Charlotte could help? After all she was there in bed with you," she said resentfully.

"Noëmi don't..."

"Do you think I want to find out the lurid details of you and Charlotte? Oh that'll be fun for me to hear! For all your intelligence you have none really do you?"

"Sorry, it was a dumb thing to ask," he snapped back.

Noëmi hung up without saying goodbye.

Desperate, he appeared on her doorstep, feeling dreadful, early that afternoon.

"N please, I'm sorry I'm just frantic," he said sitting with his head in his hands in her kitchen.

"What do you remember?"

"The three of them said all these nice things and that we were all going to a house party. Deanna was going to message you to come too, it was busy, hot, loud, lots of drinks, so many people. I do remember Charlotte coming on to me, then nothing."

"Any other details?"

"Okay so we were kissing."

Noëmi looked away.

"I have no idea why, I don't like her in that way, then the next thing is waking up and she's there, next to me, her in her underwear and me in mine..."

"Oh God they set you up, hold on."

She rang Deanna and put her on loud speaker.

"Hey, Deanna, I need a favour."

'Yeah?"

"Marcus needs some information."

Deanna burst out laughing.

"Deanna! He's really worried, he can't remember what happened."

"Well let's just say Charlotte was somewhat left flat. Her party fun didn't add up to much," Deanna laughed some more.

"Deanna what did you all do to him? Tell me!"

"Oh for God's sake the beautiful one can't hold his drink. We just helped loosen him up a little before boring old Oxford. Charlotte got nothing okay, but she really likes him so if he's there with you, tell him to call her for a proper hook up."

"Charlotte needs to call him and tell him the truth."

"What are you, the Patron Saint of having no fun? Parties are fair game, sometimes people just need relaxing, encouraging, easing into the spirit."

"If there was a house party at Ruby's, why was I not invited? You knew I couldn't get into Digital."

"Did you not get my text?"

"Deanna! Stop lying to me!"

"Well he didn't need his minder with him. You would've stopped all the fun."

"Deanna! Honestly, just sort it out!"

They waited and within a couple of minutes Charlotte rang Marcus to admit what had happened and apologise. She recorded the call.

Marcus sat with her, silent and looking down at his hands.

"Thank you Noëmi, I feel so stupid."

"Well you were stupid, really naïve. They'll have spiked your drinks, they've done it before to other guys. They hoped that you would've got some way with Charlotte, beyond kissing. I imagine they'll be sharing a picture of you and her getting off together, as we speak. But the drink spiking thing and taking your clothes off you, both are illegal."

"Yes, if a bloke did that the other way around."

"Exactly! But actually anyone to another!"

"You've saved my life."

"No, I've just cut out some worry, that's all. Those girls honestly and I can't believe you fell for it... the beautiful one..." she stopped, pondering on the nickname Deanna had coined for him, "true I suppose," she said almost to herself.

"I could've thrown everything away in one stupid moment," he said.

"Well yes, but no, you didn't do anything, remember? Ah of course you don't! You did nothing but pass out."

"Noëmi, the Charlotte thing, you know I..."

"Yeah I don't need to hear about that." Noëmi replied. "You're not the only one with feelings."

Marcus

Marcus was in too dreadful a state to respond. He still looked drained from having thrown up all morning and had been put off any ideas of romance, with any other human, ever again. Noëmi made lots of tea and toast, then they watched some episodes of *Friends* curled up together on the sofa, happy just to be close.

Donnie came home from work at about 6pm and found them on the sofa under a blanket watching one of his favourite episodes. He smiled to himself, being reminded of how he and Manon would cuddle up on the sofa in the same way. They had followed the series religiously every Friday night in the Nineties. Marcus jumped up and greeted Donnie, somewhat embarrassed.

"Congratulations on getting into Oxford Marcus," he said. "Will you be staying here for a sleepover tonight with N? A different house every night is it?" he continued with a ghost of a smile; seemingly congratulating himself on his witty comment, unaware of its irony.

Marcus felt himself blush, "Ah, for my last two weeks of Newcastle freedom I've been given a curfew, same as my ten year old sister's bedtime!"

"Terrifying! There'll be no getting out of that knowing your mother; escape from Alcatraz would be easier!"

They laughed.

Donnie got changed and went out to tinker on the old red Renault 4 that he and Manon had used when they were students to tour around France and Italy. They had kept the car as a cherished memento of a happy time. Donnie had no idea that Marcus' embarrassment was not due to the mortification he felt for the events of the previous evening, but that he was thinking how much he would have loved to spend the night with Noëmi.

Noëmi

As predicted the next day, the picture of Marcus and Charlotte kissing appeared. However, Noëmi was blindsided by the post displaying it. One of Charlotte's friends had put up a public poll on social media, asking for everyone to vote for '*Marcus McKenzie's new girlfriend*'. There was a choice; '*Gross Moron*', as illustrated by the sensible Oxbridge success image or '*totally gorgeous Charlotte*', featured in a high octane embrace with Marcus. The formal Oxbridge photo garnered a gamut of ridicule. The taunts were directed only at her, '*Of course he's seen as naturally clever and I'm labelled weird and socially awkward.*' Party photos of Marcus and Charlotte kissing only increased his *just happens to be talented in all areas*' status. Lots of comments and emojis were all over the contrasting images by the time Noëmi and Marcus saw them. She was completely devastated.

He went straight to see her and tried to persuade her to let him vote for their picture. She told him his lone vote would just look like he was 'joining in with the joke', so a tactful, dignified ignoring of the post was agreed, in the hope that it would just go away. Noëmi's upset at the post came out as a long rant about the 'shitty little town' where they lived. Warnings to Marcus not to 'feel sorry for her' and declarations of how she 'could not wait to get away and never come back.'

To try to cheer her up Marcus took Noëmi out to Durham; their place of discovery and delight. Here they could escape as they had when they first visited, the previous year on a sweltering August bank holiday. There they walked through the cobbled streets of the town. Marcus held her hand, stroked her hair and hugged her as he listened to four and a half years of hurt pour from her heart and eyes. He made her laugh. They looked at the shops, bought matching beanies, deciding this was quite the university look. Then they hired a rowing boat and took themselves up the river and under the bridges, messing about on the water. He took over the rowing and made her navigate; they ended up in a willow tree on the bank. From then on Noëmi had stopped crying and they could not stop laughing. He took his phone and played one of their favourite songs *Just the way you are'* by Bruno Mars which had come out the summer before. They had lunch in Flat White, where she had always wanted to go, having heard so many great things about the café. The famous Eggs Benedict did not disappoint and they sat next to the window, looking back over the river. Then, they walked up to the Cathedral Green, took the narrow, leafy path down to the river and strolled over to Framwellgate Bridge. There, with the river glistening in the background and the castle smiling down on them, they took a sweet selfie, with their heads together, wearing the matching beanies.

Returning to Noëmi's home later they sat in the kitchen in reflective moods. Noëmi played with an egg timer turning it up and down, watching the blue sand swap ends.

"Recent events just prove why I can't hold you back," she said, "it would be cruel."

"Recent events just prove how much you mean to me."

"You just feel sorry for me."

"I really don't."

They heard a key in the door and Donnie walked in from badminton practice, carrying his kit and a pint of milk.

"Hello you two, good day?"

"Yes, lovely Dad, you?" she quickly wiped her eyes and smiled at him.

"Happy for the holidays! We leave for Italy early on Monday!" Donnie reminded them.

"I know I need to get sorted."

"Indeed, then Marcus I hear we won't see you for a while. Marianna tells me you start Oxford in two weeks."

"Yes that's right, medicine gets going earlier than other courses."

"Okay I've got a badminton tournament all day in Leeds tomorrow so N don't forget you need to get presents for your grandparents."

Noëmi looked at Marcus.

"I'll spend tomorrow on all that matters right now..." she said.

Marcus looked straight back at Noëmi.

Later that evening, in an act of life affirming retaliation, he posted the selfie of them close together, publicly on his social media. He added the caption, *'**Fun day with the lovely Noëmi McAllister**'* followed by a heart emoji.

The next day she spent with Marcus, both dreading having to say 'goodbye'. He left two gifts for her eighteenth before he returned to his home under the terms of his curfew. The next morning she flew to Italy, puffy eyed, sorrowful and silent. She opened the birthday gifts a few days later, on 26 August, in Italy. One was a five year diary for her to write about her university experiences and on the inside front cover the whole McKenzie family had signed to wish her well. The second, badly wrapped in different paper, was a silver heart necklace that was delicate and looked more expensive than she would have expected from the family.

CHAPTER 5 – CROSSING PATHS

Noëmi

6 September 2016. Noëmi felt surprisingly bright after only three hours' sleep, having spent the night hours fleshing out Maya. Walking to work, the September sky was dappled blue and white, the breeze was fresh, all of which brightened her mood in contrast to the shock of the day before.

She got to her classroom early and pondered on where to move a couple of the girls who constantly chatted. Frank came into her class to collect her for the daily staff briefing.

"You're all jolly this morning," said Frank as they walked towards the staffroom, dodging overzealous students arriving back for their first day of term.

"Yes, excited for the new term, just like these guys," smiled Noëmi, gesturing towards the happy looking students.

"Don't give me that, you know your smile, like those smiles, will not last beyond break time, if you're glad to be back you're the only one," said Frank acerbically.

"Just feeling positive, like good things are going to happen," said Noëmi cryptically.

"Mmm you're up to something Noëmi, all this sounds very unnatural," said Frank sagely.

"Oh for God's sake I hate how well you know me. So what if I have a plan or two to distract me! No doubt I'll be seeking out you and Val for advice very soon!"

"We'll be waiting to catch you when you fall," said Frank.

Noëmi gave him a look and began marching towards the staffroom door swinging it open with a new confidence. As she did it stopped half way and catapulted her into the room throwing her towards John Dyer. She careered right into him and looked up in horror as he smiled down at her.

Noëmi jumped back, stiffened and felt ice in her veins,

That's it, he's recognised me,' she thought with horror.

"I don't think we've been introduced," he purred looking at her, giving no indication that she was familiar.

"I teach maths, got to get on," she turned on her heel and went towards the coffee area, her face reddening with shock, anger and disgust.

Maurice Mundy, Head Teacher, brought the room to attention and began his familiar motivational speech to his staff.

"Well here we are all raring to go, ready to make a difference in the lives of these young people for whom anything is possible."

"Words just words," muttered Frank so that those around him could hear.

Then in some kind of pre-arranged double act, John began a similar call to arms in order to rouse a spirit of unity and determination.

"And of course we want this to be the spirit that the inspectors see, when they visit at some point this year!"

Nervous laughter fluttered through the staffroom.

"Why would anyone be worried when we're all such conscientious and dedicated teachers? No I'm not concerned," John continued, "but I would say if anyone feels they're not up to the job, then do come and talk to me for support, my door is always open."

"Ah so thoughtful, nice to know where to go to get sacked," said Frank under his breath.

Noëmi let out a sudden burst of laughter at Frank's comment. Everyone looked round; some surprised, others amused. She sank her eyes to the floor and pretended not to be there.

"I see maths is confident then," shot out John.

"Absolutely no problem in maths!" answered Noëmi's line manager, sending her a dark look over his shoulder.

John

More notices followed, then the teachers scurried off to make a 'difference' to their students' lives. John had put his one and only class that week on cover, so he could patrol and check all was 'in order discipline wise'. He looked at Noëmi as she rushed out, avoiding his gaze.

'She must be so in awe of me,' he thought to himself, then he turned to Sarai, the admin assistant, who was washing up the cups and asked her, "Who is that dark haired maths teacher?"

"Well there are a few."

"That one in the blue dress who interrupted the briefing by laughing?"

"Oh that's Noëmi," replied Sarai, "She's a good teacher. I hope she's not in trouble." She carried on tidying up the kitchen area of the staffroom.

"Well we need to keep a tight ship, Noëmi... I'm sure I've heard that name before... somewhere... must be in a song or film," replied John, who knew it could not have been in a book, as he hated reading.

"It's a nice name, Italian," said Sarai pleasantly and she opened the back door of the staffroom to take out the bin bags. She threw some crumbs to the black crows that were gently cawing outside.

John nodded and walked out of the staffroom to begin his observations. He began going from class to class, but found that he was increasingly distracted and indeed it was Noëmi who was getting into his head.

Noëmi

Reality, in the form of meeting her tutor group, soon stopped Noëmi dreaming of her revenge. Now they were in their final school year, all were approaching their 16th birthdays. The students noisily caught up with each other; there were howls of laughter and shrieks of delight, the bell rang and Noëmi stood up to call them to attention.

"Welcome back, right we have some admin to get through this morning..."

None of them stopped talking.

"Okay we need to listen now," said Noëmi, as she had been taught, more firmly as the noise level grew.

One student, Stephanie, sitting quietly at the back playing on her phone, then made herself heard.

"Oi! just shut the fuck up and listen to Miss!"

Everyone was silent.

"Oh well thank you Stephanie, I need to see you at the end about the swearing as that is not the conduct expected here at St Wolboldo's," replied Noëmi professionally.

"Well the little fuckers wouldn't shut up and it was getting on my nerves," threw back Stephanie. Noëmi knew Stephanie liked quiet and hated any disruptive behaviour.

Fellow student Ronnie laughed loudly, impressed with her attitude, he started shouting back.

Noëmi started to address Ronnie's comments when she was drowned out by an enormous voice.

"I see we have some problems here do we?"

Noëmi looked round to see John Dyer at her doorway. The class fell into complete silence in an instant which riled her.

"No, all in hand," replied Noëmi, annoyed that his presence had made the students quiet.

"Well I think I need to talk to that girl right now," boomed John, indicating for Stephanie to leave the room.

"Ronnie just said worse and no one did anything," she shouted back at him, grabbed her bag and walked out of the class. He shut the door and the class sat in silence as they heard the muffled sounds of 'Mr Dyer' tearing a strip off Stephanie.

She returned into the classroom, red in the face, silent, furious.

Noëmi went through some details with the class, giving out corrected timetables as their original ones had mistakes. She was completely distracted by Stephanie, who had her head on the desk in the far corner, and by all that had just happened. She dismissed them at the bell and they began to speed out noisily to their lessons. She called to Stephanie to stay behind but she just walked off, then suddenly turned back, yelling,

"He took my fucking phone because of you."

Noëmi's heart sank and she collapsed into her seat, it was like the six week break had never happened.

Noëmi

The term at St Wolbodo's was now getting into full swing, being well into its first week. Running a busy secondary school, with over one thousand pupils, was a formidable task and teamwork was the key to success. It was a kind of fragile Jenga style structure that needed all to work together.

Pat Davies, the school secretary, was the leading figure in the administration team. No one was actually sure if she was in charge officially but in reality she decided what was what. She was a fearsome woman who took no nonsense from anyone, however neither did she take any sense. What Pat decided was the way to do things, was indeed the only way. She had a habit of complaining all day long about 'those who took advantage'. Pat's idea of 'taking advantage' included giving her work to do and disturbing her day. However Pat loved the power that her job gave her, especially the access to information about local families. Being the first to know something was desperately important to her. She would nosey through student data and give many sighs and knowing looks if anyone mentioned a local member of the community. She could recall, at length, a student's family background through three generations, with numerous colourful details, the more salacious the better. With an air of mystic sorcery she could recognise any student on the CCTV, even those with their hoods up and or their backs turned. Her colleagues in the office knew better than to contradict Pat and many barely said a word throughout the day. This was not because they had nothing to contribute, but simply because they could not get a word in edgeways, as Pat's live streaming monologues dominated the workplace.

Noëmi passed by to see Pat.

"Hi Pat, how was your break?"

"Well some of us were working over the holiday."

"Right, two students have brought me gifts from their holidays."

"And?" huffed Pat.

"I need the home contact details so that I can acknowledge these properly."

"I *am* busy with these lists here!"

"I know, Pat, but the safeguarding rules mean I need to do this!"

Pat sighed, mentioning under her breath 'all the bother' that it was to look up details of two students especially given how 'busy' she was. Pat huffed and puffed and made a big show of clicking in and out of screens. She wrote down some details, handed them to Noëmi and then heaved herself up, taking her bag to go for a 'comfort break' or cigarette break as most people would have called it. As she had been waiting, Noëmi noticed the lists being drawn up of students invited to apply for Oxbridge. Her mind wandered to her university days as both she and Marcus had made the grade for these prestigious universities.

CHAPTER 6 - UNIVERSITY

Marcus

September 2011. Noëmi studied maths at Emmanuel College, Cambridge and Marcus studied medicine at New College, Oxford. Leaving Newcastle and entering the undergraduate world of a top class university was intoxicatingly liberating for them both. The lectures, the new friendships and the socialising were endless sources of stimulation; they both felt indomitable and unlimited.

In true McKenzie style, the whole family had accompanied Marcus when he moved into his college. This was expected family practice and the children nicknamed such gatherings, *'McKenzies Assemble'*. His going to Oxford, to study medicine, was almost the only thing his grandmother spoke about, much to the annoyance of his siblings.

"It doesn't get better than that!" she would tell everyone she met. Raeni spent most of her time crying with pride that her 'fine grandson was going to university', hugging him and praising God for this 'miracle'.

"Grandma I worked 16 hours a day, for nine months, to make sure I got the grades to get in." Marcus explained. Yet Raeni still cited 'God's benevolence in giving gifts'.

Marcus' mother Marianna smiled and carried on helping her son unpack his things. Determined to begin his life, Marcus arranged his room himself.

"Noëmi deserves much of the credit too. From the time you started studying together your grades dramatically improved." His mother commented.

"Yeah, there's no way I could've done this without her." Marcus caught his breath and spared his mother a glance.

"And for her what an achievement! All this time, she's done everything in the house, all the cooking and cleaning, whilst studying too. Always so melancholy, although she brightened up this last year." Marianna opened a suitcase of clothes.

Marcus felt Noëmi's absence. It was painful. Then with determination he replied, "It's a new start, time to look forward."

"You helped each other so much when you were at Newcastle Green," his mother was not changing the subject. "God only knows how she made it through the last five years without a mother. Basically she's had to parent her father. Donnie's a good man, but he has no idea, remember some of those clothes?"

Marcus' mind filled with the memory of shopping trips with Noëmi. Her determination to be close to her late mother had grown into a full-blown obsession with the Eighties. She studied photographs assiduously. A wardrobe of eclectic, Eighties style outfits was purchased, with all the 'Choose Life' and 'Frankie Says Relax' slogans.

Marianna

However Marianna was mainly referring to her favourite story that she liked to repeat about Noëmi's teenage years, unaware it often had the opposite effect to the one she supposed. It was the two families' picnic outing to the beach at Seaham, to celebrate Noëmi's seventeenth birthday. Once arrived, the younger McKenzies had all run into the sea, laughing. Anthony chased frantically after them. Noëmi and Marcus slouched down on towels, well away from their parents and plugged themselves into their music.

Marianna looked sternly at Donnie. "She needs to put a t-shirt on."

Donnie was positioning his deck chair and clearly did not think Marianna was addressing him.

"Donnie!"

"Yes Marianna?"

"Noëmi needs to put a t-shirt over that excuse for swimwear."

Donnie was open mouthed, "What's the problem?"

"I have two teenage sons, that's the problem."

"Well that's unfair Marianna, she bought the costume in a reputable sports' retailer. It's good quality fabric and it was affordable. Plus what did you think she was going to wear to go swimming in August?"

"And they obviously kept the price down by removing ninety per cent of the material."

"She wanted something more fashionable! Not the school swimsuit!"

"They're growing up!"

"Yes and I think that's your problem here. But knowing how well you've raised those boys, I'm sure they've been to the beach before and know how to respect their friends!"

"But…"

"No, it's a perfectly decent costume. Manon wore bikinis like that when we were in Italy, at her parents and they're staunch Catholics. So I do know what's right for my daughter…"

Rarely did Donnie mention Manon first.

Marianna sighed and let it go as Donnie seemed wistful. Suddenly it hit her that their children were adults. She had no concern that her son would objectify Noëmi; indeed he was an honourable young man. It was how mature, close and relaxed they were in each other's company. Her discomfort grew as she noticed the pair alongside one another; invading each other's body space, holding the other's gaze and whispering shared secrets.

Donnie

Donnie was bemused. Having seen how happy Noëmi was with her purchase, he thought she had done well. He wondered whether he should be talking to Noëmi about relationships and so on. He knew that Manon had covered periods and puberty when she went to secondary school. Yet whilst she did not have a boyfriend, he thought there was no point; so he found there was never any need for awkward conversations.

Marcus

"Will you visit each other?" Marianna asked her son.

"Maybe, but we need to focus on our uni lives, make the most of the opportunities," feeling excited for Oxford but sad that his old life would never be quite the same.

"I'm just wondering how you'll manage without her," Marianna paused for a moment.

Marcus thought back.

"Yeah, it feels odd," Marcus said quietly. However he wished his mother would stop talking about her. He put his feelings in a box and packed it away, determined that university would be the fresh, exciting beginning that he needed.

Marcus had correctly imagined the opportunities university would offer and had made a plan for himself. Not neglecting his heart, he drew up his blueprint of the perfect woman, almost like he was thinking of having her made up. Various qualities appeared on his wish list; physically fit, capable, clever, kind, good looking and he added altruistic at the end.

'Just sounds like Noëmi. I need to forget and look forward,' he sighed to himself.

His plan made him feel in control and everything began to fall into place. He made friends easily, found his course fascinating and achieved academic excellence.

Time galloped on.

During his third year Marcus had started seeing a strikingly pretty, blonde girl, called Sophie. She ticked all the physical boxes on Marcus' list, but not all of the personality ones. She was also studying medicine, was highly intelligent and extremely accomplished.

Sophie De Lisle was a confident girl whose background was entirely the opposite to that of Marcus. He loved that she knew so much about life and how to be. Sophie had already travelled the world. She had attended a private school and was talented in music; playing the cello, and in sport; rowing for her school team. She was a dynamic character, if sometimes a little overpowering.

They had met properly in the first week of the third year when she made it clear that she was attracted to Marcus by sitting next to him in every lecture and tutorial. Sophie's good looks and Marcus' fine physique made them an attractive couple and after a couple of dates they were established as a pair. Sophie's assuredness swept Marcus along and with the new challenges from his course he was feeling quite changed from the person he had been.

Noëmi and Marcus both had very much their own lives. They kept in touch, although initially their communication was strained. Marcus did not hide his hurt at Noëmi's refusal to try a long-distance relationship. As their contact lessened, Noëmi's feelings for Marcus only increased. To make things worse, once at university, Marcus had stopped going back to Newcastle in the holidays. This was due to the intensity of his medical placements and the pressure of never ending exams.

Feeling lost, Noëmi missed him viscerally. *'God I want him. Why did I cut him off like that? Such highly generous, altruistic reasons? Not wanting to tie him down? Or plain stupidity?'*

She resolved to claim the place he had offered her in his heart.

'Ha, am now part of the CU football squad! Ehehe! Coming over for the inter uni tournament! Bet you're playing! We should get together! Any room at your place? Nxxx'

'Go you! Sounds great! I'm playing too. No spare room in my place but Sophie has a room at hers where you can stay over! M'

'No invite! Sophie? Why would I want to stay there!'

'I haven't forgotten it's your birthday - will bring huge gift! Who's Sophie? Xxx'

'Ah! You're the best friend ever! Sophie's the girl I'm seeing'

'Right, no worries, I can stay in the hostel with the rest of the team.'

'Friend... because that's what you are. Am I wrong to dislike Sophie even before I've met her?' She thought to herself and took a deep breath. However painful it felt, Noëmi was determined to be part of his life.

During the varsity football challenge, it was time to meet Sophie. She showed no interest in Noëmi, Marcus' 'friend from home'.

Sitting in the stands Noëmi was waiting for her match to begin and Sophie asked her the origin of her name.

"It's Italian, I'm half Italian." She replied. Watching Marcus play, all she could hear was his girlfriend, grating in her ears.

"God Italians! Italian men! When I was interrailing in the summer, they wouldn't leave me and my friend alone! They were always trying to get with us! I think it's because we're both blonde, they really are persuasive and totally full on aren't they?" Sophie shrieked.

Noëmi did wonder why any woman, whatever their hair colour, would want to be treated in this way.

"Anyway, what are your plans for the holidays *Naomi*?"

"It's *Noëmi*. I'm not sure, get a job, see my Dad..." Noëmi replied but Sophie's eyes had glazed over, so she asked, "What about you?"

"Sailing, after the clinical week is over, going off to the south west of France, off the Bordeaux Coast, with the fam it'll be a good break."

"Sounds lovely."

"Yah, such big waves though, bit dangerous really, only for the very experienced, always turning turtle."

Noëmi worked out what that could mean although she had no experience of boats. Sophie was still talking;

"...but my Dad wants to add to his wine collection, he's a connoisseur, you know, and Mum's got an eye for antiques, she collects professionally. So France it is this Easter, rather than

Dubai, bit sad really."

She did not have a chance to respond as Sophie was already talking to someone else.

Although sorely tempted to visit Marcus while Sophie was away in France, she knew that she could not interfere. Respecting his feelings, she could only regret her own.

CHAPTER 7 - JOINING FORCES

Noëmi

September 2015. Noëmi completed her MMath at Cambridge after four years. In spite of graduating with a First, Noëmi decided to become a teacher. Next, she needed to do her teacher training qualification. She chose to go to Oxford as Marcus was still there, although the official reason she gave was that the course allowed her to combine maths with modern languages; Italian and French.

Noëmi started sharing a student flat, off the Abingdon road, with an international student, Yumi Watanabe. She was also training to be a teacher on the same course, in maths and Japanese. Their flat was not far from Sophie's place at Grandpoint, whereas Marcus was in the Jericho area, three miles away on the other side of the university. Although Yumi and Noëmi had not met before, they hit it off immediately, both sharing a kooky sense of fun and a love of Eighties music.

Early in their time living together, Yumi wanted to go and support Japan play in the 2015 Rugby World Cup and she had secured some tickets for their match against South Africa.

"Brighton Community Stadium...Where's Brighton?" she asked.

"South Coast, not that far but you know what Oxford is like for trains and getting anywhere!"

"Let's go! It's on Saturday."

Noëmi knew Marcus would love this.

"Can I bring a friend?"

"Sure, but they have to wear a Japan shirt."

As predicted Marcus was delighted, so now Noëmi knew she had to ask,

"Do you want to bring Sophie?"

"No, she's already told me she's busy, out rowing at a regatta and then she's got an evening social she's organising with her friend Ben."

"Oh what a shame!"

Call finished, Yumi looked at Noëmi, "That was the most unconvincing expression of regret I've ever heard!"

"Judge me when you've stood in my shoes or whatever that phrase is." Noëmi replied haughtily.

"Shoes? More like combat boots ready to march into battle," Yumi gave her a knowing look.

Although the journey was bitty by train; having to go via Reading and Gatwick, the three were in good humour and Yumi was on a mission to enjoy herself with her new friends.

Sitting on the train already in her Japan Rugby top, she got the other two shirts out.

"You two need to put these on," offering them the red and white striped tops with the pink cherry blossom logo. "You must honour our brave blossoms," she said formally.

"How much will you pay me to wear it? South Africa are going to be all over them," Marcus joked.

"Whose idea was it to bring him? Okay if South Africa win the shirt is free but if Japan win you pay for the shirt," replied Yumi dead pan.

"Well it'll become a collector's item if they win! But that won't happen, just setting some expectations okay! Thanks for the free shirt Yumi!" chirped Marcus.

Yumi gave him a look.

The train carriage was empty so Marcus took off his jacket and t-shirt and popped the top on.

"Fit," said Yumi simply.

Without flinching Noëmi did the same.

"Seriously N you can't do that!" said Marcus.

"Why? You did! I'm all decent. It's only a sports bra," she replied.

"Oh! It's inside out," Yumi suddenly said.

The process was about to start again when Yumi finally relented,

"Oh, it's not, I'm just messing, but I *feel* the energy between you two," she added matter of factly, pointing at them both. She looked down and started browsing on her phone.

Marcus looked back at Noëmi, and he was unable to stop smiling at her. She looked down and quickly back at him and could not help her grin.

Noëmi and Marcus thoroughly enjoyed the game of rugby.

On the train home Yumi fell asleep whilst Marcus and Noëmi chatted.

"I love that they risked everything and went for the win with no time left," she said.

"High scoring match, they didn't settle for the draw, that's what we should do in life."

"So exciting, look at these stats, 122 tackles by Japan, I love that team."

"Best match ever, thanks for inviting me along, N, I loved it."

"So good to spend time with you Marcus."

"Yeah, we've been away from each other for far too long, you really make things fun. I've really missed you," he said genuinely.

Noëmi smiled at him, "Same, you seem very happy and settled here."

"Two more years, I'm doing really well on the course, Oxford's great you'll love it'

"Things are pretty serious with Sophie too, that's been a while."

"Yeah things are fine." He looked away.

"Doing the same course... do you revise together?" she asked.

Marcus looked back at her and replied. "No, no, it's not like us."

She felt a little lump in her throat and tears spring to her eyes. Suddenly he changed the subject.

"Did you like Cambridge N? I thought it was a vibrant place when I visited you those times. That Mill Road house was a blast."

"Yeah it all worked out, I had a great uni experience, no partner from it though; I'm too idealistic!"

"That's okay, no point settling for someone just for the sake of it, we're all on a quest to find love."

"True, talking of which you know I met up with your brother Jayden a few times when he started there? I've met his girlfriend Shreya, they *are* so well suited, she's just gorgeous."

"Yes!" he said, "what a great couple, now that's love! I keep in touch each week with my brothers and sister, Tianna. It's important being the eldest so much has been about me. They're all doing great, they tell me you've been helping Sai in the holidays with his maths. He doesn't like all the Oxbridge pressure from school, he'll go to London. Tianna's got no problems at school but she's the feisty one, not fond of the McKenzie family rules, plus I think she feels a bit sidelined."

"You have such a wonderful family, has Sophie met them all?"

Marcus laughed, "No, I've suggested it but I'm not sure Newcastle is Sophie's thing. Anyway we're often doing clinical placements in the holidays. Plus my mum's strict ways, can you imagine? I can't see Sophie tidying up after dinner!"

He read her mind, "Don't worry, Sophie has her good points too!"

Marcus changed the subject; he did not seem relaxed talking about his relationship with Sophie.

"Your hair looks good N, it suits you long."

"You've gone for cornrows I see, looks great, stylish."

"Let's take a selfie in our shirts that we're happy to pay for," he came and sat next to her and took the photo, "I'll send it to you," he then stayed next to her, close, talking about the time they had been apart until they reached their final stop.

Having seen the girls to their place he looked up at the dark sky and thought about the huge world he was in.

'Noëmi I can't decide if you're exactly what I need or precisely what I don't need right now.'

Medsoc…

Marcus had begun to call Noëmi more and more just to chat. Early in the spring term, they were catching up;

"Good luck with the teaching placement, rather you than me! Anyway, are you up to help with this year's fundraising events? I could do with you on the team. Plus it's my fifth year and I'm finding it too much with my clinical training," said Marcus lying on his bed, exhausted after a day in a GP clinic.

"Yeah, sounds fun, as you know I ran my college charity society for two years. This will definitely be my last too, I've just been offered a job teaching back in Durham."

"Nice one and well done on the job that's so exciting. Get some of your student teacher friends to sign up too."

One evening the following week, Noëmi took Yumi along to a charity meeting run by the Medical Society. Sitting at the front was Sophie, who was the Vice President and Marcus who was the Chair for charity events. She was reassured that Marcus looked genuinely delighted to see her, offering her a broad, warm grin.

The proposals were read out and the UK charity was agreed to be the children's hospice linked to the local hospital. The choice of which overseas charity to adopt was a topic of more debate and a number of charities were suggested. In the end it was agreed that a few small groups would research each one and present their findings the following week.

Sophie went through the list and individuals agreed to take on each one.

Noëmi instantly offered to help.

"Count me in," she declared.

Sophie furrowed her brow, "Okay and I'll join you as you're not a medical student."

"Ouch!" said Yumi under her breath, "she's nice!"

"I'm really okay with it, I just want to get involved somehow and help."

"Shall we go to the pub now?" asked Yumi.

"Yeah, I'll see you there, I just want to find out exactly what I need to do."

Noëmi walked over to Sophie who was chatting with the rest of the committee, including Marcus who smiled affectionately as he saw Noëmi approach.

"Hey Sophie!"

"Right yah, here are my contact details and I'll meet you next week so we can go over our plan okay?" Sophie gave her a printed card, which surprised Noëmi as it all seemed a bit formal. She swung round, flicking her hair and turning her back on Noëmi.

Marcus saw this, gave an exasperated sigh, then broke away from the group to talk to Noëmi, "Thanks so much for doing this N."

Noëmi looked at the card which had Sophie's mobile and email address. Quickly she took a photo of it.

"Don't want to muck this up! You know me!" She looked up bashfully at Marcus.

Marcus smiled knowingly, "She's quite business like; lacks that vulnerability people can get when they've experienced failure."

"Tell me about it. But how would you know? You've not failed at anything Marcus!"

"No, not academically but I failed to hold onto you."

Noëmi opened her mouth but no words came out.

"Anyway N, let me know if you need any help, you know where I am." He gave her a hug and went back to the committee.

Noëmi went off to meet Yumi in the college bar and ordered a diet coke.

"No vodka in that then N?" her friend asked.

"Keeping a clear head so that I can work on this project, I don't want to make an idiot of myself with that lot." Marcus' words ran through her mind.

"Cool idea," agreed Yumi and then they spent another hour discussing their teaching placements and how to manage difficult classes.

Noëmi got back to their flat and began researching different overseas charities.

"God so much suffering." she thought to herself as she delved deeper. One disease caught her eye in particular; noma.

'Noma is a cruel disease, common in an area across Africa. Noma causes gangrenous sores which destroy the faces of its victims. It mostly affects children under 10 years of age. 90% of sufferers die and those that survive are left disfigured and

stigmatised by society. It is caused by poverty but is easily cured by cheap antibiotics. The End Noma Campaign runs a hospital performing maxillofacial surgery and also helps sufferers who may not realise they can receive treatment. Another aspect of the work is to educate the vulnerable people to prevent further cases.'

Noëmi felt her throat tighten, as she watched the video of the patients and their immense suffering. It was uplifting to see the pioneering work of the plastic surgeons who would visit the End Noma hospital. She definitely felt this was the project they should support and she began to work on her presentation. A few nights later, it was complete and she sent Sophie a message.

"Hi, I've got a great presentation together. When can we meet?"

"Just send through what you've got."

Noëmi had prepared a full presentation and forwarded it all through to Sophie, who replied with a thumbs up emoji.

The following day she arrived at the meeting early and Marcus immediately went straight over to her. They then went to Sophie who was chatting with the others.

"Hey did you look at the presentation?"

"Yah, but I had to change it to suit our audience, you know doctors," Sophie said condescendingly.

"Oh… alright, which bits do you want to do?" said Noëmi.

"Don't you worry you must be so busy, I can manage on my own," she said in a loud voice. Marcus looked puzzled and glanced over at Noëmi, saying nothing.

Noëmi felt her cheeks redden.

A couple of students presented together for Oxfam. Another

presented for Save the Children. Finally, Sophie stood up and began the presentation. Noëmi noted that she had kept the presentation actually unchanged and was pleased as she had spent ages embedding the video into the slide show. Everyone voted for The End Noma Campaign and it was selected as the overseas charity by The Oxford Medical Society. The decision was proposed, seconded and agreed. The next meeting was set for two weeks' time and the group started to disband. Marcus and Sophie were at the front, chatting together looking relaxed and content, as Noëmi approached to pick up the leftover leaflets.

"Sophie you did a brilliant job," Marcus said, turning to look at his girlfriend.

"Stop it, I'm just so glad that we chose the Noëmi project," Sophie replied.

"I see what you did there!" Marcus said laughing but Sophie just looked confused.

"The disease is called noma, and my name is Noëmi," Noëmi said flatly to Sophie.

Having collected the hand outs, Noëmi grabbed her jacket and turned to leave.

"Well done N!" Marcus had quickly followed her.

"What! Oh yeah, have a look at the information, I'm glad we're supporting them." She put a leaflet in his hand.

"Can you meet me next week to talk about the fun run? I'll message you."

She nodded and left to find Yumi. Walking across the courtyard, Noëmi suddenly said to her friend.

"I'm not going to let it bother me, you know."

"What? That she took all the credit for your work, making herself look like a saint? You're so unjudged!" said Yumi with friendly sarcasm.

"Exactly, be the better person. All that matters is that those children get their surgery."

"You know Noëmi, you're amazing, your spirit defines you."

They walked home and Yumi took a call from her mother, who was waking up in Tokyo. Noëmi reflected on what she could do as an individual miles away from the noma belt. Arriving back at the flat, Yumi was still talking on her phone, so Noëmi started on her plan. She decided to set up a webpage and a blog, giving details about noma to help raise awareness. It was a basic but dynamic webpage and she put in a link so that visitors could donate to The End Noma Campaign. Work on this webpage took up most of her free time and she found that she was building up a network of supporters and contacts with whom she enjoyed working. Over time she got into a rhythm of managing her lectures, her social life and her website work.

* * *

A week later Noëmi met Marcus at his college coffee shop, to discuss the fun run.

"Hey!" said Noëmi as she rushed to meet Marcus.

"Hello beautiful, how's everything?" replied Marcus with a warm smile.

"Good, you?"

"Fine thanks, I'll get these, what do you want the usual?"

"That'd be lovely, can I get an extra shot of espresso in that?"

"Heavy night?"

"Ha! I wish, marking books, takes forever!"

"Hold on, you've got an eyelash!"

Gently he touched her cheek with his soft finger. Eyes locking they looked intently at each other.

"There you go!" He put his arm around her and they walked over to the seating area.

She sat down in a faded arm chair and he went for the coffee.

Noëmi touched her cheek. Marcus returned and pulled his chair next to hers.

"Let me distract you with more work then! Now we need costumes for the fun run."

"Okay... costumes? Not just trainers and a t-shirt then?"

"No, we need to make an impact in the town, Storm trooper outfits, Harry Potter costumes, Disney dress up you know the thing," said Marcus enthusiastically.

"I'll send a message and we can contact the drama groups to see if they can help."

"Brilliant, now the route has to be marked out early on the morning of the event. We have a few volunteers and I think we can ask some of our friends to help, if they're not running, so I'll get on with that."

"Signs and maps obviously I can sort those out," said Noëmi. "I've done all the legal admin, letting the colleges and the council know. St John Ambulance is organised, the public liability and event insurance too."

"That's awesome, thanks for doing all that, have you run the course?"

"I cycled it, running's not really my thing."

Marcus raised an eyebrow, this was typical of Noëmi, "but you will run on Saturday?"

"Yes of course, can't wait!" said Noëmi sarcastically with a ghost of a smile.

They sorted out the final details and finished their coffees. Getting up to leave Marcus said,

"It's not this year? Your Dad's fiftieth?"

"No, that's next year. Crikey tempus fugit!"

"Good, I've sent a card and we're all chipping in for a family gift."

"That's lovely. It's a difficult time for him, well, for us both. It's been ten years."

For everyone losing Manon had been a massive shock, made worse by the fact it was only six weeks from diagnosis to passing. Nothing could have prepared them for the grief that would follow.

"I can't imagine, if I'm honest. You're very brave N,"

"I don't know, we don't get a choice about some things. I miss her every day. Dad struggles, for my parents it was true love."

Marcus looked at her and seemed to almost say something but must have changed his mind.

CHAPTER 8 - FUN RUN

Noëmi

April 2016. The morning of the fun run arrived. Noëmi pulled on her Yoda costume and picked up her lightsaber. Yumi emerged looking immaculate dressed as Princess Leia; her hair up in the side plait buns, perfect make up and a long, pure white dress.

"Yumi you know you have to run don't you? There's a clue in the event title," her friend reminded her, as Yumi could not have looked more glamorous, flawless and gleaming.

"Well they also call it 'fun' and that's a lie," she gave back, "plus you can talk in that overload of plastic."

"Neoprene actually, but good point! Come on, we have to help start the race off."

"Yes, but I'm not going to sweat though," Yumi replied quite seriously.

"You know I bet you don't! In this thing I'll be sweating for both of us!" Noëmi commented.

The girls made for the start, ensuring they were early in order to check the set up. Noëmi's outfit made it hard to walk, let alone run and she was already overheating by the time she got to the registration desk. Looking around she was surprised not to see

Marcus as the start time was approaching and the crowds were gathering. Delighted by the turn out, Noëmi began to feel slight panic at having to deal with everyone on her own. She was desperate for Marcus to appear. Finally he did in normal running gear, just with a batman cape over his shoulders. He looked terrible. Noëmi gasped inward as she had never seen Marcus looking so disoriented and dishevelled and she knew this was not the time for a joke or sarcastic comment.

"M what's happened?"

"Not now, we can talk later."

Marcus momentarily transformed into an embodiment of professionalism in order to start the race. As they set off running, it suddenly dawned on Noëmi that Marcus had arrived alone.

"Is Sophie okay," she said suddenly to Marcus who was next to her.

"I'm sure she is," Marcus replied cryptically.

"Shouldn't she be here?" asked Noëmi innocently.

"Oh yes, but she's probably busy with her new boyfriend." Marcus stated simply and he sped up very slightly to run alone, as Noëmi ambled behind in her hot neoprene costume. So many thoughts ran through Noëmi's head and she felt dreadful for Marcus. Around her there was a happy murmur of noise. All those taking part laughed and joked as they jogged around the course. Yet Noëmi was falling behind because of her costume and she was distracted by concern for her friend. Everyone was overtaking her and she heard the odd "Come on Yoda" to which she replied "Yoda is trying!"

Having lost sight of Marcus, she was unable to keep up with him or anyone else.

Arriving last, she did not see him again until the end of the event as they were packing everything away.

"Marcus are you okay?"

He stopped and turned to her and put his hands on his head.

"I'm furious with the whole thing."

"Who's she seeing?"

"Some guy from the rowing team. Worst thing is that it's the second time she's done this. It happened last year too. Some postgrad student that time."

Noëmi was amazed at the audacity of Sophie, that she could simply replace Marcus so coldly like that. She could not help but wonder what their relationship was like in reality.

"Do you want to get coffee after this?" she suggested kindly.

"Yeah great let's do that, chat about stuff," he seemed grateful to have someone to talk to.

"I'll tell Yumi to go back without me."

Noëmi and Marcus strolled in the spring sunshine. Still in her Yoda costume, Noëmi was sweating profusely. Many children ran up to her. She smiled and let them take photos or hold her lightsaber which lit up and made the warring sounds a Jedi would want to hear. Finally arriving at their favourite coffee shop Noëmi felt the relief of the cool interior.

They ordered, then sat at a small lacquered table in silence for a minute and Marcus began.

"Sorry about all this, how are you N?"

"I'm fine but I can see you're not."

"I'm just so annoyed with myself and completely seething with her. See what she's like?"

"You said she's done this before, what did you think?" She sipped her coffee

"Yeah after last year I should've known better. Last time we were apart for about six months when she took up with that postgrad guy. Then he moved on and she said it had all been a mistake."

"And of course, this mistake was obviously not her fault!"

"As you say, we got back together. Now this guy. She says she's gone with him, because I was 'ignoring' her. Everyone's really busy with their clinical years, it's just an excuse."

"There's no justification. No one should ever cheat, no that's a red line." Noëmi took a sugar sachet.

"Well exactly N, finish one thing before starting another. Here's the best bit. I heard rumours from friends that she was close to this Ben person before she told me."

"Ouch that's mean, so calculated. She's made a real fool of you." She squeezed the sugar from one end to the other inside the sachet.

"And I've made a real fool of myself."

"I'm sorry for you Marcus, you know that, but she doesn't deserve you."

It seemed odd to be hearing Marcus talk like this and Noëmi felt a little overwhelmed as she had remembered feelings for him.

"I got too selfish and self-centred, caught up in the Oxford life, my plan, the perfect girl."

"Perfect?" The sugar burst out of the sachet.

"Sorry N, that came out wrong, I don't mean it like that, I mean in the sense of ticking boxes…"

"No! no! Don't worry it's all about those boxes…" She felt him look at her but she kept her eyes down.

"Well she knows stuff about how we should be and all that."

"How are we all supposed to act then? Like Sophie?" Noëmi angrily rolled her finger in the sugar.

"I know, I know…"

"What's this 'plan'?" she snapped.

"I just figured on a kind of blueprint, a set of rules of what I'm looking for in a partner. It's similar to studying, get the correct information, put in the effort…"

"That worked then!" said Noëmi sarcastically, looking away. She had made the letter **M** with the sugar.

"I don't understand, it should be like a formula,"

"You've forgotten that there has to be something stronger. Just because you're both attractive medical students at one of the best universities in the world, doesn't mean it will definitely work out."

"But it should, right?" He moved the sugar turning the **M** into an **N**.

"You may well find that the missing part of your formula is love. However I think Sophie has some work to do before she's capable of loving anyone but herself. I hate that she's hurt you like this… twice now."

"Anyway, you don't need to hear about all this." Playing with the sugar he made the **N** into a rough heart shape.

"Maybe I'm just not the best person to talk to about you and her...but you need to stop taking her back. Don't do that again. There are other options. You're missing out on those." She tidied up the sides of the heart.

"Let's forget about her now. I want to hear about you. Weren't we happy back when we were teenagers N? It was the best time," he smiled broadly at her.

He whispered in her ear. She laughed and whispered something back. He stroked the back of her hand.

"I really love that you're here. You should have just come to Oxford in the first place! You could've saved me!"

"You're difficult to save, I'm trying now!"

They sat in silence for a few minutes staring out of the window, lost in thought.

"How's the teaching placement going? It's quite a tough school I hear. Is it worse than Newky Green?"

"Ha! Not possible, you know that! Teaching maths is fine, French is tough! One student told me, *'Miss I can't do the work, it's not in English!'* How about you? What's being a GP like?"

She told him all her teaching highlights; being mistaken for a pupil, students turning her teaching computer screen upside down and falling victim to the permanent marker cat prank. He told her about his clinical placement attached to a GP practice and the variety of cases that he had seen, including a mother who was putting coffee in her baby's milk.

They both brightened up, as did the day. They decided to stay for lunch and remained chatting for a couple of hours, enjoying a Mediterranean sharing platter and drinking cider. Spring sun streamed through the grubby sash windows and mellow Magic played on the radio in the background. They chatted about the fun run and the estimated monies raised for The End Noma

Campaign and the local hospice.

Noëmi was obliged to stay in her Yoda outfit as she had not brought a change of clothes and salty sweat covered her body. Soon it was time to leave. Relaxed and happy Marcus watched aimlessly as Noëmi left the coffee shop late that afternoon. His gaze followed her out of the door and down the street. He noticed her stop and chat to a couple who had no doubt commented on her costume. Then as she walked away, alone, she started doing a little dance. Marcus burst out laughing at the sight of little Yoda shimmying through the centre of Oxford and thought how typical it was of Noëmi. He sat smiling for a few minutes then suddenly noticed the table was covered in grains of sugar and that all thoughts of Sophie had left his mind.

CHAPTER 9 - CHARITY BALL

Noëmi

May 2016. The weeks passed. Noëmi met up with Marcus a few times to check that he was alright, although the schedule of a medical student meant that he had very little free time. When they did manage to see each other, the news was very much the same, he was working hard and Sophie was still seeing Ben, the rower.

The charity ball was approaching. Noëmi was excited as she had organised a speaker from The End Noma Campaign to give a speech.

A couple of weeks earlier she had rung The End Noma Campaign Manager, Jesse O'Donnell.

"Hey Jesse here!"

"Hi Jesse, it's Noëmi Mc…"

"Oh hello you! How's it going? Your blog page is really upping donations our end!"

"That's brilliant, we wanted to know if you'd like to speak at our fundraising dinner in Oxford?"

"Sure, that'd be awesome, I've got friends there so I can stay over. If you give me the date I'll work my shifts around it."

"Brilliant!"

"I'll need you to show me around Oxford, you know I've never been there before!"

"Okay Jesse, arriving in Nigeria on your own with just a map hasn't prepared you then!"

"Easy in contrast to Oxford which sounds terrifying! Scary place! I'll need help!"

She laughed.

His background as a nurse meant that he had spent time in Nigeria helping at the hospital. Now he was doing bank work and running the charity at the same time.

They chatted through the details and agreed to follow up by email.

Opening her laptop to send the information through, Noëmi had definitely got the impression Jesse was keen to meet her. Thoughts ran through her head and she found herself fantasising about connecting with Marcus. She reasoned that since Sophie had given him up and cheated on him, anything was permissible. Wondering what to wear to such a prestigious event she knew she could not afford a new dress, then she remembered a picture of her mother in a long, tight fitting, evening dress.

She rang her father.

"Dad, you know that dress Mum wore at your engagement party, the silver one?"

"Yes of course, the sequin one, it was her favourite."

"She would've been about my age then?"

"Indeed..." the line sounded faint.

"Would you mind if I borrowed it? I'd like to wear it to the May Ball we're organising for charity. But only if you think it's something she would want me to do."

"Well...err."

"Dad, are you okay?"

"Just a bit of hay fever, don't worry, yes absolutely she would love you to wear it. She always looked so beautiful in it and I am sure you will too, my dear, I'll mail it tomorrow, do send me a photograph."

* * *

Her mother's dress arrived at her student flat a couple of days later, along with a note from her father, which read:

'Don't forget the photo, love Dad x.'

Together with Yumi, she pulled the dress out of its tissue paper.

'Is this all a massive mistake? How will I feel wearing this dress? Will it be too morbid or will I feel close to her?'

Picking it up slowly by the bodice she held it next to her and looked in the mirror.

"I'll make you proud Mum," she said quietly and carefully pulled down the zip. With Yumi's help she stepped into the dress and melted into it. She felt amazing and the fit was good, a little tight at the waist as her mother had been so slight but still it cinched all the right places.

"Never waste a waist they say," said Yumi. "You look lovely."

Noëmi was impressed; her hair was styled, blow dried and flowing over her shoulders, rather than pulled back in its usual ponytail, the dress was stunning. Instead of being sad at her memories of her mother, she felt close to her. Hoping to get together with Marcus she felt warm inside. It was time to relax and see what may happen.

The college dining room was beautifully decorated with soft lights and colours. There were small crystals scattered on the tables which caught in the candlelight. Exquisite arrangements of late spring flowers in whites, pinks and blues gave out a sweet scent. The high vaulted ceiling and wooden panelled walls added a touch of grandeur to the event. Relaxing background music was being played by a harpist and the scene was elegant. In a corner of the room, the committee was busy checking last minute details and timings for this sold out event. Noëmi was impressed with the professionalism and effort of everyone involved. For her part she was waiting for Jesse, from End Noma to arrive although she was more anxious to see the now single Marcus.

As guests began to arrive, Noëmi was surprised that most of the girls were in cocktail dresses. She was the only one in a long dress.

"I feel a bit frumpy," she said to Yumi,

"You look exquisite, I've never seen you in anything tight before."

Suddenly she caught sight of Marcus, her heart jumped, then it was pumping; she could not help her nerves. Yet he was looking right through her. Then she took in a small gasp of shock when she saw him hand in hand with Sophie, who was looking stunning in a short white dress. Her heart was racing as she realised they had reunited. Noëmi deliberately turned away to avoid seeing Marcus and pretended to sort out some registration papers, so that they did not meet her face to face. Yumi and some others were welcoming guests. Noëmi reasoned that they were doing a great job and that she was really there to meet her speaker anyway.

Sophie held tightly onto Marcus' hand but turned and looked past everyone to survey who was in the room. At the same time Marcus spoke to the team to check some of the event timings.

"When's the speaker on before or after the meal?" Marcus asked, looking at the schedule which just had *'Dinner plus speaker'* written on it.

"Not sure, Noëmi when's Jesse from End Noma speaking?" asked Yumi.

Noëmi had no choice but to turn and face Marcus, in order to answer the question.

"Well he gets here about 7:30pm and would like to speak after the main course."

She could not look at Marcus at all and felt herself blushing. She was looking down pretending to check a blank piece of paper.

"I hope that's not the schedule for the whole evening, Noëmi, it looks a bit empty!" Marcus joked. She noticed his hand holding his papers was trembling.

"Oh...I...was just...never mind," she managed.

He smiled and got a drink quickly.

Before Noëmi could even think about what had just happened, Jesse from End Noma arrived early. She was pleased to meet him and chatted warmly with him; the adrenalin set off by the encounter with Marcus, making her extremely animated.

Marcus

Marcus was distracted by Noëmi and kept stealing glances at her, as she spoke to the speaker. She had agitated him. It was not merely a physical thing however beautiful she looked tonight. It was the way he could laugh with her, be himself with her and how much they had shared. He took another drink, shook his shoulders back and focused his mind on his job that evening as Chair of the charity ball. He took Sophie by the hand.

'Noëmi has no interest in me, she made that quite clear. Sophie is part of the best life plan'

Noëmi

There was a brief break before the speaker took the stand and people went to the cloakroom and got drinks before the presentation. Noëmi went to the toilet where she stood in line and spotted Sophie and her friends behind her in the queue as she went into a cubicle.

'I can't believe he's got back with Sophie after she cheated a second time' she thought.

Yumi was after her and got the next one.

Noëmi could hear Sophie chatting with a friend.

"Back with Marcus right, what happened with Ben?" her friend asked her.

"Yah didn't work out, plus 'Slow Off' is steady you know."

"Slow Off?"

"Slow off the Marc...us! Get it!" She gave a guffaw.

"It did take him a while I suppose!"

"... and Ben can fuck off," replied Sophie.

"Whoa angry what did he do?"

"More what he was doing with some other slag," replied Sophie.

'So classy,' thought Noëmi to herself, wishing she was not overhearing this.

"Well Marcus is a stayer he won't ever cheat on you," her friend re-assured her.

"Yah, I know he's fine for now and I can't not be with someone you know," affirmed Sophie.

Noëmi felt annoyed.

"I'm pleased for you Soph."

Noëmi wished the conversation had ended there, however difficult that was to hear, as the final exchange left her bereft.

"And him being black makes me look good too," Sophie whispered to her friend.

"Yeah you two look amazing together."

"Yah, but it's not serious, he ticks a couple of boxes that's all. Plus it's not like we'll carry on after uni or shit like that." Sophie said casually.

"I see Cinderella's dressed up," commented her friend.

"That dress will turn back to rags at midnight," replied Sophie.

"When has graciousness ever turned a bloke on!" commented her friend.

"Oh God, she's so sodding pious and Marcus is so bloody protective of her, don't call her Cinders in front of him he'll go off on one," said Sophie.

The girls laughed.

Noëmi walked out, Sophie took her cubicle.

Seething Noëmi looked at Yumi. As she thumped the hand wash bottle to make it work, she said, "Can you believe the amount of racism right in front of us? In plain sight?"

"There's absolutely no excuse, you just need to keep on educating people." Yumi replied, drying her hands.

"So much work to be done it seems, especially here," and they left.

Marcus

Meanwhile Marcus was at the bar when Jesse came over, propping himself next to him. "Can I get you a drink?" he asked the speaker.

"Nice one, thanks, just a coke as I am speaking now, I'll get a proper drink later," Jesse fiddled with a bar mat.

"Sure, are you travelling back tonight?"

"No, I've got a friend who lives nearby so I'll get a cab there, make a bit of a weekend of it."

"Good idea."

"It's an excellent evening, great to meet everyone, all so friendly...and it's nice to finally meet Noëmi..."

"Yes she's done a great job setting this up." Marcus stood tall.

"Yeah, I've been working with her, she's awesome, so smart. She speaks Italian and French, so we've got things going in Europe now. So much fun too, we have a real laugh, now I find out she looks amazing... you know, I really like her."

"Yeah... she's lovely," Marcus agreed completely with Jesse's description, *'in every way'* he thought to himself.

"...but I guess she's with someone?" Jesse was obviously fishing.

"Er... no... I don't think she's with anyone," he managed, feeling anxious. He steadied himself on the bar as he felt a bit nauseous all at once.

They moved back to their seats as everyone returned to the party.

The speaker stood to talk.

Jesse explained about the work of the charity and what the funds raised by Oxford University could do. He spoke at length about the challenges facing the medical staff given the remoteness of the villages. He described the importance of building trust and awareness within the community. On the one hand there was the misguided belief that paying traditional healers would cure sufferers and yet on the other those left disfigured by the disease were shunned by their own neighbours.

Marcus listened enraptured. He knew that his heart lay in helping those in need. Jesse finished his speech by thanking the university and acknowledging the £30,000 raised, saying how much it would help the project. His final words however made Marcus rigid with surprise as Jesse said;

"To end I would like to thank Noëmi McAllister who has underpinned the success of this project through her hard work on a webpage and on social media blogs. This has raised awareness of the work of our doctors. She first contacted me when she was preparing her presentation to get your support. From that moment on, she has worked tirelessly to promote our cause and donations have increased by twenty per cent meaning we can send two more surgeons out this summer. With the funds raised by Oxford, that's a third surgeon, so it means that many more victims will receive new faces."

Marcus thanked the speaker and the society, feeling proud of Noëmi and pleased with the recognition she had received. The meal finished and the dancing began. Sophie grabbed his arm to dance and he complied, but his mind was racing over the speeches. He said over the music to Sophie, "Such an amazing result."

Sophie was dancing happily and swung her hair around. "What?"

"The money raised for Noma."

Sophie did not reply but ignored his comment.

Marcus felt awkward; he really wanted to talk about the success of the fundraising. He went to get another drink. The dancing continued, with Sophie in the middle of the mosh pit by now, her dress riding round her taut thighs.

The music got slower and Marcus noticed Jesse speaking and laughing at length with Noëmi. She was equally enjoying his company and they danced together, with Jesse very close to Noëmi, talking only to each other, looking like a couple. At that point Marcus could not deny to himself he wished that was him. Feeling sobered up, he went and sorted out the paperwork that he had to do before the end of the party, happy to get away from all that was going on around him. Having spent a good half hour getting everything paid up and signed off, instead of going back to the dance floor, he went out onto the patio into the late spring evening. He looked out at the stars, as he turned he saw Noëmi standing alone doing the same thing.

"Noëmi!"

"Marcus!" she replied, surprised to see him. After a moment she added, with a smile, "Is it Star Walk time?"

"Ha! I've upgraded to the latest version of course! What about you? Still reading things written in invisible ink?"

"Stop it! You got me all flustered!"

"Great dress, you look really lovely."

"It was my mum's, I thought I should dress up."

"She would be so proud of you, in every way."

"Oh can you take a photo of me? I promised my Dad."

Not ready for any talk of her mum, Noëmi struck a few silly poses as he clicked away.

"Your dad will love those and that dress is now my second favourite of all your outfits," he said smiling.

"What's your favourite?" Noëmi asked, confused.

"That pink bikini you wore on our families' day out to the beach for your seventeenth!"

Noëmi burst out laughing, "Oh such a great day! The best!" she laughed some more "Your mum was so angry, do you remember she was right to be? God at that age I just liked what my mum wore, I had no idea, now I realise it was a bit too much!"

"No, I think the problem was that it was a bit too little!"

They both laughed out loud together. Neither could have felt happier at that moment.

"We were so young, but it was the best day." She said.

"I wish we could go back...that day, being with you, I was happy."

"That day meant everything to me."

"Yes it did N, to us both," he took her hand, "But now I wanted to say 'well done' for the web page, you have sent two, actually three doctors out to Nigeria, well done on all you've done for End Noma, I had no idea."

"It just means a lot to me. I loved this project. Thank you for including me Marcus."

"You made it such a success, so typical of you, throwing yourself into everything."

"Actually, all that matters is those people getting their surgery."

"I know," Marcus replied, "one day I want to go out and help."

"I'm coming too, pact?"

"That's a deal then, N,"

"Just us, alright? I doubt it's Sophie's thing."

He laughed, "...you're beautiful," he took her other hand.

"But you got back with Sophie?" Noëmi said simply.

Marcus looked down and was silent, "It seemed the right thing to do, all part of the plan..."

"Oh what happened to the rower?"

"He cheated on her."

"They were well suited then."

Marcus gave a laugh although it seemed to catch in his throat.

She thought for a moment, "You have a plan again?"

"Well kind of, need to be structured, make the best decisions, take measured risks only occasionally if necessary."

"Getting back with Sophie is 'part of the plan' or a 'measured risk'?"

"Not sure, it's just after being together we have the same circle of friends, doing the same course, it's just easier, plus I have so many exams this year..."

"But she cheated on you, *more than once*. So are you telling me you're not angry anymore? You were *'furious'* remember? Now you've decided that it's okay for an easy life?"

Marcus liked the fact she was reckoning with him.

"She says she made a mistake," he said in Sophie's defence.

"Of course, another mistake. I just don't think you should be with someone who treats you like that, I'm sure being picked up and dropped, when it suits, is not in your plan. You're the one making the mistake now."

"I hear what you're saying."

"Do you? Do you really? I care about you, that's all…there are other options…I wish things were different…"

"What do you mean?" He fixed his eyes on her.

"You know what I mean. Do I really have to spell it out to you?"

Suddenly a cacophony of noise burst out onto the patio, it was Sophie and her friends.

Marcus turned away from everyone and looked out into the evening sky.

"Marcee, come on baby let's dance."

Marcus did not reply and Sophie and her friends carried on dancing around and went back into the party. They could hear the faint sound of the love songs playing in the background.

"Never mind, forget it, I start at the school in Durham in two weeks, so I'll be gone."

"Really, what? Not September? I didn't know...I have a placement until mid-August...it won't be the same without you..."

"You know I really hate being your friend Marcus."

"What do you mean?"

"Because I wanted to unbreak your heart, suddenly you had a choice and you chose her..."

"I didn't think I had a choice, I would never..."

"Thank you both for this evening and for all you've done." said Jesse, interrupting without realising.

Marcus and Noëmi stood straight and both smiled at Jesse.

"I have to go now. I'm staying with a mate. You know Noëmi, I'd love to keep in touch with you and see you again for dinner soon. Are we okay to move things from professional to personal?" said Jesse, as if no one else were there.

Marcus turned away tactfully.

"Yes of course, that would be good," said Noëmi, "We were just catching up on old times," said Noëmi.

"Absolutely," said Jesse.

"We know each other from our school days," added Marcus, noticing the silver heart necklace Noëmi was wearing.

"Okay, wow, fabulous," commented Jesse.

"Our families know each other too, they live in neighbouring streets, we're old friends, just always really, really good friends, it's just so wonderful," said Noëmi pointedly.

"Like brother and sister!" laughed Jesse.

"No, definitely not," replied Marcus, with feeling.

Jesse said goodbye to them both, shaking Marcus' hand and then giving Noëmi a tender kiss before he left.

The next morning, Marcus woke up alone on his couch. His bedroom door was open and he could see that Sophie had already left. Maybe she was rowing? He was not sorry, he was confused about his feelings for Noëmi and just wanted to be by himself. Lying, staring at the ceiling, he thought about the huge amount of work he needed to do and rolled over, not caring to face it for another hour. However, his idea to lie in was abruptly interrupted by a message pinging through on his phone, which he ignored. It prompted him, reluctantly, to get up and focus on revision for his upcoming exams. Having showered and grabbed coffee, he began to reflect on the charity ball. He wished he had not been there; his feelings were distracting him. None of this was in his carefully planned spreadsheet for today; he was losing his time and his focus. Unable to concentrate he grabbed his jacket and headed out to clear his mind and walk off this frustration.

Heading to the river, the morning shone, he could hear church bells ringing which reminded him of his childhood and having to go to church each Sunday. He felt nostalgic and suddenly missed his family. He reached into his pocket for his phone wanting to ring home to speak to his grandma Raeni. He realised he had not seen her for nearly five months, not having visited home at Easter. As he went to dial the number, he saw that he had a message from Sophie and he clicked on it. Perhaps it would explain why she had left without waking him.

'*Fuck you we're finished,*' the message read.

Marcus sat down by the riverbank and looked over at a pair of swans gliding softly next to one another. Annoyed by the fact that he never seemed to know what Sophie was about, he messaged her,

'Do you want to talk?'

Immediately she sent back, **'You're being unfaithful.'**

He was stunned. He had hung onto his plan, hoping that he and Sophie could reignite the happiness they had felt right at the beginning. He knew that they were too damaged now. He wondered why he had allowed the relationship with Sophie to continue.

When she had cheated on him, he took her back twice. He allowed this to look like forgiveness but in reality the thought of disrupting his whole life and friendship groups was the reason for the reconciliations. Yet after the evening before, he had also decided to break the relationship off.

He did not reply to Sophie as he needed time to think. Whilst he knew he was in no way being unfaithful physically, he could not deny that thoughts and memories of Noëmi were in his head.

He felt he had no structure or control, all of which made him anxious, he dialled home and Raeni answered,

"Hey Grandma, how are you? I'm coming home for a few days, can you let Mum know? I need to see you guys it's been too long."

Raeni was of course delighted and told him so, which lifted his mood.

Marcus strode back to his house and packed a travel bag, mostly with revision. He headed to the station, not even bothering to look up the travel times for getting to Newcastle. He was going home.

CHAPTER 10 – QUESTS

Noëmi

'N I'm home for a couple of days before I go to Cambodia, I'd love to see you Mxxx'

'Same, let's go to Durham I want you to meet some of my new work mates Nxxx'

August 2016. Towards the end of the summer Noëmi met up with Marcus in Durham, which was the first time she had seen him since the charity ball. He was home for two days and she wanted to show him the school where she had got her first job.

They both liked to spend time in Durham, given its relaxing vibe, plus it was a special place for them. She noticed he looked excited to see her and he gave her a tight hug.

"Do you remember when we came here those times in sixth form?" Marcus asked nostalgically.

"Last time was five years ago! Almost to the day, It was a lovely thing you did for me that day. Funny to be back up here now!"

"This place has some memories!" he beamed.

"As do a few other places too!" she smiled.

He laughed.

They made their way over the bridge to the Swan and Three Cygnets where Noëmi had arranged to see some of her new teacher friends. She was pleased that Marcus would meet them. She was sure he would get on well with Frank, his husband Val, Sarai and her husband Luca.

All were now becoming good friends to Noëmi especially as she, Luca and Valentino would speak Italian together. Noëmi loved her heritage; she used to speak Italian to her mother and did extra lessons as a child, losing herself in the grammar and beauty of the mysterious words. Valentino and Luca were happy to have met a fellow Italian speaker and found her funny and kind. Frank would raise his eyes in mock disdain when they got into an intense conversation, with all the necessary gestures.

"Those three Mafioso arm waving and reciting pasta shapes do not fool me," he would often comment about the trio.

Sitting on the balcony the group looked out at the river Wear, Noëmi turned to Marcus.

"Do you remember when we took the boat out?" she asked, taking a gulp of wine. The water below them looked cool and refreshing as the hot August sun burned down on them. Little rowing boats bobbed in the current.

"That was funny, you're rubbish at rowing," he laughed.

"You're the one who ended up in a tree!"

"And who was navigating?"

"Whatever, hopefully I'll be better at teaching."

"Clear instructions okay! Well done on the job, it's really exciting."

"I'm happy but teaching demands so much and yet I'll start on about £20K. How rubbish is that? Trainee lawyers in the City can start on £45K."

"Yes, I know, I'll start on about £27K, but people like us are not in it for the money, doctors, teachers, it's a vocation." He replied.

"After five or six years at university too. Bills still need to be paid and no one says *what a great 'vocation' I'll only charge you half.*"

A discussion on pay ensued with the others.

"Could be worse guys, you could be self-employed!" Luca laughed.

"Or have no qualifications so you end up making tea for a living!" Sarai added.

"That's not your fault Sarai!" Luca defended his wife.

"Sarai was just 16 and spoke no English when she arrived from Ho Chi Minh with her family twenty years ago. So she took no exams." Noëmi explained to Marcus.

"Listen to you now Sarai, you nearly sound like a real Geordie!" Luca laughed.

"Wey aye Pet!" Sarai tried to sound authentic.

"Getting there! A few more nights out on the Town and you'll be an expert!" laughed Marcus.

"Well I'll be bankrupt when I'm paying Frank's legal bills after he tells that mother who keeps complaining exactly what he thinks of her!" joked Val.

"No, I would never! I'll be saving my exquisitely eloquent expletives for senior management!" replied Frank.

"Oh yes, after they gave the Assistant Head job to someone else, that was dreadful!" stated Luca.

"Yes I know Luca, it was an outrage!" agreed Frank.

"I was delighted!" laughed Val.

"Luca's a fine caring man unlike my dear husband."

"Ah he really is!" agreed Sarai looking lovingly at Luca as she leant close to him.

"Don't worry guys Marcus can pay all our bills when he's a rich consultant," Noëmi joked.

"Whoa! For now I'll just get the drinks!" He moved to the bar.

Noëmi chatted happily with the others.

Returning with the order Marcus sat down and positioned himself even closer to Noëmi.

"Your work on The End Noma Campaign has inspired me. I found out when you're two years post qualified, you can go out to work in places excluded from healthcare, like parts of Africa or Asia, where there are literally no doctors." He had leant right in towards her to explain.

"Cool but that's five years away, we need to do our trip first and then I'll visit you."

"In Democratic Republic of the Congo?"

"Where in Africa is that?" asked Noëmi.

"Used to be Zaire, they have an urgent need for doctors, especially emergency specialists. People die from basic stuff, measles, childbirth, dirty water, snake bites. I want to go and help," said Marcus.

"Sounds awesome, don't like the sound of the snakes!"

With a smile he looked directly into her eyes. Puzzled as to what was funny, she suddenly realised he was moving a long lock of her hair from his pint as she had leant in so close to him. She could feel his skin against hers but she did not move away.

"Sorry, it's clean. I washed it before we came out! How's Sophie by the way?"

"Yeah, fine I think, but we broke up. That's definitely it now, enough is enough," He sounded reluctant to talk about Sophie.

"Oh you broke up! I'm sorry to hear that. Actually I'm not," Noëmi was surprised.

Marcus let himself smile, "Yeah, it's for the best, it ended that night of our Medsoc charity ball, she left me. Although, I was having second thoughts. It was more than just Ben the rower, some bloke from her old school too during the holidays," he said very openly.

"Oh!" Noëmi was stunned, "How wonderful! A third affair!"

"Yep, I know. Anyway she left in the night and dumped me by text."

"Lucky escape! For you I mean!" She laughed, finishing her drink.

"Yeah, but seriously, that was only part of it. I'd been thinking about what we spoke about. What you said to me that evening. I knew that relationship was so wrong. I'd decided to end it too."

"That's good."

"Yes, it feels so much better now. Sorry, I don't want to bore you with this." He took a drink.

"She nicknamed me Cinderella!" Noëmi said laughing.

"She didn't! Don't tell me she said that to you?" Marcus looked horrified.

"No, I just overheard it. I don't care. I think it's because of how I used to dress. Funny really."

"No it's not, honestly, you see? I just can't handle that kind of thing. She said it to me once and saw my reaction. I can assure you she never said it again, well not in my presence. God she's something else." Marcus appeared truly mortified.

"What's she up to these days?" asked Noëmi, really wondering what on earth had happened after they had gone back from the charity ball.

"I have no idea. She's with Ben, we didn't really discuss anything although I tried to. We're just ex-partners now. I know, for her and certainly for me, it was never love. But I still want the best for her if that makes sense." Marcus replied honestly.

Frank was getting the next drinks and took their orders. Marcus carried on talking to Noëmi,

"Anyway, no more messing about, next time I'll be in love. I don't care how long I have to wait, no question."

"I think you definitely know when you're in love," Noëmi stated.

"Yes, I'm sure too," he agreed.

They looked away from each other.

Marcus

Marcus was keen to move the subject on from Sophie. He had left out the bit about not sharing a bed with her after the charity ball. This had infuriated Sophie as they had not been together since their reconciliation. Marcus knew it was not what he wanted after the conversation he had had that night with Noëmi.

"Anyway, what about you? Still seeing the Noma guy?"

"Yes, but we don't see a lot of each other, with him living in London. Plus hard working student teachers are not much fun either. Especially ones whose idea of a good time is everything KPop! Yumi's fault!" Noëmi laughed. "He's nicknamed me the basement dweller."

"Oh that's funny! So, will he kill me if I get you a birthday gift?" Marcus asked, smiling.

"He doesn't own me, you know! That'd be lovely. I like gifts!" she finished her wine, "He's coming up for the weekend on Friday actually," she said.

Frank returned with a tray full of drinks, and they thanked him.

"Have you been down to see him?" Marcus asked.

"A couple of times," she said.

The awkward silence that followed lasted too long. Noëmi continued.

"I stayed with Yumi, he's moved back in with his parents, long story."

"Okay, great that you could combine the two visits." Feeling nervous, he tried to appear casual.

She looked at him with a ghost of a smile.

"It's not love but he's a good person. As you know my relationship history has been a bit of a fail." She gave a long sigh into her wine glass. "I think I've been too idealistic, chasing dreams. I suppose I need to give it a go. We still work together on The End Noma Campaign and I'm going to fundraise at the school."

"Ah that's great, the fundraising that is." He felt himself relax.

"Plus, I'm starting my proper trainee year this September. I've got plans, I'm moving out of Dad's and renting my own place in Gilesgate. Yumi's coming up the first weekend too!" She looked excited.

"Yumi? No one's safe!" Marcus was amused and took a sip of his pint. "I don't know what you mean by *'too idealistic'* though. You should chase your dreams, go for the win. Find that person who absolutely loves you as much as you love them."

They had leant in together again and more of her hair was in his beer. He could feel her right close to him, her gentle breath on his neck.

"There's always things in the way." Suddenly she noticed, "Oh God, I'm sorry, my hair's in your drink again," she said as he removed another lock. Slowly he pushed it back over her shoulder and brushed his hand through her soft hair, smiling. He could see they both felt the intense sensuality in this small gesture. Their eyes locked, neither moved apart.

They were quiet for a few moments.

"Anyway, N, I've already decided to help train some health workers. You know I'm off for a month to Cambodia to volunteer on a primary healthcare project run by Oxford. We're travelling in Vietnam for a bit first. I leave at 3am tomorrow, Dad's driving me to Manchester Airport."

He did not want to hear any more about Jesse. He explained about the work he would do in Asia. Her talk of giving the relationship with Jesse a chance made him think he could not interfere.

"Yes, amazing. Will we go to Nigeria, you and me, like we said?" She asked, reminding him of their promise from the Medsoc event.

"Oh yes we need to plan it, I'm determined to do that," he replied, "but I only want to go with you, and don't bring Jesse either," he said, stroking the back of her hand.

"Yes it will be tough, you need to have a travel buddy you can trust, with the right attitude and work ethic," she replied looking amused.

"And for me it's important that they look good too," he said, smiling at her.

"What are you like," she replied.

Noëmi

They enjoyed catching up. Sarai expressed how pleased she was that Marcus would visit Vietnam on his way to Cambodia and told him about the country. In the company of the two couples Noëmi noticed how naturally she interacted with Marcus, their soft touches on each other's arms, reassuring looks and playful ways. By the end of the evening they were still sitting so close to one another. She could feel the warmth of his body, his soft skin and the gentle vibration of his chest when he laughed. Marcus stroked her hair every now and then as he had used to do when they were in class together.

Quiet and reflective, they travelled back on the train together, then walked to their childhood homes.

"How many times have we done this?" he said, putting his arm around her affectionately. They stopped outside her father's house, playfully he added,

"Are you going to invite me up?"

"Stop it!" she interrupted, "You know I can't, even if I wanted to...and I do want to, just so you know." She could feel herself blushing.

113

"Ah yes!" He moved in front of her with a huge smile and held her arms gently.

"Oh such new information!" She leant in to hug him. "Good luck in Vietnam and Cambodia, keep in touch!" she replied, putting her head on his chest.

"I'll miss you," they said at the same time.

She looked up at him, she could feel his heart beating fast, as was hers. He put his hand lovingly on the back of her head.

Suddenly Noëmi's phone rang. She jumped and went to her pocket to get her mobile.

"Oh hey, Jesse, yes, yes, I know sorry, just out with friends...some people from my new job...okay…that's great, see you then!"

"That could have been his best timing ever," said Marcus, looking past Noëmi.

Noëmi looked down and felt conflicted.

'Definitely his worst,' she thought to herself feeling sad, but replied "Take care when you're away."

He started to walk away. Then seeming determined, he quickly turned around.

"Noëmi, one last thing on the Sophie stuff. What you said about me having chosen her, I would never choose her, or anyone else for that matter, over you. Never in the whole of time would I ever do that. Just so you know." Breathlessly he got his words out.

"Oh my God Marcus..."

"One day Noëmi, one day!"

She felt a slight panic as Marcus gave her a warm smile and a wave. He still had a year at Oxford and she would be starting her Newly Qualified Teacher year. At Christmas she would be travelling to Italy to mark the ten year anniversary of her mother's death, with her father and maternal grandparents. If Marcus was home she would not see him until New Year's Eve at the earliest.

Having reflected on her feelings for Marcus, Noëmi had thought it only fair to let Jesse know that she wanted to move things back to friendship. Undeterred, Jesse replied, *'Let's still get together and talk. I've already got my ticket!'*

However, a few days later Noëmi's new 'friendship' with Jesse, crashed to a halt when he failed to appear for her birthday weekend.

Jesse

Jesse had arranged to meet some old friends at a bar near Kings Cross on the Friday afternoon before taking the fast train up to Newcastle to see Noëmi. Having settled in, catching up, listening to live music, he found he was having such a relaxing time drinking in the London sunshine. So he decided not to get the train but to stay with his buddies. Of course, he was too far gone to let Noëmi know and whilst he felt momentarily bad; he was not sure he could be bothered. She not only waited at the station until all the London trains were in but was frantically calling and texting him to see what had happened. His drinking friends nicknamed her 'wifeline' and blocked her number from his phone which he had found hilarious. It was not until 4pm on the Saturday that she heard he was okay. He messaged that he had been out on a *'bender'*, that they should *'find another time to talk.'*

Noëmi

'Fine by me Jesse,' she thought.

115

A three week sulk from Jesse ensued.

Having heard Marcus was safe in Cambodia, Noëmi reflected on the turn of events.

A few days after Jesse's failed visit, on her twenty-third birthday, she received her birthday gift from Marcus. He had messaged her to look out for it and that he had organised it especially, whilst waiting for his flight at the airport. It was the next five year diary to follow on from the last one she received when turning eighteen. The cover was dark blue leather with golden stars, moons and comets embossed on it. He had got the front personalised, written on it was;

'Chase your dreams, Noëmi!'

And inside he had got printed;

'Go for the win. Find that person who absolutely loves you as much as you love them, All my love M xxx'

* * *

Gilesgate. Moving into her new flat in Durham and preparing for her first proper year of teaching kept Noëmi busy whilst Marcus was away in Cambodia and Jesse was AWOL. Durham was a lively, if a little cosy, city full of lovely coffee shops and bars. She now had the beginning of a hectic term to prepare for.

Her father was fragile and she was happy to be closer to help him with his anxiety. Her flat was in Gilesgate, not far from the city centre, about a half hour walk from her work. It was on the top floor of a Victorian villa; all garret windows and sloping roofs.

Noëmi had an eye for colour and before long the flat was decorated with a modern Italian style. Noëmi was happy to just rent a place rather than try to buy.

"It gives you your freedom, it is best to have no ties," her father had commented. "You must travel, see the world, live in different places!" He advised her often, although she was not sure if he actually meant it.

She enjoyed visiting her relatives near Naples; spending time in Pompeii and visiting the Amalfi coast. Each year she would go with her father. This had started the year after her mother's death but the first holiday was a traumatic experience for them both. In spite of her sadness, Noëmi, as a fourteen year old, was keen to go abroad. She wanted to get away from Newcastle with the incessant bullying and be somewhere warm and glamorous. She made sure she mentioned her holiday plans in class to give herself a more exciting image.

The day to literally 'get away from it all' arrived and Noëmi travelled on the local train to Newcastle airport with her father.

"Two weeks, Dad, it'll be great," she said looking through the blackened window on the train to the airport.

"Passports, money, tickets,"

He kept checking when they were waiting at the departure gate. Sitting on the small plastic seats Donnie was restless, he repeated the checks yet again.

"Dad, they've not leapt from the bag, you only checked a minute ago!"

Donnie put his head in his hands, began to cry.

"Dad I'm sorry, we'll be okay, be strong."

Noëmi put her arm around him. A few people sitting opposite gave them a bit of a look, no doubt wondering if the pair were alright. They managed the journey there but given that it was the first time Donnie had visited since the memorial service, the year before, he was upset as soon as the plane landed. Everything reminded him of the trauma of losing his dear wife. He was woken by nightmares of Manon falling from his grasp every night. Once awake he began getting up to check that candles were out, taps were off and the front door was locked. He would repeat the process a number of times to be sure.

Manon's parents were worried about him and after two days it was decided it was best for Noëmi and Donnie to return to their routine in the UK. Whilst Noëmi understood and wanted her dad to get well, she was aghast that she had to go home to the grey skies of Newcastle. It was not possible for her to stay; the extended family did not think it was good for Donnie to be alone. Having reluctantly accepted the situation, Noëmi was miserable and just wanted her life to be otherwise; not to be the one with the dead mother, the name calling and now no holiday. She helped her father who began to see a therapist about his grief, which was something he had never done previously. Over time, he began to be less anxious. The next year Donnie was even able to talk about Manon briefly without crying. She hated her father's suffering but was strangely comforted about the intensity and completeness of her parents' love for one another. In the following years, although Donnie still struggled, time and therapy enabled them to go to Italy successfully and enjoy holidays with the family.

Noëmi had no idea if her father would ever be well but she knew things were slowly improving.

PART TWO – REACTIONS

Il faut chercher avec le cœur

Le Petit Prince - Antoine de Saint-Exupéry

CHAPTER 11 - RESPONSIBLE

Noëmi

September 2016. The first week of term was over and the intensity of the workload was already being felt by the teachers and staff.

"It's like the summer never happened," Noëmi said to Frank in the staffroom, thinking back to various low points, top of which was John Dyer's visit to her 'learning environment'.

Noëmi was still supporting The End Noma Campaign; fundraising with different year groups. However she was distracted by her unresolved feelings for Marcus, especially as the latter was now single. Keeping busy was helpful during this time of confusion and she was buzzing with energy, especially when it came to plotting her revenge on John Dyer.

As she planned her moves on him, Noëmi kept a surreptitious eye on her target at all times. She watched as he looked women up and down, without them realising. She noted the number of times his few classes were on cover and how he would cosy up to anyone he thought had power or influence. Her disgust growing; she felt that nothing could surprise her about his low behaviour and his disregard for others.

Noëmi was therefore astounded when she was sitting in her classroom, looking over some of the work from a previous lesson when the door was flung open. It was her Head of Department who gasped out in a desperate voice,

"Noëmi quick! Come on! You're on duty at the lunch queue! It's crazy out there, you're so late."

Confused, as she had definitely checked the rota, Noëmi immediately left her desk and ran to the lunch queue. At the end of the lunch hour, she looked to see who should have been on duty and let out an angry scream.

The AWOL staff member was John Dyer. She told her Head of Department who assured her he would make sure this was followed up. However she was pretty sure he had absolutely no intention of doing so. He had a reputation of being too scared of rocking the boat with senior management and not supporting his hard working colleagues. Noëmi left for her class feeling frustrated and powerless. Why had such a seemingly little thing upset her so?

She asked Frank in the pub after school.

"Duties are such an important part of safeguarding!" she told him, finishing her drink.

"And a sensitive area for the school, you know a few years ago a student had had their arm broken during the administering of birthday bumps!"

"Where was the staff member then?"

"Having a sneaky cigarette on the other side of the building. Mmm legal case is still on-going, something of an embarrassment to Mr Mundy." Frank's lips twitched in amusement.

"That makes it even worse! Dyer stood up and lectured us about it on that first day!"

"Well Noëmi, 'tis the stuff of nightmares, that Wunderkind who is now leading our learning establishment. Him and your esteemed Head of Department. Those could be your two," he replied mysteriously.

"My two what?"

"You know that French play where there are three of you and you're trapped in a room together for eternity, then you find out it's hell!" explained Frank.

"Oh God, could you imagine?" Noëmi visibly paled. "Who would your two be?"

"The same ones probably," said Frank looking with mock horror.

Noëmi laughed and was happy to be smiling for the first time since the incident.

"What about heaven?" she asked.

"Only one other allowed to be with you, and of course any offspring you may produce," said Frank teasingly.

"I know who I'd choose," replied Noëmi wistfully.

"Do share, you know mine, after all," said Frank.

"Marcus," she replied simply, looking down at her hands.

Frank said nothing but gave her a hug.

Arriving home as the evening closed in, she threw her things down, grabbed a coke and rushed to get her laptop out. Finishing her drink she sat back and admired her work on Maya who was looking great. Now all Noëmi needed to do was to get her connected with John. Noëmi began planning her lessons but got distracted and opened a new tab on her laptop to search for information on John Dyer. Her relentless burrowing unearthed a profile on an educational consultancy site, mainly aimed at those looking to commission freelance work and keynote speeches.

"Hmm not really a place for Maya," said Noëmi to herself as she read John's précis of his services, 'one of the youngest Assistant Head Teachers in the country, talking about getting it right in the classroom'.

"Well you're never in the classroom. Your two classes a week are more often than not on cover." She scoffed.

Next she found him quite easily under his own name on a popular dating website.

"God he needs to be careful the kids don't find this," she muttered as she looked over the photos of John doing all sorts of amazing things; paragliding, standing in Times' Square, drinking at an All Blacks vs Springboks rugby match. His profile and interests made him sound unrecognisable and nothing like the prematurely promoted school teacher that he was. *'He's not even that good at his own subject'.*

With all the song writing, influencing and blogging John Dyer was clearly a busy man.

The website had a direct messaging facility so once Maya was all signed up Noëmi sent out a hook to catch John.

She decided to go right in.

'You look like someone I should more than just know!'

Noëmi was quite pleased with her work here, making sure a sexy shot of Maya was attached. She checked the bacon and lentil soup she was making and waited.

He did not disappoint.

'And you look like someone I need to see more of...'

'*I'm always keen to...*' Noëmi was typing when she got back from John.

'*You're wearing too many clothes...*'

'My God he doesn't waste time'.

'*I'm always keen to...*'

She baited him back by not finishing her sentence.

'*To what?*' he threw back immediately with a devil emoji.

She left him hanging, although she was desperate to just get on with her plan. She worked on the profile some more, taking pictures and videos from Magda's profile. She felt a tinge of guilt as she downloaded another great picture of Magda. Sending it to John, he liked it immediately. Jolted out of her reverie she then looked at the clock. It was 2am. She had to be up in four hours and she had no lessons prepared. Yet she could not sleep wondering what John Dyer was also doing online, so deep into the night.

* * *

The next day was a blur.

Fridays always started with a half hour Citizenship lesson across the school where students were taught 'useful skills' to help deal with future life. That day's subject for Year 11 was 'Money and Budgeting'. As Noëmi browsed through the lesson, her heart sank. Today the person responsible for organising the lesson, had produced many slides of illegible text in a tiny font, copied and pasted from a textbook. There were no activities or videos, just information on a screen that only those with telescopic vision could read. It would be useless as a lesson. She hastily searched on a teaching website to find a suitable lesson preferably with a video so she could catch her breath.

Suddenly Noëmi noticed Stephanie come in late, dark circles under her eyes, she looked like she had been crying. She sat down at the back, not in her correct seat, put her head on the desk and remained silent, not moving. A couple of the other students looked round, saw she was out of sorts and let her be. Ronnie, however, had other ideas.

"What a grumpy arse," he shouted out, "and she does dirty stuff."

"And you spend your time threatening people and blackmailing," yelled back Stephanie.

"No I don't threaten no one," said Ronnie quietly; "ain't got no clue what *blackmailing* is."

Noëmi sensed immediate danger on every level and asked Ronnie to collect the worksheets from the photocopying office. She had arrived at work too late to do so in advance.

"Get that stroppy bitch to do it," he replied pointing at Stephanie.

"Ronnie, you apologise for that abuse! You need to do as I ask, right now!" Noëmi said firmly.

"Can't wait to get out of this shitty class," called back Ronnie slamming the door as he left.

Noëmi asked a student to let the office know that Ronnie was roaming the school. Then she tried to start her hotchpotch lesson with no resources apart from a YouTube video about shopping. Through the chaos one student was attempting to give out the books and the rest of the class were generally on their phones or chatting; none of which was the expected behaviour for St Wolbodo's or anywhere else.

To add to her frustration the video sound would not play.

'Oh God I was supposed to get in early and sort the speaker problem out with IT!'

As the clock ticked on, the students ignored her, the noise level rose and in walked John Dyer, with Ronnie in tow.

'Of course he's on patrol, never teaching,'

He had picked up Ronnie, who was perfectly happy out of lessons wandering the corridors looking for amusement or argument. As John asked Noëmi sarcastically how her 'learning domain' was, Stephanie sat bolt upright, grabbed her bag and stormed out. John Dyer chose to ignore this and continued to talk to Noëmi about Ronnie. Noëmi was in despair but could not think straight. Feeling John Dyer's eyes on her she noticed him look her up and down and felt disturbed.

"So Miss McAllister I'll see to Stephanie next," John Dyer announced and he walked out.

"That pervert was eyeing you up Miss!" Ronnie shouted out as the door shut.

Noëmi felt even worse. The chaos continued. Suddenly the fire alarm went off. She was relieved as she had nothing to teach, but felt cursed as she had hoped to sort out her next lesson in the five minutes between Citizenship and lesson two. It was going to be a tough day.

In line with procedures she took her class out to the tennis courts for the fire safety register.

The whole school was lining up with excited students, happy to be missing a lesson which they saw as 'pointless'. Indeed most of the students wrote things like 'The most useless lesson ever' or 'Complete waste of time' on their Citizenship exercise books instead of the subject title. The students hoped that they would miss the first ten minutes of lesson two. Upon doing her register there was still no sign of Stephanie or Ronnie, and she went and reported this to her Head of Year.

Stephanie had walked out of class before the fire alarm and had gone to have a cigarette near the bike sheds, where the CCTV did not quite reach. All the students knew about this spot, as did most of the teachers. Everyone could get a good view of it from the first floor window, above the canteen, at the back of the school. Stephanie disliked John Dyer as he had confiscated her phone. Not able to get it back for two weeks, she had to use an old basic phone. Ronnie had escaped Mr Dyer as the alarm went off and rushed to find Stephanie in the smokers' corner. Having briefly seen each other over the summer, they had mutually decided to not take things 'too seriously'. He quickly found her.

"Get lost!" she yelled.

"What's the problem?" he asked quietly.

"You know."

"No, I don't."

"I saw that message, you threatening to send my picture out to everyone."

"I wouldn't do that. I've deleted it."

"Liar."

"I don't tell lies. I'd never threaten you, I like you too much," he tilted his head back.

Ronnie came and leant on the wall next to her. She silently offered him a drag of her cigarette, which he took.

"These are so expensive now!" Ronnie said to break the silence.

Finally Stephanie sighed.

"Everything's messed up in my life. That Dyer prick's got staring problems."

"He's an arse. Don't get all stressed! Come on, let's make the most of the time we've got now, on our own. The whole school is out on the tennis court like losers, and you look good," he grinned, putting a strong arm around her.

"Not bad yourself," Stephanie laughed back, extinguished her cigarette and took him into her arms.

Noëmi

Eventually almost all of the school settled on the tennis courts. A warning was given via the loudspeaker that the perpetrators of this 'prank' would be 'severely dealt with' and that 'the new CCTV system would leave them no place to hide'. Noëmi wondered what that actually meant as, more often than not, if the parents complained the sanction was downgraded.

The students reluctantly filed back in for lesson two and learning resumed. Noëmi managed to find some worksheets that gave her a minute to sort herself out. As she reflected on the fact that nothing was going well that morning, she realised that she had not seen John Dyer at the fire alarm evacuation. She was annoyed that he was too lazy to turn up to his duties, then a mandatory safety drill and that he would undoubtedly get away with it.

CHAPTER 12 - STAFFING

Maurice

Maurice Mundy was scurrying along the corridor on his way to what he knew would be a difficult meeting. Rushing past students strolling to their next lesson, he looked mole-like in his dark brown woollen suit.

Maurice Mundy was a competent teacher who had risen to his Headship position after a successful career in a neighbouring school. He spent his time either on his pension calculator, working out what he would get aged 65, or on the school calendar literally, counting down the days until the next holiday. He disliked the talk of salaries and pay grades as the paperwork always showed how his own salary was five times that of the hard working newly qualified teachers who ran around like worker ants, dealing with all the difficult students.

'Well managing different types of learners is one of the key teaching standards and we all learn by doing,' he would say to himself defensively.

In fact it was actually years since he had done any 'managing of learners' of any type, be they 'different' or otherwise. Indeed this was a fact he liked to pass over, preferring to talk at length about important meetings with the Local Education Authority, hinting at major changes and potential school closures. These meetings often involved long lunches, exchanges of titbits of gossip about other Head Teachers and they had little substance to them.

He was particularly good at reading reports on the latest developments in education. Deriving most of his answers for difficult educational questions from these papers, he liked to quote extracts from them when required. Whilst it sounded good to talk, at teacher training days, in sweeping terms about 'the need for consistency in practice' and 'the importance of inclusive educational methods in the classroom'; the day to day reality often contradicted this idealistic dogma. Teachers were stretched to the limit, indecision over how to set students and a lack of flexibility in the timetabling system, had led to significant problems in classes that were not a 'top set'. Indeed Maurice restricted his classroom visits to only those top set groups, as he did not want to have to intervene in some of the difficult classroom management problems faced by teachers each day.

Looking at his watch he quickened his pace and turned a corner into the languages' corridor where he could hear a cacophony of disruption. He crept past the door of a classroom with a significant level of sound. Through the frosted glass, there were shadows of students evidently out of their seats. Amidst the noise he could make out the small strained voice of a young teacher, declaring that she would next be "sending for senior management", to which the students laughed and shrieked even louder.

'Best not to interrupt the flow,' he justified to himself and hurried on.

Breathless he arrived at John Dyer's office to discuss redundancies that were necessary due to the overspend during the last two years. Sharon King, Deputy Head was already there. She was a tall, well-built woman with thick, cropped strawberry blonde hair, who played a power game.

John kicked off the meeting.

"Before we start, I just want to let you know we're investing in a big promotional media campaign. This will entice new students into the sixth form, to bring in much needed cash."

"Right I see, what's that then a new brochure?" asked Maurice fumbling for his papers.

"Yes and a dynamic promotional video, too! We'll be in it obviously and then the better looking teachers. You know the young ones, no one ugly."

"Great idea!" replied Sharon probably thinking she was on the good looking list.

"I'll get Pat to send emails to the chosen ones and I've organised a production company to come in."

"What sort of budget are we looking at here?" asked Maurice nervously.

"All in about 30K but it'll be worth it," replied John.

"Of course." Maurice seemed to go pale.

"Now redundancies. These old teachers are expensive and before you know it they will have days off for old people illnesses." John declared.

However the statistics for staff absence did not correlate at all with age and were more linked to general misery and therefore evenly spread over all demographic groups.

"Sexagenarians out!" quipped Sharon King, who was not far off from being one herself.

John looked up hearing the word 'sex' and appeared intrigued.

"People who are in their sixties," explained Sharon almost on cue.

Maurice bristled as he knew that he was in that demographic.

131

It was next decided that the subjects where money could be saved were maths, IT and drama.

"Let's look at who we have in maths, Will is my friend so forget that, Brianna, she's that hot NQT, so she's cheap and nice to look at so not her, what about Noëmi, Colin or Charvi?" asked John, reading through the list of names.

"Noëmi's an NQT so she's cheap. Either of the others could go although both are good teachers. Who's more expensive?" asked Sharon King.

"Charvi," replied the Head Teacher looking at his notes.

"Perfect, what can we get Charvi on?"

The Head Teacher looked over his notes and furrowed his brow, "her performance management reviews are all good, outstanding in fact, no parental complaints, results are stable, well as they can be for Foundation maths."

"What do you mean?" jumped in John.

"Well the students who can't manage maths we put into a foundation option, it's the class where we put students who are non-attenders, school refusers and the like."

Maurice knew it was unfair to judge anyone on their results for such a class.

"Charvi is the only one who will teach the group, apart from Noëmi who has a similar group in the other timetable slot. The other teachers all refuse to take them," replied the Head Teacher, feeling guilty as he knew he would not be able to manage them for even a minute.

"Perfect, bad results, not popular, troublemaker, I can rustle up rumours of parental complaints and we're all set. This is what we call 'competency proceedings' the actual definition of incompetent practice is so subjective that we can rightly apply our own interpretation to it, you know, given the high standards of St Woldbodo's. It will also scare others, so maybe more will move on, bit of a two for one, great work guys, so are we done?" live streamed John.

The group nodded and Charvi's fate was set.

Stephanie

The next day Stephanie left her home and started walking slowly to school, listening to music and checking her basic phone at the same time. Traffic buzzing busily past her, she weaved in and out of other pedestrians, ignoring the disparaging looks she got from those she was slowing down. Stephanie was excited about her day as she had a talk about A Level choices and she was thinking about her future. Wondering whether to do sciences and go for medicine, she heard a message come through. Suddenly she stopped dead, causing a rain coated business man to walk into her.

"For goodness sake, manners!"

Stephanie did not reply, eyes on her screen.

'Send me another picture or I'll email the others to your mum.'

Ronnie had started again.

Feeling panicked she had no idea what to do.

'No' she replied.

'I got my mate to film us, you know, during fire practice, he'll send that out, everyone will know what a slut you are.'

She was distraught and ran home, images running through her head.

'Don't believe you.'

Almost immediately a screenshot of them together came back and she was physically sick.

Stephanie felt she had no option but to comply with Ronnie's wishes and went back to her bedroom and sent him the picture he had described in great detail.

Her hand trembled as she pressed send and she sent a message saying, **'no more leave me alone.'**

She felt dirty and disgusting. She decided to skip school that day and looked out of the bedroom window of her small suburban home. Black mould was ingrained in the windowsill where the paint was flaking off. The rain was pouring down and it was only 8:45am, the time she should have been in registration. She had no idea what she would do all day and looked across at the scissors.

CHAPTER 13 - CHARVI

Noëmi

Dear N McAllister

You have been specially selected to represent St Wolbodo's School in the promotional video that will be shared on our website and during open days. Please understand we have only chosen those whom we feel will give the right look to the school. It is asked that you be discreet about this. **John Dyer, Assistant Head Teacher and Lead in Child Protection and Safeguarding, St Wolbodo's School, Durham.**

Even before she read the name at the bottom she had typed a reply to say that she did not want to be part of such a project for 'ethical reasons'. The whole concept horrified her.

She forwarded the email to Maurice Mundy to formally complain and to Frank to vent her fury.

On the day of filming, she saw the selected staff gathered together with the production company. All were young, apart from some members of senior management, and very white. Angry with the whole idea she sought out Frank at break time to complain.

"Well Noëmi, I obviously didn't get a golden ticket, being an ageing savant," Frank said with mock indignation.

"It's just so wrong on every level, based on looks, age and

135

whiteness," she threw her hands in the air in Italian rage.

"We could do our own version, a kind of spy on the wall, rough guide to St Wobo's," suggested Frank, sipping his coffee.

'St Woboldo's: everything right for everyone.'

Noëmi gave the project a title using the school motto.

'St Wobo's: everything ruined for everyone.'

Frank corrected her with the student's version of the motto.

Noëmi simmered with anger the whole day as she saw the comings and goings of the filming team and heard the trilling laughter of future film stars. Incandescent with rage she shut her classroom door and lectured the students on what were important qualities in a person and that 'no one should be judged on their looks'. Her young class told her nicely that they thought she was acting a bit oddly and could not see what her talk had to do with maths. Yet they liked Miss McAllister and it took up lesson time, so they did not have to do any work. Therefore everyone was happy and the students thought nothing of it, putting it down to the kind of things teachers went on about.

The Monday after the week of filming in school, staff briefing began with a preview of the video. A large projector screen needed to be set up in the staffroom and Pat had to organise this at the last minute the previous Friday afternoon. There was a great deal of complaining about 'lack of notice' and 'thoughtlessness' given 'how busy she was'. Pat had to send two emails; one to the caretaker Terry and one to Steve in the IT department. After all her huffing and puffing Pat left a mere five minutes after her usual departure time of 3:30pm.

All the staff gathered to watch the video and Noëmi had absolutely no doubt what to expect. As she predicted Sharon and Maurice had a quick five seconds each introducing the school and the rest was the John Dyer extravaganza. His idea was to take the viewer on a mock tour of the school 'in action'. This meant he was the main person in the whole five minute clip, smiling and beckoning the camera to follow him on this exciting journey. The background music sounded suspiciously like John singing, although she was not certain. Going in and out of the classrooms of the attractive teachers, he showed the school in a fabulous light. Experiments with serious looking students, eager hands shooting into the air, violin playing, displays of sport and unfamiliar pieces of artwork, which no one could recall seeing in the school. Nothing could do a better job to persuade the viewer to enrol. Up flashed excellent exam results and awesome predicted results, which somehow had been manipulated from data.

'Those figures must have been taken from a tiny subset of students,' Noëmi thought as the assembled staff clapped, someone even cheered. Everyone was buoyant and enthusiastic *'as the ship began sailing a new path'.* The staff grinned with reflected pride, apart from Noëmi and her friends who looked on grim faced.

The staff dispersed and Frank caught Noëmi's eye. He looked at her knowingly.

"What?" asked Noëmi with a presentiment that Frank had something she would enjoy hearing.

"Oh nothing, just I think the school has wasted a lot of money."

"Tell me something I don't know," replied Noëmi flatly.

"I'm sure time will make everything clear," he replied mystically.

Noëmi wondered what on earth he was talking about and went to start her lesson, now beside herself with rage about the pompous video.

Maurice

Senior management were happy with the video and were now

working hard on the accompanying brochure that would be distributed at the upcoming open evenings. Now they had to go to a meeting to begin the 'competency' discussions with three members of staff. John strode happily out of the staffroom and bounced into his office. A couple of minutes later he was joined by Maurice and Charvi.

John sat at his huge desk and picked up his silver pen. Maurice was relegated to the low sofa in front of the desk and Charvi was asked to sit on a hard student chair in front of Mr Dyer. Maurice trembled as watched the battle commence.

John Dyer started off by saying that her examination results were *"alarmingly below target…"* However, it was clear that Charvi knew her data and she informed him that this was not so. She reminded him of his own report which said the opposite. She could even quote its exact title, **'KS4 Results: Analysis and Action'.**

Charvi then reminded John that her results with a challenging class, that no one else would take, had been 'far above the national average for that cohort'.

Clearly not put off, John proceeded with some rhetoric about 'children at St Wolbodo's deserving much better than the national average'. With Charvi still able to explain why what he was saying was complete nonsense he went in for the kill. He claimed that he had heard parental complaints and comments against her that he could not 'discuss because of their nature'. Charvi appeared stunned. Both Maurice and John knew that these were, of course, totally fictitious. She looked round at Maurice who had said nothing during the meeting. Indeed Maurice was terrified by what he saw, scared, not for his loyal colleague, but in case this ever happened to him.

John finished up.

"I'm sorry but it is time that you took your job more seriously and I have to inform you that as of today you are on a competency programme that will offer targeted support to address the weaknesses in your teaching," said John formally, "if your class observations continue to be poor, the only option will be for you to resign or we will need to take further action, which will make it impossible for you to continue teaching here, or anywhere else..." said John reading the statement from a sheet.

Charvi looked from one to the other, simmering with rage, she said nothing and left. Maurice began to sweat and mopped his brow with his handkerchief. No member of the HR team was present and indeed Charvi had no representation, all of which Maurice thought actually rendered the whole meeting illegal.

During that day another two other teachers received the same treatment.

"One of my fellow teachers in drama is always off sick, and the other is about to leave on a world trip, so most of the time I'm trying to organise two or more classes at once. I've got a good record!"

Huw had been teaching for three years and was overworked. However senior management needed to find a cheap way to make him leave and competency did the job just fine. Huw left the meeting, ashen and looking on the verge of tears. Huw had been accompanied by his Head of Department, who looked uncomfortable throughout. She was a fine leader and stared directly into the faces of the two senior managers.

"Just you wait! I'll see you in court Mr Mundy and Mr Dyer."

Darlene had taught IT at the school for twelve years and was on the highest pay grade. It was decided an NQT would be a cheaper option so Darlene was to be put on a 'competency' plan too. Darlene left the meeting furious, walked through reception and carried on out of the main door, through the school gate and never returned. That evening a cartoon appeared on the front page of the school website and on every other page too. The cartoon showed a woman sitting with a cigarette and a glass of wine, the caption read:

'Once upon a time a wise woman said 'fuck this shit' and lived happily ever after.'

Maurice instructed Mrs King, who was in charge of IT, to sort it out. She tried to get the cartoon down the next day but failed. She admitted that she struggled with the coding that had been used to put it up. This was in spite of being an 'expert' in this coding, as detailed as on her CV. The only option was to shut the website down for a week and call in a specialist to rectify the situation.

Maurice returned home traumatised after the day of 'competency hearings'. During the drive home he was continually mopping his brow, fraught with worry.

'What if any of them took their case to a tribunal?'

He was not sure what the legal status of this all was. None of the employees had any notice or representation. All the allegations were fictitious, false and in fact fraudulent. John had told him that competency is how his former school dealt with staffing problems, and that most teachers did not object as they feared getting a bad reference. Arriving at his smart home, he grabbed a beer and dropped onto his sofa. He had not been sat down for more than a second before his wife rushed out of the kitchen and yelled at him to get off the sofa. She had spent the day plumping the cushions, before her book club were due to visit that evening. With that and making a fluted quiche she had been quite 'rushed off her feet'. Maurice, took his beer, went into his study and looked at his calendar. This time he was working out how long it was until his wife would be away for the weekend with her walking group. Then he would have the house, the sofa and the plumped up cushions to himself.

Eventually, John got the good news that the external consultants had finally been able to take down the unwanted picture. St Wolbodo's was back online after an interminable week. In an act of retaliation, John instructed the new promotional video to be put up on the front page of the website so that they could make up for the lost week. In addition he got a banner on the bottom of each school email which would link to the video so that it got maximum exposure. Delighted with his work and having proudly watched the video himself a number of times that morning, he was perturbed to receive a knock on his permanently shut door from Frank. Having no idea who Frank was, he welcomed him in and asked him to sit down.

Frank apologised for disturbing him from his work but explained it was urgent.

"A parent of one of my tutor group has contacted me, upset that their child is featured in the video," he explained. "They have stated in the child's school record that they expressly do not wish their child to appear in any photographs or videos publicly."

John took a minute to understand what Frank had said.

"You should have known this information about your tutor group and told me this beforehand as it is an urgent safeguarding issue," he replied coldly.

"I did. I came to see you but was told to send an email, which I did after the staff viewing, last Monday week," explained Frank as he knew how important parental consent was.

John remembered the email, which he had not bothered to read. He had assumed Frank was not important, in spite of the fact Frank had written urgent in the subject box.

"You should have followed this up."

141

"I did, with the office, each day. I was assured that you were on top of all your affairs and that the website was down anyway."

With nowhere to turn and no one to blame, John thanked Frank and said that he would deal with the problem.

The video was quickly taken down. John, being in charge of safeguarding, wished to avoid the embarrassment of having to ask the staff to identify each student in the video. So he decided that Pat could do this. That way she could check the photography permission status of each one and where necessary arrange for the face to be pixelated out. Pat sighed deeply and bit her tongue when she heard the news and set to work identifying the numerous students in the film. The additional work meant that the video was not ready for the open evenings and that just the brochure was available to promote the school. In order to explain this away to Mr Mundy, John claimed that the IT staff were late in organising the video distribution and left it at that.

CHAPTER 14 - HILARY

December 2016:

Noëmi

'Hey N, passing through on Friday with a friend I met in Cambodia, Hilary, she wants to see Durham and then we go onto Edinburgh. Can you meet for an early dinner Friday? Mxxx'

'Sounds great, she's obvs classy as she's not interested in the Toon then!'

'Def, btw us true Geordies call it the Town!'

'The Scottish Italian immigrant suggests Zen 6pm? Best behaviour! Nxxx'

'Perfect! You've got the picture! Mxxx'

Unsure exactly what the relationship was between Marcus and Hilary, she felt odd at the prospect of being the third wheel but was keen to see Marcus.

They were to go for an early dinner at Zen and Noëmi made sure she arrived later so that she would not be sitting on her own. Ironically she was the first to arrive. The restaurant was always so beautifully decorated, with pink cherry blossom trees, dark wooden screens and small Japanese lanterns. She waited in the bar and ordered a drink and then she heard Hilary before she saw her.

Hilary was tall, broad shouldered and spoke with a mid-Atlantic accent, having family in New York and London.

"Sooooo cute, my God this is awesome."

Hilary had arrived.

She steeled herself and thought that this could be a long night.

Marcus did the introductions and explained who did what and the chit chat began.

"So, I'm La terza ruota," Noëmi laughed.

"Are you okay?" asked Hilary.

"Yes sorry it means third wheel in Italian."

Hilary gave no response.

A waitress invited them to move from the bar to their table.

"Wow! Politics and International Relations, sounds amazing," Noëmi began passing round a plate of prawn crackers.

"I'll need water to eat those."

"Sorry, yes of course, what's your particular area of study?"

"Well looking at post political truth in the context of reflexivity and transpositional objectivity, kind of turning the double helix on its head." Hilary replied.

"Great!" replied Noëmi without having understood a word.

"What about you?" asked Hilary automatically.

"Oh I'm training to be a secondary school teacher, in maths."

"Hey, could I get some water?" Hilary asked a passing waiter. "So, Marcus says you guys were at school together,"

"Yeah gosh that's a few years ago now," said Noëmi.

"I get it so is Marcus like the older brother you never had?" asked Hilary looking at the menu.

"No, definitely not." Noëmi replied determinedly, recycling Marcus' phrase and he looked up.

"You'll love Oxford." Noëmi moved the subject on. She passed around the newly arrived water jug.

"I'm not so sure, Harvard was just awesome, that's where I was an undergrad, Oxford's okay a bit parochial."

Noëmi looked at Marcus; she knew he thought Oxford was the best place in the whole world.

"You do kind of grow out of it after a while I suppose," he agreed half-heartedly.

"I think graduating from Harvard is as good as it gets." Hilary closed the conversation down.

Noëmi looked at Hilary and was surprised that she was so serious *Don't say anything immature or stupid,'* she told herself.

"Will you go back to the States for Christmas?" Noëmi asked, unfolding her napkin.

"Yes I'll be flying back, although I have a research project to complete in the first term so I'll be working up to the wire."

"I'm going to see my grandparents in Italy for Christmas, but a few of us are meeting up for New Year's Eve Marcus, if you're around," Noëmi mentioned.

"That sounds just great N," Noëmi could tell he was delighted.

"That's so nice that you guys can get together, think of me, I'll be working on my eight hour flight! Got so many articles and journals to get through. Of course, I'll be having to check all the data. Nothing's ever up to date, let alone correct, these days." Hilary's authoritative voice dominated the room.

"Maybe you should plan a break too?"

"I don't think so, if you have a schedule like mine." Hilary replied flatly.

'Of course the rest of us lazy ignoramuses never have any work to do,' thought Noëmi.

"Oh, I just thought you may need it."

"It depends on your priorities and I can't afford to take time off, I guess you can as an educator, I mean those holidays are so long." Hilary said with emphasis.

Noëmi could not be bothered to say that university holidays were even longer.

Hilary left the table to go to the toilet, Marcus asked;

"What else are you doing over Christmas? Are you going to London to see Jesse?"

"No, no we broke up. It was a while ago, immediately after you and I met up. Yeah like I said before, Jesse and I are better as friends." She sighed and paused. "It turns out The Queen's Head in Kings Cross is far more interesting than seeing me for my birthday. Which I don't doubt for one second. So it's back to chasing dreams! Anyway that's enough about me scaring people away."

"He didn't come and see you that weekend then? I know you said things were more relaxed but I got the impression you were still together,"

"No. Actually in fairness it took me three weeks to hear from him properly after my birthday. I had no idea if something had happened to him. If he was alive or dead. I couldn't get through to him, Yumi had to go and find out for me."

"Worrying." His eyes sparkled his delight.

"But after that evening I spent with you, he would've had a wasted trip." She fixed her eyes on him. "So what's the situation with you and Hilary then?" Noëmi looked over her shoulder.

"No, nothing, we're just friends, sorry if I didn't make that clear at first." He jumped to tell her.

"Do you think she wants more?" Her brow creased inquiringly.

"Well I'm not encouraging anything, so I hope not." He put his hands openly on the table.

"I'm sure Hilary would just get straight to the point, so it looks like you're safe!"

She caught his grin. He was irresistible.

"Thank you for the birthday gift again, it was perfect." Her voice was slightly shaky.

"You're welcome," he said looking at her. "You're easy to buy for."

She gently took his hand in hers.

"And thanks for the quest you set me, '***Find that person who absolutely loves you as much as you love them***', maybe I should set you the same quest? Find that match in love."

"Definitely, I'm sure that person is not far away," he said, not taking his eyes off her.

"I hope they're close by," she replied, looking at him.

The frantic buzz of the restaurant fell away.

"Did you know I'm looking at a job in Newcastle from next June as a Junior Doctor?" Marcus suddenly blurted out. "At the Royal Victoria Infirmary, it's the other reason for this trip."

"Oh I heard you would be going abroad or to a teaching hospital in London."

"Newcastle RVI is a teaching hospital too, there are a number of advantages for my career, plus we would be near each other. We could see more of each other..."

Hilary returned to join them. They slipped their hands away.

The waiter came back, then asked if any of them wanted any drinks,

"We're good thanks," Hilary answered for them all.

"Actually can I get a glass of red wine?" Noëmi asked, thinking she would not get through this meal without it.

"Make that two please, Hilary, what about you?" Marcus added.

"How can you drink red wine, it tastes so bad," Hilary commented, clearly not looking for an answer.

"So Marcus, how are your placements?" Noëmi asked.

"Great, exhausting but I really enjoyed my emergency doctor training," he replied.

"Oh did you get to go in an ambulance?" Noëmi asked jokingly.

"Yeah but as a doctor luckily," he said smiling.

"God I was a patient in one once after that lower sixth Christmas party, do you remember? I had to go to A&E and get my stomach pumped. I kept the blanket as a memento, so at least I got something out of it!" Noëmi laughed, as did Marcus until Hilary spoke.

"It's just not right," Hilary said unsmiling "I spent my senior year as a volunteer educating peers about alcohol abuse and one of our projects was to go over the cost of an emergency call out."

The waiter returned with the glasses of wine.

Noëmi felt stupid and could not think what to respond so just said.

"Oh well everyone makes silly mistakes!"

"Actually, I don't agree," replied Hilary, her voice dominated.

Noëmi did not reply wondering what was coming next.

'Here we go, of course you don't agree!'

She took a gulp of her Malbec.

"Up to the age of 12, okay. But after that they are not silly mistakes are they? Just thoughtless actions, selfish really. The reason the world is in such a mess," Hilary pontificated.

Marcus looked between them and did not know what to say at first and then added,

"Yeah same thing happened to me in sixth form, but I didn't get to go in an ambulance and no blanket! So unfair!" He tasted his wine.

Noëmi's Year 12 memory no longer seemed funny. She desperately tried to think of something intelligent to say to redeem herself but came up with nothing. So she changed the subject.

"What was Harvard like?" Noëmi asked, putting the attention on Hilary.

"I mean just awesome, the level of challenge and the standard of teaching are just superb. To have so many gifted peers was a joy. I kind of have a problem in that I just don't get on with people who aren't clever. Marcus thinks I'm an intellectual snob, he keeps telling me to be kind."

"Oh I thought it was the cleverest thing in the world to be kind!" said Noëmi airily.

Marcus gave Noëmi a look but luckily Hilary seemed lost in her own thoughts and appeared not to heed the assumption made in the comment.

Noëmi backed off because she did not want to spoil things for Marcus. The meal continued in much the same vein until it was time for everyone to leave. Noëmi went with them to Durham station to see them off to Edinburgh.

Standing on the platform they had fifteen minutes before the train. Hilary went to get a coffee.

"So, it's been a great evening!" Noëmi said dryly, rolling her eyes, as she closed her coat to keep out the chill.

"Stop it Noëmi, it's so lovely to see you." He started to fiddle with one of her coat toggles.

"Hope I didn't make any more *selfish mistakes!*" she answered.

"I think you're over analysing things. You actually have things in common with Hilary." Marcus said, obviously trying to find a connection.

"Really? Such as the fact we're both alive?" Noëmi replied

sarcastically.

"You're both clever," reasoned Marcus.

"I doubt Hilary agrees not after my joyride in an ambulance," said Noëmi emphatically.

"Come on forget about it, some people are just difficult. It was that evening that encouraged me to go into medicine!"

"I'm such an inspiration!" She began to arrange his coat collar and scarf for him so he was protected from the wind. "Marcus, you know what you said, last time we saw each other?"

"No, what?"

"You know about choosing people over other people?"

"Absolutely no idea. I must've been drunk, you'll have to remind me!" he smiled at her.

"You're so annoying,"

"No, no, what exactly did I say?" he teased.

"Anyway it meant a lot what you said and well it's the same for me, I wasn't choosing Jesse or anyone over you. Never in the whole of time would I ever do that. I just had to do the right thing at that moment."

"I know, that's why I didn't push it!"

"Funny us being back here again. You know, that's the second time we've been to Zen."

"I remember, the other time was with our families. The day after your birthday."

Noëmi nodded, felt tears come to her eyes, she couldn't talk. No doubt sharing the same emotions and memories from that evening, he pulled her in tight.

"Remember those fortune cookies? Mine was right! *'Stop searching forever, happiness is just next to you'* and you were and still are!"

She laughed and wiped her eyes.

"Is New Year's Eve really the earliest we can see each other again?"

"I'm on a clinical placement the next two weekends and then you go to Italy, so it looks like it."

"God I can't wait that long."

"Hey was that a Cappuccino or a Latte you wanted?"

"Anything will do," Marcus looked to the skies, he could not care less. Noëmi smiled as she saw his face.

"The service is just so dreadful, I mean the counter was sticky and there were no napkins, then I asked for soy milk and the waitress, who had holes in her tights, looked at me like I was an alien, so as for decaf forget it, although..." Hilary's voice went on in the background. An announcement indicated the arrival of the Edinburgh express on Platform 2.

"Here we go, that's us, come on Marcus!"

Marcus looked at Noëmi who suppressed a smile.

"So many memories," said Noëmi.

"And so much that is to be N."

Noëmi waved them off and felt at peace.

On the Monday morning, Marcus texted her:

'Hey N I got the job at Newcastle RVI, so I've accepted, we'll be neighbours again! All my love Mxxx'

She jumped with delight; everything was working out at last.

CHAPTER 15 – CONNECTING

Noëmi

Stephanie and Ronnie were equally fierce, forthright and fragile. Their temperaments meant that they argued frequently and made up with as much fervour. During the first few weeks of term, Noëmi had no idea what to expect; they were either enveloped in one another or ignoring each other. However today, they were both in school and Noëmi could not help but notice that Stephanie appeared terrified of Ronnie. The latter strode in oblivious to the lateness of his arrival and threw himself into his seat. As a registration time activity Noëmi had wanted students to start thinking about career choices. She had put some instructions on the whiteboard and Ronnie asked his friend to read them out to him. Stephanie began to shake, slowly got out of her seat and went to the door. Noëmi noticed her trembling and how blanched she was. For this reason she pretended not to see her slip out of the class. However Ronnie spotted this and shouted;

"Oi! Miss! Why's she allowed out?"

"Leave it Ronnie and finish your task." Noëmi replied firmly.

Stephanie

Hyperventilating and holding back the tears, Stephanie stood outside the classroom. She was desperately trying to think of how she could escape, only for John Dyer to appear.

"And?" he said simply.

"Go away!"

"Can I remind you where you are and to whom you are speaking in such a rude way?"

"No."

"I'm very concerned about you and your behaviour, you know."

"Well don't be." She turned her shoulder to him.

"I'm hearing all sorts of rumours, you may be surprised how much teachers find out about you." He bored his eyes into her.

"Leave me alone!"

"I think you should be telling Ronnie to leave you alone."

On hearing Ronnie's name, Stephanie started walking down the corridor, only for John Dyer to block her way.

"Let me pass."

"You need to be in your classroom."

"I want to go to the office. I'm not feeling well."

"Back to your class," he yelled at the top of his voice.

Stephanie could feel hot tears and did not want to cry. She turned and walked back into her lesson, slumped into her seat and put her head on the desk.

"Young lady I suggest you sit up," John Dyer had followed her into the class.

"Lady, ha that's funny!" Ronnie shouted, but John ignored this.

Noëmi however took it up, "Ronnie don't you dare talk like that! You will apologise to your fellow student."

Stephanie left her head on the desk and ignored 'Mr Dyer'. He looked over to Noëmi, who was now sitting wide eyed observing the scene.

"Stephanie Smith needs to be put on monitoring report immediately until her attitude improves," he boomed in front of the whole class and left.

As soon as he had gone, Stephanie left the classroom and walked out of school.

John

John strode out of his office ready to patrol the corridors. Everything was quiet. Surveying the classrooms, John's mind wandered to Maya's chats. He was assuming to meet up with her at Christmas, so that she could deliver her promises and enticements to him in person. Yet for now, he was still free to find pleasure in the many other women he pursued, amongst them, Noëmi. She had definitely caught his eye. Given how aloof she was, she was a challenge. John liked that. Women who presented a strong front, he had decided, would probably be interesting in many other ways, such as taking control in the bedroom. He enjoyed the idea of a woman who could demand what she wanted in bed. Feeling confident that he could work his charm on her he began to imagine what sort of lover she may be. Never having had his advances rejected by anyone, he decided it was just a matter of time until she was in his arms.

Noëmi

Noëmi for her part, ignored John completely and only observed him discreetly after a heavy session of late night messaging to gauge Maya's progress. As this was her one free lesson, Noëmi was in the staffroom photocopying her worksheets herself, as Pat had 'an emergency'. With the faint sound of far off traffic the room had an eerie calm about it in contrast to most areas of the school.

Seeing Sarai enter, she asked her friend; "Sarai, how's the oil painting coming on?"

"Oh yes very well, this portrait is a second commission and they're paying more than last time. They're really loving my work, plus they've recommended me on their website!"

"Brilliant Sarai, you really are a talented artist!" Noëmi tidied a pile of photocopies and grinned at her friend.

"And Luca has been offered work in the US at Christmas, so I get to go too. His contact wants a family portrait in oils!"

"Amazing that's...great," she stopped as she saw John Dyer enter the staffroom.

He looked them both up and down and stared at Sarai's figure. Sarai looked around, appeared uncomfortable and went to start her washing up in the corner quietly. John acted as if she was not there.

"Busy, busy, busy," he said as he approached Noëmi.

Noëmi was not sure if he was referring to her or to the image of himself he liked to project. She said nothing.

"How's it going in maths then?" he asked formally.

She could not ignore his question.

"It's all wonderful," she lied, without looking at him.

"We're really working on getting the right people into the right positions, you know, give opportunities to those who are good.

Move on teachers who should not be on our ship, it's all about standards," he smarmed. She guessed he wanted to imply she may be promoted.

'Teachers on a ship,' she thought and could not help herself.

"Gosh it must be so hard when you have to push people off your fine ship?" She had heard all about Charvi's treatment.

"Well it is a very formal performance management process and we're looking to ensure we have only the very best here at St Wolbodo's."

"Of course but it must be hard making those excellent teachers walk that plank, people like Charvi, Huw and Darlene," said Noëmi sarcastically. All three she knew had been treated terribly.

"Anyway, never mind all that, how are you? Are you getting the right work-life balance?" he cooed.

"Yes thank you, how are you?" she immediately regretted asking him a question as she just wanted him to go away.

"Well there's never enough time to switch off is there? You know, go for a drink, relax, spend time with people you like." He said in a leading way.

Noëmi felt uneasy. His eyes were drilling into her body and she could feel him inching closer. Palms sweating, she decided it was time to leave so she ended her photocopying despite not being finished. Pressing any and every button to stop the machine churning out the fractions worksheet, she turned to go without saying anything back. He moved slightly in front of her.

"How do you like to relax?"

"I work." Noëmi replied flatly.

"Maybe we should get together for a drink sometime?"

Noëmi thought for a minute and then said, "Thank you but I don't think that would be appropriate."

"Oh don't worry about the fact I'm a manager and you're just a teacher," he replied, condescendingly.

"It's not that," Noëmi replied.

"You have a boyfriend? Husband? A great looking girl like you," he asked.

"No."

"So let's go on a date!" he suggested, "and actually even if you have a partner that shouldn't stop you taking up this chance to go out with me."

"No that won't be possible as I don't find you the slightest bit attractive." Noëmi replied formally.

John turned red. Noëmi was somewhat scared that she would be in trouble but then she reasoned she had spoken nothing but the truth and very politely. As he left John slammed the door causing both Noëmi and Sarai to jump.

"Oh my God, terrifying!" Sarai yelped.

"Yes, the drink offer! I've never been more petrified in my life!" Noëmi agreed.

Standing silently they both looked shocked at the violence of his temper.

Noëmi

Exciting news…That evening Noëmi called Marcus, as they had begun to do every day now. Their relationship was developing and there was nothing they did not share, apart from the invention of Maya.

"How long until we see each other?" She asked him.

"Twenty-five days!"

"God, that can't go fast enough! Well in other news, my failing love life has taken a turn and I've been asked out for a drink by my childhood tormentor. It all happened as he stalked me by the photocopier. I'm such a lucky girl!"

"No way! He really doesn't know it's you does he?"

"Nope, hilarious if I was not throwing up at the thought." She picked up an exercise book from the pile beside her.

"You could have some power over him now."

"That sounds a bit weird but you're right! Anyway, how are you?"

"I'm a proper doctor now," and he sent through a picture of himself in his hospital scrubs.

"You look fit, just awesome, like someone out of *'ER'*. Here, it's pouring with rain and I have a huge pile of books for company." She sent through a picture of herself in her flat, holding a red Bic biro between her teeth, surrounded by exercise books.

"You're looking very pretty N. I love your hair, perfect mouth and everything else about you. Oh and nice backdrop of books bet you can't wait to mark all those!"

"Now I have to decide whether I should go out with the person who ruined my childhood. So hard!"

"Don't let him near you!"

"Don't worry I won't! It's so annoying no one can see what a lazy, mean bully he is."

"He may have changed for the better!"

"No he hasn't. I'm watching him, noticing little things like not turning up to his duties, looking at women in a pervy way. One of my students even told me how he was eyeing me up!"

"N you've got your revenge, he doesn't recognise you and now he even wants to get with you. Don't let him into your headspace, it's not good, just forget about him."

"No, no, don't worry of course," once again she lied to the one person she was always honest with.

"Thinking of you tomorrow."

"Thank you." She whispered.

"Sending you lots of love N."

"And right back at you! Miss you," she replied.

At last everything was developing perfectly between her and Marcus.

'Really forget about him N I mean it,' he texted after the call had ended but Maya was already messaging John.

CHAPTER 16 - SARAI

Administration assistant Sarai had a number of different duties assigned to her role. She prepared refreshments, dealt with the post and helped in the school office.

Luca, her husband, was a self-employed photographer who was finding that new advances in mobile phones meant that work did not come in as often as it had before. However a collector, Corey Anderson, in the US, was a big fan of Luca's work and had invited the couple to his ranch in Texas to photograph and paint him. Luca was excited, preparing well for the visit and asked Sarai if she could leave two days before the end of term so that they could travel together on the long flight. Sarai had never missed a day's work in six years and diligently put in her request for two day's unpaid leave, two weeks before the day, as required.

Maurice

Maurice called her in from the general office and asked her to sit down. He was never very comfortable in meetings with staff members as they usually got the better of him. Here with Sarai he felt fine. This was his opportunity not to be weak but to assert his authority and do his job as a Head Teacher. He smiled broadly at her and began,

"Thank you for your leave request but I'm sorry it's not possible."

"Okay that's a shame," Sarai replied and she got up to leave.

Maurice was a bit peeved she was cutting the encounter short, as he was enjoying being the boss for once.

"Well you see, it's not personal but I am not in a position to set a precedent. If I let you take two days off then I'll be inundated with requests, do you see the problem?" he reasoned.

"Yes but there's a science teacher currently off visiting her family in Australia for Christmas. She will have a full month off with all the necessary cover for her classes. Whereas no one would need to cover for my two days, just wash the cups themselves," replied Sarai simply.

Maurice was uncomfortable, as he had not thought anyone would notice this, let alone Sarai. He had been especially clear to that teacher to say nothing, but the cover form had the holiday code on it. Pat had told him she was *'in no mood to be creative'*.

'Well no one reads that stuff,' he had thought.

"Everyone reads the absence codes Mr Mundy." Sarai added quietly.

Maurice ignored Sarai's comment. The awkward conversation was over. As she left, he said,

"Could you make sure we organise a small reception for the drama teacher who's off on a sabbatical for nine months? We want to give her a good send off. She's leaving the day before the end of term to get herself sorted, so we need to do it on the Thursday morning of that week. Maybe organise a collection for a gift as we won't be seeing her until September, and we want to make sure she comes back."

Sarai did not look back and shut the door firmly.

Sarai was therefore leaving on a flight to the US, three days after Luca. Sarai had to wait, ever dutiful, spending the time in school, tidying the kitchen area and washing the cups. She also had to clear up the wrapping paper that had been left on the staffroom floor. This was from the gifts given to the drama teacher who was off on her trip 'following the sun'. Sarai was confused why anyone needed presents prior to a holiday. Yet the vacation had been conveniently renamed a 'sabbatical for the purposes of research'.

22 December 2016, 7am.

'Search teams in Texas are at the scene where a New York Airlines flight crashed late last night. Initial reports do say that there is little hope that any of the twenty one passengers and four crew could have survived...'

Sarai felt her heart ripped out from her body, darkness overcame her and she fell to the floor. There she remained.

'At this stage speculation is rife that it is a terrorist attack as there has not been a domestic air carrier accident in the past seven years...'

The family liaison unit were preparing to go to Sarai's house. Part of the team was Guy Castle, a trainee policeman one year through his probationary period and he was absolutely terrified.

Guy's supervisor went through the procedure. By the time they arrived at the house it was nearly 4pm. Sarai answered the door and the senior policeman's prayers,

"Is it true?" she gasped.

"I am so sorry Mrs Bianchi." The supervisor said. "They have found the crash site and there is no evidence, or indeed possibility of survivors, I am so very sorry."

Sarai fainted and Guy caught her.

"Let's call an ambulance and get her to hospital."

Arriving in University Hospital, Durham, Guy waited with Sarai and explained the situation to the nursing staff. Sarai had no relatives nearby so Guy worked late into the night, trying to contact someone. He finally got hold of Sarai's stepmother, Vicki, who said she could not drive that evening, only the next day. She arrived at the hospital the next morning, but not early and, Guy thought, clearly hungover.

Guy was dynamic and ambitious. He had spent two years teaching English in the Japanese city of Sendai upon graduating in Law from Durham University. With a desire to become a detective, he had then spent a year volunteering as a Community Special Constable, prior to being accepted into formal police training.

Guy, being the link officer for St Wolbodo's, came into the school to talk to the Head Teacher later on that morning. This uncomfortable moment jolted Maurice into full Head Teacher mode and he got into action, looking up the correct plan in his handbook.

"Thank you so much, this is terrible news, we will organise flowers and suggest counselling to any staff affected by this."

"I think Sarai has been affected by this," Guy responded with emphasis.

"Yes, yes we will get HR to begin a course of action," blustered Maurice.

"And hospitals don't allow flowers these days."

"Okay, a card for now and flowers for when she's out to welcome her home," he suggested clumsily.

"She's not having a baby, she'll be planning a funeral," replied Guy.

"Yes, yes of course," flustered Maurice.

He showed Guy out and then went back to his office to think about what to do next.

Maurice

He called his Deputy Head on the walkie talkie and Sharon came along promptly, shaking rain from her coat. Maurice explained everything to her. Her first comment unnerved even Maurice.

"Well we don't want to put a damper on everyone's Christmas now do we?" she said.

Consumed by weakness and an inability to disagree with anyone stronger, he nodded.

Sharon continued "I'll send an email in the holidays as most staff won't read it until we come back in January, then we can't be accused of not doing anything. I'll mention the opportunity for counselling, of course, in case anyone is affected by this." To Maurice it appeared Mrs King would not be in need of this service.

"Yes, the staff party is tonight and we don't want to spoil that as we've paid the deposit," remarked the Head Teacher.

"Let's keep it quiet for now so as not to cause alarm," reasoned Sharon.

"I'll get HR to arrange flowers for Christmas Eve, but will just put *'hope you're feeling better soon,'* on the note," said Maurice.

"Okay we'll need someone to wash the cups today..." said Sharon.

"My God yes how will we cope?" replied the Head Teacher in all seriousness.

"The cups, everyone will be mad."

The Deputy Head and the Head Teacher stood in silence for a good few minutes, trying to think how to resolve the cup problem.

At school that day everyone was moaning about the unwashed cups but no one seemed to notice that Sarai was not there. The plane tragedy was on the news. Speculation continued as to the cause of the 'incident'. Was it terrorism? Pilot error? Bad weather?

Pat pondered loudly on lurid questions such as 'whether you would be alive as you plummeted from the plane' or 'whether your body would break up', insensitive to the fact that twenty-five people with personalities, families and hopes, were now dead.

CHAPTER 17 - END OF TERM

The staff all loved the last day of term as they had an easy half day of showing Christmas videos to their equally happy students. In the evening was the staff Christmas party. The festive film fest followed the end of term assemblies where candles were lit for *'the poor and the lonely at this time of year when everyone should be with those they love'*. Prayers were read for the needy and a Christmas collection was taken for the homeless in the local area.

Everyone felt a sense of satisfaction engaging in such a timely, hour long, community action for the less fortunate.

Maurice and Sharon continued their pact of silence about the tragedy that had beset one of their own as they had paid deposits on the vol au vents and the DJ. Pat had already bought the wine from the local supermarket.

Noëmi

Therefore, horribly unaware of the agony Sarai was experiencing, the staff all congregated for a raucous Christmas party. Noëmi arrived with Frank and both noted that Pat was already well oiled. She was being unusually pleasant as the wine flowed through her veins. The school hall was packed with garish decorations whilst staff wore an array of Christmas jumpers, antlers and Santa hats.

"This place looks like it's ready to spontaneously combust."

168

Frank muttered as he walked in reluctantly.

"It's Christmas Frank, time to be jolly!" Noëmi offered him a sausage on a stick but his expression declined the offer.

The DJ mixed **S&M** by Rihanna to ***I wish it could be Christmas everyday*** by Wizard.

A line of staff in a conga danced past them.

Frank turned to Noëmi "Can you explain why we're here?"

"Don't be a grump, we need to be sociable, it's important," she laughed, desperate to spy on John Dyer.

"Well this is two hours of my life I won't get back," he sighed.

"Think of it as research for your novel," said Noëmi in a good mood.

"God I'll be sued, please visit me in my exile."

"With pleasure, choose somewhere hot," smiled Noëmi. She pointed out the mince pies to Frank.

"I wouldn't eat that if I were you, looks homemade. Talking of all things hot, when does that lovely young man of yours arrive home?" asked Frank.

She took his advice, resisted the festive treat and replied, "Marcus? He's not quite mine, although I wish he was. Next week I believe, just in time for Christmas but I'm away so we can't get together until New Year's Eve at the earliest."

"Excellent, in time for our party. I'm sure it won't be a patch on this though! Now that's something to look forward to Noëmi isn't it?"

"Yes I'm desperate to see him and for your party too!" she replied.

"Sparks could fly all that pent up... let's say, emotion!" he said mischievously.

Noëmi replied, "I really hope so Frank."

Darlene's walk out was the talk of the evening, with many wishing they could do likewise and after a couple of drinks, threatening to do so. Charvi and Huw boycotted the event following their treatment but few noticed they and Sarai were absent. Most were just keen to get their two free drinks before it all ran out and begin the countdown to the glorious ten days off. Pat Davies was in charge of the RSVP list. She had noted those who were not attending at the last minute and kept their drinks' tokens for herself. Everyone was relaxed and happy. One exception was an assistant who kept going to the toilet to cry as she had received a pore firming face mask in the all staff Secret Santa.

Before they knew it John Dyer was upon them. John had tried to connect with Maya but she was not online so he left that idea for now. Noëmi saw him arrive and turned very obviously away, going for a drink, leaving Frank to make small talk. From her point of safety she could hear the discussion about how to organise the classes in Science that followed.

Frank joined Noëmi again, "Thanks for abandoning me like that!"

"Sorry Frank, I can explain, I just have to avoid that man, can't breathe the same air."

"Do you have any idea how excruciatingly boring that last conversation was?"

"Oh yes I think I do."

Frank finished his drink and grimaced.

"Honestly you're not doing that to me again. How cheap is this wine?"

"I can't promise."

"You *are* definitely up to something Noëmi." He put his glass down and sighed.

Finally she left for the pub with Frank, who resolutely and absolutely refused to remain at the staff party after 8:30pm.

John

John figured if Noëmi had enough to drink he could get her back to his place. In his pocket he had an extra flask of vodka which he could easily slip into her drink to help her to comply with his wishes. He never usually had a problem with getting women into bed, occasionally he had to be quite brusque to move them on the next morning. They usually got the message when he said his girlfriend Bunni would be back soon. He did not have a girlfriend, only a pet rabbit of that name. John did not like this pet as it had bitten him the one time he tried to stroke it. However tonight John had decided not to use the girlfriend line as he found Noëmi quite a challenge and thought she may be someone he would like to sleep with again. John continued to attempt to talk to Noëmi but she eluded him at every turn. By the end he was frustrated as Noëmi had left. John got chatting to a teaching assistant, who bored him but she had a large chest and a compliant attitude so he took her home instead.

Sharon

24 December 2016. At 5pm the next day, Sharon finally felt well enough to prepare an email to staff.

'Okay so message to all staff, damn how do I take her name out of that distribution list? God, why's everything so bloody complicated...maybe it'll be good for her to know that everyone knows, yes! Genius! That covers it all, and then she'll actually feel less awkward.'

Email to all staff:

'Those of you that know Sarai Bianchi will be saddened to hear that her husband was killed in a plane crash in the US this week. The staff association has sent flowers and if anyone feels affected by this tragedy the staff directive X2145 covers this and you should contact HR for counselling options.'

She was about to press send and stopped.

'Shit I hope this is not going to keep me working all over Christmas, damn...actually no one's going to read this until the last day of the holiday anyway, I'll send it then, just make sure I put an alert on my calendar, yes there we go, perfect.' Sharon sat back and took her mouse off the send button. *'Now no interruptions and two glorious weeks of rest. God what was his name...no idea of the address for flowers, well that's just a detail and she won't be expecting that. In the end she'll be getting a huge compensation pay out at some point.'*

Shutting down her laptop, she sighed, "work, work, work," and realised her Christmas food order was due to arrive any minute.

A and E. As the staff recovered from the excesses of their celebrations, the emergency team at the University Hospital of North Durham got an urgent alert. At the emergency ambulance entrance they had to meet an incoming paramedic team working on an overdosed fifteen year old. They rushed to meet the ambulance with the young girl in the back. She had been found at home on her own after she rang **999** frightened by the number of paracetamol she had taken. A team of six nurses and doctors swung into action, as she swayed in and out of consciousness. Efficiently they went over the procedures and various checks that needed to be made swiftly in order to assess the extent of the poisoning. The team worked tirelessly, the patient's stomach was pumped to remove its contents and luckily she had called for help in time. Overnight she was observed carefully, with a nurse by her side the whole time. On Christmas day Stephanie sat in her hospital bed, cannula in arm, blue blanket over her knees, staring into space. When she was ready she had an interview with one of the child psychiatrists. Having been briefed by the medical team, PC Guy Castle, still working in family liaison, spoke to her mother, Tessa.

Guy

"Hello, are you okay?" Guy asked sympathetically.

"I think so. I'm just so shocked, was she trying to kill herself?"

"Well, from what she told the nurse, she said that she had a headache and took too many pills." Guy handed her a box of tissues.

"Well that's rubbish, she's an intelligent girl and we always used to have fun carefully measuring out Calpol when she was little, I told her all about the dangers of an accidental overdose."

"What's been happening up until now, any problems?" he asked gently.

"Well she's a typical fifteen year old, you look young enough to remember what that was like."

Guy did not take this as an insult, but as more of a compliment, especially as he had been on duty for twelve hours.

"Any problems?"

"Just the usual ones, messy room, on her phone and computer too much, up in her room on her own all the time, but in general we get on."

"Never easy is it?" Guy smiled kindly.

"I work long hours as her dad doesn't pay anything towards our bills, so it's always a bit of a struggle. I'm out a lot because of work, so I do feel bad about that. I just don't know, she never tells me anything, she keeps herself to herself."

"Have her friends or teachers noticed anything?"

"She's a bit of a loner, not many friends...but she's smart, does well at school or she used to until this term started. Now I've had three phone calls about her not turning up, so I just don't know what to think and then this," explained Tessa, taking more tissues.

Guy put his notebook down and gently said, "With your permission I would like one of the Children's Services' team to assess her urgently so we can keep an eye on her. There appears to be evidence of self-harm, marks on her body, arms in particular. It sounds like she needs to talk to someone as we need to assume that she was attempting to take her life."

"Oh my God, yes, whatever needs to be done, I can't bear to think about what would've happened if she'd not called the ambulance," sobbed her mother.

"Okay we'll keep her in and get her assessed immediately, now let me just confirm the details, it's Stephanie Smith and she's, yes, fifteen, birthday tenth of July 2001, I can see her notes, and she attends which school?"

"St Wolbodo's in Year 11." Tessa's tissues had disintegrated into crumbs.

Stephanie

Stephanie was kept in for a few days. She was only discharged once another mental health assessment had been carried out, a referral was made to Children's Services and a therapist was assigned to her. Guy made a point of having a chat with Stephanie before she left.

"Hello Stephanie." Guy went to her bedside with one of the nurses. He sat down.

"Hi sir or officer or whatever." She put her right hand up the left sleeve of her sweatshirt.

He smiled, "You can call me either, I don't mind anything if it's polite, I do prefer PC Castle but that's a bit formal isn't it, so 'Officer' is fine, makes me sound important."

Stephanie relaxed visibly.

"Now Stephanie, you have your therapist to talk to, but if you ever need anything you know you can speak to someone at your school. A teacher that you trust maybe? We all want to help you with your worries, you know we really care about you and want you to have the best life you can." He moved the plastic water jug on her bedside table out of the way and put his police radio down.

"I just need to figure stuff out," said Stephanie, settling and trusting him.

"But don't rely on your own strength, talk to others, there are always solutions Stephanie,"

"Maybe, I hope so, I'm just stupid," said Stephanie, hating herself and wishing she could be someone else.

"No you're not, I know what being fifteen is like, it's hard,"

"Yeah but you didn't do stupid stuff," said Stephanie lowering her head, envious of anyone who had not done what she had.

"If you want a list of all the rubbish I did at that age I can provide a very long one! Remember what I said, be kind to yourself and talk to someone who can help. You're a fifteen year old child, however grown up you think you are."

"Yeah, but anyway thank you I promise not to do this again."

"Really?"

"Yes I don't want my mum to worry."

Stephanie said all the right things to make him stop talking, but continued to scratch the crook of her arm with her nails, until it bled.

'You're so vile and disgusting,' she told herself.

CHAPTER 18 - HAPPY NEW YEAR?

Frank and Valentino's New Year's Eve party 31 December 2016.

Valentino

Frank had decided that he and Valentino were getting too comfortable in their own company, especially given that this year none of their family were visiting them for Christmas. So he announced that they should be 'uber sociable' and have all their friends over for a New Year's Eve party.

Valentino and Frank threw fabulous soirées, and everyone was assured of a good time. They were great cooks and Valentino had an eye for how everything should be presented.

"Fireworks at midnight!" he declared and immediately thought about where to source the best ones. "And then everyone sings 'Happy New Year' just like we did in Stockholm last year and then 'Auld Lang Syne'. Yes perfect I'll organise the playlist," he said not waiting for Frank to give an opinion as he knew he would love it.

The previous year Valentino had taken Frank to Stockholm for his fiftieth birthday as a surprise and had organised tickets to Mamma Mia the Party for New Year's Eve. This was the time of Frank's life and they had never had a better evening even if it was for the most part in Swedish. His love for Frank was absolute.

He loved Abba and his husband in equal amounts during that trip.

"Wonderful!" agreed Frank, "So everyone will need to be ready to go outside for fireworks, tell them to bring jackets."

"Yes but we don't want anyone wearing fleeces or ugly things like that!" said Valentino in horror, "make sure you tell them 'no fleeces'."

"Okay my love, you're absolutely right but I think we need to soften this a bit,"

So the invitation went out to their friends to join them to welcome in the New Year of 2017; enjoying, drinks, dinner and dancing, with fireworks at midnight. Dress code; *'party glam'* and in smaller lettering underneath, *'No fleeces unless they have sequins on them'*.

Noëmi

Noëmi was thrilled to receive the invitation. It brightened her mood, which was always sad over Christmas; the period she missed her mother most. This holiday she would be spending most of it in Italy at her grandparents' home with her father, so New Year's Eve was the big night for her. Noëmi beamed with delight as she set about planning for the party, 'it's going to be unforgettable!' she thought.

Checking in with Marcus, she could tell he was excited.

"I've got some bank work at the hospital as a Healthcare Assistant over Christmas and am on duty until 6pm that night. Then I'll be right over to Durham, thanks N. I just can't wait to see you, it'll be lovely," said Marcus.

She was relieved that they would end up together at last, they had waited far too long.

Valentino was buzzing as many of their friends could make their party and he loved to organise a good time for everyone.

"How many?" asked Frank,

"We have forty-eight confirmed and three possibles," replied Valentino.

"Is Marcus coming?"

"Yes."

"Excellent, anyone not coming?"

"Jorge and Alberto are in Canada and no reply from Sarai and Luca."

"Ah they're in the US, he's got work out there," explained Frank.

"That explains it then but I was surprised not to hear back; they're such dear friends," mentioned Valentino.

The morning of the party arrived. Noëmi had travelled back from Italy that morning and had spent the day cleaning and clearing up her place. Marcus would be coming home with her. Choosing a dress, she went straight for the tightest, shortest and lowest cut one she could find.

"To hell with it all," she said to herself as she took a sip of wine "I'm going to enjoy myself tonight."

Gathering the champagne and flowers for Frank and Valentino she ordered a cab, and feeling emboldened by her pre drink she sent a message from Maya to John;

'When are we going to meet for sex?'

179

She put her phone away, jumped in the taxi and was feeling good as she arrived.

Frank and Val's house was still glittering with Christmas decorations aplenty. Soft fairy lights, delicate candles and fresh greenery gave a sophisticated yet cosy glow to the place. Noëmi always brought them a decoration from Italy as they loved the traditional carved pieces she could find in her local village. This year she had bought them a small statue of the Madonna formed in olivewood. They had laid a large table of food, fresh pasta dishes, warm salads and delicious casseroles. Noëmi spotted Frank's homemade profiteroles in the kitchen and felt warm inside.

Everyone greeted one another with big hugs and chatted animatedly about recent Christmas events and travel plans for 2017. Noëmi spotted Marcus already talking to mutual friends in the kitchen and headed straight for him.

"Wow you look just amazing!" Marcus said when he saw her. Noëmi was buzzing, this was exactly the reaction she had wanted.

"You're looking great Marcus."

They hugged each other hard and for the longest time. He clasped her closely to him and stroked her hair which felt soft and silky.

"Hey," she said "what's everyone's resolution then?"

Some general chat about weight loss and working less followed and then inevitably the question was turned to Noëmi.

"Oh well, I don't know, maybe I'll get a boyfriend," she said out of nowhere, looking straight at Marcus.

The others laughed, *'Oh my reputation for always being single is not an old story.'*

She immediately felt stupid and wished she had not said this, she put her wine glass down and filled it some more. Marcus saw this and she noticed he suppressed a smile.

He spoke to her,

"I thought that was just filled?" he told her with a grin.

"What? I know I drank it, New Year's Eve, that's all I can say!" she giggled.

"No N, I thought the boyfriend vacancy was filled!"

Her heart jumped a beat, "Ah still lots of interest but you and only you, just skip to the front of the very long queue that's forming," she joked back, delighted he was playing along and teasing her back.

The number of people in the kitchen forced them into the lounge.

"What about you? What's your resolution?"

"I've got two, avoid scheming people, and to fulfil the quest you set me,"

"What if I'm *plotting* to do the same? Will you have to stay away from me?"

'I think I could make an exception! Pick up where we left off?" Marcus laughed and he put his arms around her waist.

Valentino loved karaoke so he began singing along with various tracks and dancing began. Marcus was enjoying himself and he went to whisper something to Valentino. He looked back round and took Noëmi by the hand.

"Come on, do you remember this one? Time for us to show everyone how it's done."

Noëmi knew what was coming and as the first notes of **'Just the way you are'** by Bruno Mars played out, they began to sing together.

Their old karaoke favourite had a special place in Marcus' heart as it summed up how he felt about Noëmi. He had told her, that day on the river, *"surely you can hear the message?"* Noëmi did indeed remember and she could not have been happier.

As they sang, Frank put his arm around his husband.

"They're the perfect couple and they don't realise it do they?"

"More perfect than you and me?"

"Ah yes, well then they're the second most perfect couple," said Frank proudly. "Assolutamente," Valentino replied, hugging him close.

Marcus stayed next to Noëmi when they finished singing.

"Loved your vocals," he said laughing. Noëmi was relaxed and happy; she had a new confidence about her.

The party got hotter. The group continued to chat and the music got louder.

Suddenly Noëmi got a message, and she checked her phone. It was John,

'Sex is a great idea. How are you celebrating tonight?'

'Party of course! You?'

'Party too, but imagining you in my bed!'

'Let's make it happen!'

"Who are you messaging? Are you telling Yumi we're getting together? Or is it Deanna?" Marcus tried to grab her phone to see. Failing to get it, he wrestled playfully with her.

"Nooooo get off!" she laughed, pulling it away from him. "This is my private life Marcus McKenzie!"

"No problem, I'll check your phone in the morning!" He laughed.

"Cheeky!" she joked back.

Noëmi exhaled deeply thinking, *'delete, delete, delete'*. She put her phone away then re-focused on the group. Valentino's singing got louder and everyone started joining in. Everyone was chatting, laughing, swaying, drinking, hugging, joking, eating, dancing and singing. Soon a group rendition of **'Angels'** was in full swing and the group of friends could not have been happier.

Suddenly her phone beeped and she froze and immediately checked the message.

It was John, *'When shall we meet? I want to see you naked.'*

With everything going so well in all areas, she was on a roll.

'First I'll send you a photo, sex after that, but soon okay?' she teased back.

'I want intimate photos too, you know what I mean?'

'Sure no problem. You'll see everything.' She messaged although now feeling a bit panicky that she was getting out of her depth.

"Who's that N?" Marcus asked her.

"Oh, just a friend at school, no one special," she lied.

He shrugged his shoulders, "Why don't you turn it off? Focus on us?"

"They've got some problems," now the third time in her life she had ever lied to Marcus.

It was nearly midnight, Valentino was stressing between preparing fireworks, topping up champagne glasses and queuing up Big Ben on television for the chimes.

Everyone and everything was bubbling; it was nearly time for the countdown. Noëmi wanted to kiss Marcus at midnight. That would mark their moment. However Valentino then asked for help with the fireworks which took Marcus away.

"Five, four, three, two, one, Happy New Year!"

Everyone shouted hugging each other and Noëmi let go of her precious phone and popped it onto a side table, to embrace those around her.

Frank grabbed Noëmi and gave her a warm cuddle.

"Happy New Year my friend and I am sure it will be."

Noëmi looked round for Marcus, sipping more champagne, she then swirled round to be cuddled by Valentino. Before she knew it she had been transported across the lounge. Having hugged her hosts, she felt desperate to get to Marcus, but she had chatted with her friends for longer than intended. On the other side of the room her phone beeped.

Marcus

Marcus came back inside and took his jacket off. He began to look for Noëmi, but could not see her but he noticed her mobile on the table. Hearing her phone ping, he picked it up to take it to her, knowing how attached she was to it. *'She'll be delighted with me!'* he smiled to himself. Searching the room for her he noticed the message thread jump out at him. The last message left him devastated.

'Send me naked photos of you tonight like you promised and let

me know when you want to meet for sex…' followed by a devil emoji.

The profile picture of the person sending the message was unmistakably John Dyer.

'What are all these messages? Sex hook ups? What? Photos?'

Confused and devastated he put the phone back down.

'What was going on with Noëmi? A desire to meet John Dyer for sex? John Dyer of all people, the one who had ruined her teenage years. What was she thinking?'

He remembered John had recently invited her out on a date. What was happening? Why had she lied to him? Memories of being played by Sophie and all her cheating flooded his head. He was determined not to fall into this trap again. Suddenly feeling very sober and so very sad, he decided to slip out early; this party was over. He saw Frank going for more champagne and thanked him quietly.

"Got an early shift tomorrow," he said, and stepped out into the fresh night air.

Frank was surprised and disappointed to see him leave. He left the party through the front garden gate and walked to pick up a taxi, alone, feeling gutted, confused and angry with Noëmi.

Noëmi

Having finished chatting to Valentino, Noëmi filled her glass as the singing started, she looked round for Marcus but could not see him. She began to feel anxious, not finding him anywhere. Getting frantic she went to Frank and interrupted his singing.

"Where's Marcus?"

"He left about 5 minutes ago, he's got work early tomorrow," he replied quietly.

"No, no he's on holiday... he told me!"

'Happy New Year' by Abba was playing in the background...

With her dreams indeed confetti like on the floor, Noëmi rushed to the door and ran to the end of the garden gate. Marcus was nowhere to be seen. She went down the street a little but still no sign of him, disappointed she turned, went back to the party and bitterly wished that he had not left.

New Year's Day was bleak for Noëmi; she had a raging hangover and no recollection of how she had got home. Hanging her head over the side of the bed she saw her silver heart necklace on the floor and the chain was broken. Upset with herself, she looked through the photos from the night before and felt a lump in her throat when she saw those of her and Marcus. As she watched the video of them singing Bruno Mars, tears began to fall. She felt sad and lonely and wished she could turn back time as she would not have let Frank and Valentino delay her, she regretted not just staying by his side.

'Why?' she thought to herself, *'we were finally going to be together,'* she answered to herself. Her phone beeped which interrupted her thoughts.

'Photo?'

She was confused and looked through the messages from John Dyer.

'Oh God!' she thought to herself, *'How am I supposed to get a naked photo of Magda?'*

She put her phone face down, ignored the messages and sunk back into bed. Her day was wasted trying to sleep, eating comfort food and flicking through programmes she could not focus on. Regrets began to flood her head.

"Why am I trying to mess with that man? Why can't I just be normal? Why does Marcus date people like Sophie and not me?"

Nervously she sent Marcus a message.

'I missed you after you left.'

He did not reply immediately. An hour later he texted back.

'Thanks for the invite, it was good to see everyone, your work is very busy.'

She thought the message was most odd and cold, but left it at that. This unexpected misery of having been rejected by Marcus was a shock. Her future looked very bleak and she felt depressed, all made worse by the fact the only thing on her horizon now was a difficult term of teaching. She pulled the duvet over her head and listened to the rain on the roof and wished that things were different and that Marcus was with her.

Noëmi's Reckoning

PART THREE - RESULTS

Pardonnez sans savoir ce que vous avez à pardonner

Le Nœud de Vipères - François Mauriac

CHAPTER 19 – CHANGES

4 January 2017. The first day back to school after the Christmas holidays was bleak for all the staff when they heard the news about Sarai. Monday morning staff briefing was a sombre affair. Those who could not picture her, were upset as they imagined themselves in such a position. The Teaching Assistant, who had gone home with John Dyer after the Christmas party, let out hiccough like sobs upon seeing him again. She did not know Sarai and no one knew her tears were for the regret she felt in sleeping with John Dyer. He had not contacted her since the party. That morning he had completely blanked her, in spite of the encouragement he had given her in bed after the Christmas party.

Noëmi

Noëmi, Frank and Valentino were truly devastated. Upon receiving the email the night before the first day back, Frank broke down and could not face school that day. Noëmi was feeling so low, she messaged Marcus to tell him about Luca and asked him to call her. He rang back almost immediately. He had met Sarai and Luca when he visited home the previous summer. He had liked them immensely and it was Sarai who had advised him on his trip to Vietnam and Cambodia.

"My God what's happened?" he asked.

"It was that New York Airlines' air crash just before Christmas, I feel terrible. I just assumed they were having a great time in the US when I got no reply from Sarai."

"I wondered why they were not there at New Year."

"She's not back for a while. I've sent her a message but have not heard from her, I think it's too soon. I've no idea who'll be looking after her, she only ever had Luca."

"Please If I can help in any way at all you know I'm here," Marcus was selfless.

"Thank you, that's kind. Marcus, how are you?"

"Yeah, I'm good, just really tired, you know final clinical year is such a great gig! Plus the exams are soon."

"It'd be good to see you... I miss you, I miss seeing you," Noëmi said quietly.

"Yes I agree," he said, a bit formally.

"Or we could meet after the exams? A night in Durham would be fun, go to Klute? Not student night, although you still are a student!" she stumbled over her words.

"Okay you're doing that thing again N, I've got to go, hope your friend at school's okay." Noëmi thought it was a bit off hand and strange how he was referring to Sarai after this tragedy.

"Err?" she replied confused.

"You seemed quite distracted by them at New Year but maybe they have what they wanted from you now?"

"Sure," said Noëmi completely at a loss as to what he was talking about.

"Bye Noëmi, take care, I mean it, be careful, look after yourself," he said seriously.

"Sorry? Hope to see you soon Marcus," she replied quickly, realising he was hanging up.

Guy

The investigation into the crash continued with one side convinced that this mysterious explosion could only have been caused by a bomb, and the other saying the fuel tank must have exploded. This had been the case in a similar disaster a few years earlier with another one of this type of plane; the wiring had sparked, causing fuel fumes to ignite, leading to catastrophe. Whatever the cause, it had become apparent from the Foreign Office, who liaised with Guy and his victim support unit, that no bodies were ever likely to be recovered. The plane had suffered an explosive event at 23,000 feet, breaking up completely. Guy paid a visit to Sarai to gently explain these harsh facts and to collect DNA from Luca's personal items for identification purposes. Whilst he felt very sad having to do this work, Guy was actually most effective at helping people given his kind and thoughtful disposition. Noëmi was there to support her friend as Guy gave the devastating news. Thus with Guy's gentle persuasion, Sarai agreed that Luca would have a memorial and then a private burial when or if his body were ever recovered. Having remained in her bed, bereft, for almost four weeks, Sarai emerged for the memorial of her beloved husband.

Marcus

On a wet, grey day in January Sarai, her stepmother Vicki, Luca's elderly father Roberto and a few close friends gathered to remember Luca at the local parish church. St Oswald's was a traditional church near the centre of Durham and it was linked to St Wolbodo's. The tall spire dominated an overgrown churchyard with its many gravestones and the surrounding light stone brick wall. Sarai wore traditional black Vietnamese funeral robes, with a white headband, that her stepmother had organised. She had to be held the whole time and was helped from the car by her stepmother and Valentino. Sarai only just made it to a pew at the front of the church where she wept throughout the service. Her deep sobs echoed through the church and the sight of this tiny hunched woman, dressed in black with her white headband was making Marcus' chest hurt. She had written a eulogy that Frank was just about able to read on her behalf as she sat weeping. Next to her, Roberto was holding her hand and in his other he had a large white hankie that he used to dab and wipe his eyes throughout the service. The Priest, Attila Varga, who had recently moved from Hungary to serve in the Parish, said prayers and comforted Sarai. For such a sad event it was conducted with dignity and feeling and Luca was very much at the centre.

Although he was invited to be part of the main group, Marcus had declined. At the last minute he changed his mind and decided to travel back for the day to pay his respects. He stayed deferentially at the back of the church with Guy and some others from the bereavement support group, who had not known Luca. Marcus was horrified at this brutal spectre of death that had never met him before. He desperately tried to think of practical things like counting the number of windows and pews. He thought about how long it would have taken craftsmen to build the church, in order to avoid the raw picture of utter desolation in front of him. An empty casket, a wife overwhelmed with grief, an elderly man who had lost his son.

He could see Noëmi who hung her head and cried throughout the service. She had not noticed he was there at the back. Only at the end of the service did she see him and she tried to smile. Marcus greeted them all quietly and went home thinking about how death had brutally separated Luca from Sarai. Noëmi, Roberto, Frank and Valentino were to stay with Sarai and her stepmother that evening to pray together for Luca. So much love and prayers; that was all they could do.

Sarai

Back to work. Sadly Sarai quickly discovered that whilst her life had stopped the world outside carried on and bills continued to arrive. Along with the final demands and letters from her bank, came a letter from the Local Education Office, saying that her compassionate leave was at an end and she would need to contact the school's personnel department with a decision on her future. Whilst they were sorry for her *'distress at this time'*, they were not in a position to make exceptions to the employment contract. With a heavy heart the reality of her situation hit her and she finally returned to St Wolbodo's, her face etched with sadness. She was now the only person in the school who dreaded the weekends and her loss of routine, however dull. In order to deal with this she continued to attend church on a Sunday. By attending the early service, she avoided the crowds, clad in pastel clothes, chattering about the slow refuse collection services or the changing hours of the rubbish tip. What their reason for going to church was, Sarai could not fathom, but from her experience, it was to look respectable, score points talking about their families and to judge others who did not fit in.

Sarai struggled with her work, she found it hard to cope with the smallest of tasks, she had no energy and nothing to say. Members of staff seemed awkward around her, so they avoided the staffroom after break and lunch, when she was clearing up. She felt sick the whole time and could not eat.

CHAPTER 20 - ANGRY

Noëmi

By February the school had settled into the spring term and thoughts of the suffering of others were now over until charity week in June. One morning, as the bell rang for morning break, the teachers congregated in the staffroom for a well-earned rest.

Frank saw Noëmi and went to chat to her.

"Noëmi how are you?"

"Not great to be honest, devastated about Luca and Marcus is basically ignoring me, I don't know why, so that's just the icing on the cake... '

Frank appeared unsure how to respond to either statement when Sharon King, Deputy Head, marched into the staffroom, picked up a mug for her morning coffee, sighed sharply, shook her head and stormed out of the kitchen area. Frank looked at Charvi and rolled his eyes. Charvi laughed and said loudly,

"Cups not good enough for her highness then," as she now had little time and no respect for senior management.

Frank added, "If Sarai had any sense she would get herself back to her family in Vietnam, far nicer than this place."

"But she has no close family left, only a stepmother in

195

Manchester and Luca's father in Rome," said Noëmi, "plus she feels close to Luca in the flat and doesn't want to lose it."

"God I feel dreadful for her," said Frank.

Through the walls they heard the muffled sounds of Sharon King 'going off on one' as Pat would say.

"Delightful woman!" muttered Frank sarcastically, "clearly *mal-baisée* as our French friends would say."

Noëmi laughed as she understood the French.

"God is that just about a cup?" asked Charvi bewildered.

"I'm so confused," added Noëmi.

"We need one of your Cosa Nostra lot to sort her out!" said Frank wickedly as he always used to refer to Noëmi, Valentino and Luca as the Mafia when they were together.

Noëmi smiled at the memory and then began to blink tears away.

Maurice

The noise emanating from Mr Mundy's office was Sharon complaining bitterly about the shoddy nature of Sarai's work. He thought back to when he had seen Sarai washing up that morning. He had found her alone, sobbing loudly and crying uncontrollably. Unsure how to help he had scurried past but now he realised that Sarai had not seen the dark brown grime at the bottom of the cup for the tears. Maurice felt wretched.

Maurice listened to his colleague rant at length about 'hygiene issues', 'incompetence in the workplace' and being 'too busy' to have time to deal with 'emotional breakdowns'. He managed to calm Sharon and said that he would look into the matter. Following Sharon's outburst Maurice decided to move Sarai to a new position and he had the bright idea that Sarai could become

John Dyer's personal assistant. John had been asking for help with his workload since he arrived. He called Sarai in and spoke to her about her new position. She seemed quiet and nodded silently. John was sent an email about the decision and replied with an emoji; Maurice spent most of the next period trying to find out its meaning.

Frank

Frank had seen Sharon leave the Head Teacher's office, striding down the corridor until a small student got the full feel of her wrath. The tiny pupil had walked into Mrs King. He had been looking at his timetable changes, which were all wrong as Pat Davies had muddled up the class lists. The young boy was desperately trying to find where to go next and was becoming increasingly scared of getting a late detention. Frank heard the commotion and went out to find the child sobbing with a friend trying to console him. All students feared Mrs King but none more than Year 7 students who had heard many tales of her temper from their friends and siblings. Frank took the boy to his next lesson. On the way he told him that Mrs King was probably 'not feeling well' and that adults often made 'mistakes', especially if they were 'very busy' or 'sick'. The student smiled, Frank gave him a tissue for his tears and the student said he appreciated his kindness and thanked him; everyone liked Mr Sprague.

Noëmi

Sex?

'Hey when are we getting together then?'

Noëmi was sitting in her kitchen, about to start on her laundry, but felt frustrated. She had been enraged by the whole of the senior management team, all of which made her more audacious in her communications with John Dyer.

Immediately he pinged back.

'Ready when you are, what are you thinking?'

'Sex, sex, sex,' she replied unsure how she was going to deliver this.

'I like it, where do you want to meet?' Noëmi tried to think of a place, then remembered a scene from a recent comedy film.

'Your work, your office, somewhere we could be caught,' Noëmi immediately regretted texting this. Surely he could guess this was a big joke.

'Really? Maybe a drink first?'

'Yeah lots to drink then sex somewhere dangerous, do you have keys to your workplace?'

She carried on the idea as she seemed to have gotten away with it.

'Sure, I run that place so I can do what I like.'

'Where for a drink? What sex do you like?'

'What do you like?'

'Everything, anything, threesomes too, but that's for our second meet up.' She was now looking in her cupboard for her colour catchers and washing powder.

'You know someone?'

'Yeah a friend of mine, Lola, we can trust her we've done threesomes before.'

Noëmi was annoyed with her choice of name. It was pathetic, Maya and Lola, sounded like a pair of spaniels. Yet she was on a roll just typing away, saying whatever he wanted to hear, whipping John up into a catatonic fury. She no longer cared.

'Great sounds cool.'

'But first we need to fuck each other, then she'll be okay with it.'
She checked the temperature setting for a colours wash.

'Where and when?'

'I like to have sex on a Sunday, this Sunday evening about 7pm at the Dog and Duck in Newcastle, then we go and have sex on your desk.'

'See you then.'

Noëmi disconnected and went to put her washing on. She felt a bit sick, what had she done? No one was going to the Dog and Duck, no one was going to have sex in his office, no one was going to have a threesome with the non-existent Lola. As she sorted her clothes into piles she was astounded at herself and how engrossed she had got with this.

John

John was buzzed with sexual energy. He began counting the hours until he was meeting Maya.

The excitement of Maya's messages had energised him and he was unusually active, striding up and down the corridors, exercising his power as an Assistant Head Teacher.

Saturday came and went with John spending most of his time in bed recovering from his Friday night, fantasising about Maya and what lay in store for Sunday. He prepared well, making sure he had the school keys and the passes he needed to get into the main building. He sent the caretaker, Terry, an email saying that he was going to be in that evening to 'catch up on work'. He thought about the set up of his office, and decided he would film the encounter.

Sunday and John was careful to be on time, hanging around outside for a bit, not wanting to look too keen. At about 7:15pm he walked into the pub, blood pumping, ready to meet Maya for unbridled fun with a like minded adventurous player. He looked around the pub with its garish fruit machines, faded velvet burgundy seats and mucky tables strewn with leftover pint glasses and tatty beer mats. John saw a group of students in the corner, a couple of older men at the bar talking animatedly and a couple of pairs of middle aged women. Everyone noticed him immediately as he was well dressed; preened to perfection. He felt surprised that he could not see Maya, as it did not occur to him that she would not be there waiting for him. After all she was the one who set up the encounter out of the blue. He got a Jack and coke, sat down and checked his phone. It buzzed with a message, it was Maya,

'R u there? I'm running late, train problems.'

John tried to keep his cool but responded, **'Just arrived'**. He waited, looking around, thinking it was an odd choice for a bar as he was expecting somewhere livelier, this place looked like his dad's local, plus the lighting was harsh which was giving him a headache.

'Are you ready for sex?'

'Always!' followed by a devil emoji.

'I'm fantasising about it already.'

'What underwear are you wearing?'

'None of course!'

Ten minutes later, a message buzzed through.

'No trains.'

'Get a taxi,' he fired back, feeling peeved.

No reply from Maya, he waited and then realised he had no idea where she was coming from.

'Where are you now?'

No reply.

Then his phone buzzed, ***'Sorry can't make it, gone home, getting in the bath,'*** and a picture of Magda in a foam bath was attached.

'Can I join u?'

…

'Where do you live?'

…

'I'll come to you.'

There was no further message from Maya. Angry he finished his drink and returned home full of rage, annoyed with himself and with her for messing him around. She had enticed him with all she had promised to deliver and he was beyond frustrated.

Later that evening Maya sent a final message,

'LOL'

John threw his phone across the room in a blind rage.

CHAPTER 21 – FURIOUS

Sarai

Monday 6 February early morning. Sarai's desk had been in the general admin office but John immediately had it moved into a small corridor in front of his own office. Here Sarai felt isolated and had no contact with anyone other than John.

This Monday was Luca's birthday, he would have been 39. Sarai felt sick and had wanted to stay at home but she knew that it would be difficult to be around the flat. So she went to work to take her mind off her sadness. John did not disappoint in being able to distract her the minute he walked in. He was in a foul mood and snapped at her when she wished him 'Good Morning,' replying that there was 'nothing at all good about Monday mornings'. Whilst Sarai agreed, she was stunned by his aggression and stared at him in disbelief, then left as quickly as possible.

John

John's mind was overrun with disappointment of not meeting Maya. Tension burst through his veins. He had spent the whole of the Monday morning staff briefing fantasising about all the young women who were present in the meeting.

He had got a message from Maya earlier saying; **'I never wanted to fuck you actually'** followed by another laugh out loud emoji.

Feeling furious, he did not reply. No one ever treated him like this.

Arriving in his office he saw his desk. He was reminded of his disappointment as he sat down unable to concentrate on anything.

Caretaker Terry knocked at his door.

"Mr Dyer, you didn't turn up last night then! I kept the car park gates open well past ten just in case you know!"

"My plans changed." John did not look at Terry.

"Well just wanted you to know that everything was as you wanted it!"

'Oh for God's sake go away you annoying sycophant. No one cares about your dedication to duty!' John was getting irritated by his presence. "Splendid thank you so much Terry, that's just as I would have expected of such a committed staff member!"

Terry smiled and left.

He logged onto his computer and spent some time looking over some files then Sarai knocked and brought him a cup of coffee as she had been instructed to do each morning at 9:30am. His frustration was making him restless. He looked at Sarai with new eyes. Whilst she was very petite and always miserable, he mused that she probably had a nice body under her clothes. Apart from that he decided she could do with some attention to cheer her up. Her hair swung nicely round her shoulders, she smelt nice even if her eyes were puffy from crying.

"Sarai," he said in an unusually friendly way.

"Mr Dyer?" she replied suddenly not moving.

"Call me John," he purred.

"Okay...Mr Dyer," she said awkwardly.

"Why don't you sit down and we can see how things are going, how you've settled in," he continued.

She sat down silently looking pale.

"How are you?" he went on.

"I'm fine," she looked over her shoulder to the door.

"Do you get lonely? You know since your husband died," he asked her, taking off his jacket.

"No I'm fine but I have a number of letters to do if that's okay..." she said, getting up to go.

"But maybe you need some company sometimes, you know, so you don't get lonely," he said looking at her, "no one likes to be lonely."

"I'm fine thank you for asking but I need to do my work," she said, her voice trembling.

"How do you relax? At weekends? In the evenings?" he asked, getting up from his seat and walking towards her chair.

"I have my work which I enjoy," Sarai replied, wringing her hands.

"But maybe you need some help relaxing?" he said slowly, looking at her intensely.

"I'm fine Mr Dyer and now I need to work," she jumped up to leave.

John had now moved between her and the door which he locked with his right hand behind his back. The bolt gave a loud click.

Sarai swayed backwards.

Keeping his right hand on the door, John moved in towards her and said;

"You owe me things, things that you have to do. Getting this job, there *is* a price, you know that?"

Sarai gave a panicked cry.

He continued, "So let me fuck you and make you feel like a woman again," and he put his left hand on her shoulder and began to slide it down towards her breast. He put his head towards her, inviting a kiss.

Sarai looked at him in horror. With her right hand she took hold of his left hand and removed it from her chest. Holding on to this hand with hers she twisted his wrist right back and round. She pushed him towards the door, pinning his other hand, which was still behind his back, against it. Then she took her left hand and with all her strength she slapped him across the face with a ferocity he could never have imagined of Sarai. Snarling she hissed at him like a wildcat,

"Come near me again and I'll rip your balls off."

He stood holding his cheek which in places was bleeding, eyes smarting with pain, his wrist felt sprained and he was doubled over. Sarai shoved him out of the way with her shoulders, unlocked the door and hurtled out.

Ronnie

Agitated... Miss McAllister seemed stressed and disorganised. More so than usual. Ronnie could hear her talking to herself.

"No, no, I've forgotten to pick up the worksheets from the office." He saw his teacher searching her desk for her resources.

'She's never on it, her desk is all sprogeldey,' he thought to himself.

"Need any jobs doing Miss?" Ronnie called over to her, eager to get out of class.

Musing on this she decided to send Ronnie to fetch the worksheets.

Jumping from his seat, he strolled happily to the office and greeted Pat Davies with a big smile.

"Alright Miss, good weekend?" he enquired jovially.

"Depends who's asking, doesn't it?" replied Pat nonchalantly.

"I went riding, good times," offered Ronnie.

"What do you want?" asked Pat suspiciously, not returning his friendliness.

"Worksheets for Miss McAllister."

"They're not ready, I'm rushed off my feet," said Pat with no concern.

"Okay I'll tell her," and off went Ronnie, walking all around the school to waste time so that he could miss more of the lesson. He headed towards the toilets, where he found his friend, Albie, and the pair spent the rest of the lesson strolling around the corridors chatting and laughing.

Noëmi

Noëmi was frustrated to have to do her lesson without the worksheets and went to the office at break to ask Pat why they had not been ready. Everyone knew Pat never did two things, miss her cigarette breaks or apologise and today was no exception. However she liked to justify the missing of deadlines especially if there was some higher force or gossip involved.

"Been busy all morning, that little Chinese tea lady is upset again, been in the toilet for an hour crying," said Pat with a knowing nod, all of which threw Noëmi off guard.

"Sarai is Vietnamese," she replied firmly as she went looking for her.

In the echoing toilet block, she found Sarai who was inconsolable. She opened the door.

"Sarai what's wrong?"

Sarai could not answer but was trembling. Noëmi gave her hand a squeeze and led her out of the toilet.

"I've got a free period now, shall we go and talk somewhere?"

They walked over to the staffroom and sat in a quiet corner. Alone, they could talk freely.

"Noëmi, I've lost everyone I ever loved, my Mum, my Dad and now Luca. I'm tired and I have no hope, now I just exist every day."

"I do understand a little bit, I lost my Mum when I was thirteen and I miss her every day, but I have to live the life she would have wanted me to."

"The life I should be living is with Luca, I want to tell him I love him one last time," Sarai was desperate and grasped Noëmi's hand. 'It's agony, if I could see him, touch him, hug him just one more time. Just one more minute with him then I could tell him how much I love him. The pain gets worse, nothing gets easier."

"Sarai..."

"I can't go on like this," Sarai whispered, beginning to sob.

It was just too big. They sat close to each other for half an hour in silence which was only ended by the bell for the next lesson.

John Dyer did not leave his office for the rest of the morning and busied himself on his computer, behind the locked door. His face was throbbing and a small red hand print was clearly visible as he looked in the mirror. He also noticed that there was a bleeding welt. Sarai had lost weight since the loss of her husband and her rings were loose. Her engagement ring had twisted round so the stone, sitting in its claw, was on her palm side. So as she lashed out at John, her engagement ring, on the inside of her hand, had caught his skin. He had to attend a senior management meeting later that day and came up with a story that Ronnie had hit him to explain it away.

By chance Ronnie had been caught on CCTV strolling around the school with his friend Albie at the time of the supposed 'attack' which helped to back up John's story. Ronnie was immediately excluded without question and given a final warning by Deputy Head, Sharon King who dismissed his protests of innocence as another ruse to cover his tracks. No one bothered to ask Ronnie or Albie what they had done during the time. Ronnie, bewildered by this punishment, angrily stormed out of the school, barging through the main entrance, which was forbidden for students to use, shouting;

"I'll fucking get my fucking revenge on this place!"

Sarai

Quid pro quo. The next day Sarai got in very early and asked two students, Joel Rivera and his brother Gabriel, to help her move her desk into the main office so that she was no longer isolated with John Dyer.

Pat arrived and noted the new arrangements, as she took off her coat.

"Well the liberties of some people. That desk is now a fire

hazard. The selfishness of it! We're all at risk of a burning, grizzly death."

Sarai held her breath and the tears. Thoughts of Luca blinded her. *'Why can't she stop talking?'*

Pat stomped off, muttering, for a comfort break and an email pinged through from John Dyer. Now he communicated with Sarai only by email which suited her fine. He was not in a position to complain as he could no doubt guess the quid pro quo; her silence for him leaving her alone. Whilst John Dyer had asked for an assistant, in reality he did not need one. Therefore Sarai only got a couple of emails a day with tasks to be done, which she duly completed. This lack of work left her too much time to think. However she needed her job, as it was a struggle now only having her income. For Luca, as a freelancer, there was no death in service scheme. Although they had some modest savings, Sarai knew she had to hang onto those for more unforeseen difficulties that undoubtedly lay ahead. Between money worries she began to slip into a deep depression which was not helped by the fact she was so tired all the time and could not face food.

Rosie

For the *'attack on Mr Dyer'*, Ronnie was excluded for five days and he was absolutely apoplectic. His mother Rosie was shocked when her friend read the letter to her as Ronnie was naughty but had never been physical before with anyone. He was a gentle boy, who loved animals, particularly horses and he helped out at a couple of local farms. Ronnie had much patience and he also assisted Rosie greatly with his younger siblings, often making himself late for school. Rosie was crying when she learnt about the exclusion and feared that Ronnie would be in jail before he was seventeen, as hitting a teacher was 'bad'. Ronnie was quiet, upset, refusing to talk to Rosie all of which made her confused and keen to know why he had attacked John Dyer.

Sitting in their flat, Ronnie was watching South Park.

"Why did you hit that teacher?" she asked

"I didn't."

"I've had the letter read and it says you did."

"They're lying."

"Schools don't lie."

"Yes they do."

"That man's important, he doesn't lie."

"And neither do I, so make your mind up who you believe."

Rosie was silent, what Ronnie said about himself was true. He never lied, he told her everything, anything and never even said he liked something when he did not. She had no idea what to think.

Ronnie

Most students would be glad of five days off school, but Ronnie's veins ran cold with the injustice of the situation and the fact that he could not get anyone to believe him. Albie said that the whole thing was 'a joke' but when Albie spoke to his form tutor to defend Ronnie, he was told 'not to get involved'.

Ronnie made some wooden sculptures of birds whilst he was off and thought about how he could get even with John Dyer. Ronnie sold his birds at the fairs and horse races and his work was well liked, particularly his owls. He had a keen eye for detail and really put life into his carvings. He would search in the local woods for branches he could fashion into such pieces and spent hours tenderly carving the wood into lifelike creatures. Ronnie had had no formal instruction and his skill was the result of practice and natural talent.

When Ronnie did finally return to school he said absolutely nothing during the re-integration meeting which tested Sharon King's patience. It was left for Rosie to say simply 'Ronnie doesn't do things like that', and for her to agree to a fresh start for her son. Ronnie left Sharon's office and caught sight of John Dyer in the corridor. Remaining silent he gave him the fiercest glare which startled even this Assistant Head. Ronnie saw a large black crow appear at the corridor window and it stared silently at John Dyer. He watched as John retreated into his office and angrily banged the door shut.

CHAPTER 22 - FACING THE TRUTH?

Marcus

Marcus was frantic with his final exams and clinical placements. He had not been in touch with Noëmi properly since Luca's memorial service. Devastated by the thought of her sending naked pictures to John Dyer, he could not get the image of the sixth form bully salivating over her from his mind. The more he thought about it, the more bewildered he became by her behaviour. Had she now actually hooked up for sex with him? The thought turned his stomach, how could she even want to breathe the same air as him after what he had done to her? Unable to sleep, he did not know what to do. The decisions before him were stark; move on and start again or forgive her and win her back. He did not feel ready to do either of these. Why would Noëmi be playing the two of them off against each other? Nothing made sense and he could not understand her.

A message pinged through from Noëmi as it often did.

'Hi Marcus, I hope you're well, I'd love to talk to you. Nxxx'

He knew it was unfair not to let her know how he felt.

'How are you? How's Sarai?'

'I'm okay but Sarai's not good,' She quickly texted back.

'Please send her my love, I think about her a lot,'

'That's kind, she needs support,'

'Noëmi I hope you're alright. Actually, I feel bad writing this but I am so disappointed in what you are doing with John Dyer. It's upset me tbh.'

'I didn't plan it. Everything just happened so quickly. I know I've been stupid, I let it take over my life,'

'But why him?' He asked.

'Because of what he did.'

'To get revenge?' He began to feel anxious and stood up as he messaged back.

'Yes but it got out of hand.'

'That's an understatement,' texted Marcus.

'It was exciting at first, but it's just getting in the way of things now.'

'But that's even worse,' Marcus was stunned at her attitude. He began pacing his bedroom.

'Forget about it, it was just some silly scheming that doesn't mean anything.'

'I didn't think you were like this,' Marcus was aghast and stared at the screen.

'Like what?'

'Well without being moralistic, that you'd act so low.'

'I know it was bad, I actually thought you'd find it amusing, I'm going to stop it all.'

'Amusing? Do you even know me? It just feels like a slap in the

face,' Marcus threw his head back and looked at the ceiling.

'No it's not funny, it was stupid, I regret it,' she messaged.

'I can't believe it happened just at the time when things could have been different.'

'What? They still could!'

'It's just this, I don't know if I can handle this,' he was devastated and texted quickly.

'Don't scare me.'

'Really you need to be careful.'

'Can we meet? I miss you so much.'

'I just need some space, I can't deny how disappointed I am, I didn't think you were a player. We waited all this time too,' Marcus replied, aware of how their feelings had grown in the past year. He sat alone in his room.

'Player? Marcus please, I'm so sorry, forgive me.'

'Noëmi I just need some time, don't be upset with me but I need some space, okay, please just stay safe M.' His heart was racing and he felt sick.

Marcus was stunned.

'Finally I've confronted her about those New Year messages. I can't decide if I wish I'd never seen them. Why would she exchange naked pictures and hook up for sex with John Dyer.'

With a heavy heart Marcus decided to put her back in the friendship box and see how he fared without her in his life. In order to help with this, he decided to seek out someone else to displace her from his mind. Maybe he was just feeling nostalgic as he was going to be back in the town where they grew up. After all, he reasoned, she was getting on with her life as a strong, independent woman, so why not he with his? With his mind made up he began to discipline his thoughts and pro-actively avoid contact with Noëmi. Soon his finals would be done and he would be starting his elective, giving him the chance to find a new woman to occupy the head space she was to vacate.

Noëmi

Noëmi was upset.

'I don't remember telling him about my catfish plot but I must have done when I got drunk at New Year. He knows all about my scheming. Why did I do that? I know how much he would disapprove of me messing with someone. My head is all over the place.'

Knowing him as well as she did, she was worried by his reaction to her revenge plot and fearing she had ruined everything, she was desperate to see him. She began having dreams of bumping into him and not being able to talk. Sitting next to him and having no voice and worst of all meeting him and having no idea what to say to him. Sweating she would wake up terrified by his abandonment and her desolation. His birthday was coming up on 2 March and he would be twenty-four years old. With a heavy heart she decided to organise a gift for him anyway as they never failed to exchange birthday presents.

Marcus

Having been sent to his student house in Oxford, the present arrived in good time. He was intrigued by the package and had recognised Noëmi's writing immediately. The gift was perfect, thoughtful and tastefully put together. Struggling to understand why she seemed to be like two different people he messaged her straight away to say thank you.

'Noëmi thank you so much it's perfect, you spent time on this I can see.'

'I'm so glad you like it, what are you doing for your birthday?'

'I'm going out tomorrow with people from the hospital.'

'Okay nice, I'd love to see you when you've forgiven me I'm always here, have fun Noëmi xxx'

'N the John Dyer thing has just broken me.'

She did not reply.

Marcus looked at the message and realised he had crossed a line. Whilst honest for the most part he was not going out with 'people'. He had been set up by a university coursemate, Charlie, with a girl who actually lived in Newcastle. Her name was Shauna, she was a personal trainer and manager at a gym. She was not a student but was visiting for the weekend. The mutual friend from Oxford thought they would be well suited especially with Marcus moving up there in June. So that was how he was to spend his Saturday night. Never in his life had he not been truthful with Noëmi;

'If she's now simply just a friend why don't I just tell her about my blind date?'

CHAPTER 23 - STAY SAFE

Stephanie

Following her suicide attempt Stephanie was carefully monitored by Children's Services. She had regular review meetings with her psychiatrist who put her at ease as she was open and direct. Sitting down next to her young patient she asked;

"We need to talk about you and what's been happening."

"Stuff's been happening." Stephanie looked at her hands.

"What exactly?" The psychiatrist passed her a bright yellow anti-stress ball.

"Boy stuff."

"Can you tell me about it?"

"I don't really want to, it's embarrassing." Stephanie squeezed the ball hard.

"I know, but there are two things you need to realise, one is we all do embarrassing stuff and the second is that I'm not here to judge you, I'm here to help you." She looked directly at Stephanie.

"This boy is threatening me."

"Okay why is he threatening you?"

"He wants photos of me."

"Are you sending him photos?"

"Yes sometimes." Stephanie was clutching the ball.

"And if you don't."

"He says he'll take his revenge, send them to my mum and get me arrested for sexting."

"Alright, is there anything else you want to tell me?"

"No," she shook her head.

"Okay do you see him often?"

"Yes, he's at my school."

"We need to help you."

"No you can't, that will make him take his revenge!" She put the ball down, drew her knees to her chest and laid her head on them.

Stephanie refused to answer any more questions and her psychiatrist filed a report to Children's Services, the school and the police. This was to arrange for Stephanie to remain under the supervision of a Child Protection Officer whilst an investigation took place. The police intended to question Stephanie to find out more about the threats but it was difficult to find out if a crime was being committed if she was refusing to cooperate. A review of her case was set for the next day and she was to be placed under constant supervision, as she was still considered a risk to herself.

The next day a police car pulled into school. Guy, the young police officer, who had helped Sarai, was back. He asked after Sarai, and was assured by John that she was coping well. He then briefed them on fifteen year old Stephanie's recent visit to hospital. The senior managers listened gravely as Guy said that they were looking to work with the school to carry out an investigation regarding an allegation of peer to peer sexual exploitation. He went over the details that they knew; that Stephanie was allegedly being threatened by a fellow student and coerced into sending sexual images, but they had no concrete evidence. He emphasised that the school had to handle the situation carefully and should under no circumstances question Stephanie, as she was refusing to cooperate.

Sitting at his desk, writing notes with a fine silver pen, John took control.

"Guy, I'm very happy to lead on this and to be your point of contact. I do a lot of work with Year 11 pastorally and it is urgent that we get this resolved for Stephanie's sake."

Maurice looked delighted, wringing his hands and smiling.

"Thank you," replied Guy, leaning forward in his chair. "We can exchange contact details. We need more evidence so we want to access her school IT account. Also her current phone is new so there's nothing there, but sometimes kids have more than one, so any devices you become aware of, we will have to see. We're asking her mother for the home accounts, social media too, but that's harder as she's not giving up her passwords."

"Of course," replied John, "this is very serious indeed." He looked up at Guy opposite him.

"We must of course look after Stephanie and we would like to get a risk assessment done for her. We will set up a safety plan as we don't know the identity of the student who is carrying out the alleged abuse. We need to assign a child support worker to meet with her at any time as she is now under a non voluntary child protection order."

"We understand."

"We also need to assign an external case officer by the end of the week, I will ask them to contact you, Mr Dyer."

"John." He handed Guy his card.

"Yes, now we must ensure that staff are aware without giving too many details, especially at the moment as these are allegations," Guy said.

"Of course, rest assured we will do our bit," John fixed his stare on Guy.

"We also request that you assign a teaching assistant to her to be with her during lessons and social time, someone to whom she could relate. It must be someone of the same sex," continued Guy.

"What about Della? She's good with the girls, you know young and all that," suggested Sharon.

"Just make sure it's someone who'll keep a full and detailed account of how Stephanie is and most importantly make sure she's not alone at any time, she's still a suicide risk," emphasised the police officer.

"Of course," said John, sounding sincere.

Maurice finally spoke, "So at this stage there'll be no publicity or anything for the school to worry about? You know what parents are like!" he chortled, missing the point entirely.

Guy sighed sharply and was exasperated, "Of course not, we've not even been able to start our investigation as Stephanie will not communicate. Can I remind everyone that she has tried to take her life. Her mental health is fragile, and if we could we would admit her into a therapy unit."

Silence stood for a moment.

"Why can you not do that?" asked Sharon naïvely.

"Because she refuses and her mum supports that; she believes Stephanie 'getting on with her GCSEs' will be the best treatment for her. She knows her rights," said Guy, getting up to leave.

"Don't worry we'll keep her safe," said John confidently.

Guy nodded and walked to the door and as he was about to leave he turned to them and said, "We just need to get her to trust us."

"You're absolutely right, trust is what this is all about," affirmed John. He placed the pen in the leather desk tidy.

An email was sent out to Stephanie's teachers explaining that she had some 'emotional' problems and that all concerns and any information disclosed should be passed directly to John Dyer who was dealing with the case. Under no circumstances was this to be discussed with Stephanie and teachers were not to 'pry' or 'question' her.

CHAPTER 24 - SIXTH SENSE

Frank

Frank looked at his calendar and realised he had to be in a meeting in T minus 5. In a similar manner to the staffing figures, the sixth form applications had to be considered well before the next academic year. The school was looking to improve its uptake for post 16 qualifications and John Dyer had organised a meeting with the Deputy Head, Sharon King and some other staff members, who were on the sixth form committee.

Running, he made it in time and joined the others, assembled in a draughty science lab. John kicked off the meeting.

"Okay so great to see everyone we just need to go through our sixth form numbers for September 2017."

The process was simple enough and students from St Wolbodo's automatically had the right to stay on for post sixteen courses.

"Great news, it looks like we're full!"

Everyone visibly relaxed as this would mean the meeting would be over soon.

"Did we manage to take in all our external applicants?" asked John.

"Well yes and no, we had a few dodgy ones, you know kids from the estate, so we just binned those as they are not really the kind of student we are looking for," replied Sharon.

John took over, 'Indeed, but we had some impressive applications from some of the local fee paying schools which is good for pictures; those private school kids really have the genes for results' day photos."

"All this talk is so wrong, I warn you I'm minuting this," said Frank.

"But we have no space," said Sharon, ignoring the promotion of eugenics and Frank's protest.

"Shit we need to do something..." said John.

The room was still, faint ticking of the clock in the background.

"...well we can't do anything about the numbers we're accepting but if we look at sixth form numbers as a whole, then surely we could..."

"Get rid of any underperforming Year 12's in order to make space," Sharon finished his sentence, "Genius," she said, presumably congratulating herself.

The Deputy Head, buried herself in her notes, evidently looking for candidates whose lives she could ruin.

"According to the data there are Toby Swaines, Mercedes Benson and Joel Rivera."

Frank butted in, "but it's March already, what will they do? It could well be too late to get into anywhere else, you can't abandon them like this..."

John and Sharon looked at each other, both giving the same impression that the more Frank spoke, the more determined they would be to continue with their plans.

"And Joel is in my form and is making better than expected progress," said Frank. 'It's true that last year his exams didn't go well but now he's repeating the year, things really are looking up."

John Dyer bristled.

The school bursar who had said nothing so far interrupted,

"Joel brings in £8000 per year in Special Educational Needs funding which is very useful to the school, it paid for the new senior management offices this year...but actually it runs out soon and next year he gets nothing."

Frank felt increasingly desperate and looked at the data. "Listen, you can't do this. He's improved and his overall grade has gone from a D to a B in IT. It's great and he really has worked hard." "Actually," interrupted John, "you're right, that could be problematic."

Frank was now confused and disarmed.

"Okay," said John, thinking, "have the reports to parents gone out?"

"Yes, last week on the 4th," replied one teacher, maybe hoping that the management members at the meeting would be impressed with his exact recall of the date.

"Damn!" John said, looking lost in his thoughts, "Okay this will need some other action."

Frank was convinced Joel was now safe from the cull. John then continued, "So Joel's a bit odd right? So the parents are probably no hopers to have produced a kid like that, so we'll overwhelm them with negative information about their kid, you know from starting with the old chestnut; 'He never has a pen' and then force them to move him out, with continued criticism of all he does."

Joel's tutor Frank was astounded. "But what about his B grade, I congratulated him already and so did his IT teacher."

John turned as he was leaving and replied simply,

"Just tell the parents it's a typo."

John Dyer sent instructions to the teachers of the students on his hit list. It was decided that the cull of the Year 12 students would take a two pronged attack 'take the wind out of their sails then hit them below the belt,' as John described it, mixing all his metaphors as usual. The first part was for teachers at the upcoming parents' evening to deliver only bad news. John had provided a script to use, 'for a consistent message.' The second part would be a formal meeting with parents to agree to get them off roll by mid-July.

Frank opened his email with horror. He had not expected the management to go through with their idea. Immediately he sent an email to the Head Teacher, saying he disagreed with moving these students on, especially given how much they had improved. For him it was important to have his feelings on record.

Unusually, Sharon King dropped into his lab to see him. Frank was marking work and looked up at her as she marched, most business like, towards him.

"Can I be of assistance?" he asked dryly, returning his gaze to his pile of exercise books.

Without pausing for breath Sharon launched into a monologue.

"This school cannot accommodate students like Joel Rivera who have such complex needs. He's a drain on the staff. St Wolbodo's is not the place for him and he needs to go somewhere else for his own benefit. It is not fair on him to keep him here!"

"Oh what a kind thought and where would you suggest he continues his education?"

She put her hands on her hips, "Anywhere but here!"

"Well that's helpful. When you say he's a drain on staff what on earth do you mean?"

Sharon stood tall. "The amount of time required to mark his work. Differentiate the lessons for him"

"I'm sorry? That's why the school gets extra money for such students. Do you actually keep a record of how it's used?"

"It's not possible!"

"Really?" Frank could feel his colour rising. "You, Mrs King, are going to lie about his grades, not give him the support that his funding pays for and then just chuck him out. This is not right and you damn well know it!" Frank stated clearly.

"Don't you shout at me!"

"I have not raised my voice!" Frank stood up and flung his pile of books down on the desk. He looked directly back at her, unblinking.

Sharon puffed her chest and was straight back at him, "Frank, you stick to the script okay and think about how much you need this job!"

"Is this some kind of threat Mrs King?" Frank froze his stare.

"I'm just reminding you how grateful you should be to have employment in this day and age! The promotion you wanted went to someone else after all! Someone younger!" Sharon smirked. Some small beads of her spit hit Frank's cheek.

"I can tell you right now I have no intention of lying to anyone. My advice to you is to forget this illegal plot of Dyer's and to do the right thing!" Frank's face flushed red.

"This school needs to get rid of those students and it doesn't matter how we do it!" Sharon snapped.

Glaring at each other neither blinked.

"What's become of you? Every child matters apart from the ones you decide don't! You're a disgrace!" Frank was burning up.

Looking smug, Sharon King gave a laugh, turned and left.

Frank was glad to see the back of her, quite literally. He sat silent for a while, reflecting on the disappointment he felt in his management team. Beginning to wonder why he stayed in this job, he thought of the young people he taught.

Resolute, he decided to forward the directive, about 'getting rid' of the students, to his home email in case he needed it in the future.

Too early... Joel Rivera remained on the hit list to be removed from the sixth form to make space for the new high achieving students. Frank knew the family well. His parents, Luis and Penelope, worked long hours as nurses at Newcastle RVI hospital. They had two sons, both kind, sensitive boys, clever in their own ways. Each morning, in order to arrive at work on time, Mrs Rivera would drop them at school at 7:20am with a freshly packed breakfast. 7:20am was over an hour before registration and the boys' parents were the only ones in the history of St Wolbodo's to receive a letter home complaining they were bringing their children to school too early.

Frank, being Joel's tutor, was copied into the letter, which was truly bizarre reminding the parents to;

'reearly the reason for the earlyness to the school office by 9am," and *'that given that these were not isoearlyed incidents'*, the parents should *'contempearly the reason for their child's behaviour, take action to reguearly it and seek to emuearly the behaviour of other students who were never early'* and more

seriously *'Failure to do so would escaearly the matter which could transearly into a poor future reference'*

Going to see Pat to find out why such a letter had been sent he was met with a barrage of self vindication.

Pat Davies moaned that she was 'too 'busy' to write a new letter so she had simply taken the late letter template and had done a find and replace; exchanging late with early. She muttered furiously about 'exploitation' and 'slave labour'.

Frank could see Pat's use of find and replace was extremely basic, plus the threat of *'tardy monitoring report'* was left in as she obviously did not know what tardy meant.

"Did you re-read this?" he asked exasperated.

"Not paid enough and too busy" she replied and turned her back on him.

Frank shook his head and went to phone Joel's mother to explain.

CHAPTER 25 - MIDDLE AGED SPREAD

Sarai

Sarai woke up each day, tired from her lack of sleep due to the night terrors she was having. She put one foot in front of the other and carried out her day. Sarai realised by about 9am each day that whilst she was having disturbing dreams, her waking life was in fact the nightmare, and by 9:01am each day she wanted to die. As the weeks passed she resolved that being alive was important if only so that Luca could be remembered.

She sat at her desk all day and saw nothing but Luca's face; she fell into a reverie and took herself back to the days when they were together. She woke at the end of the day and felt terrible that she had done no work but had evidently fallen asleep at her desk. As the spring term drew on her tiredness grew worse and although she no longer felt nauseous when she woke, she suddenly noticed that her clothes were tighter round her waist. She was jolted out of her somnambulant life by the disturbance of having to find some bigger clothes. As she had not eaten properly in months and had in fact lost weight, she had no idea why her stomach was distended. In a frantic panic she wondered what was happening, she always had Luca to sort things out but now he was not with her. Unable to focus she began to cry, searched 'distended stomach' on the internet and realised she was suffering from malnutrition.

Pat Davies saw Sarai arrive each day, sit unhappy at her desk and then leave. Although technically Pat never actually saw Sarai leave as Pat was out of the office by 3:30pm each day whilst Sarai stayed until 5pm. However, for all of Pat's jobsworth attitude and nosiness, she was intrigued by Sarai.

"So what's China like then?" She asked out of nowhere one day, as they queued to do some photocopying.

"I have no idea I used to live in Vietnam."

"Well China, Vietnam same thing, wherever all you Orientals live, seems so far away." Pat sighed.

Noticing Sarai's distended stomach with her beady eyes Pat suddenly announced to her as they waited at the photocopier,

"You're getting middle aged spread, you need to watch it."

Pat could never have been accused of having any artifice or being anything other than direct.

"I don't understand." Sarai was confused.

"Well don't say I didn't warn you. My knees are playing up. I need to sit down."

In spite of not having finished her task, Pat grabbed her papers, returned to her desk and announced she was off for a comfort break. Sarai stood shocked. Why was the malnutrition getting worse? She was setting an alarm so that she remembered to eat three times a day. With trepidation she decided she should go to the doctor and see what was wrong with her, confused and upset she arrived in front of her GP, whom she had not seen for a few weeks.

Sarai entered the small doctor's surgery that was housed in a clinic built in the 1960s. The room was clean. It was practical with linoleum flooring, useful in case anything needed mopping up. It was dominated by an examination couch, surrounded by a sky blue curtain. Doctor Chaudry had a large leather chair and an oak desk which looked oddly out of place. A large box of tissues sat on the edge of the desk next to some hand sanitiser.

"How may I help you today Sarai?" asked Doctor Chaudry kindly as he knew she was recently bereaved.

"I've got a stomach problem; it's becoming distended from malnutrition."

"Malnutrition? Why do you think that?"

"Because after my husband died and I couldn't eat, and I felt sick so I searched on the internet and I found I must have malnutrition,"

"I'm so sorry to hear about your husband, I hope you are getting support?"

"I... I, yes of course my employers are good," Sarai lied as she did not want to start crying.

"Okay," said Dr Chaudry unconvinced "Obviously I don't dispute that, but who cares for you?"

"I care for me."

"And how do you feel?"

"Sad, I miss my husband, but it is my stomach that is why I've come today," she was feeling raw as Dr Chaudry was touching a nerve. She could not cope with talking about her feelings.

"I understand, I will set up some counselling sessions, these can really help, having someone to talk to. You'll be entitled to time off work. But you say you have a stomach problem?"

"Yes it's distended, malnutrition but I am making an effort now to eat."

"Okay I think you need a scan but tell me what about your menstrual health, do you have regular periods?"

Sarai was dumbfounded.

"I'm not sure."

"Let's take a urine sample now, and I'll refer you for a scan."

Sarai went into an echoing cubicle with a bright white Armitage Shanks toilet and peed into a specimen tube, wondering when she had last had a period.

"It must have been before Christmas," she reckoned.

She waited whilst Dr Chaudry performed a few dip tests and then took off his glasses and looked at her straight.

"Sarai, from my tests it looks like you are pregnant."

Sarai fell backwards into her chair with shock. Slowly she began to understand what the doctor had told her. Heart racing, she felt tears begin to run down her cheeks.

Sarai and Luca had wanted children but since their marriage nothing had happened. Although disappointed, they consoled each other with the knowledge their love was already entire for one another. However before Luca left for the States they had intended to go to get help from the doctor as Sarai was now in her mid-thirties and they were keen to see if they could be parents. Luca knew the money from the Anderson project, in the US, would help towards any potential treatment, all of which had made him keener not to miss the opportunity.

"Sarai, are you okay?"

"Yes, it's what we always wanted." She gasped, breathlessly, her heart full of Luca.

"Now you must go for a scan so that we can see how advanced the pregnancy is and that the baby is growing well. Do you have any idea of when conception could have taken place?"

Sarai assured him that she had had no relationship with anyone other than her husband and that their love life had been very happy but that she had no recollection of a last period. She told him it may have been November but she could not be sure.

This news gave Sarai a new perspective and whilst it did not diminish her sadness or loss, it gave her further reason to live. She felt absolute joy in knowing Luca would live on in her child. God had blessed her. For the first time in months she smiled as she rushed to the hospital for an urgent scan.

CHAPTER 26 - ILLUSIONS

John

John had stopped contacting Maya, furious with the fact that she had not turned up for their rendez-vous. Staring back over her profile and messages with his mobile in one hand, he thumped the desk hard with his other. His eyes smarted as this left wrist was still painful from Sarai's retaliation. Standing up he paced his office and let out a growl of anger. *'No one rejects me!'* he thought, bitterly.

His one lesson that week was on cover so that he could supervise a trainee teacher for a formal assessment. However he decided to use the time instead to look over Maya's pictures and see if he could check out her version of events. John took the first of Maya's pictures and he did an image search which brought up her modelling and fitness pages. Delving further into the searches he then started looking for a name. Finally he found M Jankowski. Excited, he searched now by name and started looking over the results. Infuriatingly Maya Jankowski was not producing anything. Indeed, by the by, he found that the name 'Maya' meant 'illusion'. In time he found Magda Jankowski and saw that her image matched that of Maya.

"Maya must be a shortened version of Magda," he reasoned. He now had her full name and surname and he began to get more luck in his results. John switched onto social media sites and quickly looked over the profiles for Magda or Maya as he knew her.

He was relieved that she was real and not a fictional character. He poured over her profile; happy that all he had seen was true; every picture. Yet she seemed a lot quieter and more serious in her social media than the woman who wanted *'sex, sex, sex'* on his desk. Indeed the more he looked the more perplexed he became. Whilst her photos were a confident show of a good body, it seemed much more linked to sports physiology than an overt sexual display. John now had a number of tabs open and he was searching further into her profiles, most of which were not private. From her personal information he saw that she was in a relationship, which brought a sly smile to his lips. He liked the thought of a woman who would deceive to get her sexual satisfaction. However as he scrolled over her profile picture he noticed the likes and froze as he recognised Noëmi's name as one of her friends who had liked her picture. He sat back completely puzzled as to what this could mean and for once he was speechless. He quickly took out his phone and messaged Maya to say,

'It looks like we have a mutual acquaintance doesn't it?'

He sent it quickly to her to see what she replied. No response and his mood grew darker as he reflected on Maya and Noëmi. These were two women who had not played his game and who were not falling for his charms, which perplexed him. He wondered how friendly they may be and it dawned on him that he may well be the victim of a prank. Angry he stormed out of his office, with no plan but to move. He immediately bumped into the trainee teacher, whose lesson he should have been assessing.

"Mr Dyer! Where were you?" She looked confused.

He feigned a look of exasperation and disappointment and snarled at her;

"Serious child protection case came up, nightmare."

He did not elaborate further, merely furrowed his brow to give the impression he was stressed out by this fictitious event, then he continued,

"...and of course I cannot discuss it, we'll need to find another time for the observation."

He went to walk off.

"But I spent the whole weekend preparing! I missed my friend's thirtieth birthday party! I made individual information sheets on each of the thirty children..."

"A good teacher is always prepared for anything." John snapped back without turning his head.

The teacher watched him leave and began to weep. Her hot, futile tears ran down her face as she watched him stride into the distance.

Noëmi

Noëmi heard her phone ping and she looked down with interest to see who was messaging her during the school day. Her students were working quietly and she quickly looked at her phone.

"That should be confiscated," quipped one of her young students.

"Absolutely! You're right, I'm going to do that straight away!" she threw back with a smile.

The student grinned and settled back to work. Everyone liked Miss McAllister.

She saw the alert had come to Maya's dating profile and popped her phone in a drawer and sneakily opened the message.

'It looks like we have a mutual acquaintance doesn't it?'

Her blood froze, what did this mean? Trembling, she began to close the drawer. She then pulled it open again. Her stomach was rising into her throat.

Fingers shaking, she clicked on the message again. Was he onto her? How could he have made the connection? No way was that possible. As she racked her brains she suddenly became aware of the noise level rising and then suddenly the room going completely silent. Noëmi swung round and shut the drawer and saw John Dyer at the door, stopping off on one of his patrols. He said nothing, looked at the class, stared darkly at Noëmi, remained silent and walked off.

CHAPTER 27 - EASTER

Noëmi

The Easter holidays had arrived and everyone was delighted as it had been a long and gruelling term. Noëmi would spend the second week in Newcastle with her father Donnie, as it was his fiftieth birthday. The pair had decided to visit their old home village of Kenmore for the middle weekend, staying at the Kenmore Hotel on the banks of Loch Tay.

Being a fit man with a full head of chestnut hair, Donnie appeared much younger than his years. He enjoyed the outdoors so they took a boat out on the loch and walked to places like Menzies Castle where they admired its turrets and fine walls. They made up stories about unquiet ghosts that now inhabited the castle and imagined the past lives of the spirits. On their way back they took silly photos next to the sign for Dull, twinned with Boring. However behind this jolly front, Noëmi was feeling very low but she hid her sadness from her father. Just as he would hide his from her. She had not heard from Marcus in weeks. Since their last message exchange he had been distant, not replying to her messages immediately as he used to, and he was always too busy with studying to talk. In addition to this disappointment, the dark looks John Dyer had been throwing her made her suspicious that he was onto her game and she felt worried that she could lose her job. Anxiety filled her mind whether it was to do with John or Marcus, so she tried not to think about either.

Arriving in Newcastle for the second week after a wonderful few days, she arranged to join her father for a social get together with his work friends. Donnie's colleagues wanted to take him out to celebrate his upcoming milestone. They knew Noëmi, enjoying her company very much, as she always accompanied her father to the annual Christmas party.

They chose a charming family run Italian restaurant called Ricci's that had a relaxed vibe and excellent food. Old style mirrors decorated the walls and pictures of Italy, from days gone by, were everywhere to be seen.

"N typical of you to do all this for me, I really don't like being the centre of attention you know that!"

"Relax Dad, it's going to be a wonderful evening! Fifty!"

He gave her a look, "And you can stop age shaming me right now!"

She grinned. Donnie's friends were delighted and all greeted him, slapping him on the back, hugging him and starting the jokes about Zimmer frames and stair lifts. Sitting in the softly lit restaurant as a small group of eight, Noëmi was listening to the chitter chatter about Donnie's work when she suddenly saw Marcus walk in.

'My God, he's home for Easter!' Frozen to her chair, her heart leapt at the possibility that she could go and talk to him. *'I have to talk to him, find out what's going on.'*

In close pursuit, an attractive redhead followed behind him. Marcus did not see Noëmi across the crowded restaurant. She simply watched as the two of them sat down together, chatting happily. They seemed at ease and Marcus looked like he was enjoying the company of this woman whom Noëmi did not know.

'Just a friend? Maybe a medical contact?'

Then she saw Marcus reach for the woman's hand and hold it affectionately. Slowly he gently leant across, kissing her on the cheek, as the latter laughed shyly.

Noëmi looked down at her pasta and was no longer hungry, she turned her chair so that Marcus and his date could not see her. She picked at her food, but had a big lump in her throat.

"And of course then he realised he'd ordered A1 instead of A4, it was enormous!" One of the group finished a long anecdote and Donnie's colleagues laughed loudly.

"But he thinks his nickname *'A1 man'* is a compliment!"

More merriment followed. Miserable, she nodded every now and then so that the group would leave her alone. She tried to smile but tears began to fall from her eyes. Marcus had moved on.

'Well of course he has,' she thought, *'He's just everything a woman could want, who wouldn't want to love him. Oh God, is he in love?'*

She looked round and they were still settled, seemingly deep in conversation, and it was time for her and her father to leave as arranged.

"N are you feeling alright? You look so pale!" He fixed his eyes on her.

"Yes, fine Dad, just tired!"

They said goodbye to the group and slipped out of their table easily getting to the door, where the restaurant owner insisted on marking Donnie's birthday with cheery conversation. Enthusiastically he recited a proverb and got Noëmi to translate it into Italian, which she could not avoid doing, her voice was thin and breaking.

Count your nights by stars, not shadows

Conta le notti con le stelle non con le ombre

Count your days by smiles, not tears.

Conta i giorni con i sorrisi non con le lacrime.

And on any birthday morning, count your age by friends not years

E per ogni compleanno conta la tua età con gli amici non con gli anni.

Marcus

The burst of happiness from the cheery restaurant owner, at hearing this Italian, made Marcus look round. His heart jumped from his chest, *'Noëmi!'*

She avoided his gaze as she left with her father. Donnie spotted him and gave him a big smile and a huge wave.

"Noëmi! Look, it's Marcus right over there!" and he clearly saw him tap Noëmi on the shoulder to alert her to her friend's presence. Noëmi did not turn around but shook her head and carried on walking. Donnie gave Marcus a mock confused shrug to indicate that he did not understand his daughter's ignoring her old friend.

Marcus watched as they walked away,

'Oh God she's seen me with Shauna, what am I doing? No remember she's a player. Be strong! Oh should I go after her?'

"Are you okay?" his date, Shauna, asked.

"Oh yes, sorry, just tired, you know."

The redhead agreed and spoke at length about her upcoming

schedule, but Marcus zoned out, *'Remember those messages, she's not what she seems...you don't miss her, it's just nostalgia. Memories of feelings that's all!'*

At the end of the week Donnie had a low key open house on the day of his fiftieth birthday which was Easter Monday 17 April. Marcus had been working until 8pm and by the time he got to Donnie's to drop off a present, he had missed Noëmi.

"Oh what a shame you've missed N, she's got school starting tomorrow you know. She's been here all day greeting everyone, serving canapés, cake, and champagne."

Marcus was not sure if he was disappointed or relieved.

"Very Happy Birthday Donnie!" Marcus replied looking around at the house all decorated with helium balloons, flowers and streamers. There were pictures of Donnie from his fifty years all displayed with funny comments. Immediately he recognised Noëmi's handiwork.

"I told her no fuss, but she's organised so much for me; took me to Scotland last week and next weekend she's taking me to my folks in Leeds."

"Was that a birthday meal earlier in the week then?"

"Ah yes at Ricci's, of course, she organised that with my colleagues from work, I'm blessed with the most thoughtful of daughters," he mused, feeling warmed from a day of drinking champagne.

"Yes you are," he saw that Donnie was sorting a number of photos on the kitchen table.

"And did you know her friend Sarai is pregnant! It turned out she didn't realise. They conceived just before her poor husband died. Such an awful time, but this is wonderful for her!" Donnie shared the news and Marcus felt uplifted.

"That's fantastic!"

"And you look like you've found happiness too Marcus!" Donnie was on a roll as the birthday drinking continued to keep him chatting, "Good for you! What a lovely looking girl too!"

Marcus could feel himself blushing.

"It's very, very early days, I wouldn't take it as anything serious Donnie, we don't even live in the same town," he emphasised, unsure why.

"You know Marcus, I really wish N could find someone, she's not seen anyone since that charity guy who let her down," Donnie's face was red. Marcus was not sure if it was the champagne or that he was angry with Jesse for failing to turn up to visit Noëmi back in August.

Marcus clenched his jaw as he thought of Jesse. He noted no mention of the Assistant Head Teacher in her relationship history.

Marcus glanced down at the pictures on the table, there were some from the charity ball,

"I took those!" he commented. "Almost a year ago!"

"Doesn't she look beautiful, you're welcome to take one," Donnie replied, so Marcus did, spending a couple of minutes to choose his favourite. Noëmi had her mother's dark, thick Italian hair and her father's blue Scottish eyes. He found a shot of her smiling, looking radiant and her hair around her shoulders that he particularly liked. Putting the photo in his wallet he looked around her old home and remembered all the times he had spent there with her. Unsure what he was feeling he asked Donnie in all honesty.

"Is Noëmi okay? It's strange being here without her, you know."

Donnie looked at the photos of his daughter and shook his head.

"I don't know, she's really not been herself recently and this week she's been so low, she thinks I don't notice but you can't help but see it as a parent," Donnie sighed. "Maybe you could talk to her, you two have always been such good friends. She was so very excited at New Year when you were coming home. I think she needs cheering up."

Marcus felt conflicted and contemplative. Noëmi's feelings for him were evident. He walked back to his parents' home in the half-light of the spring evening. His life could be so different had he not caught Noëmi agreeing to send John Dyer naked pictures. He felt so very sad.

CHAPTER 28 - YOUNG LIVES

Sarai

The Easter holidays were now a distant memory as everyone began to prepare for the upcoming exam season. An air of optimism and calm filled the school and no one felt this more than Sarai. Beside herself with joy that hers and Luca's child was growing inside her, she furiously researched her final trimester of pregnancy. Sarai caressed her growing stomach with soft, soothing strokes and spoke to her baby gently,

"I will love and protect you, just as your father did me."

As she shut her eyes she cupped her hands over her stomach and she began to cry, wistful that Luca was missing this.

With a renewed vigour for life, Sarai made a calendar to count down the days to her due date, estimated to be the first week in August. She wrote out all the days and ticked them off, keeping a diary of all that happened in school plus her feelings.

Back in the office Pat noticed, with surprise, a supply of health foods had appeared all of a sudden on Sarai's desk.

"She won't lose that tummy if she eats all that," she sighed to her colleagues.

In between John's work requests, Sarai read voraciously about pregnancy and thought of nothing else. Sarai also began to take an interest in the school and her work, which meant the day passed quicker and the moment of meeting her baby would arrive sooner. John and Sarai still communicated by email.

One bright morning, Sarai settled down at her desk and read through her emails. Not long after Pat arrived and was all a flurry. 9am the office phones began to ring. Ignoring them Pat began to rant.

"No one appreciates how much I'm put upon. I'm treated like a slave at this place. Always at full pelt the whole day long, day in day out."

She sighed loudly, made a cup of tea, huffing and puffing, took her bag and walked out again.

"I'm off for a quick comfort break."

This meant to those that knew her, a cigarette break.

Sarai thought to herself *'Surely a break comes between two periods of work?'*

Clearly that was a misconception when dealing with Pat. Sarai sighed and opened her *'to do'* list from John. As always it was delivered in a blunt, unfriendly tone and this day was no exception.

'Find my report templates should be on my drive.'

During the time they used to speak to each other, Sarai remembered him telling her about these templates. She recalled how the story summed him up.

John had a 'clever' way of saving time on this key reporting process. When he was Head of Department, he had got a trainee to compose a series of reports for male and female students of all abilities over all key stages. This had taken the young teacher their entire Easter holiday. He then used them as a base for writing any reports required, as he had only to replace a code with the name and with one click the report was done. This had served him well throughout his teaching. He had even told Sarai.

"Only one awkward moment when a parent had contacted me as her two children had exactly the same wording on their report. I explained this away as my secretary mixing the two students up and told her that I would look carefully into why this had happened."

Now being his current secretary, Sarai wondered what wrongdoings had been laid at her door. John continued that he felt no guilt when he got emails about how much these reports meant to parents or carers, nor when he overheard a young student say how much they valued what had been written. "Empty words gain me time!" he would say.

Sarai looked over the shared folders she had from John's drive and found very little and nothing like the blueprints for report writing of which he spoke. She decided to go and look in his office in case there was a hard copy or anything else to help with this search.

Sarai checked his diary to make sure he was out of school and entered carefully, lodging the door open with a large unread book, lest he returned from his child protection meeting early. She noted he was due back in fifteen minutes.

The office seemed relatively tidy with the desk clear. A row of books with impressive titles such as 'Ensuring Academic Excellence in Education' and 'Diversity and Inclusion in Secondary Education' were positioned behind the desk. Nestled in between were the complete works of Dickens, Jane Austen and Shakespeare. Beyond those was a book about the Second World War and the SAS. When she first started working for him and before the assault, she would make conversation.

"Which is your favourite?" she asked him as she had brought in the 9:30am cup of coffee.

"Sorry?"

"Which novel, Emma's my favourite."

"Yeah Dickens is a good writer, can you make sure you don't move my computer, I've got the video camera all set up to capture the bookshelf."

"Of course."

"Got a video call with all the local Head Teachers soon."

She opened a few drawers to see if there was a hard drive or memory stick. In the first drawer was chewing gum confiscated from students that John used for himself, a box of tissues and a couple of mobile phones belonging to students. Another drawer had a few pens, a spare tie and condoms. Sarai felt anxious and made a note to wash her hands.

A further drawer had some folders and blank paper. A final drawer at the bottom Sarai was unable to open as it was locked. Sarai began to wonder why John had a locked drawer and could not help but feel a frisson of excitement that she may find something interesting in it.

With surprising energy she looked around for a key and was disappointed to find nothing. She sat in the chair and imagined she was John, knowing how he liked to have everything easy to hand so he did not have to get out of his seat.

She swung round and looked about her. Feeling over the shelves and surfaces she found nothing and sat back resigned to disappointment. Her baby kicked and she jolted up in the chair and felt something on her upper leg. Under the front of the desk she looked and she saw a key sellotaped to the underside of it.

Instantly she knew she had found the key and excitedly took off the tape, making sure she left it in the same place. Her hands were shaking as she unlocked the drawer but she found nothing inside.

"No! why's it locked if it's empty?" She glanced up at the clock; he was back in ten minutes.

Thinking again, she felt the top inside of the drawer, which was hidden from view, and found a memory stick taped there.

Sarai logged on to John's computer as a general user and put in the memory stick, which she saw contained a number of folders; 'Keynotes', 'Presentations', 'School Work' and 'Child Protection!'. Her eyes glanced at the exclamation mark and she was confused as to why that was there. Curious, she clicked slowly onto this folder and saw that it needed a password.

"Damn!" she said out loud and began to think.

She used the password he usually had for things which was 'Password1' but it did not work, she tried 'Password 2' but that was also no good. She stood and was about to go when she tried '1drowssaP' and she was into the folder. Again she checked the time.

It contained two more folders, one called 'Pictures' and the other 'Videos' so she clicked onto 'Pictures'. As the thumbnails opened she began to tremble. The images looked odd, things she had never seen before, she made the screen bigger and she began to see what the pictures showed. Her heart jumped in her chest and her throat tightened, unable to breathe she let out a shallow scream, she pulled the memory stick from the computer and ran out and into the main office where she grabbed the nearest bin and was violently sick.

Pat and the other office workers looked across at her shaking at the bin and Pat sighed,

"It's all that food you've been stuffing your face with," and turned back to her screen.

Sarai, sobbing quietly, pulled herself back up and returned to John's office where she shut down the computer. Two minutes. She replaced the memory stick and locked the drawer, desperately wishing she could turn back time and unsee what she had seen.

Pale and quivering she walked out of his office as John turned into the corridor, eyes down, checking his mobile phone. Turning her head away she waited for him to slam shut his door. Dashing to the toilet she was sick many times. Returning to her desk she sobbed for the rest of the day.

As Sarai dashed out again to be sick, Pat began to moan that the crying was putting her off her work.

"I tell you that Sarai, with all her malingering, is a drain on anyone trying to do a decent day's work to earn an honest living."

CHAPTER 29 - GETTING RID

Penelope Rivera

Mr and Mrs Rivera sat outside the Head Teacher's office, confused and uncertain as to why they had been called in. It looked serious; they were outside the most important office in the school. Their son, Joel, joined them and they sat in silence thinking their own thoughts.

The office foyer was a sixties style breeze block building with a small black sofa and a window from the reception area into the school office. The plastic leather look sofa was where Joel and Gabriel used to sit when they arrived early at school, but now they waited outside the main building after they were sent the warning letter. A few silver trophies sat proudly in a display cabinet, giving an air of success to the school. If you looked closely you would have seen that the dates on the cups and shields were all from two decades earlier and that there had been no recent sporting triumphs.

Suddenly the Head Teacher's door opened but it was the Deputy Head, Sharon King who came out, half studying paperwork. She greeted them with a hearty,

"Okay guys thank you so much for coming in," as she ushered the family through.

Penelope Rivera replied sunnily and politely.

"Thank you for inviting us in to update us on Joel's progress," hoping that her optimism would be contagious.

Sharon carried on "Okay well guys the thing is that we really don't think St Wolbodo's is the right place for Joel to continue his education."

"Oh and why is that?" Joel's father asked, looking taken aback.

"Well based on his performance so far he really is struggling," replied Sharon, knotting her eyebrows.

"Struggling?" repeated Mrs Rivera incredulously.

"Yeah academically which means he's finding his subjects really hard," replied Sharon in a somewhat patronising manner.

"Yes we understand what you're saying, what is the evidence for your conclusions?" asked Luis Rivera sensibly.

"Well guys his last report, you know that piece of paper with grades on, that's the evidence!" continued Sharon smirking.

"But he's improved in IT," stated Mrs Rivera who knew the report inside out as she had been delighted to receive it. "Yeah, but if we look at the actual data it is a different story," explained Sharon.

"How so?" asked Mr Rivera.

"I'm sorry none of this makes any sense," interrupted Mrs Rivera.

"Well guys we're happy to get someone in to help you with the English and basic comprehension if you need it," simpered the Deputy Head patronisingly.

"No we have no problem with English, it shows here he improved in IT from a D to a B over the last term," replied Mr

Rivera.

"Yeah, but guys as I said it doesn't actually mean that and in fact that B is a typo," explained the Deputy Head.

"A typo?"

"Yeah guys it should be an E not a B, see they sound similar," explained Sharon.

"A typo?"

"Yeah the letters even look the same," continued Sharon thinking how ingenious this sudden idea was.

Joel interrupted, "But the teacher congratulated me..."

"Yeah but guys I think she was being nice, you know finding something positive to say," explained Sharon.

"No, she told me how well I'd done getting a B grade," said Joel defensively.

"I am sorry but the report has a typo," said Sharon, getting fierce.

"So, why did you send it out then? It's signed by the Head Teacher," asked Mrs Rivera.

The Deputy Head interrupted nastily, "Guys, can I remind you this is a Christian school? You need to be less harsh on our admin staff; they're rushed off their feet dealing with serious educational issues, Jesus."

At that moment Pat sauntered past the office window off on a comfort break.

"Are you telling us the grade is a typo?" asked Mrs Rivera.

"Exactly!" replied Sharon.

"I'm sorry, but I don't believe you," stated Mr Rivera firmly.

"Well guys what we need to do is to think about what's best for Joel," continued Sharon ignoring the parents.

"So what are you suggesting?" asked Mr Rivera.

"We suggest he goes to a technical college to complete his education as he'll find it a lot easier in a place like that," said Sharon.

"But it's the same subject and the same curriculum," said Mrs Rivera who had done her research. "The course at the technical college is actually worth three A Levels," said Mrs Rivera.

"Yes, great isn't it?" said Sharon.

"And it's the same exam board?" said Mrs Rivera.

"Fabulous!" asserted Sharon.

"Well, how is it that he cannot manage one A Level here, but if he leaves he'll be able to do a qualification worth three A Levels?" asked Mrs Rivera incredulously.

"So they teach better over there?" said Mr Rivera simply.

"Mr Rivera, can I remind you again not to insult our staff, Jesus!" snarled Sharon.

"How would you explain it then?" asked Mr Rivera, staying calm.

"Well they are more used to dealing with students like Joel."

"So you are telling us that he will easily succeed in a three A Level course over at the technical college and yet a single A level course here is beyond his capability?" stated Mr Rivera. "Great, you've got it! We'll do the paperwork, so that's decided then guys I'm so sorry I've got to dash to an important meeting, you know child protection, can't discuss it, and I'm like back to back all day. So busy," and just like that, the Deputy Head ended the meeting.

Being in charge of IT, Sharon King felt exasperated as she had relied constantly on Darlene. Since Darlene had walked out, following the competency threat, Sharon was struggling with supply teachers. Time had come for the seen IT exam papers to be sent through to the students, in order for them to prepare for their database question.

"This is truly a lovely paper" trilled Sharon. "I don't think I've seen a better paper, now you need to go over it and work out all the formulas you'll need. I'm sure you'll all score well."

Joel felt uneasy in class and preferred not to ask questions for fear of annoying Mrs King. Therefore he got on as best he could and he had the support of Della, his Teaching Assistant, for half an hour a week. Yet Della spent most of her time looking beyond Joel through the window into the fields outside and replying to every one of his questions with

"Well, what do you think Joel?"

Having looked at the information, he decided to talk to his dad rather than Mrs King. He was concerned she would use his questioning as evidence of his failing.

Luis Rivera sat with Joel at the end of a long shift at the hospital. They looked at the seen exam materials and spreadsheet over a few evenings and felt happy with the questions. It looked very easy, working out the stages for a rally car race and ensuring all the different criteria were met. As Luis looked more at it and the structure of the exam, he did wonder whether there was another aspect that the students needed to know in order to calculate the results.

"Surely the teacher has taught you about the Vlookup function?" he asked.

"No," replied Joel.

"Are you sure, I don't see what else they could ask you, it would be logical."

The thought bothered him so he sent an email to Mrs King, who was in regular contact with him regarding his son's perceived lack of progress in IT.

Dear Mrs King

On the spreadsheet task for the exam (the rally race) we spent quite a bit of time on it over the weekend. Joel knows the equations and I'll go through it again with him this weekend

I wonder if in the exam they might give the actual race results for them to do some modelling on, like to calculate who wins the race after the different stages - do you think they will?

Best wishes

Mr Rivera

Very soon, according to the 24hour reply rule, Mrs King replied:

Dear Mr Rivera

Re: the exam, he will only have to complete the formulas in the model and to understand the key facts relevant to what the model does.

The model has no formulas on anything related to 'who wins the race', it is solely about planning the route of the 6 stages in the event.

Kind regards

Mrs King

Luis thought it was strange and was sure there must be more to this paper. Although he was not an IT aficionado he knew about the Vlookup function from his work at the hospital and went over it with his son as he felt that the exam board could well be asking for that skill.

CHAPTER 30 - STEPHANIE

Noëmi

Stephanie was refusing to talk to anyone and was spending all her break times in a stuffy little room away from her friends. Eventually it was decided to give the 'supervisor' a break and that Stephanie could spend some lunchtimes with her form tutor, Noëmi.

To tell her the news Noëmi went to the recently organised 'supervision centre' which was at the back of the school above the gym. It looked like it was an old store cupboard for PE items no longer needed. The hastily arranged room had a high ceiling but no natural light. A broken goal was in one corner along with punctured footballs and basketballs that no one thought to repair. Some items of discarded kit were in another corner, the 'supervisor' and Stephanie were at tables with uncomfortable looking chairs.

Noëmi saw Stephanie slumped over with her head buried in her arms, no earphones, no phone, just prostrate doing nothing. The teaching assistant come 'supervisor', Della, was on her phone but quickly put it away when Noëmi appeared.

To everyone's relief, Stephanie seemed delighted with the new arrangements. They began to watch films together, even though Noëmi was losing time on her work for this, Stephanie mattered more. 'Finding Nemo' was Stephanie's favourite and she began to smile.

"Nemo means 'no one' Miss," announced Stephanie.

"Yes in Latin," replied Noëmi.

"You speak Italian don't you, Latin is ancient Italian,"

"That's right, how did you know?"

"When you count out loud you do it in Italian and they say that if you are bi-lingual then you always count in your mother's tongue,"

"That's really insightful." Memories of Marcus came to her mind.

"What was Cambridge like?" she asked out of the blue.

"It was brilliant, hard work and loads of fun, are you thinking of applying?"

"If I get the grades."

"I hope you do," Noëmi was pleased that Stephanie was thinking about her future, "let's arrange to have a session to talk about what you need to be doing now to make sure you get in."

Stephanie smiled warmly back at her.

One lunchtime, Della, the TA, stopped to talk to Noëmi, on her way to pick up Stephanie.

"Oh hello Della can I help? Is it about Stephanie?" replied Noëmi.

"Yeah, she needs to have one to ones with the safeguarding officer, so she can't come to watch the films at lunchtime anymore," said Della flatly.

"Okay who decided that?"

"Not sure but I got an email yesterday telling me to let you know."

"Which safeguarding officer?"

"Jo… err … Mr Dyer," said Della.

"What does Stephanie think?" asked Noëmi.

"Dunno, it's just what has to happen in this kind of case," and she left, looking down at her phone.

Stephanie

Della needed to tell Stephanie about the new arrangements but had been busy messaging and left it to the last minute of lunchtime. The first bell went, which jolted Della out of her social media frenzy. Stephanie started getting ready to go to her next lesson.

"Oh we've got new arrangements for lunchtimes on a Monday now," blurted out Della.

"I go to Miss McAllister on Mondays," said Stephanie.

"Now you have a one to one with Mr Dyer, no more Nemo," said Della plainly

"What do you mean?"

"He has to talk to you each week and see how you are, innit," said Della trying to sound like a teenager.

"No I won't go, he stares at me."

"You have to."

"I'm telling you no!" shouted Stephanie.

"If you don't do as you're told, young lady, you'll be excluded from this school!" said Della, trying to sound tough, ignoring how fragile Stephanie was.

"Fuck this school! And fuck you! Nemo, that means no one, you're no one! You're not the boss of me, I'll exclude myself!" and with that, after weeks of steady progress, Stephanie kicked the door open, started walking along the corridor to the main entrance of the school. She walked boldly through the main visitors' reception, flinging the door behind her and exiting through the entrance which was forbidden for students to use. This shock caused receptionist, Jan Pritchard, to let out a small yelp of shock and to fumble for the phone to alert senior management.

Stephanie kept walking, just as Darlene and Ronnie had and did not stop, chucking her text books out as she went. Senior management, in the shape of Sharon King, arrived to see Stephanie far away in the distance emptying her school bag down the drive. Jan was sitting motionless, startled, with her mouth hung open like a baby bird. Della was looking down at her phone.

Noëmi

Frantic phone calls were made to alert Stephanie's mum and Guy, the Police Officer. A note was sent to Noëmi, as her form tutor, to attend an urgent meeting. Entering John's office, Noëmi, whose arms were full of things she had needed for her next lesson, missed her footing, stumbled over and dropped everything. Her planner, reward stickers and identity badge fell to the floor. She quickly scrambled to pick them up. Noëmi's cheeks reddened as she flustered around, then stood to attention given the serious stares of everyone around her. Guy looked at her with a ghost of a smile. Everyone sat down in John's office silently. Sarai brought in some water and tea and looked quietly at Guy and Noëmi who both nodded back to her.

"Terribly awkward this," started John.

Noëmi said to herself, *'You never feel awkward about anything.'*

"Right I need to know where she could have gone," said Guy, "Has she confided any special places to anyone?"

Della looked blank. Noëmi thought hard.

At that moment the door swung open and Jan Pritchard brought in Stephanie's mother who looked ashen.

"Who spoke to her last? We need a timeline," said Guy.

Maurice looked up from his paperwork, "Della she was with you?"

"Yeah," replied Della nonchalantly.

"How was she?" asked Guy, creasing his brow.

"She was fine, about to go to her lesson as the bell went and then she walked out,"

"This is very odd," said Stephanie's mum, Tessa, "she was really perking up."

"Right we need to talk to any of her friends," said John "What about Ronnie?"

Noëmi wondered how he knew Stephanie and Ronnie were friends.

"She doesn't have many," mentioned Tessa softly "Ronnie knows her but they annoy each other now. She refuses to have anything to do with him."

"Maybe in school but it's a start," replied Guy, "Let's get him here, from the rest of you I need accounts of your time with Stephanie and any information you think may be relevant."

Guy took the opportunity to talk quietly to Noëmi. She

remembered him from the memorial.

"Hello, spectacular entrance to the meeting just then!"

"Sorry I'm so clumsy, I completely careered over... so career over!" she laughed.

"Very drôle! How's Sarai getting on?"

"Well she's found out she's pregnant with Luca's child. It's been tough for her but this baby is giving her hope."

"Good, please let me know if she needs any support for anything...and you too, you know, for walking through doors!"

Noëmi smiled back.

Guy then went with Stephanie's mum to the police station, the others dispersed quietly from the meeting. Noëmi stopped to talk to Sarai. Della lingered in John's office and he shut the door behind them. Noëmi rolled her eyes at Sarai who smiled.

"Horrible man," said Noëmi.

"I know I avoid him since the time he tried to seduce me," admitted Sarai finally.

"No way! He tried it on? My God he's an animal. Did you report it?" asked Noëmi.

"Noëmi I'm too scared of losing my job because I hit him, who would believe me? He's like a God, he can do no wrong," Sarai sighed.

"Well that's not true, but you must report this behaviour, it's not safe for you to be near this monster," stated Noëmi.

"No, he avoids me now, which suits me fine, we communicate by email. You know I have things to tell you," said Sarai seriously.

"Let's meet up soon for a chat, I have to go now because my class was put on emergency cover for this meeting but I need to set them homework," said Noëmi at the same time desperate to know more.

"Okay..." Sarai began as an email from her boss pinged through.

'I'm in a meeting with the TA going over Stephanie's case, I'm not to be disturbed,' she read out loud, at the same time they heard the office door lock, Noëmi and Sarai looked at each other.

Sarai

Della left John's office with her head down, but not checking her phone for once. She slipped past Sarai, who said nothing. She noted that it was past four o'clock and Della usually left at 3:15pm on the dot. As she pondered her next move, a call came through from Stephanie's mum to say that her daughter was safe and had returned home. She would email formally but Stephanie would not be returning to school and she would like to make special arrangements for her exams. Sarai acknowledged this and made sure everyone knew that Stephanie was safe. This urgent news meant she would have to speak to John directly. She saw him walking out of his office, on his way to the bathroom and said as loudly as she could, without looking at him.

"She is safe and at home."

"What? Who?"

"Stephanie Smith." replied Sarai.

"Oh, they've found her," he said casually.

Almost immediately some parents of a student and their form tutor arrived for a meeting. John strode forward to greet them, shaking all their hands and led them into his office.

Sarai sat back and trembled. *People need to know what he is, I just can't carry on.'* Shuddering she listened to the muffled sounds of obsequious parents listening to the vaunting rhetoric of Mr John Dyer.

CHAPTER 31 - DOING THE RIGHT THING

Sarai

'Luca! I need to get to you, why have you not seen me? Why have you gone? Why did you not talk to me? Luca I can't understand you! What is that accent? Luca! I...I...,'

She sat up sweating, it took her a few moments to discern what was real and what was a nightmare. Tears fell from her eyes.

'How can I ever look after a child?'

Sarai's nightmares became even worse, since she had found the secret memory stick; she could not get the images from her mind. Her baby kicked and turned the more anxious she became. She was tired and confused. Sarai did not know what to do or to whom to turn as senior managers, John Dyer and Sharon King, were in charge of safeguarding. As usual she kept the thoughts to herself, afraid to speak of anything. However one wet Wednesday morning fate paid her a visit.

"Hello Sarai," chirped Sharon King, Deputy Head, who was walking past into John's office.

No one usually noticed Sarai, let alone spoke to her so she was taken unawares.

"Hello!" she managed in reply.

Sharon was in the office for about fifteen minutes. Then she came out and stopped to talk to Sarai.

"How's it going?"

"Yes, good, and how are you?" Sarai had learnt that you needed to ask the same question back in order to be polite.

"You know, snowed under, not sure how I've got the time to stop here to be honest but hey!" said Sharon.

'She always has to say how busy and important she is'. Sarai sighed to herself.

"Yes, yes, me too, so busy," Sarai had learnt that if someone went on about being overworked it was best to respond similarly.

"So how's it going working for John?" asked Sharon quite innocently.

Sarai misreading her friendliness took the moment, looked down and said,

"He's *a perv, a sex pest,*"

"Oh, oh... can I please remind you where you are and your position in this school," said Sharon, turning fierce and snarling at this tiny woman.

Sarai jumped back and replied with a suddenly very thick Vietnamese accent;

"Sorry, Sorry, my English, he's *superb, just the best* sorry!"

Sharon looked her up and down suspiciously and left saying nothing. Sarai felt a lump in her throat and grabbed a cereal bar to eat.

Within fifteen minutes Sarai had received an email from Deputy Head, Sharon King, asking her to come and see her. She pulled on her coat, although it was May, in order to cover up her pregnancy. Unsure of her rights, she was hiding her condition from the school. She walked to Mrs King's office.

Sharon King was in her very bare office, sitting in a chair which overlooked a low sofa. A small cactus was the only ornament on her desk. Through the dusty window Sarai saw the rain had stopped and sunlight now glistened on the leaves outside. Sharon welcomed Sarai and invited her to sit on the low sofa which meant she was towering over her. Sarai could see what this meant and felt her blood rise at how she was being treated. The scene was quite odd with the Sarai perched on a low sofa in a huge coat as the sun now burned into the small beige coloured office.

"How are you?" asked Sharon fakely with a false smile.

"Fine," said Sarai quickly.

"Okay, how's your new position going?" asked Sharon.

"It's great I love my job," lied Sarai putting on her accent again, just in case.

"Good and how do you get on with John?"

"Great," lied Sarai.

"Good, what do you think is his best quality?"

"Err...Mmm. I don't know there are so many," Sarai lied, accent falling away.

"Well, choose one."

"Mmm err...he is so... err ... good at IT!" Sarai managed struggling.

"Yes so important," replied Sharon, "You know Sarai, we're concerned that you are not 100 per cent for St Wolbodo's."

"No, no I am, I love the school, the kids are wonderful and there are so many lovely teachers, Frank, Noëmi, they're such great examples of dedicated professionals, you know the givers in life," Sarai retorted in perfect English.

"And is John one of them?"

"He is... err...mmm, special," spluttered Sarai.

"Of course, you know Sarai, we're concerned that you are not completely behind your boss."

"No Maurice can be a good Head Teacher I think," she replied, faking a bit of an accent again.

"I mean John."

Sarai looked into her lap and said nothing.

"I'd like to see some improvement in this area, you should be grateful for this job and this opportunity to be involved with senior management," said Sharon, "there are people queuing up for a job like yours."

Sarai said nothing and waited, looking at the floor.

"Do you want to tell me anything?" asked Sharon.

"No I love my job," lied Sarai.

"Okay, but I'll be looking for improvement, Sarai," said Sharon, nodding over her shoulder at the door, indicating that Sarai could leave.

Sarai took a deep breath and began.

"He tried to seduce me, locked me in the office. I had to fight to get away from him. Plus he has a memory stick with bad obscene child pornography pictures on it, weird sexual stuff. He keeps it locked in his desk drawer." Sarai blurted out with no accent,

269

putting her head in her hands, relieved to be sharing the awful information.

Sharon looked taken aback, said nothing, thought for a minute and replied.

"Sarai, do you have mental health issues? You're making some bold statements here."

Sarai looked down at her hands.

"The memory stick is bad, you need to see that," Sarai said, sacrificing herself, "He keeps it locked in his bottom drawer of his desk, you need to look at what he has on there."

Sharon stared coldly at Sarai.

'Not all men are perfect you know, some men need pornography, I suggest you take some time off and think carefully if you want to continue working here," said Sharon, ignoring the red flags Sarai had given.

"It's not women in the pornography, it's children. The girls are very young, that's all, children, so, please do something," said Sarai, knowing she was making it worse for herself but desperate to offload the terrible burden of what she had seen.

"Can I go now?"

Sharon

Sharon nodded at the door and Sarai rushed off, leaving Sharon to wonder what was going on in the office. Sharon, the Deputy Head, had admiration for John and how he managed to have such a powerful effect on staff and students alike. Given how easily he could control the students; their respect for his rules, she could not do without him.

When she spoke he would listen attentively looking deeply at her, he laughed loudly at her jokes and during one to one discussions he would lean in closely to her. Sharon in return got a flutter of excitement to have a good looking man, thirty years her junior, paying her such attention; in John's company she could be decades younger.

To hear Sarai talk like this shocked her and she did not know what to think. Could she be wrong about John? Many strong young men had desires and she could not see what would be wrong with John admiring the odd photo. Sharon began to imagine herself in his powerful arms, with his dark gaze looking down at her. She checked herself and felt herself blushing at the thought.

Again she shook herself to reality. What was she to do? She had not seen anything in his behaviour to concern her, surely Sarai must be mistaken? Sarai had been off work after Christmas, although Sharon could not remember why, and then a memory of the warm and friendly Christmas card John had left on her desk floated into her mind. How he had known what her favourite wine was she had no idea, but she had felt touched and a smile leaked onto her lips. John was a wonderful man and whatever Sarai thought she had imagined. Sarai must be mistaken, delusional even. She thought no further of Sarai's allegations. Opening her emails, she concluded that this was all down to mental health problems.

'Must be the stress of seeing how busy senior management are.'

CHAPTER 32 - BREAK IN

Noëmi

8 May 2017. The exam period approached with students and staff becoming increasingly nervous. Notices about revision sessions and posters with motivational advice were suddenly popping up in every corridor. All at once, students were wanting to buy revision guides, which stressed Pat out, as it meant that she had to work over lunchtime. In recompense she took her lunch hour between two and three pm. This meant her afternoon work amounted to a few minutes at the end of the day, excluding the time she took for a comfort break.

Noëmi arrived at school one morning to see a police patrol car outside and a couple of officers talking on radios. Students were being ushered in by Deputy Head, Sharon King who was acting like a policewoman taking control of this dramatic crime scene. She assured everyone,

"Nothing to see here guys, let's just get on with learning," which was of course the last thing the students wanted to do.

Noëmi went into the staffroom to find out what was happening. She met Frank who rolled his eyes. "The office of the great John Dyer was broken into last night, everything smashed up and ransacked, shame he wasn't in there really." Frank took a sip of his coffee.

Feeling her eyes widen, Noëmi began to wonder who could be behind this crime. Why John Dyer? Why his office only? Who had done this? Naturally everyone was thinking the same, although most thought it must be someone looking for a key to the safe, where the exam papers were being kept. Indeed the exam boards rushed representatives down to the school, where they spent the day cross checking all the papers for the centre, to verify that no exams had been taken or tampered with.

Meanwhile a rumour swirled round the school that the GCSE exams would be cancelled because of the break in. Another story was that all the papers were now on social media. Extra details were added and by ten past nine some had heard it confirmed *'that students across the country would be getting their mock grades'.*

Many were now in tears. By half past nine the school office was being called incessantly by worried parents, causing Pat to unplug all the phones and take an extra-long comfort break. The calls all then started going to Jan Pritchard in reception, who had no idea what to tell parents. After asking for help, she was told to say that the website would be updated as soon as possible. During this frantic toing and froing of information, speculation and rumours, teachers found it hard to settle their students. Many students decided to organise protests at the injustice of not being able to take their exams as planned.

Frank looked out at a group having a 'sit in' outside on the grass in the sunshine, and commented loudly,

"That's quite ironic, given the lack of homework Elizabeth Stoney has produced this year, her mock grade is probably higher than anything she'd get in the real exams."

"How so?" asked Noëmi.

"Well I had to be a bit generous otherwise she'd give up completely and that would leave five months of her disrupting my lessons. I think they call it *being positive.*"

The scene in John Dyer's office was catastrophic and he was attempting to clear up some of his belongings. He was very quiet and ashen faced when he realised some items were missing. Police were taking fingerprints and Sarai was equally shocked and pale, as she sat at her self-exiled desk, watching proceedings unfold. Sharon King was striding around throwing unfriendly looks at Sarai, no doubt wondering if this was anything to do with her. Pat spent the time live streaming her thoughts to anyone who would listen. "If people did an honest day's work, as I do, there'd be no crime. When I was young, if I stepped out of line I got a clip round the ear. Everyone just takes advantage of people like me working to earn an honest wage."

Finally she ended, "I just don't know how much longer I can go on being the one person in the school holding everything together."

Guy arrived and Sarai was desperate to talk to him about the memory stick and what she knew of John. However before she could, Sharon King ushered Guy into the scene of the crime. Sarai could hear muffled voices and sounds as if decisions were being made. As they left Guy stopped to speak to Sarai, with Sharon King remaining close by.

"How are you? Great news about yours and Luca's baby," he said with a warm smile.

"Baby?" echoed Sharon King.

"Yes, it was a shock but I'm happy."

"What's gone missing?" Guy's partner asked, as he passed by.

"Just the usual stuff, a laptop, computer equipment and some other things like a bottle of vodka, a few files, here's a list," he said as he handed over a piece of paper.

Sarai wondered if the memory stick was amongst the things missing.

"Do you want me to type it up for you?" she offered. 'It won't take a minute."

"Thank you, okay then," said Guy, handing the list to Sarai.

Nervously Sarai took the paper and glanced quickly up and down. She saw no mention of the memory stick, although clearly each drawer, locked or otherwise, had been ripped from the upended desk.

Sharon King stopped in front of Sarai's desk, she snarled in a loud whisper, "I hope all this havoc is nothing to do with you!"

She then left.

When the office was empty, Sarai checked the scene. The desk lay upside down and the upside of the drawer was visible, with sellotape hanging loose. The memory stick was gone.

John

Later John stood alone in his office and was also wondering who had been out to destroy his space. Out of the window he saw a large black crow looking through at him. He punched the window frame with his fist.

He, alone, had been targeted. Who could be behind this?

His thoughts turned to Maya, or Magda as he now preferred to think of her, especially as she had promised him sex in the office and was now ignoring him. He had seen that Noëmi was a mutual friend and this was bothering him. It was too much of a coincidence, too close to home, something was not right. He looked around the devastated office and picked up a few folders from the floor. He saw some pens and papers under the upturned desk and started picking them up. He noticed one of the small bits of paper was actually hard white plastic. Turning this over he saw it was an ID card for a member of staff. The name jumped out at him, *Noëmi McAllister*. That name again, what was happening here? Why was she connected with everything that was going wrong for him? Agitated after the disruption to his day, annoyed by the inconvenience of not having his private space and anxious about some items that were missing, he took his phone out. He looked Magda up and this time messaged her via social media, not the dating app.

'Hello, I got in contact with you via that dating app. I think you owe me an explanation. John.'

A few minutes later a message pinged back, *'Who is this?'*

'John' and then he sent a screenshot of her profile and another one of their conversation arranging to meet.

'WTF, I don't have a profile on that site.'

'Yeah right.'

'No I don't, you've been played,' Magda replied.

'How do I know you're not lying again?'

'Someone has faked a profile using my picture, plus my name is not Maya and I don't tell lies.'

'Why should I believe you?' threw back John

'I like women,' and Magda sent a screenshot of her profile from a lesbian dating app. *'Can you send me the details? I need to look into this, I'm angry, someone's been using me as a catfish.'*

'Alright, give me a few minutes and I'll send you everything I've got.'

He sent all the details to Magda who thanked him and then sent back jokingly, *'You perv, who wants sex on a some teacher's desk? Lol.'*

'Assistant Head actually.'

'Whatever, I'm annoyed at whoever's done this. I'll let you know what I get cheers.'

'By the way, how do you know Noëmi McAllister?' he messaged. Magda was now offline and John did not get an answer to the question that was tormenting him.

His mind turned back to how Noëmi was connected so conveniently to Magda. John brooded on this and was angered by thoughts that raged in his head of a conspiracy between the women. He was determined to know more and also to find out who was behind the vandalism of his office. John quickly decided it was unlikely to be Magda as she lived in Bristol. He could see that she had been in the gym the previous evening, as she had posted her training statistics on her social media.

With Maya and therefore Magda out of the picture, John began to think who else would want to get back at him. A number of women came to his mind. However most of them he thought were either too *'unimaginative'* or *'stupid'* to cause this kind of destruction. He could only conclude that it must have been the jealous boyfriend or husband of one of them and that this third party was responsible. Whilst this gave him some relief, he was bothered about the things that were missing and he wondered who had them. Being without control was an unusual and uncomfortable place for John.

The mess was tidied up, the damage repaired and St Wolbodo's swung into full exam season. There were pre-exam breakfasts, last minute catch up sessions and weighty revision guides finally ready for students to collect.

CHAPTER 33 – WISDOM

Marcus

June 2017. During the Trinity term Marcus had focused ferociously on his work. Nothing was more important to him. Finally the exams were over, his elective done and he passed with a flourish. He had gained a First in medicine, much to the delight of Raeni and his whole family. Trashing done; he was beginning his new job straight away. Donnie and Anthony had helped him move into a rented flat in the Jesmond area of Newcastle, a twenty minute walk from Royal Victoria Infirmary (RVI). He was now a Junior Doctor.

Marcus was on a shift in A&E as part of his training; he was exhausted. The day was getting busy. First a baby with suspected Meningitis. Marcus carefully followed his protocol for such cases; the baby was fine. The parents, relieved and grateful, thanked him most sincerely. Next, a head wound on a toddler who had fallen off a sofa. He comforted the mother who was upset about the accident and who blamed her husband. Marcus could still hear her telling him off as they left. Next was a teenage boy, who had decided to experiment with gin, wine and beer in quick succession. Having put the young lad on a drip he consoled his mother who had no idea 'why he had helped himself to the contents of their drinks' cupboard. Finally he was done, but he had a medical examination of his own to attend.

St Woldbodo's got on with the exams and the school was bubbling with tension. Frank's husband Val, unconcerned by all this hysteria, enjoyed the calm of his dental practice. This was based near Newcastle RVI, so a number of NHS employees were patients. Today one of those was Marcus, whose wisdom teeth had been playing up.

"Ah my friend, come on in, pop yourself in the chair, don't worry I'll be gentle. I know you doctors are the worst patients!" Val was pleased to see Noëmi's friend, having recognised the name on his list. "This man is my friend, so only the best treatment, just in case we end up in his department one day!" Val joked to Solange, his Dental Nurse.

"Thanks Val, I know I'm a real wimp when it comes to drills and things."

"Don't fret, I only over drill and under anesthetise people I don't like, so stay on my good side!" he joked.

Marcus was unsure if he was serious or not but did not intend to find out.

Marcus opened his mouth.

"Oh nice teeth, someone has good hygiene, I love it. At our next party I'll tell you some horror stories!" Val was enjoying himself here.

Marcus, although unable to respond, felt a bit happier.

"Now these wisdom teeth, oh yes, luckily they're not impacted but the lower two will need to come out as they are growing at an angle, so at some point they will push into the other teeth and we can't have that. Now how much pain are you in?"

"Yes a fair bit but I'm using some gel."

"Of course, perfect, you docs are always ahead on the pain relief!

I guess you can grab some at work; perk of the job!"

"Well yes and no, I did go and buy some, but I knew exactly what to get from the chemist."

"You see Solange, so honourable. I've been telling her all about you. Now we need to make some appointments for you to come in and we'll whip those out, first I need to take two images so just one moment." Val made it all sound so straightforward.

Val and Solange did all the necessary for the two X-rays.

"Solange please get the diary for me," and the nurse popped out.

"How are you Marcus?"

He began to think this was no longer about his teeth.

"Yeah okay, working hard, busy over there you know."

"Well personal happiness is so important too. Don't forget that! So many sad people. Such a shame. Sometimes people just need to talk and then before you know it people are all jolly again! So, for example, if you were feeling, maybe, a bit melancholy, you could talk to your friend! Now let me think, oh, say Noëmi, and you would feel better! Also if she was, for any reason, feeling extremely low, as she has been recently, she would feel much improved too, does that make sense?"

"Thanks Val, it's all been a bit of a mess. I don't know what to think, there was something going on with her and someone else at New Year and I didn't realise."

"What?" Val looked stunned, for once he had no words.

"I came back to Newcastle, for her, I just need to work through it."

"I don't understand she's been single forever!" Val was

incredulous.

"But thanks, I appreciate it, I really do."

Val was dumbfounded, after a few moments he managed, "Please make the appointments with Solange on your way out."

Astounded Val sat down and messaged Frank.

Frank replied that he had no idea what to make of Marcus' comment.

Vlookup. For one student, Joel, exam time at St Wolbodo's was bittersweet as he would almost certainly be moving on afterwards.

The day of Joel's seen IT exam came and he was fully prepared for the paper, having worked tirelessly to master the formulas. He turned over the paper and worked steadily through it. Upon reaching Question 3, the modelling question, he came to a halt. The question asked for the results based on the information given in each stage. Initially he had no idea how to approach this and started frantically trying to add up all the scores but realised this was taking way too long. Then he remembered his father showing him how to do the Vlookup function. He got himself into the swing of this and did what he could. Joel realised the rest of his class would be completely stumped as they had not been taught anything about Vlookups.

Sitting in her office at the end of the exam day, Mrs King opened the exam paper. One student had come to her office and knocked, which she ignored, but she wondered what they had wanted. She looked through the paper she smiled to herself, pleased that she had cleverly worked out the first question. However her smile dropped when she got to Question 3 and saw the question asking for results, which would require the Vlookup skill.

"Damn, we can't teach these idiots everything in five hours a week," she said out loud to herself. Her sick feeling became panic for herself. She quickly turned to her computer, did a search on her email for Mr Rivera and deleted all emails either from or to him, lest her incompetency be discovered.

'No proof of anything at all,' she thought. All feelings of responsibility left her, although she knew deep down, as an IT 'expert', that deleting emails did not mean they no longer existed, but at least they would not bother her.

CHAPTER 34 - VAL'S BIRTHDAY

Frank

Exams had been stressful for all concerned. To ease the strain Frank had arranged a small Sunday lunch gathering, for about fifteen close friends. This would take place at his and Valentino's exquisite Durham townhouse, which was set on three floors, overlooking the River Wear. The lunch was also to celebrate Valentino's birthday which coincided nicely with the end of exams. Having mutual friends meant that Marcus and Noëmi would be coming together for the first time since New Year's Eve and Luca's memorial. Marcus phoned to accept and asked if he could bring a guest. Unable to help himself, Frank had replied *'Of course, no problem, I'll make sure I tell Noëmi so she's prepared. You know she still has feelings for you.'*

Noëmi

Noëmi had been delighted that Ronnie and Stephanie had come in for all their exams. Both had special arrangements; Stephanie took hers in isolation and Ronnie had taken some entry level exams with a reader. Ronnie dropped by Noëmi's classroom to say goodbye.

"I want to do well in life." He looked out of the window at the late June sunshine.

"Good, your mum wants you to be more settled."

"She worries too much." Ronnie turned in his chair to look at his teacher and smiled warmly.

"Mum's do though."

"Does your mum worry about you working in a shithole like this?" He gestured at the rundown classroom with its mismatched tables and broken blinds.

Noëmi smiled at Ronnie's description of the school.

"Actually my mum died of blood cancer when I was thirteen Ronnie."

"Sorry Miss." He looked shocked and genuinely concerned.

"No. It was hard and I miss her. And yes my dad worries about me the *whole* time!"

"Suppose so, my mum thinks I'll get into trouble, but I want to do plumbing, make money, help her out. My brothers and sisters have to go to school and learn. She lets them get away with too much. She's actually pretty useless, but she loves us."

"Well you're really turning things around Ronnie, keep up the good work!" She stood up, indicating he was free to leave.

"Sure, I won't let you down Miss."

He ran from the form room and immediately Noëmi could hear the cacophony of Ronnie meeting up with his friends. Flopping back into her chair she smiled.

No sooner had she got back to marking books, when Frank arrived.

"It gets worse, the more I teach them, not better!" Noëmi gave him a cheeky smile.

Frank looked forlornly at her and sat down on the chair next to her. "This is hard to say."

"What?" her eyes widened.

"On Sunday, Marcus is bringing someone he's been seeing for about a month; her name is Shauna. I wanted to warn you."

Her heart stopped. Noëmi turned away, she could feel her lip quivering.

"Maybe it's best I give it a miss."

"Noëmi, as the host, I can tell him no."

She thought for a minute; she had to face up to her failure to win his heart.

"No Val would want us both there, time for me to be a grown up eh!" Throat lumpy she saw the kindness in Frank's eyes. He gave her a hug.

"I understand it's hard after the New Year debacle. He seems to think you were involved with someone else then?"

Noëmi gave a start, "What? The only relationship I have is with this job! Why would he think that?"

She began to tidy her desk. "If we could have talked, it would have helped but now he's involved with someone else. I can't interfere."

"You know I really admire the respect you have for others." Frank sighed.

Nodding, with her eyes welling up, she said 'thank you' to her friend but no words came out.

Noëmi was nervous about seeing Marcus after so much time; she thought of nothing else.

Sunday 2 July 2017. To keep some aspects of the lunch secret from Valentino, Frank arranged for Noëmi to get his husband out of the house. Frank decided a long road cycle that morning would do the trick. Noëmi had dropped her things off the day before and duly took Valentino on a fifty kilometre ride over the County Durham countryside. A puncture delayed them by about half an hour so when they arrived back the guests were already assembled. Noëmi trembled as she locked up her bike, walked to the house and took off her cycling shoes.

As they walked into the hall Val exclaimed.

"Quanto amo mio marito!" Tears sprung to his eyes.

"Così bello!" She replied, voice shaking as they saw the magnificent balloon arch Frank had organised to surprise Valentino. Rushing to hug his husband Val left Noëmi alone. Immediately she saw Marcus standing with the redheaded Shauna, whom she had first seen in the restaurant at Easter. Luckily, he did not see her and she rushed upstairs to get changed.

Marcus

Marcus was determined to move on.

However, in the run up to Val's party he was anxious. He was nervous about seeing Noëmi after so much time; he thought of nothing else.

As she arrived back from her cycle, Marcus instantly saw through the window in her lycra. His mind wandered *'God she looks just gorgeous. So toned, her plaits look cute. Well Shauna's a personal trainer so being physically fit is not an unusual thing…'*

Valentino apologised profusely for his lateness.

"A small technical issue," he explained.

"Isn't that your day job? Small technical issues!" Frank joked back.

"A puncture is never easy, but luckily I had Noëmi with me and she got it fixed."

"You always need help Val!"

"Indeed, it would appear I can only repair teeth!" and everyone laughed.

Marcus was unsettled, she was now mending bikes. *'Many people can do this kind of thing,'* he reasoned to himself.

Noëmi showered, changed and quickly brushed her hair out and then came in nervously to the gathering. Marcus raised an eyebrow to say 'hello' and turned quickly back to the conversation he was having with Valentino's practice hygienist about flossing.

Valentino called over to Noëmi, "Tutti dovrebbero avere un bellissimo meccanico di bici come te Noëmi," as they had spent the morning conversing in their language.

She replied, "Sei il fortunato non dimenticarlo!"

Now she was speaking other languages that he could not understand. Marcus, unnerved, told himself, *'Well of course she's clever, it's what attracted me to her in the first place. All my Oxford friends are intelligent. Nothing remarkable there.'*

"A drink Marcus?"

"No thanks Val, I'm on duty at six, a week of nights!"

"Ah you should've been a dentist, no one wants their teeth done at antisocial hours!"

"Yeah although many of the people I see on nights end up

needing exactly that!"

Solange and her partner now joined their fun group. Shauna was laughing and talking to the hygienist's partner, she was bubbly and relaxed.

"Hair of the dog!" she laughed as lycra clad Valentino kindly filled her glass again.

Noëmi

Shauna was tall with stunning, long, flowing red hair. She looked trendy in painted on jeans and a well-tailored top. Noëmi suddenly felt very boring in her old floral tea dress. Noëmi's hand was shaking as she put her gift for Valentino on the table. She then took a drink and sat in the corner on the soft white sofa next to Sarai.

"Sarai, how are you feeling?"

"I can't really stand for long, I'm thirty-five weeks now, excited but anxious. Plus it's day one hundred and ninety-two of being without Luca…"

Noëmi pulled her friend in for a hug.

"What about you? Frank told me about Marcus bringing the guest."

"Yeah, not great to be honest, she looks vaguely familiar, but I can't place her."

"She likes her wine!" Sarai sighed.

Noëmi looked away and wondered what Shauna was like. Sarai whispered the odd comment about Shauna in her ear every so often.

"Look! Another huge glass of wine and no food," she murmured, scowling at Shauna.

Frank came and sat with them and squeezed Noëmi's hand.

"I can arrange a hit if you'd like, I tell you Val has connections, the world of Italian dentistry is very dark you know."

Noëmi tried to smile and shook her head.

"Honestly, I guess it wasn't meant to be. As long as he's happy that's the main thing."

Marcus

Marcus noticed Valentino open Noëmi's gift. He realised how well Noëmi knew her friends as it was a large coffee table book about the entire history of Eurovision, complete with a DVD. Val was overwhelmed with delight and gave Noëmi a huge embrace. *'She really knows how to make people happy, her birthday gift to me was just perfect'.* Val insisted on putting on the DVD and dancing around to various songs whose complete backstory he knew.

The sun glistened on the marble fireplace and Noëmi started to chat quietly with the group of friends. Inevitably, given the small number at the gathering, they all had to face each other. Noëmi sat forward on the sofa which seemed to be eating her up. Marcus found it hard to look at Noëmi, given the effect she was having on him. He thought she was looking beautiful with soft curls framing her face and a feminine dress that showed her figure well. The silver heart necklace, she had got repaired, rested gently just below her neck. He noticed her chest rising and falling as she breathed shallowly. Again he told himself, *'many women are good looking and I know I've never been attracted to anyone else in the way that I am to her, both physically and emotionally…'* He noticed her eyes looked sad and she kept them lowered when he came over.

He gave her a quick peck on the cheek to say 'hello' she smelt fresh and lovely. Playing with his glass of water he thought to himself, *'looks can be deceptive'*. A memory of her intently messaging John Dyer on her phone and offering to send him naked pictures came to his mind. *'Shauna Is the kind of girl people like me go out with. She's fun, fit and flirty... mature and self-assured...steady job and a large group of friends. This is the type of grown up life a man of my age and position should be enjoying. It feels so strange and uncomfortable but hopefully I won't be this unhappy for too much longer, I need to protect myself from scheming people.'*

Euphoria played out with Val singing along.

"Sarai, Noëmi, this is Shauna,"

"Hello," they both replied.

Although he had written her a note he said.

"Thank you for the birthday gift again. It was perfect," he wanted to add *'like you'*.

"What did she get you?" Shauna asked, refilling her wine glass.

"An album of the photos from my travels around Vietnam and Cambodia. It must've taken ages,"

"What was the point of that? It's not like she was there!" Shauna quipped.

Marcus looked away.

Each photo was printed out, dated with the time, place and the **What3words** for each location, which he loved. A caption from the accompanying message that he had sent her was underneath. Noëmi nodded and looked down;

"Sorry I had to change the messages a bit, I didn't know who might be reading it." She turned her glass in her hands.

He had noticed that she had edited out the words of affection *'and yet so much love went into this gift'.*

"Yes, I saw."

Taking a gulp of wine, Shauna asked them, "Did you both come alone?"

"Oh us? Yes, yes," Noëmi jumped in immediately.

"No partner either of you? Not seeing anyone? What about you, there's obviously someone responsible for your condition!" Shauna laughed, pointing at Sarai, who recoiled slightly in shock.

Before Marcus could change the subject, Noëmi rescued Sarai.

"Oh no. God no time for relationships, teaching is very intense and anti-social. I bet if you ask Val he'll tell you how awful it is to be married to a teacher. The amount of work you have to take home in order to do the job properly is insane. A friend of mine in maths wanted to go part time to see her children more because..." she kept on talking about anything for no reason other than to protect Sarai from getting interrogated on this painful subject. Marcus knew exactly what she was doing.

"...I've been single since I started at the school... such fun," she continued.

Marcus raised his eyebrows. What was she saying here? Her relationship with Jesse had broken up when he let her down the weekend of her birthday. Yet what about John Dyer? She gave no indication of this liaison. Was she now a liar?

"Yeah, the gym's not like that. That's where I work," replied Shauna, finishing her wine, "there are loads of people to meet, I got 20 Valentine cards this year." She seemed to have missed Noëmi's point.

"Great I'll have to work at a gym," joked Noëmi and off she went again "I'm a Valentine's disaster zone. My dad sent me a card when I was fourteen. I don't think that counts. He was trying to make me feel better as I was very low then, but I knew it was from him as he signed it *'love Dad'* which kind of gave the game away..."

Shauna turned to fill her wine glass.

"I sent you some." Marcus said quietly, looking directly at her. Noëmi took a sharp intake of breath.

Marcus felt his chest tighten and his heart racing. He shut his eyes. What a fool he had been. She was not lying about anything. He understood that meeting him with Shauna must have been so hard for Noëmi. Her feelings had never changed. He put himself in her place, and reflected on his own actions, justified by her *'sharing her bed with John Dyer'*. For exactly six months he had ghosted her. From warmly reciprocating her love to freezing her out; how that must have hurt. Now she was determined to help out Sarai in what must have been the most painful of meetings. Her humility had torn down the last of his defences.

'I'm so utterly ashamed of my cruel behaviour, I can't believe how I've treated her, how I've ignored her. She is the first and only woman I've ever loved, we've shared everything, my feelings have never changed. I love her. She's the only one I'll ever love. I can't imagine my life without her. Nothing matters anymore, naked pictures, relationships with John Dyer, nothing.'

Noëmi

Noëmi was overwhelmed, Shauna not having heard Marcus' comment began talking about herself again. Shauna was getting louder and slurring slightly. She steadied herself on the arm of the sofa.

"At the gym. That's how I met my Marcus," Shauna said, smiling at him.

Marcus looked uncomfortable.

"A mutual friend set us up on a blind date. He was trying to get over the last girl, he caught her sexting," Shauna had no filter and Marcus looked horrified. Noëmi was confused, Sarai even more so.

Was she thinking of Hilary? In her polo neck sweaters, she did not strike Noëmi as someone who would take, let alone send a naked picture in a million years. Her brow furrowed as she tried to figure this all out, Marcus had not mentioned anything like this to her and they had still been close at that point. Shauna then continued in a kind of stage whisper to Noëmi and Sarai,

"I think it's affected him as he's a bit slow off the mark, if you know what I mean. Most men want to get me into bed the first time I see them," she said pointing at her body, "But not him, I'm still waiting but I think it'll be worth it, don't you girls?" Shauna overshared then adding "unless he's struggling with his sexuality?"

"Maybe he's a gentleman?" suggested Sarai.

"God yes but we all have needs now don't we ladies," Shauna had obviously decided Noëmi and Sarai were her new best friends. Noëmi was not sure what of this Marcus had overheard but he looked quite alarmed.

Before anyone could say anything else, Shauna pointed at Noëmi and shrieked;

"Oh my God, were you at Newky Green? You were, weren't you? Oh my God it's you, you were in the year above me!"

Marcus definitely heard this and immediately looked round, Noëmi felt her throat tighten and her palms got sweaty.

"Gross Moron, it's you!" Shauna said in the loudest voice possible, as if they were long lost friends.

The room went quiet and everyone looked round as Shauna's voice got louder and louder, partly thanks to the bottle of wine she had now drunk.

"You were the one everyone bullied, 'Gross Moron', we called you, 'Gross' for short, that was so funny, we had a secret club in our year and you could only be in it if you swore you hated Noëmi McAllister," she continued oblivious and insensitive to the fact that no one could ever want to be reminded of, or if they were unaware, informed of, things like this.

Silence, followed by more long silence.

Trapped, sunk into the luxurious white leather sofa with Shauna standing over her, Noëmi was completely humiliated. The seconds that followed lasted hours. Marcus had a look of horror on his face. Shauna was laughing, congratulating herself upon noticing the coincidence. Sarai was extremely confused. Frank, Valentino and the others all looked embarrassed and bewildered. Marcus quickly took charge of the situation.

"You need to go outside now and wait for me there!" he said to Shauna sternly. "We have to go straight away."

"Oh for fuck's sake!" Shauna replied angrily, clearly unable to think what the problem was and she downed the rest of her wine in one, grabbed her bag and stomped outside.

"Noëmi I am so, so sorry," he said in all honesty, evidently reeling that he had not been able to protect her.

Frank quickly started talking, loudly;

"Well the Tour de France is just going to be spectacular this year, so many talented cyclists who all unfortunately suffer with asthma!"

Valentino helped, "You're such a cynic, sport asthma is a thing you know. Anyhow, the Giro D'Italia is far superior because it's in Italy. This other so-called tournament is meaningless!"

Many groans followed.

Marcus went to Noëmi. Kneeling before her, he put his hand on her arm.

"I, I…don't want you to feel sorry for me," Noëmi could barely talk, she gave up, everything was too much, she hung her head and large hot tears filled her eyes. Sarai hugged her friend.

"I have to take her home but I won't be seeing her again." Marcus stated firmly.

Sarai hauled herself off the sofa to tactfully get a glass of water and left Marcus and Noëmi to talk by themselves.

Marcus sat down next to her and turned towards her. Noëmi could not look up. His hand brushed the side of her cheek gently and a large tear flooded out onto his fingers.

"I'm sorry for your relationship, I ruin everything it seems," she finally said.

"No it's not serious. You need to be aware of that…"

"It's really none of my business, it's your life Marcus, you're free to do as you wish," she whispered.

"We have to talk, there's things I need to say to you, I have a night shift now but I really need to see you. Just us. Like we were before."

Noëmi sighed, "I'm not sure it's that easy."

"I've been so cruel in how I've treated you and I feel utterly ashamed of myself," he admitted.

"But that was your choice, you could have talked things over with me. I still have absolutely no idea what terrible thing I've done to deserve such treatment. Can you imagine how that feels? No chance to put things right, that hurts! Especially when it's us!" She said simply.

"Noëmi I know I've made so many mistakes, please!"

She took him into her arms. They held on for as long as they could, feeling each other's breathing. She felt his skin on hers and his heart beating fast. Marcus clutched onto her desperately.

"Noëmi I have missed you so much," he told her as they unlocked from their embrace, she could not reply, everything was too raw. The taxi pinged through and he had to take Shauna to her home and go to work.

He thanked Frank and Val and apologised for the behaviour of Shauna and for bringing her. As he left he looked round. Noëmi's head hung low.

Frank went over to Noëmi who remained quiet following Shauna's detailed public derision.

"What a lovely girl!"

"So tactless and blessed with an elephantine memory," Noëmi managed to say.

"Maybe I'll organise that hit after all," Frank said back and Noëmi tried to smile.

Frank held her as she rested gently in his arms, letting out little sobs every now and then. The rest of the party had moved into the small riverside garden that Valentino had done out like an Italian terrace. His favourite plant was the white lilac, which had grown from a cutting from Donnie's garden. It was already taking well in the wonderful green backdrop of shrubs and bushes. Olive trees and fig trees lined the sides and the south facing aspect caught the best of the British climate. Val was complaining that his lemon trees could only grow in a greenhouse in this 'shocking English weather'. As the evening drew in, Noëmi and Frank could hear their friends' distant chatter whilst they sat together looking out onto the warm setting sun.

CHAPTER 35 - SHOWTIME

John

John had received a message from Magda who was incandescent with rage that her pictures had been used on a fake profile.

'John, I'm kind of grateful to you, I suppose, for letting me know about this shit and I can tell you I want to rough up whoever's behind this, but I guess you do too as this person has fucked you over big time. So I checked with the police and it's not illegal to use someone else's pics on a dating profile, apparently lots of people do it. It's not nice they said, like yeah! You should be able to see from the IP address where the messages were coming from, so I'd check with your IT department. That Naomi person I don't know her really, I just met her at a yoga camp a couple of years ago and we all hung out and added each other on social media. She's not a proper friend. I've not had any contact with her since. She was nice I thought, but not into girls so that was that. Anyway if you find out anything I'd be interested to know what went on here. I'm changing all my privacy settings now. Good luck Sherlock and have a great sex session on that desk with anyone other than me!'

John smiled, he liked Magda's style and felt certain she had no interest in destroying his office. Indeed her references seemed to confirm she knew nothing of his vandalised desk. He was inspired by her idea to check out the IP address, so he went to see Steve, one of the IT technicians, with Maya's first message.

Steve was a sallow looking, self-professed IT geek in his late twenties, who enjoyed taking computers apart and rebuilding them. The IT office on the top floor of the school was alive with bits of equipment whirring, buzzing and flashing. Steve sat up there with two other IT workers who played online games all day. The whole area was hot, very untidy with boxes of leads and cables, piles of papers and old coffee cups everywhere. Photos of the IT boys on various nights out and daytime bonding activities filled the walls, along with large posters warning;

'IT problem? Send a ticket' and **'Need IT help? Send a ticket.'**

John walked into the IT den without knocking. He found Steve, sitting, headphones on, clicking through a series of screens as he hummed along tunelessly to whatever music he was listening to. He turned round unapologetically and pointed at a seat. Taking off his headset he began.

"It's busy up here. Since Darlene left we spend all our time trying to sort out all those IT teachers who don't know anything. Darlene was the only decent one," said the IT technician, completely unaware of the events that had led to her walking out and never coming back.

"So I got this message and I'd like to know if you can see what device it came from, you know from the IP address?" said John ignoring the first comment.

"Got a ticket?" Steve asked.

"No bruv, too busy," John said.

Steve sighed. Everyone knew that senior management never followed the rules like the rest of the staff, always assuming they were a priority. He took the laptop.

"You look like someone I should more than just know..." the IT technician read the message.

"Wow hot bird, you suit guys get all the luck."

"Yeah well not that great actually," said John trying to avoid any further messages being seen.

The IT guy did some clicking through some black and yellow looking web pages and wrote down a long number which he then entered into an IP lookup function.

"Well it's been sent from one of our devices, I would need more information to pinpoint which one, you'd have to give me full access to the accounts."

"It's alright, I think I know what's been going on. Cheers!" said John and he left the dingy, little IT office. As he walked away, he smiled to himself and said quietly "Okay showtime..."

Frank

Goodbye... Frank was finishing up on a Friday afternoon. His lab was neatly laid out with light blue melamine tables and neat displays of work. Around the top edges of the walls he had rows of inspirational quotes from great authors and scientists whom he admired. When he struggled he would bolster himself up with these words and they truly motivated him. It was early July, the exams were over and he was getting the results for different year groups into the spreadsheet, for the final end of year reports.

As Frank got to his final set of data, he was on the home straight. He was looking forward to a weekend with Val, when Joel walked in.

"Do you have a minute sir?" he asked.

"Well it depends who's asking now!" replied Frank with a smile "Come on in Joel, just leave the door open okay."

Frank knew all the rules.

"I've come to say thank you and goodbye sir," Joel handed over a small box of chocolates.

"Oh! So you *are* leaving us?"

"Yes I'm hoping to go to the technical college and get my A levels finished there."

"Well I'm very sad to hear that and I hope that you can get onto the course there."

"Same, I just need to see if I can sort it all out on Monday. I've just seen the Deputy Head, Mrs King, and she's writing to my mum, but her decision is final."

"Even before any results come out..."

"I know, but I need to hope it'll all work out. I'll just do the three A Level IT course."

"You know they have a great team over there; their A Level section is top notch."

"Thanks sir, I would've preferred to stay here but it was getting me down all the emails home about how I 'don't have a pen', 'don't have any idea what the questions are asking' and all that. It's relentless."

"I understand Joel, we'll miss you from the form group and I hope you get on well. Keep in touch in case you ever need any help. I'll be here to write any reference you need."

"I think Mrs King says she has to write my reference."

"Of course..." said Frank, angry at what he was hearing.

"But in the future if you need any help you can come to me, you have my school email address. I won't be going anywhere for a

301

while, unless I win the lottery, of course, in which case I'll be off!"

Joel laughed, 'I'll hunt you down sir."

"Keep safe and remember one thing, as Buddha said '*Three things cannot hide for long: the Moon, the Sun and the Truth.*' Got that?"

"Very intellectual sir!"

Joel smiled and left. Frank sat back in his chair and sighed. His eyes went from the small box of chocolates to the card with its mismatched envelope. He would miss a polite, hardworking student like Joel, whose future really depended on the reliable input of adults during his education. He made a note to mention him to his friends over at the technical college but was aware it was a huge place. He exhaled deeply and looked up at his classroom display of inspirational quotes, one jumped out at him instantly.

'In a time of deceit, telling the truth is a revolutionary act.'
George Orwell

Frank knew immediately what to do.

Noëmi

Friday, late afternoon, Noëmi was also busy getting her final assessment results into the various databases before the deadline at six that evening. Marcus had sent two huge bouquets of flowers, one to her and one to Frank and Val, to apologise for the birthday debacle. The card for Noëmi read;

'Please forgive me. I've been heartless, selfish and immature. I need to see you, all my love Mx.'

He messaged her every day to apologise for Shauna's behaviour numerous times. He wanted to meet up to talk as soon as possible. Noëmi was keen to meet him but their work patterns were genuinely incompatible that week. Marcus was working nights and Noëmi each day. All week she was out on end of term day trips to a high ropes activity centre with the younger year groups. Then she needed time at the end of each day to get all her marking finished and the results entered.

She was glad for the space however, as Shauna's outburst had brought back painful memories. Once again the reminder of the bullying made her feel worthless.

'Maybe he just feels sorry for me…'

Entering the final end of year grades for her classes she had an hour to go. Her hands hurt as she had blistered them abseiling with a group of twelve year olds. In order to lighten the mood from Marcus' intense messaging, she sent him a picture of her hands with a note.

'Abseiling with Year 7, living the dream!'

He messaged back straightaway. **'Come to A&E now and I will make you better xxx'**

She smiled for the first time in a week and wished she could just go. Maybe things were getting back on track.

The work to complete all the spread sheets was relentless and she had already spent countless evenings marking the numerous assessments. Exhausted, she sat at the computer in her classroom, which was growing colder in spite of the early July evening sun.

Suddenly a message pinged through on her computer. Tempted to ignore it, she clicked to see who was contacting her on a Friday evening.

'Come to my office now for an important meeting,' with the formal signature of **John Dyer, Assistant Head Teacher and Lead in Child Protection and Safeguarding, St Wolbodo's School**

- *Everything right for everyone.*

Confused and feeling sick, Noëmi wondered what to do. She had to get her data entered, so she decided to finish up and then go to his office. Noëmi was engrossed in her Year 9 spreadsheet when an ominous yet familiar figure appeared at her door. She looked up and saw John Dyer filling her escape route.

"So Nemo or whatever your name is," he started aggressively.

"Yes?" she squeaked her throat tightening.

"Nemo means 'no one', just like you, a nobody," John obviously thought he was being clever.

"I believe so in Latin," her voice trembled, but she could see he was not here for a language lesson.

"Did you see my message?" he asked plainly.

"Yes but I…" she stuttered, unable to lie as he bored his eyes into her.

"Well did you understand it?"

"Yes but I have to get these results in before 6pm so…"

"So I have to wait for you?"

Noëmi had no reply.

"A Senior Manager sends through an urgent request and you ignore it?"

Noëmi hated him even more but felt awkward as she was used to doing the right thing.

"Never mind, I'll tell you that you are hereby suspended from teaching. You will be investigated for destruction of property. I have the paperwork here so I am issuing it now."

Her mouth got dry, her heart began to race and she could feel herself hyperventilating.

"What? You can't suspend me...I've not done anything wrong and HR have to be here anyway for something like that," said Noëmi, her voice thin and raspy.

"Well, let's think about that shall we? Evidence you were at the scene of the crime," he said holding up her lost ID card. "Not the behaviour we expect of a teacher."

"That has got nothing to do with me, I lost my card that's all."

"Evidence that you've been misusing your school laptop to solicit sex."

Feeling her colour and panic rise, she lied, "I don't know what you're talking about."

"We have the messages you've been sending from your school laptop. The IT technicians have all they need," said John sternly.

"I have evidence the senior manager was keen...and joined in enthusiastically. So I'm told by a friend," replied Noëmi slowly.

"As part of our behaviour observation strategy the manager in question was instructed to play along so that we could gather evidence and catch the person responsible."

"Of course..." said Noëmi flushed, eyes burning.

"So basically, you're suspended with immediate effect or you have the option to quit, given that the harassment has extended to destruction of school property," said John.

"I had nothing to do with that," said Noëmi quickly.

"Well the evidence points to an inside job and an investigation will be carried out and criminal charges brought. You're in a lot of trouble **No-enemy**, actually you've made plenty of enemies now haven't you? Sorry, what should I call you? Maya?" said John.

"So...I'll think about it all over the weekend thank you," said Noëmi slowly. "I need to finish these assessment reports now."

John seemed annoyed that there had not been more fireworks and stayed to torment her further. "Whatever happens this'll be on your record, so your teaching career is over. You'll have a criminal record. Nemo, just a little nobody, you'll almost certainly go to jail. You know this really is your own pathetic plan backfiring," he said.

She did not look at him.

There was a silence and she felt his eyes on her.

At that moment the caretaker Terry came barging in noisily and started emptying the bins and shutting the windows, on his evening tidy up.

"Sorry you lot I'm locking up, ten minutes till chucking out time. When you're paid a pittance by the hour, like me, you have to get on."

John Dyer turned on his heel and left. Noëmi let out a gasp of relief and burst into tears. Terry stopped, looked at her and offered a tissue. The small act of kindness made her more upset but she thanked him through her little sobs.

"Terry I'm sorry just ignore me!"

"Don't you worry, you're not the only one. I'm finding people often get upset around John Dyer, Miss."

CHAPTER 36 - TELLING IT AS IT IS

Marcus

Friday afternoon, 7 July 2017. Sitting staring at his Americano Marcus was deep in his own thoughts. The coffee shop was virtually empty and he had a final night shift before a weekend off. Friday afternoon sounds of people getting on with their lives buzzed outside, whilst Marcus sat in his reverie. The more Marcus had tried to force Noëmi from his mind, the more she had entered it. The events of the Sunday before had left him bereft. Why had he just given up on her? Why had he not fought for her? Why had he not protected her from John Dyer?

He thought about his embrace with Noëmi, how he had felt her long soft hair. Shauna's hair had big clips next to her scalp that attached all her fake hair extensions.

During the trip in the taxi on the way back from Val's lunch party neither he nor Shauna had spoken. Marcus was consumed by his thoughts and Shauna by the wine and her anger in equal measure. When they arrived at Shauna's place Marcus said politely.

"Shauna I have immense respect for you, but I'm sorry I don't think we're well suited and we should stop seeing each other."

Whilst the second reason was true, the first was certainly not. Marcus had no respect for her following her cruel outburst. He was not in the mood to start educating her.

307

Shauna simply replied. "You'll be sorry!" then turned and swiped him hard round the cheek. Holding his face Marcus felt only relief when she left the car and his life. Having witnessed the slap the driver looked at Marcus in the mirror, past the yellow fir tree air freshener.

"That's on camera if it helps, sir."

"Well I hope that's the last I see of her but if it's okay I'll take your taxi card, just in case I need it, thank you very much." Marcus' cheek was smarting.

"Did you know that was going to happen? Is that why our next stop is A&E?" the driver smiled.

"No! I work at A&E. I'm a doctor there. Why do you need a camera in your cab?"

"Abuse, racist comments, people not paying, threats, all sorts of stuff."

"I'm sorry you have to put up with all that."

"Most are fine honestly, just the odd idiot but I think you see as many of them as I do in your job! Gets me down a bit sometimes though."

"I know what you mean," he said to the taxi driver and himself.

Reflecting on these past events had brought him to the conclusion that he had to see Noëmi to resolve this once and for all. Whilst friendship was important he could not deny what he was feeling and friendship was not compatible with his future plans.

His coffee was now cold and he pushed it to one side.

'Call Frank? No, I'm still undoubtedly persona non grata there. Go directly to Noëmi and be honest with her?'

Having gone over what he should say, time after time, he decided not to call but to write her a text message. In desperation to get the words out he pressed send by mistake half way through and he ended up sending two messages.

Noëmi was struggling to finish her data entry and process how John Dyer had found out that Maya was her. She was worried in case she had done anything illegal. How was she to prove that she was not behind the destruction of John's office? The caretaker, Terry, happily stayed with her as she felt uncomfortable alone. What would John Dyer have done to her if Terry had not come along?

She collected all her things, and went to leave, not knowing what to think. As she went out of the door she thanked Terry with all her heart. She turned and caught sight of Sarai walking slowly down the school driveway. Sarai had trouble walking now as her pregnancy was advancing, estimated at about 36 weeks. However given her small frame she looked larger than this.

"Sarai, wait," Noëmi shouted, running to catch her up.

"Noëmi, it's good to see you."

"How are you feeling?"

"Fine, just tired, glad it's the weekend, what about you? After last Sunday?" Sarai said.

"Oh, everything's going wrong and now I think I'll be sacked. Our favourite person is trying to pin the vandalism of his office on me," said Noëmi.

"That man," said Sarai, shaking her head. "Did you do it?" she asked in all seriousness.

"No of course not!"

"Well I would've if I could," said Sarai plainly.

"We need to report this man, he locked you in his office."

"The attempt to seduce me is his word against mine, who will believe me? They think I'm just some irrelevant nobody."

"No we need to report it, also what's this memory stick you mentioned?"

"He has bad things on it, that's all I can say. But the memory stick has been stolen in the office vandalism, so that evidence is gone." Sarai's voice was thin.

"But we should tell the other managers..."

"I told the Deputy Head, Sharon King, about him locking me in the office and the memory stick."

"And?"

"She questioned my mental health and warned me about losing my job. Noëmi I need this maternity pay otherwise I cannot survive, already I'm in debt trying to buy stuff for the baby."

Noëmi forgot about her personal vendetta and thought about the poor woman in front of her.

"I'll help you Sarai, I have some savings but we have a duty to tell what we know of John Dyer. We should contact that policeman Guy."

"Right, he gave me a number if I needed anything after Luca died."

Nodding to each other they went to make the call.

Guy

Guy arranged to meet the women at Sarai's small, sparsely

310

furnished flat. He walked to the door and remembered the last time he had been there to break the news of Luca's death. All those memories came flooding back and although it was just over six months ago it felt like six years.

"This job is aging me," he said under his breath as he knocked at the door.

Noëmi greeted him and he saw Sarai lying on the sofa, although all he could really see of her was a large baby bump. He was wondering what this meeting was about.

"I'll make some tea," offered Noëmi, going into the kitchen.

Guy spoke briefly with Sarai, checking she was well. He then followed Noëmi into the tiny, old fashioned kitchen with its Formica worktops, small light blue aluminium table and ill matching oak chairs.

"How's she doing?" he asked kindly.

"I really don't know, I feel terrible. I've hardly seen her and it's been so busy, but now she's opened up to me and we need to help her," said Noëmi, preparing Guy.

"Good, she seems so alone, will she be okay with the baby?" he asked.

"Yes, a few of us are setting up a support rota, then her cousin is coming over from Vietnam for when the baby arrives, which should fall during the summer holidays, so that works well."

"That's kind. Anyway, what about you? Not too burnt out with all those kids!" said Guy taking his tea.

"Ha, ha, I can tell you it's not the kids who are the problem in our school. Anyway I hope you're not coming across any of our lot in your work, kids or adults!" She handed him his drink.

"Couldn't say if I did! Actually I'd quite like to come in and talk to students about staying safe online," said Guy.

"Great idea! I'd love to help with that. I spend my time sorting out social media stuff, kids don't realise once something's online anyone can get it."

"Absolutely, everyone needs to be careful these days, no one seems to know the laws," said Guy sipping his tea.

"Actually on that subject," said Noëmi thoughtfully, "is it a crime to make a fake dating profile?"

"Sorry what?"

"No just a friend of mine asked me so..." said Noëmi awkwardly

"Well it's not nice, but no...not a crime."

"Even if you use a picture that's not you?" asked Noëmi wide eyed.

"Well you could say most people on dating sites look nothing like their picture anyway! *So a friend told me,*" He emphasised ironically "but no not breaking the law unless the perpetrator uses it to commit a crime, like fraud, grooming, harassment," replied Guy.

"Oh okay I see," said Noëmi, obviously thinking hard.

There was a long pause.

"Will that help your friend?" asked Guy with an old fashioned look.

"Oh yes, yes, of course, I'll let them know," said Noëmi breezily and they walked back to join Sarai in the sitting room. Settling down, Guy was ready to listen.

"We need advice on a problem we have," said Noëmi, taking the lead.

"Happy to help if I can," said Guy.

"Can we talk off the record as it were?" asked Sarai, looking scared.

"Well I *am* a police officer so I can't ignore any crimes you must realise that?"

"Never mind," said Noëmi, brushing Sarai's words aside. "We have concerns about John Dyer."

"Okay what sort of concerns?" Guy sat forward.

"About his conduct and what he likes to look at," said Sarai.

"Right, have you contacted the safeguarding lead at the school?"

"Well that's him, but yes I did tell the other one Sharon King, Deputy Head."

"What are you worried about?"

"First, he tried to ask me out with no encouragement," said Sarai.

"A crime most people may have committed," said Guy smiling.

"No that came out wrong, he was quite intimidating. When I was given the job as his assistant, he came on to me and pushed himself at me. He touched my breast through my clothes, offering me sex to help me get over my loss of Luca. As he did that he locked the door so I had to fight to get out," said Sarai struggling.

"Okay sexual assault and false imprisonment, we need a statement Sarai, any witnesses?"

"No,"

"Don't worry, but we need you to make a formal statement as this sounds like an attempt to force himself on you. God I'm shocked we only ever hear good things about him," said Guy not sure what to think.

"Do I have to go to the police station?"

"Yes, usually, but I can arrange for a couple of officers to visit you here Sarai, to make things easier."

"There's something else," said Noëmi, nodding at Sarai.

"He asked me to find something on his computer and during my search of his office I found a memory stick, locked away in a drawer, well hidden. I thought the files he wanted may be on it, but on the memory stick were sick pictures...I can't describe, very young girls, you know, bad stuff. Child pornography." Sarai could hardly breathe.

Guy clenched his fists and felt his pulse quicken. *'God have I missed something here? How long has this been happening? I need to get that man away from those kids now.'*

"This is serious, right, we need to get all the details straight away, dates, times and so on. I think we'll have to go to the station, I'm sorry. Where's this memory stick now? Do you know?"

"After the break in I noticed it had gone," said Sarai.

"Never mind our IT experts can trace anything, we'll get onto the case right now. Noëmi, Sarai, can you come with me to the station?"

"Yes of course," said Noëmi, "let me gather up some things. Sarai, what do you need?"

Noëmi busied herself with grabbing water, snacks and a cushion for Sarai as Guy took some notes and made some phone calls in advance of their arrival at the police station.

CHAPTER 37 - FRIDAY EVENING

John

7 July 2017, Friday evening, sitting in his office, John was alone.

'Why does Noëmi McAllister want to play games with me? Why has she done all this? Who is she?'

Deciding he needed to know more about this mysterious employee, he went into the school personnel database.

'She went to both Cambridge and Oxford Universities!'

He felt his brow moisten. He scrolled down and stopped; completely stunned.

"Newcastle Green Academy!" He said out loud. "We went to the same school! She left three years after me...did our paths ever cross?"

He looked closely at her picture but could not place her. In spite of his lack of sensibilities, he knew this was not a coincidence. Beginning to sweat in the hot July evening, the black crows began calling outside his window. His mind began to mull over his behaviour at secondary school and he felt a disturbing unease which was a new sensation for him.

"Locking up time Mr Dyer!" The caretaker jolted him back to the present.

John shouted back, "Five minutes."

He gathered his things and he quickly sent the messages he had been preparing, checked they were delivered and turned out the lights as he left the office.

Ronnie

Friday evening, Ronnie was feeling hot and stressed out by the noise of his younger sister. She was having a tantrum about the TV not working. The internet was out and his mother, Rosie, was moaning in case it was another bill she needed to pay. Vacuously, she smoked a cigarette out of the window.

Ronnie went out for a walk to meet up with his friends. In the summer's evening he felt calmer and his thoughts turned to the plumbing apprenticeship he would be doing next. He was excited.

'I'm alright at fixing stuff. I think I'll do good on that course. Soon I'll make two hundred quid a week! That'll help Mum. Maybe I'll get my own place. See Steph more.'

Thinking of Stephanie he missed her and he sent her a message.

Frank

Friday evening, a difficult year was coming to an end and Frank had kept a detailed record of it all in his diary. He carefully crafted a factual account of what he had witnessed, made a list of his concerns, attached the relevant evidence and pressed send on his computer. He thought he should have done this a number of weeks ago but he had hoped that right up until the end the outcome would have been different. He checked the information had gone through and reflected on his actions. Nothing would change but his conscience was clear.

Friday evening, sitting on her bed Stephanie was relieved she did not have to go back to St Wolbodo's again. She felt optimistic about sixth form at another school or college. She heard a message ping through to her phone.

'Send me another picture,' Detailed instructions followed.

'No,' she was determined to end this and stop Ronnie's demands.

'If you don't I'm emailing all the others to the school, your mum and uploading them onto social media.

'Meet up?'

'Go away, leave me alone,' replied Stephanie.

'You've been warned I need it this weekend or I'll take my revenge.'

She drew her breath and put her shoulders back. How she had become ensnared by the manipulations of someone she had trusted?

The first time it seemed easiest to acquiesce and keep him quiet. Terrified and small, she could not find resistance. The barrage of demands was unassuaged by her meagre offerings it would seem. He displayed his battery of email addresses, phone numbers and social media channels, which he could use to distribute the material. This had terrified her so much that she continued to comply, as she assumed that at some point he would stop because she was being nice, but he never did. Every now and then he would send her a screenshot of herself with the caption *'Everyone will see this'.*

She was too embarrassed to tell anyone. If they knew what she had done.

It was all her fault because she was *'vile, despicable, ugly, dirty, cheap, revolting, repulsive and better off dead'.*

Stephanie paced the room trying to think what to do, feeling terror and anxiety rise in her. She went downstairs. Her mum was watching TV. She ate a pack of biscuits, stuffing them in her mouth, not tasting them. She took a pair of scissors. She went back upstairs.

Noëmi

Friday evening, Guy had taken Noëmi and Sarai back in his police car. Arriving at her flat, Noëmi decided to take a walk by the river and tried to get her head straight. She could hear groups of students in the background celebrating their graduations and felt safe. She turned on her phone for the first time since that morning and opened her messages. The first was from Magda. Noëmi took a breath and braced herself;

'When I met you I thought you were alright. Now I see you are the worst, evil, oxygen stealing piece of shit that ever landed on this earth. Fuck you for using my photos for your silly infantile plan to mess with some worthless dickhead, you must be such a child to think that it's okay to do something like that. I can't wait to steal your lame photos to make a fake profile but looking at how boring they are, the only site worth putting them on would be to warn your neighbours that a dangerous weirdo lives in the area. So fuck you and fuck off and don't think I won't tell the world what a loser you are. Shame it's not a crime as I'd love to see you locked up and actually I'm still asking my lawyer to look into this. A thousand curses on your pathetic life.'

Noëmi could not stop her tears. Her hands shook as she opened the next message; *'N hope you're okay, I missed you tonight, I thought you were coming over for dinner, let me know everything's fine. Dad xxx'*

She now sank onto the river bank and felt hot tears stream down her cheeks.

'Oh Mum's birthday anniversary! I'm so useless,' she quickly replied, **'I'm so sorry, I'm okay don't worry xxx'**

She curled up hugging her knees into her neck.

The third message was from Marcus. Fingers trembling, she fumbled to open it.

'No I've deleted it, oh no it's still there!'

Quickly she clicked. It read simply;

'The past week has been too hard for us both, I don't know how to tell you this but I just can't be friends anymore.'

Noëmi let out an agonised howl. Her mobile fell from her hands.

'How have I managed to ruin my one chance of happiness?'

Lying prone on the wet river bank she sobbed as she had never done before. Slowly the shadows gathered.

"Are you okay?" A couple of students arrived at her side.

Nodding, she pulled herself up.

"Yes sorry, I'm just...it's been a bit of a week."

She felt her mobile crack like ice beneath her foot.

"Can we call someone for you?"

Her shoulders began to shake.

"No, no, no, what have I done, it's all my fault, I've just ruined everything," she broke down and began to gather up the shattered remnants of her phone.

Helping her up the two students saw back to her flat.

"I'm not sure you should be on your own."

"No don't worry, I'm alright, thank you for being so kind." Her lips quivering she smiled to assure them she was safe and shut her door.

The hot, dark summer night slept over the fragile, troubled souls entwined by the roots of an unbound revenge, until a thunderstorm broke and beckoned a new reckoning.

PART FOUR – RECKONINGS

Et toutes les étoiles rient doucement

Le Petit Prince - Antoine de Saint-Exupéry

CHAPTER 38 - MONDAY MORNING

Sarai

10 July 2017, Monday morning, Sarai was getting on with her work, when suddenly she saw two police officers arrive. Nervous and excited she smiled and offered them tea as they passed on their way to John Dyer's office.

Police often visited the school so there was no surprise at their presence although Pat was commenting loudly in a knowing voice that it would be 'about the break in'. The police officers spent some time with John before removing his desk computer from his office. John was taken to the police station although the staff assumed this was to help with enquiries concerning the vandalism of his office.

Penelope

Monday morning, Penelope Rivera sighed as she looked at the letter in her hands.

Dear Mr and Mrs Rivera

We confirm that Joelle will be leaving St Wolbodo's at the end of Year 12 and we wish Joelle all the best for the future. Please ask Joelle to get in touch with me directly for a reference.

Kind regards

Sharon King

Deputy Head and Safeguarding Lead, St Wolbodo's School, Durham.

St Wolbodo's - Everything right for everyone.

She had spent the last few days investigating the IT course at the local technical college, Durham College of Technology, DCoT. This college did not enjoy a positive reputation amongst the more middle class parents in Durham.

"You can't send him there!" cried one of the admin team at her work. "It's full of unruly students sitting on desks and hurling abuse at teachers, who hide, terrified, in cupboards."

"Oh! Who do you know who goes there?" Mrs Rivera asked, wide eyed.

"No one but our boss' cousin's friend's boyfriend's colleague's mother works there in the office."

Penelope looked up the number and rang the Head of IT early that morning. There was no reply, which she had almost expected, so she left a message asking for a call back in order to discuss her son's future. As she finished the call, she felt hot tears prick her eyes and then steeled herself to be strong for Joel. Within seconds her phone rang back.

"Mrs Rivera? Head of IT at DCoT, how can I help?"

They spent some time discussing Joel's case.

"Why don't you come to the open day today with Joel and we can sort out how the college can help."

With a feeling of air beneath her feet and renewed faith in humankind, Mrs Rivera's confusion turned to optimism. She raced with Joel down to meet the Head of IT, at DCoT.

Noëmi

Monday morning, Noëmi had decided to ignore John's apparent *suspension* of her.

Besides, no letter or email had been sent by HR.

So she arrived at work as usual. She felt terrible, having not slept the whole weekend and having spent her time weeping uncontrollably. Frank found her sitting in the staffroom and immediately went to her.

"Noëmi what on earth, are you okay?" he asked.

Noëmi promptly burst into tears, unable to speak to her friend. He held her and tried to comfort her, ignoring the prying stares of Pat who had just come in to put the post into the staff room pigeon holes.

Joel

Monday morning and the DCoT open day was buzzing with excitement. The staff had done their departments proud. Smart displays of course materials and student work were ready to view on well-presented stands with pop up banners and smiling teachers. Students showed prospective pupils around, answering questions about their positive experiences.

Joel and his mother met the Head of IT. He took them through how Joel could complete the three A Level qualification in one year. He assured Mrs Rivera that he had no concerns about Joel's ability, clearly impressed with his attitude. Joel looked up in silent prayer.

The Head of IT also mentioned that Joel would need to think about his steps after college and what he could do then.

"What do your students usually opt for?" his mother asked carefully.

"A mix really, some get jobs, others apprenticeships and a fair few go onto university," he replied matter of factly.

"Well we know Joel won't be able to go to university," replied Joel's mum.

"We don't know that. You may well be surprised."

Joel felt his body lift.

They shook hands with the Head of IT. Penelope rushed to call her husband to tell him everything. Joel put his shoulders back and breathed out slowly as he waited.

Across the hall he spotted Stephanie looking around on her own. Watching her he wondered what she was doing there. Suddenly he recalled how he always used to see her up in the school support centre, red eyed and silent. She was looking at the A Level section too, but seemed jumpy and fidgety.

'I wonder why she's on her own?' All the other students were accompanied. Joel found himself at her side.

"Hey!" Joel said warmly and smiled at Stephanie.

"What?" she replied sharply, not returning his smile.

"Didn't expect to see you here, I assumed you'd stay on for sixth form at Wobo's."

"Well, you assumed wrong didn't you," said Stephanie, sounding like she wanted him to go away. Joel reminded himself that she was struggling with some kind of upset.

"I got chucked out for no reason," said Joel, just like that.

"Lucky you, I had to organise my own departure from that place. No one can stop me, especially as today is my sixteenth birthday. I'm old enough to decide what I do."

"What was the problem for you there?"

"At the moment the only problem is that I can't get away soon enough," she replied.

Joel laughed.

"I'm actually sad to leave, I don't understand why I can't stay. My work really improved," Joel said reflectively.

"Honestly, just shut the fuck up will you," said Stephanie rolling her eyes. Suddenly she glanced back and added. "Sorry, that was mean."

Joel put his hands in his pockets and shrugged his shoulders.

"Don't worry about it! Why did you decide to leave?"

"I need to get away from stuff and that place is toxic." She picked a brochure up from the table and flicked through it.

"What courses are you looking at?"

"A Levels of course. I want to go to uni. Cambridge, that's where my tutor went," said Stephanie plainly.

"You'd have more chance at Wobo's," Joel replied.

"I refuse to stay there. It was messing with my head." She sighed, looking away.

"Sorry. Which subjects?" They moved slowly past the many stands.

"Dunno, maybe maths, I like maths, not sure what they do here, that's what I was looking at."

"I'm doing IT, that looks good."

"IT is an option too."

"Well that has to be better here than at Wobo's."

Stephanie laughed, "Oh my God were you in King's class?"

"Yes, after my first teacher left, Mrs King was so stressy."

"Useless at IT too," added Stephanie, "I used to give her the answers!"

Grinning, she turned to him. She seemed at ease and leant back against a display stand.

Joel was relaxing into a comfortable conversation when Stephanie's phone pinged with an update. She immediately took it out of her pocket and checked the alert. Her face went white and she let out a gasp, her hand began to shake uncontrollably.

"Are you okay?" and without thinking he caught the phone as it fell from her hand. He looked at the screen.

'Thought you would see if I meant what I said did you? It's all uploaded for everyone, you know, to enjoy, shame your efforts to kill yourself didn't work, maybe you should try again. Looks like I've got my revenge!' It said simply followed by a devil emoji.

"Stephanie what's this? Who sent this to you?" said Joel, confused and shocked.

Stephanie did not answer and sank to the floor. A number of staff members came over to help and take her to a first aid station. Joel watched helplessly, still clutching her phone. Joel's mother saw the commotion from across the room and rang for an ambulance to take Stephanie to hospital. As the group left the open day display area, Joel looked down at the phone again and saw that the sender of the message that had so devastated Stephanie was Ronnie Young.

Monday morning and Marcus was exhausted. Two of his co-workers were sick and he was now the only Junior Doctor on the shift, which was supposed to be a quiet one. However today, the RVI Accident and Emergency Department seemed to be the place of every drama you could imagine. A mother was hysterical, convinced that her seemingly very happy two year old had swallowed a fifty pence coin. A teenager, whose over microwaved ready meal had exploded in his face, was terrified he was now blind. A drunk woman had assaulted the receptionist and had to be restrained by Marcus whilst the police were called.

Standing at the A&E reception desk Marcus got an alert that an ambulance was bringing in a collapsed teenager. Details were scarce as Marcus got his team together unsure what to expect.

Stephanie had been taken to RVI in Newcastle as the Durham hospital was dealing with a motorway pile up. At the emergency ambulance entrance Marcus took charge of Stephanie who arrived with Penelope Rivera, Joel's mother.

* * *

Stephanie could not speak and sat rocking on her bed, sobbing.

Having been thoroughly checked over, she was admitted to the paediatric unit for observation. Children's Services were alerted and also Guy's team. As Marcus wrote in her notes, he said firmly to the nurse, "Stephanie's been hospitalised before after a non-accidental overdose. She's high risk and must be on suicide watch; accompanied at all times."

CHAPTER 39 - TUESDAY

Sarai

Tuesday, Sarai had overslept and although she was not late, simply on time, she arrived at her desk well before Pat. She could hear the voices of John and some others in his office, sounding relaxed and jovial; she was puzzled as to who could be in there. Pat came in, put her bag down and was about to go for a comfort break when Sarai asked.

"Who's in the office with Mr Dyer?"

"God knows, all sorts of weird things are happening in this school. Just yesterday I saw Frank being, well I can only say, unfaithful, to his wife in the staffroom," exclaimed Pat.

In spite of her trouble with some English customs and her never-ending difficulty in understanding Pat on any level, Sarai saw the problem in what Pat was saying immediately.

"Unfaithful?" she questioned.

"All over her he was," said Pat with a look, delighted to have an audience, as the other office workers turned, open-mouthed, to listen. "His poor wife, Val, isn't it? How she must be feeling and so blatant right in the middle of the staffroom, unbelievable!" continued Pat.

Sarai questioned her further.

"What was Frank doing?"

"Cuddling that maths teacher Noëmi. All over each other, disgusting, you couldn't make it up, all sorts of sounds I can't tell you, his poor wife," she tutted loudly as she turned and saw a small student with wide eyes, waiting to pay their lunch money onto their account.

Sarai was instantly concerned as to what could be wrong with her friends so she sent Noëmi a message.

John's office door opened and she saw John chatting happily with two officers, one of them being Guy.

"No need to worry, you have to do your job and respond to anything you hear," said John jovially, giving Guy a pat on the shoulder.

"Glad you understand," replied Guy smiling.

"Honestly I just don't know who would make up things about me like that!" John said, for once, not making a pointed comment.

Guy noticed Sarai in the corner of his eye and looked awkward.

"Well sometimes people can misinterpret things," he said, no doubt for the benefit of all.

Sarai slumped back in her chair. Slowly she began to understand that John had managed to manipulate this whole scenario somehow. How had he managed to extricate himself from his downfall? Now he had engineered everything so that he was the victim of some dreadful slur.

Guy

Guy and his colleague were seeing themselves out when Guy stopped. Asking his co-worker to wait, he went back to Sarai.

"Have you got a minute?" he asked.

"Yes of course," replied Sarai, fumbling to get herself together.

"Can we go somewhere quiet?"

"Shall I see if I can get Noëmi?"

"Good idea."

Sarai tried Noëmi's mobile but it went to voicemail.

"No reply, maybe she's in the staffroom," said Sarai.

Pat

They walked out in silence, through the office and into the staffroom. Pat was beyond desperate to know what was happening. She was about to go after them, when a pupil arrived at the office window for the toilet key.

"Who let you out of class?" she boomed at this small student who looked terrified and could only mouth inaudibly the name of the offending teacher.

Guy

Frank was sitting marking some internal exams with his face either grinning or grimacing as he read the answers written by his students.

"Hello Sarai, no doubt I'll be sacked when our wonderful management team sees these results!" he said with mock concern.

Sarai laughed, "I hear you might be sacked for cuddling Noëmi, is she okay? I can't get hold of her."

Guy was confused as he could not think why Noëmi and Frank would be cuddling.

"She's all over the place, your lovely boss has apparently suspended her. Don't worry, she's ignoring it!"

'What?" Sarai was shocked.

Guy asked, "Is this a good time?"

"Yes of course, sorry," they sat down on the pastel coffee stained chairs.

Guy looked sincerely at Sarai.

"The thing is we looked into the allegations you made against John Dyer. We removed all his computing equipment from his office, as you reported seeing the files there. I'm afraid to say we've found no evidence of any wrongdoing. Certainly no child pornography. Upon talking to him he reminded me that, as Lead Safeguarding Officer, he would have all types of documents and manuals. He suggested that maybe a bystander could confuse this type of information with something more sinister. The Designated Safeguarding Lead is also required to have drawers they can lock in the case of an incident and they need to secure evidence."

"I know what I saw, the man is up to no good," replied Sarai simply.

"I am very sorry but without physical evidence, it's so hard, we've investigated as far as we can," said Guy, not knowing what to think.

"What about the sexual assault and the false imprisonment?" asked Sarai with a small voice.

"I *am* absolutely still investigating this, rest assured Sarai. At the moment Dyer denies everything so we need to prepare a case, which we *are* doing," said Guy.

"I have told you the truth," replied Sarai defiantly, looking away.

"Indeed I'm not giving up on you, it just takes time," Guy said.

"Okay you know what, I'm tired, not feeling so good," said Sarai, leaning backwards and stretching out her back.

"Are you okay Sarai?" said Guy as he looked at this tiny but hugely pregnant woman next to him.

"I've got about four weeks to go, can you believe this?" She stretched out and then sat up quickly, looked down at her legs and went white.

"My waters have gone! It's too soon, my baby! I need Noëmi, she's my birthing partner," she began to cry, blanched with panic.

Guy went into emergency mode and called for an ambulance, then sat with Sarai, asking Frank to get Noëmi.

Frank

Frank ran to Noëmi's classroom but her class had been re-roomed.

Dashing to the school office he ran in and asked where Noëmi's class was.

Pat laboriously got out of her seat and moved herself to her daily rota and sighed heavily as she looked down the rooming allocations.

"Quick this is urgent," said Frank, getting impatient as Pat seemed to be taking her time.

"Excuse me I'm very busy too," said Pat indignantly, giving him a stare. "The class is in one of the terrapins either B1 or B2 it says here," she continued unconvincingly.

The terrapin huts were a good ten minutes on the other side of the school so without replying, Frank sped off in their direction.

As he left he could still hear Pat.

"See what I mean?" she said, turning to her open mouthed co-workers who now undoubtedly believed every word Pat said, "Can't keep his hands off her, disgusting it is if you ask me."

Marcus

Tuesday, A&E, Marcus was back on a long shift with the reduced team and it was not getting quieter. Ambulances continued to arrive with various cases ranging in severity. Sarai was in one of them, as RVI was her delivery hospital. Marcus came out to see how she was before she was taken up to the maternity ward.

"Don't worry Sarai, you'll be fine, your baby is well and we'll get you up onto the maternity ward for observation. Now do you have someone who can be with you?" Marcus asked kindly.

"My friend, Noëmi," Marcus gave a start upon hearing the name.

"Okay one of the nurses will contact her and make sure you're fully supported," he wanted to spend longer with Sarai but the department was so busy.

* * *

Having had a stable night, Stephanie sat on her bed, head hung over her knees that were drawn up to her chest. She sat rocking back and forth and said nothing to anyone who spoke to her. Marcus got to her again and was soon joined by Guy and Penelope, who was now on duty. Having checked her over, Marcus updated Guy on her condition.

"Hello, Marcus McKenzie, Junior Doctor."

"Guy Castle, Police Constable, I'm working on Stephanie's case, how's she doing?"

"Well Stephanie is physically stable now, she was in shock. All her signs and stats are good now though, so it's absolutely fine for you to talk to her. We have a nurse, Penelope, here. By chance she was at the same event as Stephanie when she collapsed. She will stay as a chaperone, Stephanie is comfortable with her."

"We'll need to be quite direct with her, are you sure she's strong enough?"

"Physically yes, mentally, very difficult to say, she definitely needs to talk though, something is tormenting her. There's much evidence of self harm."

"Thank you. I've noted that. By the way, you've recently joined my gym, right?"

"Yes, I've just changed gyms." Marcus nodded, smiling.

"Plus we've met before haven't we?" Guy pointed between them.

"At the memorial for Luca Bianchi, sadly. Sarai's doing well, I know you brought her in."

"Glad to hear that, yes that's all been terrible, did you know him?"

"Not really, I met him a couple of times through a mutual friend, Noëmi, she works with Sarai."

"Oh yes, yes, I know, she's great. I was with her and Sarai discussing a case, just on Friday night. Now everything's kicked off!"

"Oh... right. You know Noëmi?" Marcus looked up open mouthed.

"Yes from my dealings with the school, I'm the liaison officer, always something going on at that place! She's Stephanie's tutor you know."

Marcus' pager called him back to A&E reception.

He left Stephanie with Guy and Penelope.

Marcus walked back. He desperately wanted to ask Guy about Noëmi. Questions flooded his head;

How had Noëmi been?

Why had they all been together on Friday?

Why had she not replied?

Everything was getting worse. Nothing made sense. His pager went again. He put his mind back on his job and his thoughts to the back of his mind.

Guy

Guy went and sat down next to Stephanie, saying nothing. Penelope pulled the beige curtain around the bed.

"Hello Stephanie, you know me and Penelope who's here to support you."

"Go away." Stephanie put her head back on her knees.

"You and I need to help each other," said Guy firmly, he dragged his chair closer. "We have evidence that a student called Ronnie Young is the one who's been threatening you, is that correct?" He loosened his tie slightly.

Stephanie said nothing, and pulled her knees to her chest.

"I'll take that silence to be a 'yes'? I'm sure he'll tell me that he wasn't threatening you. That you were happy to send him photos. You can tell me your version of events if you like." Guy sat forward, elbows on his knees.

"Are you saying you don't believe me?" said Stephanie, turning away from him.

"I'm saying that without your statement Ronnie will get away with it. Peer to peer exploitation is against the law, plus he may be doing it to others," said Guy flatly.

"No," said Stephanie darkly, lowering her head.

"Stephanie, can you please tell me what has been happening to you so that I can help? Penelope's here, you're safe. We need to get these pictures removed."

Silence stood.

Stephanie gave an agonised cry. Her body shook sporadically as she tried to speak. Penelope put her hand soothingly on her forearm. Finally, her voice breaking, she spoke in gasps.

"I was seeing Ronnie... over the summer holidays, before the start of Year 11. It was nothing. We mucked around. We ended it before it got serious. I'd sent him a picture. We reconnected but broke up... and it all began. He said he'd email the picture to my mum. He had her email address. God knows how. I sent the pictures to shut him up. Then it got worse. He wouldn't stop. I told him at school but he pretended not to know what I was talking about. He was never there. Absent. Excluded, but just demanding more and more."

"We can make it stop," assured Guy.

"No one knows where he is and he says he's uploaded the stuff, I can't bear to look, I'm dead," sobbed Stephanie.

"Right, give me all your electronic devices, your phone, your computer, your passwords, accounts and our team will be on it. Our experts will be discreet and they have ways of immediately isolating a face in a picture so your dignity will be intact. Whatever's been uploaded will be taken down. We can sweep sites by image. Trust me Stephanie."

"It's been hell," Stephanie said through her sobs.

"We need to move quickly, are you feeling okay to cooperate?"

She nodded, head bowed.

"Don't worry I've got this, but you promise me this one thing."

"What?" Stephanie looked up at him. He was supplicating.

"You won't attempt to take your life again."

"I definitely want to live," Stephanie's voice was hushed. She kept hold of Penelope's hand.

* * *

Chester Le Street. The team moved quickly to begin investigations into the threats that Stephanie had been receiving. A warrant was issued to bring Ronnie in for questioning. Technology forensics began looking through Stephanie's communications over the past ten months.

Eventually through Guy's local contacts, it was discovered that Ronnie was spending most days in one of the local pubs drinking, playing pool and gambling on a few horses. Guy wondered to himself how this was being financed and if the landlord had done any ID checks. However, he was content just to have Ronnie in the vicinity. He knew he would need Ronnie's mother to come too as Ronnie was a minor in the eyes of the law. He dispatched a colleague to pick up Rosie.

Ronnie

Questioning. Ronnie sat in the interview room with his mother, a policewoman and a duty lawyer by his side, saying nothing. The room was sparse, with a few plastic chairs and a wooden table and there was little natural light. Guy checked Ronnie was okay, explained his rights and gave him a glass of water,

"We have reason to believe that you have been threatening a fellow student."

"If you're talking about that prick in Year 10 who stole my bike, yes I threatened to beat him up. You lot should be arresting him for stealing," replied Ronnie.

"Can we go now?" asked Rosie naïvely. Ronnie knew she would be desperate to get out of the police station where she felt very uncomfortable.

"No, the threats involve asking a fellow student for sexually explicit pictures and threatening to share these online," said Guy sternly.

"Dunno what you're going on about mate," said Ronnie smiling.

"I'm not your mate."

Ronnie looked up at the ceiling. *What on earth are they talking about?'*

"What do you say about these allegations?"

"They're lies, I don't ask anyone for pictures," Ronnie said a little bewildered.

"We have evidence of an account you've been using to demand photos from a fellow student. Do you want to tell me about it?"

"I don't *demand* photos." He rolled his eyes and slumped back in his chair. Then he added in a small voice, "I use a couple of sites; you can look at my phone," said Ronnie as he handed over his mobile.

"I only have pictures of my horses," he said rather quietly.

"We are going to have to search your place, Ronnie and thank you for your cooperation; you'll need to stay here whilst we do that. We already have a warrant."

Having no idea what this was all about Ronnie thought to himself. *'Mum's going to love that; police searching the flat. This whole thing is a total headfuck. Photos, threats... warrants, whatever they are. I'm meeting Albie this afternoon and I'm stuck here.'*

"Fuck this shithole! Fuck all you useless bunch of wankers!"

Ronnie kicked the empty chair next to him. The sun was peeking through the window. Dust danced in the sunbeams. Rosie started crying and the female officer put her hand on her arm to comfort her.

Noëmi

Newcastle RVI. It seemed ages before Noëmi was permitted to see her friend. Sarai was in bed on a drip with a monitor checking her baby; she was being observed carefully as she was only 36 weeks pregnant. The medical team wished to give her baby as long as possible before inducing labour. They chatted some more and Noëmi gave the nurses her school number and her neighbour's landline as ways for Sarai to contact her.

"Where's your mobile, you're always on it?" asked Sarai innocently.

"Oh I lost it," She lied, picturing the broken mess of her phone on her kitchen table. *'Sums up my shattered life. Can't even get the sim out.'*

"That sounds expensive."

"In so many ways it has cost me dearly," Noëmi agreed.

"I need to ask you something." Looking down she played with the strap of her hospital gown.

"I have some distant relatives in Vietnam but no one close. If I die can you look after mine and Luca's baby? Teach the baby Italian and Vietnamese, especially Vietnamese cooking."

"Of course, don't worry Sarai, nothing will happen to you and I'll help you all the way," said Noëmi, momentarily wondering how on earth she could be expected to be able to teach Vietnamese in the event of such a tragedy. Sarai's faith in her touched her.

"Thank you Noëmi. That doctor friend of yours can help me too."

"Oh you mean Marcus, he works here you know," Noëmi said with a shudder.

"Yes, he triaged me, I arrived in an ambulance, never been in an ambulance before. Have you?"

"Yes unfortunately, my own fault of course, like all my other mistakes," recalling the evening with Marcus and Hilary.

"Are you okay?" Sarai reached across and touched her hand thoughtfully.

"Of course," said Noëmi brusquely and she changed the subject.

Later she left, walking through the maze of buildings that made up Newcastle Royal Victoria Infirmary. Noëmi knew that Marcus was here working in A&E and was worried about seeing him, after the message she had received and definitely not understood. She was also looking dreadful and wanted to hide from the world having spent the last three days sobbing. Luckily she did not see him. Then she took a bus home, staring out of the mucky window, exhausted and desolate.

CHAPTER 40 - WEDNESDAY

Guy

Guy met with his colleagues in forensics to go over their findings. They had worked through the night and were exhausted. Now in a police station meeting room, sitting around a large table with folders everywhere, the team was ready. They had endless cups of strong coffee to drink and much to report.

"We've looked through all the devices. We found evidence of Stephanie Smith being asked to send explicit photographs, which she did. We found demands to keep sending sexually graphic material. Many threats that the photos would be shared publicly." Said the Head of Information Technology Forensics, handing out copies of their report.

Guy sat back, *'Soon we'll have this all wrapped up and I can reassure Stephanie we've nailed Ronnie.'*

Turning to his colleagues he asked. "Have you got the exact details? The number of times he demanded explicit materials? The dates of when he threatened to share them? We can charge him with peer to peer exploitation, sexting, sharing images and harassment. That should mean juvenile jail time."

"Hold on, I have to tell you that Ronnie's devices were clean. However there was a mobile and a laptop belonging to another user that has the evidence we've been looking for."

"Another user, what are you saying? If they belong to Ronnie then that nails it!" reasoned Guy, picking up his coffee cup.

"There's no evidence that Ronnie has used these devices. The log in details and set up appear to belong to someone other than Ronnie, even though some of the accounts use Ronnie's name."

"Who do these devices belong to then?"

"Well we're not sure but we're looking into it, getting the IP addresses and going from there. I have to tell you they're definitely not linked to Ronnie. Maybe you can find out from him where he got them?" the officer suggested.

"There was also a memory stick with child pornography on it, we're looking into that too."

Guy put his hand to his mouth. For a moment he was lost in thought. Then suddenly he seemed to have an idea.

"Right I know exactly what to do, get Ronnie in here now I need to charge him."

Ronnie

Charging. Ronnie shuffled into the questioning room, bewildered, tired and resentful at being held. He had no idea what he was supposed to have done. Behind him Rosie, her social worker and a duty lawyer followed all equally absorbed in their own interpretation of things.

"Take a seat Ronnie."

He dropped into the chair and slouched, looking away from Guy.

"How long's this going to take?" Ronnie asked abruptly.

"That depends how co-operative you are. Now we need to record this interview so I want you to be aware of the procedures and your rights."

"I've briefed everyone," mentioned the lawyer, pushing his glasses back into place.

"Great, well Ronnie You are under arrest on suspicion of breaking into an office at St Wolbodo's school on the night of Sunday 7 May 2017. You do not have to say anything, but it may harm your defence if you do not mention, when questioned, something which you later rely on in court. Anything you do say may be given in evidence."

"What the fuck? What's all this about?" shouted Ronnie.

"You tell me Ronnie, we found items lost in that robbery in your possession. You're under arrest for this theft, what can you tell me?"

"My mate gave them to me," said Ronnie.

"Which friend?"

"Can't remember can I." Ronnie looked down at his hands.

"Come on Ronnie, we both know that's not what happened," said Guy.

Throwing his shoulders back, Ronnie put his foot up against the table in front of him. He looked to one side, *'So unfair I'm now going down because of that wanker, Dyer.'*

"Okay so what if I borrowed a few bits. I was planning to give them back. I just wanted revenge, get back at that prick Dyer who excluded me for no reason," sighed Ronnie.

"Explain please."

"He said I hit him and I never did and he got me excluded and my mum got all upset. So I just did over his office and took stuff to make life difficult for him. I've not used it, probably full of boring old man stuff. I was going to give it back, I just forgot."

"Forgot did you?" said Guy sarcastically, smiling.

"That can happen."

"Indeed, right, that's been really helpful, so you say the items came from the office of Mr John Dyer."

"Suppose so."

'No that really helps me Ronnie, thank you, let's get a full statement now and then we'll be in touch. You're going to be held a bit longer whilst we investigate a few final things and then you can go home tonight. You've been really helpful, thank you."

Now Ronnie was totally confused.

"Am I in trouble or not?" He looked between the adults in the room.

"Yes, but we can work something out so we don't have to charge you with robbery or destruction of property. If you just tell us the truth, okay?"

"I always tell the truth, on the big stuff that is. I mean your haircut's weird but I'd tell you it's alright. That's a lie I guess, but not about right and wrong. I don't lie about that."

"Exactly Ronnie. We're finally agreeing. Don't worry I'm sure you'll be happy to help us, and we can help you," grinned Guy.

Rosie saw Guy smiling warmly at her son and turned mystified to her social worker.

"I'll explain everything," she promised confidently. However, she then added, "Actually, sorry I can't. I have absolutely no idea what's going on here."

CHAPTER 41 - THURSDAY

Guy

Thursday, having collated all the statements and evidence Guy went to visit Stephanie with a chaperone, in order to explain everything to her. Having been discharged that morning she was huddled in a blanket on her sofa. Tessa, her mum seemed very stressed; apologising for the state of the house and offering tea at equal intervals.

"This is Karen, a chaperone and liaison officer, she's here for you. Karen will help you, explain things to you."

Stephanie nodded that she understood and took a gulp of water from a plastic bottle, closing the lid firmly afterwards.

"Now you've given us your statement. The first thing I need to tell you is that you've been the victim of a serious crime. You're innocent, you've done nothing wrong and I can confirm that we've made an arrest." Guy was clear.

"Oh my God, I'm scared. What's going to happen to Ronnie?"

"Nothing. Ronnie is giving evidence to support you. Ronnie is innocent of any crime towards you. He is guilty of destruction of property, theft, possessing weed..."

Stephanie laughed at the last part, which made Guy smile.

"...that's all, but of nothing else."

"That's so weird, I'm confused," said Stephanie, maybe looking relieved.

"Let's go through what's happened here. Stay strong Stephanie, this is difficult to hear."

Stephanie looked at Karen who took her hand.

"You were in a brief relationship with Ronnie and you shared an intimate photo with him. He kept the photo safe, deleting it as you told him to when you finished the relationship at the end of the summer holidays. Then you were in trouble at school and your phone was confiscated. It would seem that you did not have a passcode on your phone."

"Yeah it's extra effort when you want to use your phone in class."

"Your phone was then taken by a third party who saw your photo. They saw your message history and found a way to persuade you to send photos. All the time threatening to share them if you didn't comply."

Stephanie was quiet and wrapped her blanket tighter.

"Let me assure you that none of the images have been shared or uploaded anywhere. We have checked thoroughly. Sorry I should've told you that first."

"Oh thank you, thank God, I was so ashamed." Stephanie, visibly relaxed.

"Only the person we've arrested viewed any of the material you sent, and so rest assured on that point. I wouldn't lie to you. I'm telling you everything straight. I've not seen the material although I know you sent a total of 25 pictures to this person. Rest assured your dignity is intact."

"It's okay, I was so worried it was everywhere, thank you, I feel like such an idiot."

"None of the pictures have been shared. We've performed advanced internet searches; computer checks. Nothing's out there. However you've been a victim of a serious crime as you were fifteen when this happened and the offender knew this. They're guilty of many things; possessing illegal images of a child, procuring illegal images of a child, grooming, sexual assault, blackmail and threatening behaviour. It may come as no surprise that when we investigated this person further we found other illegal images of children in their possession. Plus other attempts to connect with children for sexual purposes."

Stephanie sat up rigid and Karen held her hand tightly, to support her.

"Can you tell me who it was?" she asked, her body was shaking. She looked so small on the sofa.

Guy felt nervous, he knew this was going to be devastating. Karen held Stephanie.

"Take a breath Stephanie, remember they're already in jail,"

'I need to get this right. It's so big.' Guy looked at the young victim in front of him. Ten months of suffering had reduced her to nothing but a shell of terror and torment. His heart pounding, *'If I could take all her pain I would do so in a heartbeat.'* Moving a little closer and as calmly as he could, he spoke.

"We've arrested one of your teachers at school. Mr Dyer."

Stephanie's head rolled back and her breathing quickened. She ran out knocking the tea tray over as she fled. Karen immediately went after her.

Guy could hear Stephanie retching into the downstairs toilet as she was violently sick.

Guy stood up and turned to the window. *'If I could get my hands on that man I'd tear him apart,'* He peered through the net curtains. Outside the world buzzed on. Lorries rumbled by. Children walked home from school with others, their laughter and chatter filled his ears.

Guy picked up the cups and rearranged everything, using the napkins to mop up the tea dregs from the carpet. It was some time before Stephanie returned with Karen. Shivering she sat down, giving hiccough like sobs every now and then. She looked even smaller than before.

"I'm so sorry. Please, know that the case we have against him is very secure." Guy said reassuringly.

"He took my phone, that's how he did it," Stephanie realised.

Gently Guy helped with the details.

"He then posed as Ronnie making fake accounts, which is why you thought it was your friend all this time."

"My God, it all makes sense now. The demands I was getting were so full on... Ronnie can't write that much. How did I not realise?" Stephanie bit her lip.

"To give Ronnie his due, he's very protective of you, he's fully cooperated and his testimony makes it clear that he was not involved at all. He was the one who broke into Dyer's office. Then we were able to retrieve the devices that Dyer had used and retain all the evidence of his vile crimes."

"That man is horrible," Stephanie said quietly, "I nearly killed myself..."

Guy sighed and bowed his head.

"We also know that Ronnie was not involved as we found footage of you with Ronnie on Dyer's phone too."

"Oh my God, during the fire alarm practice. We snuck off together."

"He followed you, spied on you and filmed you both, that's another offence, but it confirms Ronnie's statement of events."

"We broke up again straight after because of the threats."

Karen gave Stephanie's hand a squeeze.

"But I want to testify or whatever it is, like on TV, go to court and tell my story. Make sure he goes down."

"The trial's a long way off, but rest assured we'll work with you if that happens. He's in custody, that is prison, so he cannot get to you in any way."

Guy saw Stephanie nod slowly, she was red eyed and pale. *'She's going to need therapy now, during the trial and forever afterwards. It'll be so traumatic. I hope to God he just pleads guilty'.*

"Don't worry, I'll go to court and say how it all was... he's ruined my life."

"Now we're going to get you the rest of your life back Stephanie, so I need you to trust in some adults."

"Sure, I trust you, thank you for finding all this out, I thought I was going mad, you guys are restoring my faith in old people!"

Guy laughed, "Hey watch it, I'm twenty-six! Mind you this job makes me feel fifty years older!"

Stephanie gave a small laugh through her tears.

Thursday morning and a 5am raid had been carried out on John Dyer's flat in Newcastle. Guy made sure he was there and that he did the arrest. Waiting by the front entrance of the exclusive wharf side block, overlooking the river Tyne, Guy noticed a few black crows gathering on the rooftop. Their gentle cawing was interrupted by his fellow officers dragging a handcuffed John Dyer out of the main door.

Guy walked over and looked him straight in the eye.

"John Ricketts-Dyer, you're under arrest on suspicion of possession of illegal images of children, grooming, intent to distribute illegal images of children, blackmail, sexual assault and theft. You do not have to say anything, but it may harm your defence if you do not mention when questioned something which you later rely on in court. Anything you do say, may be given in evidence."

Staring him out, Guy did not hide his disgust and contempt. John Dyer was fighting back tears but remained silent avoiding eye contact with everyone. Suddenly Guy felt a hit of spit in his face.

"And you're under arrest for assaulting a police officer, that's another offence."

Watching him being taken away, he thought to himself, *'I don't care what you do to me, as long as we get justice for those you've abused and we will.'*

At the same time John Dyer's office was searched again and all computer equipment removed. Officers remained at both scenes until they were satisfied that all evidence had been recovered. An officer stayed on at the school to interview Steve in the IT department to obtain IP addresses, device information and account details relating to the accused.

Following that, Guy went to see the Head Teacher, Maurice, to explain the situation to him under caution. Police officers would need to collect statements from staff members and an action plan needed to be set up to identify and help potential victims of Dyer's crimes. In addition Guy had to discuss, at length, a strategy to deal with possible and indeed in his mind, probable, new victims coming forward. This was in view of the publicity that would be generated once the news was in the public domain. Both wished to handle this within the school community first.

Maurice

Maurice was shaken to the core. Never had he imagined that the impressive young interviewee could have been such a threat to children. He had always viewed these dangers, from which he was to protect his students, as far off distant events that did not happen in the real world. John had appeared like an answer to his prayers, embodying all they wanted in a new Assistant Head; youth, good looks, strong behaviour management. He had that aura of authority, with a hint of enjoying a pint at weekends, which was, in itself, reassuring. Of course this fine young man was not a menace or a pervert. Everyone knew that because he looked so honest, good and wholesome. Not a whiff of impropriety or deceit. How could it be that he had not seen through this facade? Had he done the right background checks? He went over the interview and yes he had asked the safeguarding question.

"Well thank you John and I must say it is very refreshing to have such an enthusiastic, young and ambitious application."

Nothing could have prepared Maurice for the brutal realisation that a paedophile, intent on nothing but their own gratification, would of course be clever enough to charm their way into his and everyone else's trust and into a position from which they could fulfil their desires.

CHAPTER 42 - FRIDAY NIGHT

Marcus

Friday evening, Marcus was exhausted after another long shift in A&E. Having grabbed a pizza on the way, he travelled back to his flat in Newcastle. He flopped onto his sofa with a beer, frustrated and angry. His shift had been stressful; he had to restrain a drunk man, who went for him, as he tried to examine his leg wound. Then a young girl, with a sprained ankle, was admitted. She kept asking him, 'Exactly where are you from?'

Mindlessly watching the late night news, he went to his phone to check his messages. Still Noëmi had not replied. It had been a week since he had sent the message. Throwing his head back, he tried to block from his mind the many times he had ignored her messages over the last six months.

Enough was enough. He rang her number. It went directly to voicemail. He sent a quick text to Frank, trying to sound as casual as possible.

'Hey Frank, sorry to bother you but can you please ask Noëmi to call me, cheers.'

Finishing his beer, he heard Frank ping back.

'She's in a bit of a state. Upset. She's got stuff going on at work but of course I'll tell her if I get hold of her. She's not replying to

anyone, very odd, Fx.'

Marcus stood up. Unable to rest, he paced the lounge. Looking at the clock, it was just 11pm so he decided to ring Donnie. Looking out of his bay window into the isolated street, a fox darted across the road.

"Hi Donnie, how are you?"

"Well fine, is everything okay Marcus?" Donnie sounded surprised.

"Yes, I was just trying to reach N. Is she there?" His voice rose in hope.

"Oh, join the club. I think she's at her flat, been difficult to contact all week. I just don't think she's well if I'm honest. Forgot her mum's birthday meal last Friday. Never has she missed one, not in ten years. Then not replying to messages, and when I did finally reach her she began talking of leaving her job, going to teach abroad, it's all so worrying." Donnie sighed.

Marcus could feel his heart begin to race, he breathed in deeply to calm himself.

"If you get hold of her please tell her to call me, really, I'm desperate to talk to her." His voice was breaking.

"Yes of course I will, take care." Donnie sounded concerned and confused.

'Missed her mum's meal? Going abroad?' Marcus ran his hands through his hair and looked at the clock.

It was 11.15pm. He had to see her.

Marcus grabbed his jacket and ordered a taxi, checking her address.

Once arrived, it was already midnight.

"No A&E tonight then sir?" The taxi driver gave him a smile.

"Oh sorry, hello, I didn't realise…" Marcus was all clumsiness.

"You looked completely distracted! Like a zombie sir!"

"It's been a terrible couple of weeks." Marcus leant forward.

"Don't worry sir, things can only get better!" Fumbling for his wallet, Marcus paid the taxi driver and almost fell out of the cab.

He walked up the stairs to the front door with its royal blue peeling paint. He buzzed her flat. No answer. He felt weird that he had never been there before, all his self-centred, so called self-protection, came back to haunt him. Never more did he regret not saving her from John Dyer. *'Why on earth did I just toss her aside?'*

No reply.

Looking at the other numbers he wondered if it was too late to get another resident to let him in. He knew no one would.

Just to see, he pushed the main door, it opened.

'Great security,' he said to himself. Blessing his luck, he bounded up the two flights of stairs to her flat on the top floor. The door was shiny red, undoubtedly painted by Noëmi, with a carved name plaque, **N McAllister.** It was the one she had done at school. For a moment he was back in that woodwork class when the teacher announced who had done the best one. Of course it was Noëmi. Modestly she had played it down and joked about the fact she had been given a book on wood turning as a prize. *'So useful…for wedging doors open!'* she had laughed.

The large fern plant in a bright yellow planter, cheering up the hallway, was certainly another of her touches. Everything was brighter when she was around. He knocked hard.

"Noëmi," he called out. No reply. Ringing the bell this time. He waited. No reply. Through the door he could see there were no lights on. The door of the flat opposite opened and, peering out past the brass safety chain, a young woman called out.

"She's not there, a friend had an emergency, she's with them, they called me to let her know."

"Thank you, I am so sorry for disturbing you so late." He noticed she was in a fluffy dressing gown.

"It's okay, I'm Yolanda, who shall I tell her called?"

"My name's Marcus. Do you mind letting her know I wanted to see her?" He wondered what this emergency was.

"Yeah of course Marcus, also can you check she's okay if you find her, she seems upset the whole time."

"Oh no that's bad..." he thought out loud. He turned to leave, stopped and swung back round. "Actually do you mind, do you have a piece of paper? I need to leave her a note... thank you Yolanda."

"Sure, one minute, do you need a pen too?"

He nodded and after a few moments the neighbour gave Marcus a biro and a bit of A4, smiling as she shut her door.

Marcus was not able to concentrate. *Noëmi distressed. Which friend? What was this problem? Where was she?'*

Desperate he wrote her a quick note and now he could only return to his flat. Unable to sleep, he woke extremely early. He headed into work, trying to deal with the feelings of anguish at not being able to find her.

Newcastle RVI. Sarai's labour had been delayed for five days but was now unstoppable. At almost 37 weeks it seemed her baby would be healthy. However, every precaution was being taken, given the history of her pregnancy. Noëmi had been phoned via her neighbour Yolanda's landline and went to her bedside. It was Friday night and a week since Marcus had sent that message. When she arrived Sarai was in the delivery room, with a midwife. The baby's heartbeat was being monitored carefully.

"Luca would love this," Noëmi said.

"He's with me."

Sarai seemed strong, she was breathing deeply and refusing any pain relief.

"It might hurt the baby, I'm using mindfulness to stay relaxed, I've practised."

Noëmi smiled, she was impressed with Sarai's focus and she knew she would be thinking of Luca.

"Did you decide on names?" Noëmi asked.

Sarai nodded and turned away for a moment.

Noëmi looked down. *'How is Luca not here to share this? It seems so unfair.'*

The labour was long and Sarai seemed to be progressing well. After four hours, Noëmi wandered out to get a coffee and she looked at the hospital, which felt dark, lonely and clinical. She began to think it was odd that Marcus was somewhere in the same building and she wondered why he had been so brutal and cold, cutting her off like that.

Putting the plastic coffee cup to her lips, she began to think about work and all that had happened in the past week; she could feel her body tighten and her pulse quicken.

Having returned to the labour suite, Noëmi rubbed Sarai's back through the hospital gown.

"Focus on your breathing, it'll soon be over." By 4:30am the contractions were a minute apart. Another midwife arrived. It was tough going and although Noëmi kept away from the 'business end' as her father would call it, she could see that progress seemed slow for the effort put out. She began to feel panicky. *'How must she be feeling?'*

Sarai pushed hard. The midwives looked at each other. One suggested they call for a doctor.

"Come on Sarai, you can do this. Not long now, give it everything," Noëmi squeezed her hand encouragingly. The midwives checked for signs of distress. The baby was fine but they continued to wonder if they needed a doctor.

"Who's on duty tonight? Is it Dr McKenzie?" Noëmi froze at the sound of the name. That had to be Marcus.

"Let me look, no it's Dr Pandey."

Noëmi gave an audible sound of relief, which no one understood but her.

"I'll put a call out just in case," the midwife decided.

Fearing something could be going wrong, Sarai gave an almighty push. Then the midwives worked quickly as the baby slid out of Sarai.

"5.01am 15 July," one midwife shouted.

"It's a girl!" the other shouted to Sarai.

They took the baby to clear her airway. That minute, Sarai and Noëmi heard a high pitched cry. The baby was weighed, quickly checked, tagged, wrapped loosely in a soft sheet and placed on Sarai's skin at her chest. Sarai was smiling, crying and praying all at once. Noëmi was not surprised to feel herself crying too.

"Do you have a name for this beautiful little girl?" asked the midwife, grinning.

Gazing at her child, Sarai could not stop the tears.

"Yes I'm pleased to introduce Lucia, her full name the Vietnamese way is Bianchi Truong My Lucia, Truong is my family name, 'My' means 'pretty' and Lucia is for Luca."

Noëmi's gave up. Her tears flowed. She hugged Sarai, being careful not to crush the tiny pink Lucia. As soon as her hands had stopped shaking she took some photos and video on Sarai's phone for her. Noëmi used Sarai's phone to call the new baby's grandfather, Roberto and Sarai's stepmother, Vicki.

Both were ecstatic at the arrival of Lucia. Roberto was especially emotional and luckily as Noëmi spoke Italian she was able to explain all the events, how well Sarai had done and how perfect Lucia was. Sarai sent both grandparents lots of pictures with the heartfelt message, *'Luca will forever live on in his daughter Lucia. We will make him proud'*.

CHAPTER 43 - HAVE A GOOD WEEKEND?

Marcus

Marcus did not sleep.

Arriving at work early, he got an Americano from the staff canteen and marched to the emergency department. Unable to concentrate he cursed himself as he absentmindedly split coffee on his hand. Sighing, he checked his schedule for the day. He had half an hour before his shift, so he went to the maternity wing.

He let himself believe he was checking on his friend, Sarai, but in reality he was desperate to find out whatever he could about Noëmi.

As he reached the ward he saw Sarai sitting up with a baby in a cot next to her. A smile broke onto his lips.

"Sarai, how are you doing?" He walked over to her.

"Tired but happy, this is Lucia. They've put her on a special monitor because she was premature. I need to take this equipment home but they are being unreasonable and say I can't." Sarai did not take her eyes off her baby.

"Sarai, don't worry. You and the beautiful Lucia here will not be discharged until we're confident that she's well and you're both safe." Marcus saw the baby stretch and relax.

"Then I'll be staying for at least a month, maybe two," Sarai's voice was defiant.

"How was the birth?" He watched Lucia yawn.

"Not too bad, I was scared but Noëmi helped me, she kept me calm."

'She was here! This was the emergency!' Buoyed up Marcus could almost feel her presence.

"Good, she's gone home now then?" Marcus looked surreptitiously at Sarai.

"No she's gone to get a coffee, she has a day off today."

"Of course, where did she go?" Marcus asked, trying to sound casual. His heart began to beat hard.

"Not far, she only just left. I told her not to be long. I need someone to keep checking if this monitor is working. Is that light supposed to be on?"

"Sarai, please relax, everything is fine, you're in the best of hands, I know this team, they're awesome." Half stumbling in his haste, he went to find Noëmi.

Marcus tried to think where someone would go for coffee if they did not know the hospital. Out of the maternity unit, he walked towards the main entrance and saw a vending machine with some bright blue plastic seats. He gave a start as he recognised Noëmi sitting on one, staring into space. He smoothed out his scrubs, put his shoulders back and thought what to say. Soon he was at her side.

"Well done I hear you were the perfect birthing partner!"

Noëmi gave a small shriek and jolted her plastic cup spilling some coffee on her hand. She looked at him, her face was pale.

"Are you okay?"

Bush baby eyes stared up at him. "No, I don't think so".

"I tried to call you."

"Oh." She averted her gaze. "I lost my phone."

"What's been happening? We've all been worried." He felt himself trembling.

"Stuff. Not sure you want to know really, I talk to Frank, *he's my friend,*" Noëmi said pointedly.

"And I'm not?" He sat down next to her.

"You tell me?" She chewed on her coffee cup without looking at him.

"I'm so sorry, Noëmi, I know I have treated you badly, I can't tell you how ashamed I am." Marcus was supplicating.

"But I got your message, that made everything very clear." Her voice was strained.

Marcus recalled each second of texting Noëmi that night and his upset at getting no answer.

"But you didn't reply?" Marcus shook his head.

"You made it quite unmistakable how you felt." Noëmi stretched to put the coffee cup in the bin.

"Yes, I know it was hard."

An industrial cleaning machine entered the far end of the corridor.

"The problem is that I actually feel the opposite way." She put her elbows to her thighs, leaning forward.

"Oh God Noëmi," Marcus said looking down, *'Please not again, don't do this to me again'.*

"Plus I've made some mistakes." Her hair fell forward as she hung her head.

"Sending the photos?" He moved to look at her.

"What?" Her eyes were questioning.

"Weren't you sending photos to someone?"

A large group of healthcare assistants walked noisily past on their way to a briefing. Leaning back in his seat as they went past, he noticed the confusion in her eyes.

"Well, yes but no, not me." She put her head down. "I'm so ashamed Marcus."

"Don't worry, we all make mistakes. It doesn't matter to me. I thought it did but I've realised it doesn't, not one bit. Only you're a teacher and you need to make sure those photos are not out there."

"I don't understand." She turned towards him.

"Naked photos, that's bad, especially for a teacher. If the kids find them online..."

"Good God no! I've not sent any naked pictures of myself to anyone, you know me." Open mouthed, she looked astounded. Marcus jolted back. Looking skyward for answers he remained resolute.

"The thing is, Noëmi, I saw your phone messages on New Year's Eve."

She paused, then her face contorted with horror.

"Oh no, no, no I was playing a stupid prank on John Dyer." She flung her hands onto his arm, frantically shaking her head.

"What?"

"Those messages on New Year's Eve, I was pretending to be someone else, they were all fake to wind him up. I've never sent a naked picture in my life, of myself, or anyone else. And certainly not to that man. Oh my God, that's why you thought I was seeing someone." She gasped, raising eyes to the ceiling.

Marcus was shocked, six months of thinking the wrong thing. *What on earth had she been playing at? Why had she not mentioned this before?'*

"I have to tell you that I've been struggling with the thought that you were actually involved with him in some way...sexually."

"That's why you avoided me. You thought I was with him..." Now stupefied, she gazed at him, open mouthed. Marcus leant forward to look her in the eye.

"But I then came to the conclusion it didn't matter, not one bit. I didn't care. It didn't change how I felt about you."

"It would matter to me!" laughed Noëmi bitterly.

"We were completely at cross purposes." Marcus' voice was slow as he processed her words.

"A catfish. I did it to get revenge, I'm such an idiot," Noëmi paled and fidgeted awkwardly.

"Are you in trouble?" Marcus looked intently at her.

"I hope not, I wanted to make him suffer and it's all backfired. He's found out my plan. I'm in a bit of a mess."

The huge disinfecting machine whirred past them. Lost in his thoughts Marcus was trying to piece together what had been going on.

She continued, "Why would you care what I'm doing? It was you who said we *just can't be friends,*" She sat up resentfully, air quoting with her fingers.

"It was hard to say that then. Now I know how you feel. I wish it was the other way around. I always have. I realised what I've been wanting us to be all this time and I'm sorry I couldn't say it in person." Marcus admitted heavy heartedly, staring at his hands.

"It hurt to see that," Noëmi's voice was breaking.

"It was hard for me to send those messages. Not knowing how you would react, but I meant every word I said," Marcus could feel his throat tighten. *'Why would it hurt to know my feelings?'*

Noëmi looked puzzled.

An alert beeped on his phone. He had to report for duty in five minutes.

"Can we keep in touch though?" Marcus almost whispered.

"Yes... sorry I've got no phone at the moment but I'll get Frank to give you the number when I get organised," Noëmi seemed distracted. The hum of the automatic floor mop faded out. *'Time to go, nothing more to say.'*

"You know, I really care about you N." Eyes stinging he stood up and began to walk away. Head heavy he suddenly realised she had followed him.

"Messages?" Noëmi called after him.

Marcus turned around and looked at her. Two nurses rushed past them chatting.

"What do you mean?" he said.

"You said 'messages'. I only got one text message," Noëmi replied, breathless.

Marcus unravelled the past conversation slowly.

"I sent you two messages that night, sorry I pressed send half way through by mistake as I was texting so fast, I was so desperate to contact you."

"I got one that said *I just can't be friends.*"

"Yes. Did you not get the second? I sent it right afterwards," asked Marcus, his heart was pounding.

"No only one message. Although I may have deleted" She put her hand to her mouth. "Oh God, then I broke my mobile," replied Noëmi, biting her lip.

"You didn't see the rest?" Marcus suddenly understood. Now her words made sense. He realised what she had been saying to him.

"What rest?" asked Noëmi.

"You didn't see my second message? It said it was sent...okay wait there, I'll show it to you." He felt the hairs rise on his neck. Hands clammy, he got his phone out. Going to his sent messages and he showed the screen to Noëmi who gasped as she read.

'I want us to be much more than friends, I'm in love with you and have been for a long time now. So can we go for the win? Complete each other's quest and finally be together for good?'

"Noëmi, I'm just so in love with you, it's unbearable,"

Noëmi's lip started shaking and she flung herself at Marcus

"God, I love you so much!"

Taking her in his arms, he pulled her into his body.

"I've always loved you, all this time, Noëmi." He clung onto her.

"Marcus, I never stopped loving you."

The hospital paled to nothing. Everything stopped. Only Noëmi stood before him. Their eyes spoke their love for each other. Resistance finally redundant, feverishly they kissed.

His alert beeped again. They gently pulled apart.

"Damn I've got to go!" He looked at his phone and then back to Noëmi. "Can you meet me at the end of my shift?"

"Yes! When? Where?"

"6pm at the Leazes Wing entrance, I have to go," Marcus started to leave only to turn back again. He kissed her and left quickly not wanting to show his tears or the huge smile that had taken over his face.

Marcus was on a high. Whatever trouble Noëmi was in, it would be sorted out. Thoughts flew through his head as he ran to his department.

'She can move in with me, we can live off my salary, it'll all be okay.'

Every minute he looked at the clock. The day was in rewind. Why was it not already six pm?

His energy levels were buzzing. He felt scared at how close he had come to losing Noëmi and he was now determined to make up for lost time.

At six he left straight away, turning down drinks with his team.

"Ah Marcus it's Saturday!" They moaned.

"I've got plans!" he beamed, "I promise I'll come next time."

His consultant looked at him with amusement. "What's going on

367

with you then, my serious little protégé? So you can smile!"

Excited to have the evening and Sunday off with Noëmi, he waved goodbye and raced to the entrance.

CHAPTER 44 - SILVER HEART

Noëmi

Noëmi had been there since 5:30pm, having checked four times that this was the 'entrance' to the Leazes Wing. She was desperate not to muck up anything else in her life. The receptionist at the main desk kept eyeing her with suspicion.

'If I ask about the number of entrances again she looks like she'll have me chucked out.'

Having found out Marcus' true feelings she had rushed back to see Sarai. Next she had rung Frank from Sarai's phone to make sure he and Valentino would visit Sarai that evening.

"We've all had an email Noëmi, John Dyer's been arrested," Frank told her.

"What?" Noëmi was astounded, and put the phone on loudspeaker so Sarai could hear.

"No reason given, there's a special all staff meeting on Monday morning and we're banned from talking to any press, we think it's financial irregularities, that's what Pat Davies has been saying."

"I think it may be worse than that," Noëmi said, smiling at Sarai. "Let's just say I think this is Nemo's reckoning."

"Nemo? What do you know? God tell me! Imagine making us

369

wait all this time, it's an outrage!" said Frank, desperate to know the gossip. Noëmi smiled thinking how Pat would be beside herself to know the truth.

"I'll see you Monday."

"Why aren't you going to be there with Sarai tonight? We want to see you Noëmi, Val will be mad, you know," said Frank.

"I've got plans Frank, have to go!" She said, on a high that John Dyer was no longer a problem to her.

* * *

She rushed to her flat, as she entered she found a note pushed under her door. Thinking it was from her neighbour she did not read it straightaway. Instead she showered, blow dried her hair and packed a little overnight bag; she had absolutely no intention of going home without Marcus that night. Just before she left she took a quick look at the note.

'Noëmi please get in touch. I'm so worried about you. I mean what I said in my messages. I'm in love with you. I always have been. Please call. All my love Marcus.'

She was floating with happiness.

As she ran out of her flat her neighbour passed by and called out to her,

"How did it go?"

"Brilliant she had a baby girl, Lucia. Wow, it looked like hard work all that giving birth!"

"God, I bet, no need for us to worry about things like that for a while. Also some good looking guy was at your door last night, left you a note... I'd give him breakfast any day... if you're not interested that is..."

370

Noëmi laughed "Thanks Yolanda you know what they say, what nicer thing can you do for someone than make them breakfast!" as she sped off.

"Well I can think of a couple, but have fun!"

Waiting outside the hospital, she suddenly noticed Marcus running at full speed towards her. She burst out laughing. They threw themselves into each other's arms. As they embraced, at the door of the hospital, they were oblivious of time and others. These two were in love. A couple of passers-by smiled and looked away. The receptionist's eyes nearly popped from her head. Dr McKenzie had caught everyone's attention when he arrived at the hospital around four weeks ago. Marcus took her hand as they finally walked away but Noëmi spoke first.

"I'm never letting you go."

"And I'm definitely never letting you go!" He squeezed her hand tightly.

"Marcus, we found out that John Dyer's been arrested, we think we know why, Sarai was right."

"No way! You have to tell me everything! So what do you want to do? Go for a drink? Get food? There's a new Thai restaurant just opened..."

She stopped and turned to look at him.

"Marcus, after all this time? Let's go to your place immediately, now, pronto," she replied.

She clutched her little overnight bag.

"Okay I get it, absolutely fine by me!" he smiled.

"Now let's go!" she said smiling.

* * *

They got to Marcus' flat very quickly indeed. Situated in the Jesmond area in a terrace of old Victorian villas, Marcus had the ground floor of an attractive three story building. Three steps led up to the shared hallway and Marcus took Noëmi into his place, which he had been renting since mid-June. He had done it out in a simple but stylish way and had a number of plants that he carefully fed and watered. Everything was tidy but not obsessively so and the place was clean; Marcus had been brought up to keep house. The warm July evening was streaming through the back of the flat. The French windows from Marcus' kitchen and bedroom gave out onto a small terrace. This was not overlooked as allotments were on the other side of the high wall that surrounded the garden area. There was a front room with a TV, sofa and a work desk with papers and medical journals, a bedroom, a well-stocked kitchen, a spacious bathroom and a separate toilet.

Marcus showed Noëmi in, opened the French windows and put his things down on the kitchen table,

"I need a shower, it's been so hot at work, help yourself to a drink of whatever you want. Oh I don't need to say that! You know this is your home too! I'll be quick," He rushed off to the bathroom.

Noëmi put down her bag, put the food and wine she had brought into the fridge and looked around, just taking a glass of water. Everything was very Marcus, well thought out, not pretentious or ostentatious.

She looked on a shelf and saw a picture of his family which warmed her; they meant so much to him. She laughed when she saw the picture of the two of them that the local newspaper had taken when they got into Oxford and Cambridge. This was sitting beside his Graduation photo; she had exactly the same one next to hers. A huge message board had lots of Polaroids of fun times at university with his friends and she saw that she appeared in a number of them; in their Japanese rugby shirts, in her Yoda costume. Noëmi felt her eyes sting when she saw he also had one of her from the charity ball. She was also pleased to see a number from their teenage years, including a picture from her seventeenth birthday of them on the beach together.

The album she had given him for his birthday was open on the kitchen table as he had obviously been looking at it. The messages he had printed out again. This time with their words of affection. He must have been trying to see how to swap these with the old ones. He rushed out of the bathroom dressed in a small towel around his waist, holding his clothes. She went over to him and took his things and put them on the table. They kissed softly and tenderly then she led him into the bedroom, both of them feeling the intensity of the moment and excitement for what was about to happen.

* * *

Waking up together the next morning they were exhausted from all their intimacy, and lay holding one another, talking.

"No more friendship."

"I never want to be friends ever again."

A message pinged through on Marcus' phone.

"... it's Grandma's birthday... there's a cake thing at three. We need to go to that."

"No problem, it'll be lovely to see everyone," agreed Noëmi.

He replied to the message, "I've told mum I'm bringing my girlfriend, it will be a total surprise for them after all...a good one."

She hugged him and said, "We can pop in on Sarai on the way

home if you want."

She was hot and pushed down the sheet to let the large ceiling fan cool her body. She sat up and as she turned towards him he noticed her silver heart necklace, she looked so beautiful. Everything about her was perfect. He sat up and stroked her neck and shoulders, then he held her close.

"Actually I've always wanted to ask you. When I was eighteen, does your mum know that she bought me a necklace?" she asked.

"Okay, in a way she kind of did alright!" he said smiling at her.

"It was you, wasn't it?"

"Yeah, but I used the money she gave me for my birthday six months before so technically from mum, like I said at the time."

"It means a lot to me I knew it was you," she squeezed him tightly.

"Do you remember what you got me for my eighteenth?" Gently he pushed her long hair back over her shoulders.

"Stop! It was only one of your gifts. I took you to that Newcastle Everton match too! Even if Newcastle did lose...anyway I wanted to go to that concert!" She laid her head on his chest.
He laughed some more, "Exactly! A gift for yourself!"
She gave him a look. "No escape for my hero!"
"Ah you know I loved it because I was with you. N, I've still got a gift for you at my parents' home from that time."

She looked curious and he wondered if she remembered.

"The t-shirt? No!"

He nodded and she hugged him.

374

Eventually they got up and quickly got themselves ready.

They made their way from Jesmond to Marcus' family home in High Heaton which was about a twenty minute walk away. Strolling in the sunshine, laughing and joking, they could not have felt closer.

They arrived together which did not surprise anyone, but when Marianna saw Noëmi she said in a matter of fact way.

"Marcus, I thought you said it was an actual 'girlfriend', you could have just said Noëmi, then it wouldn't have got us all so worked up. We were getting curious to finally see you with a partner. I never met that girl from Oxford so this time we really got our hopes up! Oh well one day Marcus, one day!"

Marcus knew she was completely missing that what she had always wanted to happen had materialised and was right in front of her.

Marcus and Noëmi looked at each other and smiled.

"Would you like tea Noëmi?" Marcus' mother asked.

"Oh, yes please I'd love one, I've not had one today, we've only just got up..."

"...here, we've only just got up here," Marcus added quickly.

"Well yes I can see that," Marianna replied and she rushed off to put the kettle on.

Tianna, Marcus' sister, smiled and simply said,

"Mum's just so thick," and put her earphones back in and walked off.

Raeni

Raeni had noticed straightaway that they were holding hands with interlocked fingers, how they looked at each other, how he moved her hair that had fallen across her face and the tenderness between them. She was absolutely delighted and knew they were perfect for each other.

"My dear Grandson, how good of you to take time off from saving lives. Noëmi my dear, you doing a fine job in education too. This is such wonderful news," she greeted them smiling broadly.

"Happy Birthday Grandma! You know, I work as part of a great team doing the lifesaving bit so I can't take credit on my own. Noëmi is the one who needs the praise, people just don't appreciate teachers. Yes we're so happy, but today is about you!" and he handed over a gift and a card.

Noëmi

Noëmi loved his thoughtfulness.

She had bought a large bouquet of flowers on the way which she gave to Raeni. All the rest of the family were there; Jayden back from finishing his finals at Cambridge with his girlfriend Shreya, and Isaiah having just done A Levels and Tianna GCSEs. They were all ready to relax and catch up. Everyone chatted and lots of stories were exchanged, Jayden, Shreya and Noëmi spoke about Cambridge.

Tianna was very fond of Noëmi and asked her about the maths GCSE papers that year, then she added about her eldest brother.

"Finally it looks like he's cheered up, since New Year he's been miserable as f... " she did not finish her sentence no doubt as she was at home, which made Noëmi smile.

She emphasised "No, like really sad, not like him at all. Wouldn't talk to anyone."

"I think it's okay now, don't worry," Noëmi reassured her.

"Don't break up please, I can't face him moping around anymore, or even worse being with that Sophie again," Tianna replied.

"I promise we won't."

Throughout the afternoon, they could not take their eyes off each other. About half an hour after they arrived Donnie popped by for some cake and was shocked to see Noëmi there.

"N, I didn't know you were coming or that you were up in Newcastle. We've all been worried about you."

"Oh yes, I came up yesterday. Everything's good," she replied and Donnie suddenly looked baffled.

"And where's my birthday hug Donnie?" demanded Raeni, very obviously diverting attention away from Noëmi's comment.

"Well Happy Birthday you," quipped Donnie as he gave Raeni a large potted plant and a card. "N I'll get your bed made up if you want to stop over tonight."

"Donnie, have you seen my cake?" Raeni asked before Noëmi could reply and Marcus smiled.

No one really noticed, or so she thought, that they were next to each other the whole time although Tianna rolled her eyes and threw a cushion at them when they fed each other cake.

After a couple of hours with the family they said their goodbyes and left to go to the hospital to pop in on Sarai and Lucia.

"What train are you getting N? You need to get moving, it's Sunday," Donnie called to her as she left.

"The first one tomorrow morning,"

"But...where will you stay?"

"With Marcus,"

"But he doesn't have a spare room and that sofa is tiny, where..." started Donnie who knew Marcus' flat from having helped him move in with Anthony.

"Bye Dad, talk soon!" she interrupted and left with Marcus who put his arm around her and she put hers around him. Smiling at each other they kissed and walked off down the street.

Donnie

Standing at the McKenzie front gate, Raeni waved them off and looked over at Donnie. "Don't go worrying Donnie, he's a doctor, he'll make sure no harm comes to her."

Next to them, Tianna laughed out loud, "I love how Mum completely missed the one thing she's always wanted!"

Marianna heard this and hurried out with Anthony to see what Tianna was talking about. They could see Noëmi and Marcus entwined together, walking off into the distance. Marianna shrieked with delight and hugged her husband, who himself wiped a tear away.

Donnie was completely speechless with total astonishment. Then he could not help smiling to himself at how naïve he had been. With a lump in his throat he thought how wonderfully everything was working out.

CHAPTER 45 - ALL STAFF

Noëmi

Noëmi took an early train to Durham on Monday morning. Having stopped off at her flat, she headed to work, for the last two days of school before the summer holidays. However Noëmi still had no phone;

"I'm going to get one sorted this week, after school. In the meantime I'm sure Frank won't mind if you message me via him," Noëmi assured Marcus.

Arriving at St Wolbodo's early, Noëmi was itching to know what would be said during the special meeting at 8am that day.

The staffroom was packed and everyone was there, all the part time staff, even the evening cleaners had come in especially to hear this serious news. The email had stated quite emphatically that anyone talking to the press or anyone outside the school, would be liable for prosecution as there was a 'gag' order in place."

Frank had also arrived early and was on his phone, when Noëmi went in and sat next to him.

"Hello Noëmi, I'm going to start charging for my services, how many of these am I going to get?"

He showed Noëmi his phone screen:

'Hey Frank this is for Noëmi, *Missing you, can't wait to see you tomorrow xxx',*

"Of course I replied that I missed him too. He is so hot that man, Oxford educated emergency doctor with a great body, wonderful manners, lovely hygiene habits, a good sense of fun… and it would appear he now has an immaculate taste in women, which is of course most disappointing for someone like me."

Noëmi smiled. "Sorry, I'm getting a phone later. I thought you wouldn't mind."

"Anything for you my dear."

"Frank thank you, please can you tell him to meet us all at the Swan after work tomorrow? And can he stay with me afterwards?"

"Well now you're just showing off Noëmi," Frank smiled, "seriously, I'm so glad things are working out, I think I can guess who you were with this weekend," he said, giving her a huge hug.

"I'm so happy, Frank. It was all a big misunderstanding, but I was an idiot too, that's another story. Thanks for what you told him about my feelings, it helped a lot."

"I just said the truth, remember I did say we'd catch you when you fell…"

"I know, why do I not just listen to you?"

"Val's Marcus' dentist you know." Frank gave her a knowing look.

"Yes, he's taking out his wisdom teeth, he was telling me yesterday."

"Val had put an extra thirty minutes onto his next appointment so he could talk to him, man to man, sort him out. Rest assured it was time to take action. We did that for another couple and it worked brilliantly. We were best men at their wedding."

"Thank you Frank, for everything. Tomorrow, I'm making lasagne with homemade pasta and my mother's gelato. You and Val must come and eat with us after the pub."

"We'd love to come, thank you." He hugged her again.

Pat

Pat Davies noticed their hugging from her vantage point at the back of the staffroom. She gave a loud tut. Having set three alarm clocks that morning to come in early, she was desperate not to miss this deliciously serious meeting.

'Had someone died? Had a body been found in the school? Or a number of bodies?' her mind was racing, hoping it was not something mundane like Ofsted. Keeping quiet was very difficult for Pat but the threat of legal action had scared her enough to not breach the terms of the order.

Maurice

Guy walked in with Maurice Mundy, to a hushed staffroom. Maurice looked like he had not slept for weeks. Indeed he had spent the weekend at the police station, giving statements, along with the rest of the senior management. In addition to these woes, that Monday morning he had received a legal notice of unfair dismissal claims to be brought against the school by the three teachers who had been forced out of their jobs with fraudulent allegations of incompetence.

Deputy Head Sharon King was absent, having had an extremely uncomfortable time during her interview with the police. In May Sarai had given an account of her concerns to Mrs King who had not followed the correct procedures. Had she followed the proper protocol the memory stick would have been found two months earlier, before the robbery and destruction of John's office. Sarai knew exactly when each conversation had taken place as her *'countdown to meeting our baby calendar'* had a detailed note of all events and incidents in school. Unable to account for her failure to comply with the requirements of the position of trust she held, she had been obliged to resign with immediate effect.

In addition, Sharon King was required to attend one final meeting; the Special Educational Needs Committee at the Local Education Office had summoned her to discuss the case of Joel Rivera. They gave details of a whistle-blower's serious concerns. These were the misuse of Special Educational Needs money, the discrimination faced by Joel and the conduct of senior staff at St Woldbodo's. With John now under arrest, she would have to face the panel alone and account for the actions of the school. Maurice was copied into the letter but had told Sharon that she was *'on her own'* as he already had enough problems.

Pat

Before Guy spoke Maurice asked if there were any general notices, Frank took the floor and announced the birth of Sarai's daughter which broke the tension and made everyone smile.

The mood then returned to sombre as Guy began to talk.

"I have to give a statement that on Thursday we have taken into custody and arrested a 28 year old male teacher from St Wolbodo's on charges of possession of illegal images of children and of grooming. Unfortunately we know at least one of the victims of exploitation is a pupil from this school. There are some other charges, sexual assault, false imprisonment, blackmail and other related charges. We have obtained a gag order to ensure that the privacy of any victims is respected. It is important the case is not discussed, as any media reports could prejudice a jury and cause the trial to breakdown..."

Pat Davies almost fainted with shock. She put a hand on the

chair in front to steady herself.

How had she missed all this? All this had been happening right under her nose. *I'm always the first to tell everyone what happens in this place, how on earth did I not know this?'*

Maurice then read out instructions for the day;

"In order to continue the investigation, we have contacted parents and will shut the school from today. The police need to take statements from everyone here, so you can imagine it is a huge job."

Frank

Frank had to relay all this information to Sarai, Marcus and Valentino and was getting confused by the different replies pinging back. Pictures of Lucia, declarations of love and a rant about having "looked in that man's mouth" buzzed through to him.

"Noëmi I can't cope, why don't you look after my phone?" he said, handing his mobile to Noëmi.

CHAPTER 46 - SUMMER HOLIDAYS

Noëmi

McKenzies Assemble 30 July 2017. To describe Marcus' family as proud would be an understatement; they were bursting with joy. As with all the McKenzie family events, the whole family was to attend the graduation. Hot on the heels of his brother Jayden's graduation from Cambridge, they were now celebrating this. Jayden would make his own way there and Marcus had also gone on ahead to do a final sort out of his student house. However, only Marcus' parents could attend the actual ceremony, given the two tickets per family limit. They had a seven seater car and as there were two spare places Marianna invited Noëmi and her father, at Marcus' behest. Although Marcus had attended Noëmi's graduation from Cambridge, she had hardly seen him. Sophie had dropped him off and then quickly picked him up to drive to her parents' place in Norfolk for the rest of the weekend. This time things were very different.

The early morning sun burned down on a glorious July morning as the group prepared for their four hour drive to Oxford. Spirits high, they chatted, sang and told stories as Anthony drove merrily on the way to another son's graduation. Noëmi felt almost scared at how happy she was. Sitting reflective in the car she knew she had to address one thing. Something she had been putting off. Shoulders back she took a deep breath and sent Magda a message to apologise.

Dear Magda,

Please read what I have to say. I need to say sorry with all my heart for stealing your photos and using them. I have been immature and selfish. I did it to get revenge on John Dyer. My plan completely backfired and risked my own happiness. I have to let you know that there have been some developments and I can give you more information soon.

With sincere apologies,

Noëmi McAllister

To her relief, Magda pinged back straightaway:

Hey, no worries, I was mad with you but we all do stupid stuff. Let me know what happens!

Bye and don't worry I'm over it all really!

Magda

Upon arrival in Oxford, Marcus greeted them all warmly outside the Sheldonian theatre where the graduation would take place.

"A lot of it will be in Latin Mum," he told Marianna who really could not have cared less what language it was in. Her son was graduating with a First in medicine from Oxford and it just did not get better than that. The good news was that Marcus had managed to get a spare ticket and without question it was Raeni who would join to see the ceremony. Noëmi took lots of pictures of the family group for them.

Raeni, Marianna and Anthony were overwhelmed by the tradition of the ceremony where Marcus went from Graduands to Graduate. A reception in the college followed and the drinks flowed. Marcus was busy with his friends and in demand for various group photos the whole time. Looking around the quad, Noëmi remembered her Cambridge graduation ceremony, two years previously, and how much it had meant to her. The day drew to a close with shrieks, tears and laughter as they all celebrated. Suddenly she became aware of someone approaching. Noëmi looked up and saw Sophie. At the same moment she looked her way. It was too awkward to not say something.

"Hi Sophie, congratulations! I'm Noëmi, we worked on the charity project together."

"Yes, I remember," she said dramatically.

Noëmi assumed that was it and turned to find the family group again.

"I see you and Prince Charming are finally together then."

"Sorry?" although she knew immediately Sophie was referencing her nickname for her.

"Don't act so coy, you and my ex-boyfriend. All this old friends from school business, poor little orphan, innocent girl next door. You've been after him the whole time haven't you? Your immature teenage crush. Is that what you came to Oxford for?"

Noëmi bit her tongue and waited for a minute. Finally she replied, "I'm not an orphan, dad's just over there. Anyway you know what happened between you and Marcus. It's graduation, let's move on," she said earnestly.

"Oh whatever, *I couldn't care less*," Sophie said with emphasis. "Marcus was never the one for me, far too sensible, I'm engaged now you know."

"Congratulations, that's fantastic news for you."

"Good luck with Marcus, you'll need it, I mean he can be a bit slow off the mark. We used to call him, 'Slow Off' you know, 'slow off the Marcus," she laughed at her own joke.

"That's so unnecessary, Sophie. I know how good he was to you."

"Of course, you would say something like that. Does it come naturally being so goody two shoes perfect?" Sophie's voice pierced through her, "Oh look at me I'm so casual and authentic, unfettered by materialism in my horrible clothes, doing all my charity work for the poor people in Africa." Emotionally exhausted, she desperately wanted Sophie to stop.

"There's no need to be like that." Noëmi managed.

She then looked Noëmi right in the eye and said smugly, "If you say so. Finally *Naomi,* after all this time, we have something in common, don't we? Does he look after you the way he looked after me?"

Sophie enjoyed saying the last part with a malicious glint in her eye, in an attempt to torment Noëmi. She swung her hair round and walked off to join her new fiancé who grabbed her waist with appreciation.

"It's Noëmi and like I said we both know the truth; you know yours but you certainly have no idea about mine now do you?" she said out loud to herself. As she went to rejoin her group she could hear Sophie giggling with happiness in the distance.

Sophie

Sophie's relationship with Marcus had finally fallen apart following the charity ball the year before. She yearned for adventure; excitement, Marcus yearned for academic excellence. Coming home from the ball together Marcus had wanted to go straight to sleep, on his sofa and not with her. This rendered Sophie furious. She lay awake in his bed, jaw clenched. *'What's the point of a boyfriend who doesn't give me attention.'*

In the night she heard Marcus murmuring Noëmi's name. Sophie had left and sent Marcus a text to finish the relationship, accusing him of being unfaithful. Marcus had accepted this, tried to see her to end things properly but had moved on without question. She had felt humiliated by how her placeholder relationship had finally come to an end. Today she was glad to have been able to say her piece to Noëmi.

Noëmi

Noëmi saw Marcus on the other side of the quad, champagne glass in hand, laughing with his coursemates. Seeing her approach, he ran across and put his arm around her. His eyes were sparkling.

"I've just had a delightful conversation with Sophie." She said casually not wanting to spoil his day. They rejoined his friends.

"She's angry today, even though she's just got engaged. I wonder when it started with Charlie." He finished his drink and stretched out his arm for his friend to fill his glass again.

"She's enraged!" Noëmi joked.

Marcus laughed and swung her round playfully.

Noëmi continued, putting her arms around his neck, "She's just so immature, I don't know why she cares, she left you."

Marcus stood still and looked at her, "It's because for me and her it was never love and we both knew that."

They took each other by the hand and held on tightly. Refocusing on the precious time they had left to enjoy graduation, thoughts of Sophie faded away.

Marcus was going to London that evening with Jayden. The following week he was to attend a course in ethics and emergency medicine, as part of his new job. Noëmi and Marcus said goodbye to each other. Jayden waited patiently checking his phone. The rest of the family left them to it and walked slowly to the car. Finally Noëmi caught them up.

"How long is Mr Perfect away for?" asked Tianna.

"Six days and don't call your brother that," replied Raeni.

"Whoa, N, how many hours is that?"

Noëmi looked round at her and was greeted with a mystic smile.

"You're so like your brother you know that's exactly the kind of thing he would say."

"He learns from the best," Tianna had the final word.

Marcus

Jayden walked with Marcus to the station, both pulling their cases behind them. Having got onto a graduate training scheme with a prestigious firm of management consultants, Jayden was excited to be moving to London. He would stay with Shreya's family whilst they looked for a flat. The sun was lowering and the day was cooling as evening began and the brothers chatted happily about their recent celebrations. Suddenly Jayden put his free arm affectionately around his brother as they strolled along.

"I love that you and Noëmi are together, it makes the world seem right."

"I would agree Jay."

Jayden stopped, "Bro, I'm sorry I just have to ask you."

"Ask me what? Sounds ominous."

"Given how long you and Noëmi have known each other. Considering how you were never apart, revising I think you called it…"

"Yes, where's this going?" Marcus asked, tilting his head back.

Jayden continued. "I have to ask, did you ever get together before? You know, a little trial run?"

Marcus now put his arm around his brother and they started walking again.

"I always wanted us to be together, she did too, we both made mistakes. It's taken far too long!"

"Damn." Jayden furrowed his brow.

"I know it was tough." Marcus added.

"No, I owe Shreya ten quid."

Pausing, Marcus relaxed his shoulders.

"Okay then... to be fair, when we were...no I can't say! Actually she owes you the tenner."

Jayden swung round, eyebrows raised.

"What on earth does that mean? You're not getting away with that!"

"One day I'll tell you." Marcus stared forward and smiled.

CHAPTER 47 - FINDINGS

Sarai

15 August 2017. Sarai had recovered from the birth and returned home with baby Lucia but without the hospital breathing monitor.

One morning, whilst busy soothing her baby, Sarai got a call from Guy. He had decided the time was right for her to meet at his office to discuss the findings into Luca's death. Sarai knew she needed to hear whatever Guy had to report, however painful it may be. Guy had to do this formally in his office in order to document the conversation for further questions and future reference. Immediately she rang Noëmi for support. Everyone rallied round.

Sarai arrived at Guy's office with Attila the Priest, Noëmi and Marcus. Guy had suggested having a medical doctor there to explain that Luca would have lost consciousness immediately as the plane decompressed; he would have felt nothing. Noëmi suggested Marcus, who readily agreed to help, knowing it would be important to hear this from someone she trusted. Sarai could barely walk, as the reality was hitting her that Luca was never coming back. They sat in a row in front of Guy's desk. Sarai was hunched over with dread.

Guy began by confirming that the assault on her by John Dyer was part of the charges in that case. Indeed what she had suffered had pushed over the very first domino. In addition what she had reported seeing on the memory stick had enabled Guy to solve the case and complete the domino run.

Secondly it was now right to go through the preliminary findings of the investigation into the New York Airlines crash, in which Luca had died.

The investigation had been formidable. The black box and cockpit voice recorders had been found and all evidence pointed to a catastrophic incident where the plane broke up. No one could have survived and it still could not be ascertained definitively why there had been this mechanical failure. However, given the plane's service history, initial reports pointed to an engine fire followed by the fuel tanks exploding. Luca's DNA had been found at the crash site, Guy told Sarai. This confirmed beyond any doubt that he had died. Collapsing forward onto the desk her shoulders shook; she could not hold back the tears.

Attila held her hand and Noëmi put her arm around her. Marcus gently assured Sarai that Luca would not have suffered. However it did not give Sarai any consolation; she was still living without Luca. Attila tried to give Sarai some solace;

"Sarai, when faced with this darkness, faith can help. Luca is now with God. His soul lives on. You will be reunited in Heaven."

Given that there was no other way to move on, Sarai clung onto these words of comfort.

Head down she left as quietly as she had entered with her friends.

Guy

As he left Guy thanked Marcus for his help. The men got along particularly well as professional colleagues and were now firm friends. They had got to know each other recently when Marcus changed gyms to avoid seeing Shauna and, by chance, joined the same one as Guy. The pair began to meet up for a drink or a game of squash regularly and enjoyed one another's company, sharing the same interests and sense of humour.

Asking for a friend. Half an hour later, Guy was in his office when he got a call from Marcus.

"Hey Guy, sorry to disturb you but Noëmi wants a chat if you're still there."

"Sure no problem, mate, I've got half an hour, come back over."

A number of staff members had wanted to talk to him. They either wanted to give extra bits of information, make allegations or ask questions away from other colleagues.

"Hey bit chilly for August," Noëmi said as she walked back in with Marcus, who gave Guy a nod.

"God, that was tough. If Dyer doesn't plead guilty, Sarai will be called to give evidence. She'll need people around her then."

Noëmi continued, "Yes of course. We have a rota of people helping, so we can carry on with that."

"Good, anyway what's all this about?" Guy asked.

"I want to talk to you off the record if that's okay?"

"Hmm. Here we go! I'm an officer of the law. If you confess a crime to me then I can't ignore it!" Guy said with a laugh.

"Yeah well the friend I told you about who made a fake dating profile..."

Marcus gave her an old fashioned look.

"Yes, I remember," Guy said, looking at her directly with a ghost of a smile.

"It was to try and mess with someone. Nothing happened but

this person is feeling terrible in case this sparked the behaviour in John Dyer and caused all this," Noëmi offloaded.

"Why does *your friend* think this?"

"They promised to send him naked pictures and didn't, they promised to meet him for sex and didn't show up. They wound him up to mess with him, torment him..."

"Ha! *Your friend* should know that we have evidence going back over the past six years. Basically ever since the accused entered teaching, there may even be stuff from before then too. You know he changed his surname from Ricketts-Dyer to plain Dyer, which is making it all longer to investigate."

Noëmi looked miserable, "I feel terrible, I just wanted to mess with him to get back at him for bullying me." she offered.

"Maybe you helped reveal his crimes?"

"I actually ended up nearly ruining my own life instead of his."

"Careful what you wish for eh? But Noëmi, scheming really doesn't seem to be you somehow! You're just not conniving, I can see that!" he smiled.

"Tell me about it."

"You say he bullied you?"

"It was at school, he went to my school, Newcastle Green Academy, I was in Year 9 and he was in sixth form,"

"Dyer didn't remember you then?"

"It would appear not, but I never forgot him, you don't forget the people who bullied you as a child."

"If it helps I made sure I was there to arrest him, which I may have enjoyed." Guy added. "I always find that bullies are

394

narcissists; cruel, selfish, insecure. We might come back to you to find out a little more, in case other people come forward when the trial is public. There could be victims at your old school," explained Guy.

Noëmi shuddered at the thought.

"We were all at the same school, I remember him, he made a racist comment about me, lots of rumours of his antics even back then," added Marcus.

"You two were at school together?" Guy asked, smiling.

"Yes, we sat next to each other, she needed my help, you understand."

"Yeah right, why do I think it was the other way round!" Guy laughed. "You two getting together has certainly cheered him up, but definitely not improved his dreadful squash game!"

"Ah no we've got a match later haven't we? Another brutal humiliation awaits!" Marcus put his hands to his head, resigned to his fate. Guy grinned broadly. Noëmi reassured, they thanked Guy and headed off.

Staring out of the window from the police station, Guy saw the couple leave across the car park laughing with each other. Looking back to his desk he sighed.

'I just wish I could find that kind of happiness.'

Sharon

16 August 2017. The summer A Level results were in and senior staff members were able to see these the day before the students. Mrs King snuck into the school to get her students' results, as she could not remember her log in for the online results' portal. She looked down the list of students and her heart sank. None had scored above a C apart from Joel who had secured a B grade and was the highest achieving student. There was no way to describe this as a 'typo'. There would be no photographs of smiling students jumping in the air. Mrs King knew that one pupil's plan to apply to Cambridge depended on an A grade. She scurried out. Sharon spent the day in her garden with a bottle of wine, the one she had bought to celebrate her 'amazing results'. For company she had her small terrier dog, who kept tugging at her skirts for a walk.

Donnie

24 August 2017. The following Thursday, Noëmi was in school for GCSE results' day. She was feeling relaxed and revitalised as she had just flown back from a week in Italy with Marcus.

Together with Donnie, they had stayed with her mother's parents. As they arrived, Noëmi's grandparents ran to her and hugged her tightly.

"If you add how much you love her and how much I love her and multiply it by about a million you get somewhere close to how much they love her." Donnie told a smiling Marcus.

As they took their cases to their rooms in the vast old Italian farmhouse, Noëmi insisted Marcus have the double guest suite, that she have the neighbouring single and Donnie the single down the corridor.

Coming down the stairs Donnie looked at his daughter.

"Okay Noëmi McAllister, don't think I don't get the logic behind your room allocations. Just be discreet and remember how important being a good Catholic is in their eyes."

Noëmi looked sheepish.

"And when I used to wander the corridors of this house, to either check your mother wasn't lonely or when I was ill after her death, it didn't take long for anyone to notice!"

Donnie was slightly wistful as their intense young love brought back fond memories for him of the times he had spent there, with Manon, relaxing in the hot summer sun. He did find that the amount of time the inventive pair needed 'to rest' was somewhat excessive. They both cited the reasons for their frequent naps to be that they were 'tired by the journey', 'suffering from jet lag', 'exhausted by work', 'struggling in the heat', 'worn out by the sun'...

Noëmi

Charvi was in school for results too. The hall was laid out with tables where students could all collect their GCSE results. Seeing each other, the two friends hugged.

"How was Italy Noëmi? Something's changed, you look elated!"

"Ah everything's good! I'll tell you at the Swan later!" Her eyes sparkled.

"I love that handbag, is that from Italy too? Gorgeous leather, mustard, such an awesome colour!"

"Yes I know Marcus got it for me, an early birthday gift! But what about you Charvi? Best results in the school! Congratulations!" Students picking up their grades milled around the pair excitedly.

"That'll show everyone eh?"

"We all know there's nothing to prove. The managers are all getting their comeuppance now with the unfair dismissal case!"

"Serves them bloody well right. Hey I got that job at the academy in Newcastle. A much higher salary and the team are absolutely delighted to have me! My girlfriend teaches there too! So win, win, win!"

Charvi smiled broadly and relaxed, leaning back on one of the tables. Noëmi did the same.

"I bet, I'll miss you so much but I can't wait to hear about it. I went to that school, Newcastle Green! It's come on a lot since my day!"

Noëmi became aware of two pupils standing quietly waiting to talk to her. It was Stephanie and Ronnie.

"Well done you both did amazingly!" she said smiling as she saw them, "Now you're both going to the Technical College?"

"Yes, can't come back here you know that, but they're going to support me for Oxbridge. I've got a mentor, they're really excited. It makes a difference when the teacher cares, like you did Miss. I'm so sorry when I was rude," Stephanie said quietly.

"Stephanie, stop! After all you've been through! You can't be a teacher if you don't understand how hard it is to be a teenager."

Ronnie looked over his shoulder restlessly and put his hands in his pockets.

"Ronnie, just give me a minute!" Stephanie rolled her eyes.

"I don't feel good here, that's all."

"Me neither, but we're done with this place, just needed to see Miss, say thanks."

Ronnie whispered something to Stephanie, her eyes glinted.

They said goodbye and Noëmi saw the pair walk off in the direction of the main door, forbidden for students to use.

A grin took over all their faces.

CHAPTER 48 - THAT'S HOW MUCH SHE MEANT TO ME...

Donnie

The summer gave into autumn and a new routine set in. Marcus and Noëmi began to make joint plans! To move in together the following year and visit The End Noma Campaign hospital in Nigeria. Donnie was pleased to see his daughter so safe and happy.

One early December evening, busy in his kitchen cooking a vegetarian chilli, Donnie got a call from Marcus who wanted to talk. Within the hour Marcus was on the doorstep. Smart shirt, well-polished shoes, holding a good bottle of Malbec for Donnie.

"Ah is this to impress your girlfriend's father?" Donnie joked as he looked from Marcus to the bottle.

'I think I know what this could be about!' Donnie smiled inside.

Chatting about their day they then sat in the kitchen and Donnie described his plans for his garden and the different plants he wanted to introduce. He watched as Marcus seemed to be preoccupied with his own thoughts.

'I remember it was the same for me!' he chuckled to himself.

Marcus helped him prepare his chilli sauce. He knew where everything was and felt very much at home in the familiar cottage style kitchen with its red and white gingham curtains.

Marcus glanced over at the picture of Donnie and Manon on their wedding day in Italy, looking so young, happy and fresh.

"How old were you when you met?" Marcus asked.

"She was eighteen, I was nineteen, day one of university, both looking for the same lecture and that was it, as they say. I considered myself very lucky, she could have done better!" He laughed.

"So about twenty years together."

"And three months! It's lucky we met young. I did count up the exact number of days once but it just made me sad."

"She was so young when she died."

"It came out of nowhere, no family history. Apparently leukaemia is just like that, she put the tiredness down to too much work and a busy life. There was nothing they could do. You don't expect that in medicine do you?"

"No, we always believe we'll save everyone."

"As you know I miss her terribly. I still talk to her every day, not sure that's healthy but I don't want her not to be in my life." Donnie said, looking at his hands.

Marcus could understand that.

"But you know Marcus, even if I had known that I could have only twenty years, or say ten years maybe only one year. Even just one day of the happiness I felt with her and a lifetime of pain afterwards, I would still choose that over any other option. She meant that much to me."

Sitting close to Marcus, it seemed Donnie could now talk of his feelings. The journey had been long and gloomy. It was never going to be over but Donnie had evidently come far. Marcus thought back to when he had first met Donnie ten years previously, in the same kitchen and how warmly he had welcomed him into their home. Memories of Donnie helping his father fix his bike and coming along to watch him play football drifted in his head. However as a fourteen year old, he had soon noticed that Donnie was often sad. It made Marcus feel embarrassed, maybe helpless? Marcus had watched Noëmi guide her father through the darkness and was impressed by her compassion and resilience.

Marcus gathered his thoughts.

"I don't know how I would cope in your shoes Donnie. A message for us all to avoid petty arguments and bad moods; not to waste a minute of our time together, hey?"

Donnie nodded lost in thought.

"Do you know why I wanted to come and see you?" Marcus looked over at Donnie who stirred his sauce.

Donnie

"Well let's have that wine and you can tell me! I may have an idea it's to do with Noëmi." Marcus poured their wine, as Donnie spoke. "It's funny because you have always been such good friends but over the years I've seen things change between you two."

"Yeah, although not really change. We liked each other from when we were at school, truth be told." He took some wine.

"Oh? Really? I thought you were just good friends," Donnie

stood for a minute and thought of the times when he had left them alone together without a second thought.

Marcus laughed, "Don't worry, we were unfortunately... apart from when ...there was a time when...no never mind,"

"Don't tell me any more! It never occurred to me! Which is a bit silly considering how your mum would sigh when I left you in the house together." Donnie gave a nervous laugh. He was still actually terrified that Marianna would be after him, even now, if she learnt of some past incident of his daughter tempting her son away from the path of righteousness.

"And it's taken you both all this time!" Donnie was amazed.

"Well I brought it on myself, I was a bit of an idiot at Oxford. Immature and selfish. I got caught up in a clique, so probably for the best. Gave me a chance to grow up."

"I think you're being a bit hard on yourself Marcus, you've always been selfless with me and N. We were both so lonely when we moved here."

"No I've needed you guys just as much!" Marcus put his foot on his knee and leaned back into his chair.

'Is he going to get to the point?'

"I thought I should tell you, I'm going to ask Noëmi to marry me." Marcus tilted his head and looked across earnestly at Donnie.

"Well Marcus, did you not think you should speak to me first?" Donnie put on a serious face.

Marcus jolted forward and appeared mortified.

"Oh sorry! Yes of course, it's just you don't seem that traditional. I mean, you're more like my friend than a future father in law!"

Marcus felt himself burn up.

"Oh I see!" Donnie mocked indignation.

"No I mean, that's a good thing…" Marcus got all fidgety.

"You could at least do your *friend*, as you call me, the courtesy of asking for his daughter's hand! I mean I've only got one daughter, this is only going to happen once!" Donnie pulled his lips together to look stern.

"I'm really messing this up aren't I? Donnie, could I have your permission to ask your daughter to marry me?" He asked formally, looking a little scared.

A huge grin burst onto Donnie's face. "Oh Marcus, you're so easy to wind up! It's the best news ever!" Donnie wiped tears of many things from his eyes. Marcus gave a massive sigh, presumably of relief. The men had a long hug.

"You had me going there!" Marcus shook his head.

"Does she have any idea?"

"No, whenever I mention it, she keeps saying we're too young."

"When will you ask her?"

"I was thinking of New Year's Eve. I hope she'll say 'yes'. I'm pretty nervous."

"How perfect! It would be a surprise for her! I did that to her mother, Manon. We'd only just graduated, even younger than you!"

Marcus listened.

"Feels like yesterday I went to see her father, Giuseppe, now that was terrifying. I didn't speak very good Italian and he viewed me as this Scottish student with no prospects for his daughter.

Anyway he was fine, very happy in fact, but told me he would kill me, assuring me he had the means to do it, if anything happened to his daughter." Donnie pointed at Marcus with his wine glass.

"Okay so I guess you'll tell me the same!"

"Actually now I come to think about it, that sounds like a plan!"

They laughed together.

For a moment Donnie was contemplative. "Okay let me give you this."

Donnie went to his dresser and took out a small box which he handed to Marcus.

"Go on, open it!"

It was a diamond solitaire engagement ring.

"That's stunning!"

"It was Manon's engagement ring. Obviously as a poor student I didn't buy it! Her father gave it to me when I went to *ask his permission* to marry her."

"You did it properly!"

"Indeed, they *are* very traditional! It's a family ring dating back to Manon's great grandmother, on the Santoro side. You don't have to use it if you have other ideas. You're welcome to refashion it, but as the next generation you should have it!"

The stone sparkled in Marcus' hand.

"It's perfect. Donnie, thank you. It must be hard to let it go."

"Marcus, it's true the ring holds memories. I can still see her face when she saw it for the first time!" Donnie looked across at their wedding photo. "...but my heart still holds all the love. For you and Noëmi to have this ring is certainly what Manon would want."

"It's just exactly what Noëmi would want too."

Sitting enjoying the moment Donnie broke the silence.
"The McKensters or the McAllizies! What shall we call the new clan?" he joked!
The men bonded over wine, a few beers and some Scottish single malt whiskey, talking for a good few hours about life and love.

CHAPTER 49 - NEW YEAR'S EVE TAKE TWO

Marcus

31 December 2017. A new year was dawning and Marcus had one of his plans again. Between detective work to check the size of the ring and proposal plotting, his mind was definitely elsewhere.

It was busy in A&E as party season always increased the number of revellers getting into mishaps. After a number of frantic shifts, he finally had a day off. It was New Year's Eve! He arranged to meet Noëmi at her flat in Durham that afternoon. That evening they were joining a large group of friends for a party at a restaurant in Durham. Some were visiting from London, including Yumi. She was staying at Noëmi's flat but also intended to visit her aunt who was working at the Japanese University in Durham.

Donnie was invited to spend the evening with the McKenzie's and was excited that they would undoubtedly be celebrating good news. He hoped Marcus would not leave the proposal until midnight as the suspense was too much already.

Marcus arrived at her flat, flustered, and dumped his bag inside.

"You didn't have lunch yet?" he spoke without taking a breath.

"No I did as you said, Yumi's here but has just gone shopping.

Are you okay?"

"Yes, why?" he said too quickly.

"No reason, you just seem a bit on edge. Stressed."

"We're going out," he announced.

Noëmi looked bewildered for a moment.

"Okay give me a sec," she padded off to get herself together.

"I need you to get your beanie," he called after her.

"What?" She looked back at him.

"The one that we bought six and half years ago after A Level results. I know you've got it."

He had seen hers in one of her drawers that happened to be open, which had given him the idea. Noëmi gave him a wry look as she went to her bedroom. She finally returned, *'on point university look beanie'* in hand.

"Oh wow I remember this," she said as they pulled them on and headed out "Did you buy another?" They walked out into the low December sun.

"No, I kept mine." He smiled.

"Same as me! Do you remember that day?" She grabbed his hand.

"Every second," he said quite seriously.

"For me, it was a bad day. I'd messed everything up, then that...yeah horrible day." Noëmi blinked and had a faraway look. "What I wouldn't give to change all that."

"Well for me too, so I thought we should put it right! Go back to that moment and play it differently!" Marcus was upbeat.

Noëmi

They retraced their steps, almost to the minute but this time there were no tears. They visited their best loved cafes and did all the same things. They took out the rowing boat, albeit in the winter cold rather than the August sunshine. She knew Marcus must have arranged this specially, as they did not run out of season. She laughed when he reminded her that her rowing had definitely not improved. The Christmas lights still glistened as the evening drew in. It was cold but dry. After their boat trip they made it to Framwellgate bridge, the wide street was still busy with shoppers making the most of the seasonal sales and the holiday atmosphere.

He took her to the same spot from all those years ago. They stood by the stone wall and looked at the early evening lights on the river which was becoming shrouded in winter mist.

"Do you remember the selfie?" He asked.

"Oh yes and you putting it on your social media like that was the loveliest thing anyone has ever done for me."

"Oh I'm glad it was me then!" he smiled.

"Can we take it again… if we're doing that day again. What is it… six years and four months on?"

"Before the selfie, I have something to ask you."

"Okey dokey, fire away!" said Noëmi nonchalantly.

Marcus

He waited for a minute, unsure why he was feeling so scared; What if she gave him one of her 'we're too young' speeches? What if this was not special enough? What if she said 'no'? He could just stop and give her the kiss he planned.

They gazed out over the river as the cathedral bell struck five. The soft lights from the cafes and bars lit the water, a few late rowers drifted along and the gentle buzz of others surrounded them.

"First I've got you a special New Year's gift."

He went to his rucksack and took out a large, slightly crumpled box, which he gave to her.

"Wow! Thank you! I didn't know, I've not got anything for you, I feel really bad. Shall I open it?"

"Yes, go for it," he stood next to her as she undid box after box until she got to a tiny box at the bottom with a gift tag.

"Read the message first, I know you, diving straight into the present!" He joked.

Looking at the message on the gift tag, she knotted her eyebrows.

"I can't, the writing's so tiny, hold on, *mi vuoi spossare?*" she looked at him stunned. "Do you want to exhaust me?"

"Sorry?"

"Why are you asking me that?"

"I thought we should be more official, make a public statement if you like," He felt slightly cold all of a sudden.

"A public statement?" She studied his face.

"Yes, show the world how good we are together." His eyes searched hers.

"Alright that sounds interesting, not sure how we would do that really. It's a bit personal." Now she was looking down at the box.

409

"But it's important."

"Oh, yes I know, but..." Her voice trailed away.

He was a bit underwhelmed by her reaction but it was not a 'no' so he knew he had to do it and he got on his knee.

"Noëmi, will you marry me?" He was simply too nervous to say any more.

He saw her jump up and then she dived into his arms. Her face was electrified.

"Yes, yes, yes! Oh my God! Absolutely a million times yes!"

A small cheer went up from some passers-by who had stopped.

"Sorry, I can't say it in Italian!" He lifted her as he stood up.

"Oh my, I know, I've just realised, you didn't! 'To marry' is **sposare**, just one *s*"

He looked at the tag.

"Oh sorry, what does **spossare** with the double '*s*' mean then?"

"**Spossare** means to wear someone out, you asked me, *Do you want to exhaust me?*"

"Well that too!"

"The answer to both is a definite yes!" He swung her round and she screamed with delight.

Once they had stopped laughing, he gave her that kiss. Noëmi opened the small box and he put the ring on her finger. One of the bystanders offered to take their picture for them of this perfect moment.

Marcus explained the history of the ring and added how Donnie would kill him, no doubt with the help of her Italian grandfather, if anything happened to her. Noëmi kept checking her hand; it was a perfect fit. They recreated their teenage selfie this time in December moonlight and continued walking around the town. He did not need to explain why he had chosen New Year's Eve; they were both grateful to exorcise the demons from the previous New Year. Their friends all joined for a raucous party at Zen in Durham that evening. Yumi was running late so she agreed to join them there.

Guy

Guy noticed his friends arriving so he marched straight over to catch up and get the first round in. Chatting away, he handed out the drinks and noticed there was a spare gin and tonic that had been ordered.

"Whose is this then?" He looked at Marcus puzzled.

"That'll be mine thank you!" Yumi's hand swooped in and claimed the drink.

"Oi that's theft! Give it back!" He gave a laugh.

"Not a chance!" She took a large gulp.

"Guy this is Yumi," Marcus introduced them and then slapped his friend on the shoulder, "...you're on your own mate!"

"Ignore Marcus, he's terrified of me!" Yumi had a glint in her eye.

Marcus raised his eyebrows, "It's got something to do with those things called boundaries! Ever heard of those Yumi?"

Yumi gave him a look.

All of a sudden Guy was enjoying himself even more. He made sure he sat next to Yumi during the meal, shoving someone else's stuff from the seat next to hers to make it happen. For once in his life, Guy did not care about what was right or wrong.

"So you were all at Oxford together for a year?" Guy asked Yumi.

"Fun times, although I'm the clever one."

"I don't doubt that, not for one minute, Yumi." He leant in closer to her.

"Your friend knows I've got him sussed, he's like an open book."

"Something tells me I can't wait for us all to spend time together," Guy laughed.

"You see I could feel immediately it was true love between those two, the first time we all met!"

"It took them far too long to get together."

"Absolutely, I think you can't miss opportunities especially when they look this good," she said gazing at him.

"Oh I completely agree I would never let that happen. You know Yumi, I really like your initial reactions to people, I think they're spot on," he replied, smiling back at her.

Noëmi and Marcus did not make a formal announcement, but Yumi did not miss the evidence; the sparkling engagement ring on her friend's finger.

"Look at that!" she whispered to Guy.

Guy did not let the newly engaged couple escape!

"Congratulations you two, don't worry Noëmi, I'll keep reminding him how lucky he is!"

Everyone rushed to congratulate them as Guy spread the good

news.

Guy and Yumi found that they had many interests in common, given that he had lived in Japan and enjoyed rugby. Guy suggested that she help him improve his Japanese. Equally she proposed he stay with her as soon as possible in London to see some of the shows and exhibitions they both found they were desperate to see. To ensure they organised these visits properly Guy invited Yumi to dinner the next day, which she eagerly accepted.

Marcus and Noëmi

The restaurant had music and dancing set up for everyone to see in the New Year and the group had a fabulous time enjoying themselves. Noëmi and Marcus made sure they were right next to each other ready to kiss at midnight. Then Marcus posted their second bridge selfie onto his social media and wrote the caption, ***'She said 'yes'!!! Got engaged to the lovely Noëmi McAllister,'*** with a heart and a ring emoji.

Indeed for both of them, New Year's Day 2018 was exactly the one they had hoped for the year before, but even better.

CHAPTER 50 - SO MUCH LOVE AND PRAYERS

Attila

Sunday 4 February 2018 was a bright day and two days before Sarai's late husband's birthday. Luca would have been 40 years old. Sarai had decided on this date for Lucia's christening even though it was not the usual Sunday service where baptisms took place. The vicar, Attila, had capitulated as he quickly saw Sarai was never going to relent. Attila had been keeping an eye on Sarai and he was relieved that she had the support of her good friends. The four Godparents; Marcus, Noëmi, Frank and Valentino were sitting in the front row waiting for the service to begin. All the McKenzie family and Donnie, of course, were also there for the service to see Lucia My Truong Bianchi be christened.

Marcus

"Is Guy not coming?" Noëmi asked Marcus.

"No he's visiting friends in Clapham."

"Clapham? Friends? Of course he is," Noëmi mused.

"Plus he wanted to leave a bit of professional distance, you know with the trial and everything. What are you doing? We're in Church."

He had noticed that Noëmi was getting her phone out.

414

"I was just going to see if Yumi was having a good weekend," she smiled at Marcus.

"No you're not! Leave them alone N! Remember sometimes it's fun when things are your own secret!" he laughed.

Noëmi agreed, "I loved our day!"

He squeezed her hand and smiled at her. "Which one?"

Sarai

Val and Frank had offered to host the reception afterwards but Sarai was desperate to repay the hospitality and kindness her friends had constantly shown her. Therefore she had organised with her step mother Vicki and Luca's father Roberto, to take the Godparents for lunch, given that her flat was too small. Roberto had flown in from Italy and was pleased to spend time with his grand daughter, whom he called 'his greatest blessing'. They had chosen 'The Cellar Door' with its fine food and views over the river from the terrace. The Godparents insisted on paying for the wine and had brought their Goddaughter a number of fine gifts.

Roberto made a speech saying how he was pleased to meet everyone at a happier occasion. He told how his son's friends had been such a comfort to him since that dark day. Noëmi and Val, the Italian speakers, kept in close contact. Every day, Sarai sent him pictures of Lucia. Roberto said as he raised a toast;

Noi non potremo avere perfetta vita senza amici.

It is not possible to have a perfect life without friends

Bright sunshine welcomed them in spite of the winter cold and it was an uplifting day. Lucia was passed around and giggled with delight at being the centre of attention. Surrounded by friends Sarai was peaceful, thinking of the joy that Lucia was bringing her in the ever painful absence of Luca.

Back from London, Guy was ready for a stressful week. The evidence against John Dyer had been collated by the detective team. The Crown Prosecution Service presented the case to the court and the lawyers representing John Dyer reviewed their position. Background, personality and psychological reports revealed no mitigating circumstances and he showed no remorse. Given that he had been in a position of trust his defence team could offer nothing, so reluctantly he agreed to plead guilty. A number of victims had been identified and each was assigned a team of specialists to help them rebuild their lives.

Watching the press coverage of the scandal and guilty plea on the early evening news with Marcus and Noëmi at their flat, Guy sighed heavily.

"Such a fucking wanker. I can't and never want to discuss some of the stuff we found out."

"Lowest of the lows. You've done a brilliant job especially as the victims don't have to go through a trial." Marcus commented.

"They've still got a life sentence. He'll get fifteen years tops, if he behaves out in half that time, so seven years and counting." Guy shook his head.

"Can't the judge impose a minimum term?" Noëmi asked.

"We're hoping so, we're asking for at least ten. Sentencing is in six weeks." He moved out of the lounge and stepped into the small terraced garden area to get some air. Guy called Yumi, who gave him comfort. His conversation over, Noëmi followed him outside.

The dark early evenings made it feel much later than 6:30pm and Guy was reflective in the obscurity.

"Are you alright?"

"Yeah, my first big case, there were so many of us working on it. All the charges were upheld, I've seen all the victims, including Stephanie and Sarai. I don't think Stephanie could have handled a trial, whatever she says." He seemed suddenly drained.

Marcus joined them.

"Guy, you've really given your all to this. You couldn't have done any more." Marcus put his arm around his friend.

"Thanks mate, I appreciate that. You know, that Dyer pervert never said much, but he did ask one question which was if you, Noëmi, knew him at Newcastle Green. He couldn't place you. This was outside of the case so we never discussed you, don't want to put you at risk."

"My personal vendetta seems a little silly compared with what those victims went through."

"Indeed what someone like Stephanie experienced at the hands of this evil low life is beyond compare, but it doesn't mean your suffering is not valid, Noëmi. There's a whole spectrum of abuse. Damage is damage. Suffering is very personal."

They were silent for a few moments. A fresh breeze jolted them from their thoughts and they went back into the kitchen and shut the door on the darkness for now.

Noëmi

February 2018. Half term and Donnie was excited to be hosting an engagement party, with about fifty family and friends coming. Noëmi had gone to stay at her old home to help her father prepare everything. They had spent a busy few days organising drinks and food, cleaning the house and tidying the garden for the celebration. Donnie insisted on getting caterers and a DJ for the gathering as he wanted to enjoy the moment Noëmi got engaged. He was especially fond of her fiancé and was delighted that they had finally got together. Life was taking a new turn.

Donnie had, of course, unearthed pictures of Noëmi as an awkward child and she smiled when she saw them.

Importantly he had albums of himself, Noëmi and Manon together and they spent a couple of hours chatting about their time as a family, which helped Donnie enormously and he could now speak of Manon without so many tears. Noëmi could put herself in her father's place realising that he had loved her mother with all his heart and soul and still did. She recognised that this was just how she felt about her fiancé.

Saturday 17 February 2018. The morning of the party arrived and it was a beautiful February morning with blue skies, promise of gentle sun and a light wind moving the trees. Noëmi and her father had just decorated the marquee with fairy lights and balloons and they were now sitting in the kitchen drinking coffee. She noticed he was unusually quiet.

Noëmi had a number of appointments that day and her father then asked her what her plans were for the day.

"I'm getting my hair done at 2pm. Then Yumi, who has already come up from London to stay with Guy, will come over to do my make up at 4pm. My dress is ready to pick up from the dry cleaners so I'll collect that first," she replied.

"Make up..." Donnie said almost to himself, thinking intently.

"Yeah Dad I'm a grown up now!" Noëmi replied, giving him a playful hug.

"Well maybe I should give you this now, I wasn't sure when to do so but now seems right and it has to be today," he replied mysteriously and he turned to the dresser behind them in the kitchen. He took an envelope out of a drawer.

"What's this?" she asked, puzzled. He had already given them a present of a Japanese Maple tree in a large ornate planter with a matching vase filled with roses.

Donnie took a deep breath and struggled to talk.

"When your mum found out she was not going to recover, she wanted to write you a letter. She chose for you to receive it, 25 years after she found out she was pregnant with you. That she always said was the happiest day of her life. She wanted it to be on the very day, which is, by happy coincidence, today 17 February 2018. She thought your actual 25th birthday may be too much so she decided on this day. Prophetic I would say knowing Manon. It has been sealed for over twelve years now and I have not read it of course."

Noëmi was speechless and could not believe how much restraint her father had shown in following her mother's wishes. She felt her heart beat faster as she slowly opened the letter, her mother was talking to her woman to woman.

She took a breath and said to her father.

"Read it with me Dad," and they went out to the garden. They sat down together, close to one another, on the bench underneath the white lilac they had planted for Manon as it was her favourite plant.

Bella Noëmi,

You will be a woman now so I hope Dad does not feel too old! I chose for you to receive this letter on the anniversary of the best day of my life. The one when I found out I was pregnant with you! Twenty-five years ago. I was twenty-four, as you are now, and you came as a beautiful surprise to me and Dad. From that day on you were loved entirely and completely by us both for we were blessed. And so it has been ever since.

Yet I cannot deny, my Noëmi, that it is hard for me to leave you and Dad. I am so sorry. My body is very weak; I know it is soon. I must admit I am a little scared as I have no idea what to expect in death, does anyone? However as Robert Burns said, 'If there's another world I'll live in bliss and if there is none I've made the best of this.' Living with your father has made me appreciate all things Scottish! I know I can leave in peace. The happiness I have had with you and Dad is more than I could ever have wished for.

The love I have for you and your love for me will never die. Our love is a flame that cannot go out and it will keep us both warm when life is cold. It will light our way when dark times come. Although we are not together physically, we will always share that love and it will bridge the void that separates our worlds. It will comfort us both in difficult times. For when you share so much love it means there is so much sorrow in being apart.

As when you were born I wish you every joy and happiness in this adventure of life and I hope this is your truth. I wish that you find love of the kind I feel for your Dad, and that you are loved as much in return. When you find that love, protect it. Do not be afraid to surrender yourself to it in your entirety. For you and your beloved will become as one person together.

Please look after Dad and comfort him, for ours was the greatest of loves. Now that you are a grown woman please help him to be at peace and encourage him to think of his own happiness. The love I shared with him will always be true but now he must live his life.

Let us have the happiest memories of our time together and let us not be sad. Remember how we laughed until we cried, times we shared the stillness, the adventures we made. I am ever grateful for our life together.

Remember time is short, it is precious and it is never enough. You do not get it back so live your best life.

Be kind, be honest and be wise.

Remember the Italian proverb I used to say to you:

'Vivi con passione, ridi di cuore, ama profondamente'

Live with passion, laugh from the heart, love deeply.

It is an honour to be your mother and remember that I am always with you, Noëmi.

420

Ti amo.

All my love Mamma

They sat quietly together in each other's arms, let the tears pass and felt peace come over them, as the soft lilac rustled in the gentle breeze.

THE END

(To be continued…)

ABOUT THE AUTHOR

Thank you for reading!

This is the first book in the *Scheming People* trilogy, detailing the life of Noëmi McAllister.

K McCity was a secondary school teacher for 16 years and is now training for a role in the NHS.

Find out more: www.noemisreckoning.com

Printed in Great Britain
by Amazon